Joseph Anthony's fine historical novel *A Wounded Snake* presents a compassionate, yet unsentimental, study of race, politics, law, and lawlessness in the near-South, turn of the 20th Century city of Lexington, Kentucky. Local information about events and personalities is set up as precisely as lead type placed, letter by letter, onto a printing press, to reveal line by line, in stark black and white, how a century ago "a good truth....did more than a fist in the face could ever do." In today's atmosphere of renewed racial tension, A Wounded Snake serves to remind the reader that "we cannot be in this place we've been." For although "forgetting is what we do best in the South," it's time to remember and change.

—Christina Lovin, author of *A Stirring in the Dark* and *Echo: Poems*

Praise for *Wanted: Good Family*:

"The book is masterfully written and well grounded in Kentucky history and mannerisms. It explores race, class, relationships and the potential for change-- issues that are as relevant today as they were when this story takes place more than six decades ago."

—Tom Eblen, *The Lexington Herald-Leader*

OTHER BOOKS BY JOSEPH G. ANTHONY

Peril, Kentucky, Wind Publications, 2005
Camden Blues, Wind Publications, 2009
Bluegrass Funeral, Wind Publications, 2012
Pickering's Mountain, Old Seventy Creek Press, 2012
Wanted: Good Family, Bottom Dog Press, 2014

BOTTOM DOG PRESS

HURON, OHIO

A Wounded Snake

A Novel By
Joseph G. Anthony

"Never wound a snake; kill it."
Harriet Tubman

Appalachian Fiction Series
Bottom Dog Press
Huron, Ohio

ISBN: 978-1-94-750408-0
Bottom Dog Press, Inc.
PO Box 425, Huron, OH 44839
Lsmithdog@aol.com
http://smithdocs.net

CREDITS:
General Editor: Larry Smith
Cover & Layout Design: Susanna Sharp-Schwacke
Cover Art: University of Kentucky archives
Author Photo: Elise J. Mandel

ACKNOWLEDGEMENTS:

Appreciation goes to the following: Yvonne Giles, Fayette County historian, who helped guide me through African –American history in our county. Dr. Randolph Hollingsworth, another historian, whose writing on Fayette County schools made sense of a very complicated situation. My wife, Elise Mandel, and son, David Mandel-Anthony, whose editing was keen and insightful. Susanna Sharp-Schwacke, editor, and Larry Smith, publisher, who were patient and helpful. Lexington's Central Library, especially the staff in the Kentucky Room, who aided me in years of research, and the computer staff who rescued me more than once.

DEDICATION:

To the African-Americans of Fayette County for their courage, grace, faith, and hope—who have been crossing boundaries for centuries.

PART 1

CROSSING BORDERS

CHAPTER 1

Noah Webster, May 1898, Lexington, Kentucky

I don't know how Mr. Benjamin keep from being shot.

If there are two words a colored boy hear over and over again, they're "be careful." "Be careful, son. White folks don't like it when you look at them straight up." "Be careful, boy. You headed to a beating." "Be careful. You think you white?"

Robert O'Hara Benjamin is not afraid to say anything—in his newspaper or in the courtroom where he lawyers. I work for him on *The Lexington Standard*—the best colored newspaper in the Commonwealth. The best newspaper. Says anything.

About anybody. And writes it like he ain't colored. Like he forgot his place.

Or like he remember it.

Mr. Benjamin the only one tell me you can be too careful.

Be careful, boy. You might careful yourself out of a life. "Son," he tell me, "you live your life just trying not to be shot, it's not much of a life. Especially if you're a Negro in the South."

A Negro in the South. Sometimes Lexington, Kentucky don't feel like the South. We just come through the meanest April we've seen in twenty years, Mamma says. All my life and then some. A snow storm a week ago. In April. Dogwoods white on white—blooms on the end, snow on the branches. Tulips open and close back down, like they thought better of it. Everybody shaking their head like they ain't ever seen anything like it.

Of course they have. They just don't remember. We talk about our past, but we don't really remember it. We don't want to. Forgetting is what we do best in the South. As soon as the sun peeks through, you wouldn't know we'd even had a winter: the dogwoods shake off the frost and if their tips are burnt you can't see it. Or you don't want to.

Magnolias, big pink waxy blooms, almost choke the branches. Us, too, with the smell, but Mamma can't get enough of them. The little path of dirt in front of our house barely got room for the dogwood Mamma planted let alone one of those big magnolias. But I go over to Fayette Park, act like I'm raking those big lawns clean and fill sack after sack with them. The smell almost knock you down.

Mamma take them and spread them thick over our dirt, like a pink rug. Sometimes I see people walking by baffled, looking around for the tree. If Mamma's on the porch, they might ask her, "Where's the tree?"

Mamma will look confused. "Well, that's a puzzle. Where *is* that tree?"

Where is that tree? It's our joke whenever we can't find something we need. A whole bunch of things we run short of: rent money, coal pieces, warm coats. I start to complain, and Mamma puts a hand on her hip: "Where *is* that tree?"

Mr. Benjamin lived up North for years and he say the winters in Lexington as mean as they are in New York. The people, too. Only in New York, they mean outright. In the North they know cold weather's coming; they build their houses with that in mind. A lot of our houses don't even have no foundations—just a few boards leaning in on each other with cracks so wide in the sides you might as well be sitting in the yard with a rain slicker pulled over you. Row houses are better. Mamma and me live in one of those. At least the wind blowing in only one direction.

Of course, some white people got some mighty big houses. Ashland and Fayette Park. Gracious living, they call it. Ashland its own park practically. Used to be even bigger, they say, owned halfway down to the city.

Owned half the people, too.

And the yards so big in Fayette Park you can't see the end of them. Which is good 'cause the end of them is Smithtown, where their colored help lives. Don't want to see them shacks. Fayette Park people don't own the Smithtown folks. But they sure like it that they handy nearby.

And out of sight. Of course you smell them if the wind blowing. Not just Smithtown. Some folks claim they can pick out a neighborhood with a whiff.

"That's Adamstown," our neighbor lady, Miz Wilkes says. "Whooeee. They need to clean that privy."

Privies a big problem in this town. I seen one frost-proof closet serve nine families.

Frost-proof my eye. You sit on one of them seats in February, you slide right off. Or you freeze stuck. We all got pink bottoms in February. The pipe full of ice half the winter. Need to wait till April to do your business. Or hightail it to your neighbor's bushes three blocks over. Or to the nearest saloon.

Ain't too much gracious living in Adamstown. Or down by Deweese. Not just coloreds. This town full of poor white. Mamma always taking pity on some sad white folk. Fill our yard with pink petals; fill our kitchen with pink faces. I think some of Irishtown make Yellmantown look good. Or Chicago Bottom. Bottom of the pit, I say.

Not much gracious living in Irishtown.

Poor whites might worry about filling their stomachs or keeping warm. But they don't worry much about the other stuff.

They poor but they white.

I'm working part-time at *The Standard*. That means I put in about forty hours for ten hours pay. All Mr. Benjamin can afford. The rest of the time I work at George Thomas saloon over in Yellmantown, where I do everything from bartending to easing drunks out into the street to cleaning up what they left behind.

Could use some of Mamma's magnolia petals to soften the odor, though those waxy blooms wouldn't wear well at George Thomas. Yellmantown is a whole different kind of South than Fayette Park. It just a few blocks all bunched together, kind of squeezed between Davis Bottom and Irishtown.

Coloreds got to squeeze in where they can.

Lexington's full of little neighborhoods an outsider would never know about and which ain't on any map. You got to live there to know the boundaries. You might think there ain't any boundaries because nothing's marked, but you cross the wrong boundary and you know it quick.

Mamma says the world's full of boundaries, not just Lexington.

"You just need to know where you belong."

"Are you telling me, Mamma, that I belong on my side of the fence? Safe there. Won't get hurt that way. Well, maybe I shouldn't even get out of bed."

She gonna slap me if she get to me but I'm on the other side of the room. My side of the boundary.

"Nobody safe anywhere, even in bed. But you don't need to be always knocking down fences."

I took a moment. "Only thing, Mamma, seems like a colored boy can't move for fences."

Mamma looked bothered, like she don't know what to tell me. It was okay to come near her then. She didn't look like she was gonna smack me anymore.

It looked a little like I smacked her.

"I know it do, son. And I ain't saying you wrong or that you shouldn't try. You just got to be careful. Colored boys got to be careful."

There's those words again. Mr. Benjamin telling me it not much of a life if I spend it just trying not to get shot. Mamma telling me it ain't worth anything if I do get shot.

Mr. Benjamin doesn't much care for my other job. And he sure doesn't want to hear me complain about cleaning up the damage I "helped inspire."

"What do you expect? You helped pour the garbage in. Only right that you clean up the mess when it comes out. That's what's wrong with this world. Nobody wants to clean up the mess they helped make in the first place."

We not talking about George Thomas anymore.

One of my jobs at George Thomas is to make sure the drunks move on when they get too mean. You're allowed to be mean when you're drinking at George Thomas—the hooch we sell either knocks you out or makes you holler. Just not *too* mean. Shooting mean. Everybody carrying in Lexington. We all just trying not to get shot.

White boys, too. They get shot on a regular basis. Colored boys just seem to get shot at a lot more often.

I was thinking that working the newspaper was the safe job before I see the column Mr. Benjamin write on that Mississippi shooting. It started when a cracker sheriff and his three deputies came to devil a boy and his daddy on a farm they owned. That was the first trouble: colored folks owning a farm in Mississippi. Asking for worry. When they didn't agree to be bulldozed off the place, the sheriff just shot his daddy down. That's when that boy pulled out his own gun: killed three of the deputies and sent the sheriff hightailing off.

"Shame he didn't get the sheriff," I said when we first read the news in *The Morning Herald*.

"A damn shame," said Mr. Benjamin. "But we don't live in a perfect world."

He went in and closed the door. Meant he was writing something special. Something that might get us all shot.

"Just set the copy, boy," he tell me. "What am I paying you for?"

You paying me to dodge the bullets, I think. *Just like George Thomas.*

But you don't speak to Mr. Benjamin like that. At least I don't.

Mamma's not sure about him. She don't say much when I talk about him. She say I talk about him all the time. I see that look she give me. I know that shake of her head means she thinks Mr. Benjamin not careful. Worse, he don't push me to be careful, either.

"People need to be pushed," I say to Mamma. "And he about the only one around doing the pushing."

"Just so he don't push himself off a cliff," Mamma say. "And you with him."

Mostly at *The Standard*, I'm setting type or mopping floors or trying to get stores to keep a bundle of *Standards* for sale—colored grocery stores or barber shops. Or anywhere that coloreds shop. But a couple of times Mr. Benjamin let me write a little column here and there. Of course, he marks out half what I write and rearranges the other half, but he let me do it. Ain't nobody else in town gonna let a nineteen-year-old colored boy with only six years real schooling even come near a typewriter. One time he even told me I got promising.

"You got promising, boy." That after he got me writing a column on household hints. "If after washing a chamois, there seem to be harsh places, rub them steadily but gently through the hands and soon they will quite disappear."

What's a chamois is first thing I wanted to know but we were "borrowing" the piece and rewriting a little. "For the ladies," he said. I wanted to write about the election coming up and how the Republicans were just using us again. "All in good time," he told me. "Meanwhile just be sure you spell chamois right—whatever it means."

I can tell you what it mean: it mean promising.

Promising. Don't know what Mr. Benjamin's Mississippi column is promising. Says the Negroes of Mississippi should give William Littlefield a pension for killing those three deputies. Goes on to say that they'll probably catch him and kill him so put up a monument instead—monuments like the Daughters of the Confederacy want to spread out all over Lexington.

"We were defeated in battle, but our cause lives on," I heard one Colonel say when they pulled the blanket off a statue of some other Colonel. This town full of colonels.

"It not only lives on, it rules on," Mr. Benjamin said. We were in back of the crowd—the only coloreds there. We got some mean stares, but Mr. Benjamin didn't care. He spoke up like he was an invited speaker. They just forgot to put him on the podium.

Only William Littlefield's monument might say we still fighting the war. Don't mean we winning it, but we still fighting.

> If they are going to kill us, then we should go down fighting. An eye for an eye; a tooth for a tooth. Are we to be lynched, burned at the stake, and be totally annihilated by the white man as we peaceably sit by? Shoot and shoot, kill and kill, fight and fight, curse and curse, damn and damn. Hurrah for William Littlefield.

"He leaving town?" Mamma ask when she read that.

"I'd leave town with him," I say. I feel bad when Mamma jump. But I would. But Mr. Benjamin ain't leaving.

Not too many people read *The Standard*. No whites that I know of. Maybe only a couple hundred colored people. Until that column come out. That column get read by every colored man and woman in town. We sell out and have to print two hundred more copies. Stores actually ask me for copies instead of me begging them to carry them. Those that can't read get the column read to them. Coloreds make up almost half the town of Lexington so that a lot of people.

I kept hoping that maybe white folks won't even notice. Lots of things go on with coloreds that pass right by the whites. But then *The Morning Herald* jump in. "Murderer praised by colored editor," it says on its editorial page. "Shoot to kill his motto." Then it print the whole column. White Lexington reading the same thing we reading:

"Shoot and shoot, kill and kill, fight and fight, curse and curse, damn and damn."

"What's he mean by 'damn and damn?'" Mamma asks me the next day, still studying that column like it one of her Bible verses. It read like one of those verses. Old Testament. Mamma more New Testament herself. "More Jesus than Moses," is how she put it.

I wondered the same thing myself when I set them, *damn and damn*.

"I think it mean when somebody damn you, you damn them."

She let that sink in. "Everybody's damned then, ain't they?"

What you supposed to do then? Let them curse you and not curse back? But she was my Mamma and whether I was in reach to get slapped or not, I couldn't say that. "He's just saying we got to fight back. And we do, Mamma. We got to fight back."

"Of course you got to fight back, boy. Your daddy and me didn't raise no weakling. But damning? You don't need to be damning anyone, son. You don't need to be putting your curse on anyone."

I'm raking up the old magnolia petals from our front space now. They don't last but a couple of days before the stink even start to bother Mamma. "Back to the dirt," Mamma says. Three days of pink and a whole year's worth of dirt. And mud and snow. I don't think it worth the trouble for a little bit of pink but I don't say nothing—don't let Mamma hear my cussing as I try to scoop up all them rotting flowers. Mamma don't need to hear my cussing.

She don't curse anything. Don't even curse the horse that kicked Daddy into his grave. If anybody in this family gonna curse, it gonna have to be me. If I'm gonna learn how to do it proper, it can't be Mamma showing me. It gonna have to be Mr. Benjamin. He's good at it. He let out curses the whole town of Lexington heard. Read all about it. And I set the type. Make me feel like I'm on the front lines. Make me feel like I'm holding the banner.

I'm nineteen years old and I know all about fighting. Ain't a night go by it seems some boy ain't wanting to see what I got in me. White boys see me crossing Deweese Street and they start hooting. Too many of them I duck in an alley till they pass. Lexington full of alleys. You can weave through the city and not see a main street. But the city so crowded, sometimes there are buildings blocking the end. Dead ends. Then you in real trouble. Worse I ever got beat is when I took a dead end.

But mostly you can slip around the alleys when you got to. And I got to about once a week. One or two boys I figure I can handle. Colored boys out looking for trouble, too, but most times they let you go by. Just jade at you. Jade too much, though, and we gonna mix it up. But white boys ain't just jading. I try to look nice for my job at *The Standard* and maybe that what they can't stand.

"Who you think you are, nigger?" they yell when they see me. I'm too young to be a preacher or a doctor. They know I ain't got more money than they do though some of those Irish boys got less. So how come I got on nice pants and a collar shirt? Who do I think I am?

Mamma don't understand it. Can't see why I can't pass on by, let their insults and name-calling just roll off me like rainwater drip off a cap peak. Don't understand why she have to be sewing up my nice collar shirt or try to salvage my nice pants twice a week, or keep dabbing at cuts or bruises with iodine that sting worse than any boy's jabbing.

"You think your daddy fight every man who looked cross-eyed at him? You think your daddy need to prove he a man all the time?"

Maybe if Daddy stood up more, he tell John Fielding that horse not safe to be around and he wouldn't of been kicked. Can't say that. But I can't let insults go by either. I just can't. Bad enough I got to keep shet around just about everybody. Wouldn't be nothing left of me if I didn't stand up to some Mick who ain't barely got his feet dry but who think he own the town. Excepting it's pretty clear to everybody he don't. Don't own much of anything. He know it; we know it. But don't tell him. Worst insult you could give him. "Worse off than a nigger."

So he got to fight me. And I got to fight him. They don't even like it that I'm fighting back. Trying to get up in the world. Seem like the more I get up, the deeper they sink. Or maybe the higher I get, the lower they feel.

I don't know why they feel like that, but they do. Maybe all white people feel like that. At least the Micks say it out loud and bring their fists with them. High-class whites keep their words in their head, but they don't keep them off their faces.

Wish they'd throw a punch or two. Then I could throw one back.

One part of me is real proud that I'm working for a man who wants to fight—not just for himself, not just the name-calling fights that wear me out, but for the rest of us, too. For the colored man. The Negro. I'm proud and I'm right there with him. And he never almost never raise his voice, either. Except in print. He fight. I fight. And we fighting the right people.

But another part of me think like Mamma. He jumping off a cliff and taking me with him. Taking everybody with him.

"Somebody gonna start shooting. You move your desk away from the windows," is the first thing Mamma say to me. Mamma usually don't read anything but her Bible, but of course she read the column. "And what do you mean, the 'right' people?" She looking at me, waiting for an answer. "You mean white people? Like that boy in Mississippi? He hanging from a tree yet? I ain't heard."

"Nobody's heard yet. No news is good news. Maybe he escaped up North. You think he did wrong, Mamma? They shot his daddy down. Maybe he should have just turned the other cheek?"

Like Daddy, I almost said again, but didn't. As it was, Mamma was leaping out of her chair, grabbing the umbrella by the door and beating me with it. Mocking the Savior. When Mamma ain't scowling or smiling, she's "correcting" me as she put it.

Those boys on Deweese Street ain't got nothing on Mamma. *Kind of funny*, I wanted to say, *you hitting me because I teased that line about turning the other cheek*. More than my life was worth to point that out. She stopped after a bit—more worried about her umbrella, I think, than me.

"Don't disrespect the Lord, son. You're gonna need Him."

"But what you want that Mississippi boy to do, Mamma?" I asked again, after we both caught our breath. I was too old for Mamma to be beating on me, but she didn't seem to think so. "What should he do?" I ask again. "They killed his daddy and were probably gonna kill him."

"I don't judge him, boy. I don't praise him, either. He did what he had to do. I know this, though. You begin talking about shooting and we the ones gonna get shot. Coloreds always the first shot and the last shot. You think about that."

I think about it. But I think about Mr. Benjamin, too. Only so much a man can take without going crazy. Maybe we all crazy. Maybe that's what we need to be. Like Mr. Benjamin say: won't be much of a life if you live it just trying not to be shot.

Especially if you're a Negro in the South.

CHAPTER 2

Noah Webster, May 1898, Lexington, Kentucky

The column was all they talked about down at George Thomas. George Thomas is a white man, though everybody in his saloon is colored: the bartenders, the drinkers, the pimps. There's a little room in the back where the pimps rent out their ladies, so tiny I don't know how they do it. I steer clear of that room, tell Jake the bartender I won't even clean it. Jake look at me like he's wondering how *young* I am, but then he nod. Said he'd take care of it.

Mamma don't know about that room. If she do, I be looking for another job. That'd be a shame. George Thomas is good money.

George Thomas come by once a night—sometime just to check on how much money in the till. Not just the till, but the pimp back-room and the card game over in the corner. He get a cut of it all. Sometimes he sit in a table by the other corner. Two or three white friends of his might join him. The only white men in the whole place. A little white corner in a black room. He a skinny fellow. Dark skin for a white man. Black Irish they call him. Irishtown just two blocks over. No line for the border between Yellmantown and Irishtown but everybody know where it is. Of course, Micks right off the boat land anywhere they can, so sometimes we got white neighbors. They allowed to come live into a colored neighborhood. Be hell to pay if we tried to move into one of theirs. But they move on after a few months. Move all the way over to Irishtown. Only place in town where colored and white live together regular is over at Davis Bottom. Side by side and ain't killing each other.

At least not on any regular basis. At least not much more than they kill their own.

The pimps come by one by one and give George Thomas an envelope towards the end of the night. Somebody from the card game give him one, too. He don't ever count it but if it short, the pimp ain't there the next night. Or the next. He be begging his way back in for weeks, toting another envelope which George Thomas just pocket without a word. After maybe a week or so, he might nod his head and the pimp be back in business.

You don't short George Thomas twice. It cost too much.

An hour before closing, Jake bring over the bulk of the money and it get put in the safe. Sometimes maybe close to two, three hundred dollars—a 4th of July, maybe, where men be drinking all day and there a line for the back-room. Or the day after election day when saloons been closed and everybody built up a powerful thirst. And maybe they celebrating.

I don't know what colored men have to celebrate after elections. Doesn't matter who gets elected, things stay the same. We get nothing for all our voting. Some stringers might pull off a job—janitoring mostly. Only hear of two colored clerks the city hired. We half the city almost but two colored clerks a reason to celebrate. Wonder why we even celebrate the 4th.

I sometimes make three dollars on the night. Almost never less than two. And last 4th I made five whole dollars.

Guess that's a reason to celebrate the 4th. Most nights, though, the saloon ain't see more than fifty, sixty dollars in the till. Yellmantown is a poor place. One thing: George Thomas ain't stingy. Of course, he don't do much to earn that money except take it. I ain't never seen him smile. The white men he sit with laugh a lot—they ain't paying for the beer they drinking so maybe that make them happy, but George Thomas just sit there, not saying much. Nodding. Eyes get all squinty when Jake come over with his books—maybe ask him a question or two, but then he goes back to listening. Make my skin crawl all over looking at him. Not that I look at him too much. I know he there. I'm hoping he don't look at me, either. I'm hoping he don't half know I'm there.

But he do. The night the column come out, he catch my eye. I just finished escorting a fellow outside who thought he got a singing career only the other fellows at George Thomas weren't appreciative. He was singing up a song so loud they might have heard him at the Opera House a half-mile off. Only I don't think they sing those kinds of songs there. And I know there ain't no colored singers. Good big old fellow, kept wrapping his arms around my shoulders like I was his sweetheart instead of the fellow trying to bounce him onto the sidewalk.

I was wore out, which probably had me looking George Thomas' way. I knew better. He waved me to come to his table. I froze for a second. Nobody but Jake and the pimps ever went to his table. He looked at me and waved again.

"Noah?" he said when I got there, and I felt my breath go out my mouth. I ought to of known he knew his workers' names, but I never thought about it. Jake gave us our money. I managed to nod my head somehow. "You work for that colored newspaper, don't you?"

I couldn't talk for a second. I could hardly breathe. Him knowing my name was one thing. Him knowing I worked for *The Standard* was another. I never talked about *The Standard* or Mr. Benjamin at George Thomas.

"Yes, sir, I set type, clean up."

"Do any writing?"

"Not much. Not yet."

He turned to the three white men who had paused in their drinking. "How about that? Got me a budding colored journalist sweeping my floors." The three men didn't look much impressed. "Tell your boss—your other boss—he should be careful what he writes in that paper. More than just coloreds read it."

Then his face turned off. Well, his face never turned on. But the conversation was over. He didn't expect no answer which is good because I didn't give him any. I wasn't gonna pass on his warning to Mr. Benjamin. Mr. Benjamin's life full of warnings. He didn't need no more. George Thomas was saying, "Be careful, Mr. Benjamin. Don't try to live no life."

That's the only time George Thomas ever mentioned my other employment, but Mr. Benjamin would ask me questions about the saloon all the time. Listened like I was describing another country rather than five blocks from our office. Almost never went to a saloon himself and then just to meet people, not to drink. I don't think he liked me working at George Thomas any more than Mamma did, but couldn't really say much considering how little he paid me. I tried to keep everything separate: George Thomas, *The Standard*, Mamma, and church.

All my worlds.

Mr. Benjamin got a lot more worlds than I did. I read his books about the Negro. Read them with my sixth-grade education, looking up half the words. Read about places I'm never gonna see and never even heard of. Good colored boys got home and church. Bad colored boys spend their time at George Thomas. Nothing else for a colored boy.

That's what I want to tell Mamma: that I want the whole world to wander in, not stuck worrying about what neighborhood I can't cross into. What words I can't say. What thoughts I can't think.

Mamma wants the best for me, but her best is a narrow little street called "good colored boy." Tell her things I want to do and she look at me like I'm crazy. "What's that got to do with us, boy?"

She wants me safe. But safe ain't what I want. Safe ain't even safe.

Mamma made one big move in her life when she marry Daddy and move from Frankfort, twenty miles away. Lexington the big city. "Ain't moving anymore in this life."

She felt bad when she take me out of school and me just eleven. The school weren't much, but it something. Daddy sick to dying and she need my help. Sixth grade is about four grades more schooling than she got and about six grades more than Daddy got. He ten year older than Mamma. Mamma just six years old when freedom come. Got two years of a Freedom School. Enough to cipher a bit of Bible reading. Or to pick out the verses the preacher talk about.

Daddy almost sixteen years old when he got his freedom. Only he stayed on John Fielding's farm where he'd been born. That farm stretch halfway to Frankfort. Daddy kept working horses. Moved into town when he married Mamma. When that colt, name of Fielding's Fist, kicked him, he was still an exercise boy. Forty year old. Too big boned for a jockey.

Daddy just thought he broke a couple of ribs at first after that colt kicked him—not a full-out kick, just a side meanness that would have just been bruises if that foot had landed somewhere else. Daddy even joked that he was glad Fielding's Fist hadn't aimed any lower or it'd be sure I'd stay an only child. He and Mamma never understood why no more children came. But Daddy kept aching even when the ribs healed. Then he couldn't hardly walk. Then he couldn't eat. Couldn't keep nothing down no matter what Mamma cooked. Then he lay down. Said maybe Fielding's Fist had hit lower than he thought.

Then he died.

Fielding's Fist went on to win a whole gang of races. I hear John Fielding brag on him race after race. Said that colt's fist just shot through them other horses like John Sullivan knocking down farm boys come to challenge him. Some owners offer him thousands of dollars for the horse, but he wouldn't hear of selling. "Be like selling one of my family," he said. That colt kicked a few grooms in his day. His own colts and fillies scattered all over the Bluegrass. He pass his meanness down. More than one exercise boy wishing they cut Fielding's Fist way back when he kick Daddy. I'm wishing they cut him before that.

They give me a job cleaning stables and grooming after Daddy die. Mr. Fielding said it was only right seeing as how he knew Mamma needed my wages. Wanted me to exercise horses, too, but Mamma wouldn't let me. Even promised to train me as a jockey, but she wouldn't hear of it.

Wouldn't have worked out anyway. Got my growth when I was thirteen. Would have stayed an exercise boy all my life just like Daddy. But they fired me after the first year. Think they forgot why they hired me in the first place. Said they couldn't really use me if I weren't gonna exercise. Had plenty of boys to clean out the muck. Mamma said it just as well. Thought she'd scowl when I told her I got fired, but she smiled instead. I didn't want to clean out any more muck, anyway.

Of course, I'm still cleaning out muck, or tossing it out into the street. But George Thomas pay more and most of the time people ain't kicking at me. Or shooting.

But without my job at *The Standard*, I'd be feeling like I couldn't breathe. Like Daddy. Too big to be a jockey—too colored to do anything else. I want to ask Mamma why Daddy never found something else to do. Why he stayed on John Fielding's farm even when he got his freedom.

That freedom? I want to ask Mamma, but things you can't say. Especially to your mamma.

Mamma read the Bible verses she know how to read and when I still so restless I get fevered, but she can't find what ails me, she get scared. Like when Daddy was dying and she couldn't find a food that he would eat, find a drink that he could sip without it coming up. So she called the Reverend Pickering to come talk to me. The Reverend Pickering marry Daddy and Mamma. He bury Daddy. He stand over Daddy's grave and he say, "He free now." And all the colored folk nod and say "Amen. He free now."

Only Mamma don't say that. She raise her head and look at me. *That ain't freedom*, her look say, for all Mamma being a Jesus woman. *Your daddy dead because a mean horse kick him*, that look say. *Because a mean horse worth more than your daddy.*

Still she call in the Reverend Pickering when her boy restless, when she so worried that she don't know what to do.

"A demon's got this boy," Reverend Pickering told Mamma, who closed her eyes. Her eyes shut, you can see the lines just don't stay by her eyes—they're little black scratches that almost reach her chin. She covered her face with her hands. Revered Pickering opened his Bible to a place Mamma never go to. "Isaiah 57, verse 21," he said: "But the wicked are like the tossing sea, for it cannot be quiet, and its waters toss up refuse and mud. 'There is no peace,' says my God, 'for the wicked.'"

Mamma opened her eyes. She pulled herself straight. The faraway look passed from her eyes and she don't look scared anymore. She not scowling. She shook her head. *No, you got it wrong*, that look say just like she almost say when Daddy died. Only this time she speak up.

"My boy ain't wicked, Reverend. He just want more than I can give him. Maybe more than anybody can give him. But he ain't the wicked."

And the Reverend Pickering look like he been slapped because nobody talked back to him, especially no woman. Especially not Mamma.

"Sister," he started to say but Mamma shook her head and waved her hand at him like he was just some fly buzzing at her ear. Call her sweet boy wicked? Say he headed for trouble because this world ain't kind to colored boys who are restless. Say he needed to listen to his Mamma more because his Mamma remembered what slavery was when you couldn't walk past the fence gate without the Master's permission. But wicked? She walked to the door and opened it for the Reverend Pickering, not saying anything more. He don't even try to talk to that face. She don't slam the door. She shut it quietly. But it stays shut.

She look at me a long moment after Reverend Pickering leave. That look made me squirm. That look says if it's a choice between her church and me, she gonna pick me. But it's not a good choice, not a choice she want to make. It's me choosing to work for George Thomas because he pay enough to let me work at *The Standard*. It's Daddy staying on his slavery farm exercising mean horses because that was the work he could get.

It's stealing sweet magnolia leaves from your neighbors for your own little bit of dirt and closing your eyes and dreaming a little, smelling the borrowed sweetness, making it your own while it lasts. And raking it back up when the bloom turned sour. Because just about everything turn sour if it hang around long enough.

"Ain't no peace for anybody," she say, finally. "Not just the wicked."

Then she smiled. And when she smiles it like we got three magnolia trees all blooming at the same time—all dropping sweet petals. When she smiles, we up to our necks in petals. And none of them sour.

"But you ain't wicked, Noah. You your daddy's freedom, not that grave they put him into. Kicked him into. Ain't no peace with you. But you ain't wicked, Noah. You Jesus' gift."

CHAPTER 3

Judge Frank Bullock, September 1, 1898, Lexington, Kentucky

Usually Billy Klair had more sense than to come sit in the courtroom waiting for me. I could see that he is bursting with some news. He was, of course, the head of the Lexington Democratic Party, and it is not exactly a secret that I am a Democrat. But I am also a judge and politics and the courtroom should not mix.

Unless they absolutely have to.

Not that there was anything "noble" going on in my courtroom. The Major warned me I might as well open a saloon as preside over a courtroom.

"But Father, a man must have some profession. And as you've often said, I am too short for the army."

"Too short" was a polite evasion the Major rarely used.

"If I did not trust your mother, I'd wonder at such a shrimp springing from my loins."

My *honest* mother would soothe me later.

"A man who rode with Morgan cannot be expected to have parlor manners."

Cannot be expected, she meant, to pay attention to a son's feelings.

Parlor manners. Not a burden for the participants in my court, either. I looked at the roster: John Thomas—known as Big Jack, such a familiar in my court and the city jail that I sometimes feel I am his personal judge. An unsavory character, a colored man of the very lowest demeanor. If I owned a saloon, he would not be allowed to enter.

But we do not discriminate. My court receives the lowest common denominators of all the neighborhoods: Irishtown, Germantown, and of course every one of the myriad of colored neighborhoods which make up half the city. Any neighborhood with a particularly violent turn will appear before me. Big Jack, as I recalled, was a resident of Smithtown, but known to frequent other precincts.

The Major may have caused more violence, but I have dealt with the results as frequently as he. And perhaps prevented some violence—a claim the Major never made. I don't run a saloon. I clean up after them.

Big Jack was not the defendant today, but the victim, shot down by one Annie Miller, his sister-in-law, eleven o'clock in the morning, at the corner of Fifth and Campbell Streets. Annie claimed that Big Jack struck her sister, Mandy, numerous times with a heavy cane.

"A heavy cane?"

"Yes sir. He carved it himself."

I waited for her, but she had nothing further to say, not the first person in my court to be struck dumb. The shock of being here in the court—I have not seen her before—often makes a person lose track of all context. She sat quietly, almost as if what was to come was nothing that she could do anything about at all. Almost a dignity about her. Shock again. She had shot someone. It was no small thing.

The bailiff lifted the cane for us all to view. I was impressed. I did not think Big Jack's talents went beyond a capacity to imbibe huge amounts of cheap liquor.

Annie Miller gave her head a tiny shake as if to wake herself. "And then he started throwing stones at Mamma's house. We was washing clothes on the front porch and he's telling me the next time one of us met, somebody was gonna get killed. Then he leave, but I go in and get my revolver."

"Did you go looking for him?"

"He say the next time we meet, one of us is gonna be killed. He was carrying a razor when we met. He showed it to me and started to cross over to me."

"But you went looking for him."

She stared at me a second, not confused any more it seemed. "I wasn't gonna wait."

Of course not. Nobody in Lexington, black or white, was going to wait. The whole town was as armed as a military camp but with less discipline. Father's Morgan's Raiders would feel right at home.

Or perhaps not. People might actually have shot back when they rode through town. So many people praise my lineage—as if Father and Morgan had been a band of gallant cavaliers, though the Major, to his credit, never said that. "Just boys licensed to shoot," is how he put it.

Much of Lexington feels the same way, though they are not particular about the license. Even the women.

"Did you report Big Jack's threats to the police? Perhaps they might have prevented this?"

Annie Miller's eyes widened. She did not answer for a moment. I started to feel impatient.

"Judge," she said, in a puzzled voice as if I had asked her something absurd, "police don't care about a colored man threatening a colored woman. They'd tell me to stop wasting their time."

Patrick, my court officer, let out a loud guffaw that he attempted to turn it into a cough. I gave him a hard glance. Wasting time. I turned to this colored woman whose self-possession was beginning to annoy me.

"We have only your word that it is self-defense. You do not even claim immediate self-defense. The law is very clear. You cannot simply shoot someone whom you think might harm you."

Annie Miller just nodded, as if she'd already come to that conclusion. I could not really doubt her: I had seen enough of Big Jack. But the statutes concerning self-defense were quite clear. Of course, Annie Miller had made the bargain she needed to—a few years in prison as opposed to being killed by Big Jack. And she had not killed him. He might be waiting for her when she got out. Probably not, though. Someone else would have shot him by then.

In self-defense. The Major's world and mine sometimes did not seem so far apart.

Billy was still waiting as I entered my chambers—looking as entertained as if this was a vaudeville show at the Opera House. I let my irritation show.

"I've asked you before, Billy, not to wait in the courtroom. Politics and the court do not mix."

"The politics made you a judge," Billy said to me, but I just stared him down. He doesn't usually have to have the obvious pointed out to him. He's barely old enough to vote, but he's naturally discreet. Somehow he was born knowing the power of the secret. I hold high hopes for him. His background—he is the first of his people to be born here—should keep him from the top offices of the Commonwealth, although these days even the meanly born rise to the top—like fat congealing. At any rate, his birth will not keep him from power. And power is worth more than any title.

He had good news for me. That unsavory colored editor, Robert Charles O'Hara Benjamin, had decided to run for Congress. As a Republican.

Robert Charles *O'Hara* Benjamin. I had not heard his middle name before. I smiled at Billy. "With a name like O'Hara, I imagine that the Irish will be supporting him."

Billy gave me a wide grin in return. "You'd think that, wouldn't you? Unfortunately, he's running as a Republican and there's just some lines we can't cross."

20

"We, Billy? Aren't you only Irish by marriage?"

"Good enough for my people. Born German, converted Irish. Best of both worlds."

Lines, or borders, were there for the crossing as far as Billy was concerned. He'd be a Republican in a minute if it paid more. Right at the moment, though, it was more profitable to be a Democrat. An Irish Democrat if it suited him. Having a Negro Republican running for Congress was a good reminder to his Irish constituents, his German ones, too, as to where the respective political parties stood on the question of race. Race and class.

But race was the ultimate line. At least in Kentucky.

"Sam over at *The Leader* showed me the letter Benjamin sent announcing his candidacy. Sam wasn't happy."

He wouldn't be. Sam Roberts at *The Leader*, our Republican paper, had a hard enough time electing Republicans. Benjamin's candidacy would make it impossible. At least in the seventh district.

"Benjamin's letter went on and on about how the Republicans are just 'using the Negro.' Never giving him any of the spoils."

"Do you think that's what this is about? Trying to get appointed to something?"

Billy was a small man, not much bigger than me. Skinny. He shrugged his shoulders. That was what it was always about according to Billy.

"What'd Woodford say when they tried to pass that Civil Service bill?" Woodford Dunlap was one of the other Republicans running for the seventh. "To the victor belongs the spoils." Billy just about doubled over laughing. "Good old Woodford. He never was what you call subtle."

He straightened himself up. Back to business. "I don't doubt Benjamin wants something. But he talked the usual hooch about Lincoln, the party losing its way. Here's some lines I copied down." Billy had a whole sheath of papers. He was taking Benjamin seriously, more seriously than he ever took Woodford. He began to read, in a deep sonorous voice, as if he were some Negro Baptist preacher. It was all quite amusing.

"The Negro has no disposition to leave the Republican party, but the party seems inclined to leave the Negro. I am trying to prevent it from committing suicide. Parties have characters as men have characters, and parties make and mar their characters much as men make or mar theirs." Billy put the paper down.

"Oh, Sam was steamed about that line, saying the party has no character. He took it personal."

He would. Sam Roberts, as editor of *The Leader*, was the Republican party, at least in Lexington. But the metaphor intrigued me. The character of political parties. What an interesting idea. It was not my experience that the presence of character had ever troubled them—Democrat or Republican—at least not in Kentucky

"Why do you think Sam Roberts shared this letter with you?"

Billy got that cagey look on his face. Billy Klair had the flat face of his German parents and the Irish tongue of his neighbors, but I could imagine him Italian when that look passes over him, a combination of wary and gleeful. A Florentine instead of a Lexingtonian.

"Well, we're old friends. I used to sell his newspaper." Billy's childhood had been rough, I give him that. He never spoke of it. But then all childhoods are rough as far as I can tell, one way or another. His took the shape of a father who decided early on that family life was not really his preference. He left Billy at thirteen to support his mother and siblings selling newspapers, the half dozen papers that keep our small city uninformed. *The Leader* was the main paper in those days—before *The Morning Herald*. But Billy did not care about a paper's politics in those days. He would have sold *The Standard* if it'd been around then. From selling papers to a page job in the legislature, though those jobs are hard to get. You need connections. But Billy made his own connections.

No Majors in his life—with or without parlor manners.

"Call me Billy." And everyone did, even his enemies. At twenty-three he had more of them than he should have. Outnumbered only by his friends. I sometimes wondered which I was: friend or enemy. Somebody told me he had spotted Billy's father in Cincinnati looking prosperous and fit. A bit stout, but with a young girl on his arm, probably younger than Billy. It was a subject no one broached with him.

We all had parlor manners enough for that.

"You're right. My Republican friends don't usually call me for party strategizing. Even Sam. But I got an idea. It's just a hunch, though."

I waited. Billy waited, too, for a moment. It meant that he hadn't come just to gloat over Republican bad news, bad news that I could read in the next day's papers along with the rest of Lexington. It meant that he wanted me to play a part in something. I felt myself tense. "Look at what Benjamin claims in another part of the letter."

> They have completely ignored the Negroes, who are the only genuine Republicans. The Negro Republican vote of Kentucky numbers 65000. This vote makes it possible for the white Republicans to keep together and maintain their organization, and yet every one of the Federal offices in the State are being filled by white Republicans.

I was incredulous. "Sixty-five thousand? That's an exaggeration, surely."

"Maybe. But there's a lot of them. Too many. And that's the Republican predicament, the bull's horn they're stuck on. They can't get elected without the coloreds but every time they bring a colored into the tent, a white vote goes out the other flap. Already people calling them the Nigger Party."

I looked at him.

"Yes, sir. I'm one of them." He smiled. Not many coloreds called him Billy.

"So, what do they do? They're the Nigger Party to my folks. They wouldn't touch 'em. Sooner get them to wear orange on St. Paddy's day. 'Cause they ain't any more the Nigger Party than we are. Benjamin's right: just take their votes and run. But now Benjamin wants something for those votes and you know he ain't the only one. But give them any spoils—other than a couple state janitor jobs and maybe some principal or teaching jobs in the colored schools—and Republicans can kiss off any hope of being elected anything in this state."

Billy paused, pleased with his analysis. "What's that saying about the camel's nose in the tent? Benjamin's the camel nose. Only if he gets in the tent, the whole tent is gonna collapse."

I didn't understand the problem. "So let it collapse. Why should we care? In fact, I think we'd like that."

Billy shook his head. He was always one step ahead of me politically. Oh, two steps.

"No. We need the Republicans. They're about the only thing that keeps us a party. If you can call us that half the time. Look at The *Herald*. It's the Democrat paper and all it does is rant on about Goebel, the best Democrat we got in the state. If we didn't get to hate the Republicans, we'd be reminded of how much we hate each other. We don't need reminding."

He paused as he let me think about that. "Besides, there's those sixty-five thousand votes. Republicans have been winning more and more lately. Look at our governor. It's getting annoying."

It was more than annoying. William O'Connell Bradley, our first Republican governor. Maybe not our last if we kept fighting over free silver and Goebel. And Negroes. Yankees keep saying we hate Negroes. Ridiculous. That would be like hating the bluegrass itself. Negroes are part of the landscape. We might as well hate horses. Horses and Negroes were all you saw when we took a country drive, their cabins crowded into every level spot that wasn't a pasture or garden. One big house and a dozen shanties.

"You think there are any white folks in this county?" I asked Grace last time we ventured out into Woodford.

She just shook her head. "Only the ones we're visiting," she answered.

What we hate is all this stirring up. And what's worse, it's not Yankees doing the stirring. Our own home-grown Republicans, trying to get the war started again.

Of course, some of our "educated" Negroes are edging them on. That column Benjamin wrote was the latest. I thought he ought to have been indicted for trying to incite a riot. "Shoot and shoot, kill and kill, fight and fight, curse and curse, damn and damn."

The Major would have recognized the sentiments and returned it in kind.

I was on my way to swear out a warrant myself when Billy got wind of it and persuaded me not to. He said Benjamin's arrest might cause the riot he thought Benjamin was looking for.

"But we can't let this incendiary behavior go unpunished. We mustn't let our Negroes think we tolerate this kind of speech."

Billy just nodded. "Oh, we won't forget. By the time we're done, the niggers will know what we won't put up with."

I had to swallow my indignation—something I have had to do a lot lately.

Benjamin was wrong about the governor, too. Seems to me, seems to most of us, that Bradley had been working overtime for the Negro in this state. O'Connell Bradley. Some of Billy's Irishmen must have voted for him. Certainly the coloreds had voted for him. And for all Benjamin's railing against them, Bradley had come through. He had just signed the anti-lynching law. An unnecessary law if ever there was one. It was already against the law to lynch anyone—white or black.

"Our Negroes do not need special treatment," I said to Grace.

"But, dear, they are the ones being lynched."

I looked at her. Sometimes she could be obtuse. But she is a woman.

"So enforce the law on the books. We do not need a new law."

I turned to Billy.

"So, what does Mr. Roberts want to do? Get rid of the Negro vote?"

Billy chuckled at that. "That'd be a tall order—not something anybody could make happen. Outside of Alabama. Besides which, they need the colored vote. They simply don't need it to be so visible. No, nothing like that. Just make it less annoying, less pushed in our face. I think if they were just a few—maybe a few colored teachers here or there or a dozen or so clergymen—maybe it won't be the first thing the good white voters of Kentucky think about when they think Republican. Or so is the hope of good Sam Roberts."

"He said so?"

It was Billy's turn to give me a pitying stare. A young man—a boy, not half my age—teaching me the ways of the world. "Not in so many words."

"And what do we get out of it?"

"Those annoying sixty-five thousand votes. Maybe we get it down to five or ten thousand."

I shook my head. The whole conversation felt like a conspiracy. "Annoying or not, there doesn't seem to be much we can do about it, other than repealing the 15th amendment."

"Lots of things we can do without starting that fight. Look at all our sister states down south. Look at Alabama. Ain't nobody talking about repealing any amendments. Don't need to."

"Are you suggesting we revive the Klan, Billy?"

"No need for that, either. Don't think my folks care much for the Klan. Especially the Bishop."

"He lives in Covington. No need to worry about him."

"Well, *I* don't care for the Klan. They don't discriminate enough in who they hate. Coloreds. Catholics. Irish. Now the Red Shirts over in North Carolina. They zero in more."

The Red Shirts were near to terrorizing the last Negro out of the voting booth, the last Republican. They still had that colored congressman, the last one in the country. I couldn't see much difference between them and the Klan. But then I am not a Catholic.

Billy could lounge away the afternoon in talk like this. I needed him to get to the point. "What do you want from me, Billy?"

I thought he looked a bit hurt at my brusqueness, a reminder that we were profession-al—no, not professional, political—associates. We were not social acquaintances. Our wives would not entertain each other over tea. The thought almost made me chuckle: Grace making small talk with Emma Slavin, daughter of the very prominent grocer and alderman, John Slavin. Grace was a magnificent hostess, able to make anyone feel at ease, but that situation might put a strain even on her abilities.

Billy straightened up and got to business.

"Those other ways of skinning the cat that we were talking about. Well, some of them might involve court proceedings. And that's where you might prove helpful."

Patrick had come to the door with some papers for me to sign. I waved him off. "And please close the door, Patrick." I turned back to Billy.

"My courtroom will not be a political backroom, Billy."

"Of course not. Wouldn't want it to be. But we got to make sure votes are legitimate. Colored so-called voters, rounded up by the hundreds. Told who to vote for." He paused a second, long enough for both of us to picture the voting orders handed out regularly by precinct captains in the 32nd and every other ward in town. "That's all we want: our right to challenge any voter to make sure he has the right to vote. We bring the challenge, you rule on it."

"I could make a ruling that all the challenges were bogus. I could hold you in con-tempt for wasting the court's time."

Billy shook his head. "Now that wouldn't be fair. That's not the way we'd expect a good judge to rule. Especially a good Democratic judge. We need to make sure that the elec-tion's right."

"Right?" Billy didn't respond. "And what about the voter's time? He might have to wait all day, take a day off work. Might even lose his job coming to court just to defend his right to vote."

Billy looked pained, as if it was his job about to be lost. Or one of his Irish constitu-ents. But then he shrugged. "Well, what's that fellow, Jefferson, say: the price of freedom ain't cheap."

"He said the price of freedom is eternal vigilance."

Billy accepted the correction smiling. He was the respectful young man again, I the venerable elder.

"Well, that, too. But let me tell you, Judge. These days, vigilance cost a pretty penny, too."

Chapter 4

Noah Webster, September 1898, Lexington, Kentucky

At first it seem like we got ourselves a horse race, Mr. Benjamin running for Congress. The day his letter printed in *The Leader*, a half-dozen people drop by *The Standard* office to tell him it about time. Next day a dozen crowd into our small office to tell him it about time. About time, they keep saying that like they amening the preacher. About time we had a genuine colored leader speaking up for us. About time the Republicans stopped treating us like we had to vote for them since our only other choice was to vote for some ex-Confederate Democrat. Sometimes not even ex. Well Mr. Benjamin would give us a choice. Give the Republicans a scare if nothing else. About time.

Mamma wasn't in the chorus. She just shook her head when she saw how excited I was. We had printed out some handbills:

ROBERT CHARLES O'HARA BENJAMIN
YOUR REPUBLICAN SEVENTH CONGRESSIONAL DISTRICT

I had just come back from plastering the whole of Deweese Street and was headed over to Davis Bottom. "He's not *my* Republican," is what Mamma said. She softened a bit when she saw my look. "Well, I can't vote anyway. Except in a school-board election. And you can't vote, either. Not this election." I was a year and a half away from being twenty-one.

"I want to make sure I can vote even when I'm of an age. Mr. Benjamin working for that."

Mamma had that look on her face that said she wasn't sure what Mr. Benjamin was working for. But she didn't say it. "They're not going to let any colored man run for Congress. Not in Kentucky. Even if he win, they wouldn't let him go in."

"What you talking about, Mamma? Lots of colored men been in Congress. Still got one. Mr. White from North Carolina."

"Mr. White?" Mamma just let that name hang in the air. "What happened to all the others you say we had?"

I shrugged. "They forced them out. Changed the law."

"They gonna force out Mr. White by and by."

Sometimes Mamma the gloomiest person. I know things ain't good and getting worse, but we have to keep fighting. She get that far-off look on her face when she remembering.

Mr. Benjamin says I don't understand. "Your Mamma grew up in Reconstruction days. Everybody thought things going to get better and better in those days. You didn't invent hoping, boy. Colored congressmen, colored judges. Those days twenty years ago, we thought everything possible. We didn't think we'd have to wait twenty years for our first black judge in Kentucky. And the way they carried on, looks like Judge Harper'll be the last one for awhile."

We was walking through Davis Bottom, trying to find people to talk to about the election. They was hard to find. The amen chorus had disappeared. Mr. Benjamin kept his head up. If he was discouraged you wouldn't know it to look at him. You'd know it to look at me.

"You blame your Mamma for not being hopeful, but look at you. Too up last week and too down this week. You got to keep trudging, boy. You your Mamma's hope. Why would she care about some politician?"

The white man staring at us from his front door put his hand out real slow to shake the one Mr. Benjamin thrust at him. But he took it. Davis Bottom used to be about all colored, but more and more whites living there now. Come down from the mountains to work in the railroad yards. "I'm running for the Republican nomination for Congress and I'd sure appreciate your support," he told the man whose wife and children crowded up to the front door behind him. Looked about six or seven children there, though I couldn't see all of them. The houses in Davis Bottom ain't more than three rooms deep. Nice houses except they flood about every two years. Hardly get the mud scraped off before another layer sets itself down.

"Congress?" the man said. I looked down so he wouldn't see me smiling. He was just getting used to having colored neighbors and now one of them was running for Congress. Not something he had heard of much back in Harlan, or Hazard, or wherever he was from. Mr. Benjamin might as well told him he was running for state bird and could he help him fly to the Statehouse.

"That's right," Mr. Benjamin said. "The seventh district, right here in Lexington."

The man just stared. Mr. Benjamin gave him a big smile, waved to the children and nodded to the wife. The man didn't smile back but he didn't yell either. Didn't reach for a gun. He even gave us a little nod. That was progress. At least in Lexington. Mr. Benjamin almost bounced down the steps.

"Now I don't say that man is going to vote for me. But at least now he knows that he could vote for me."

But by the end of the block, when he couldn't get that man's colored neighbors to even open their doors for him—pretending they weren't home though we had seen them peeking at us through windows our whole trek through the neighborhood—even Mr. Benjamin's gait had slowed down.

"Of course your Mamma's discouraged. We wait twenty years for one judge but he's still looking out at all white jurymen. The Supreme Court says you got to have colored jurymen, so they change the law but they keep doing what they did. Could be just a coincidence, they say, that they end up with all white juries. Every time. When a colored man's in court, he's looking up at the judge. They got Judge Harper stuck off in some office doing paperwork mostly, so it's going to be a white judge.

"If I'm their lawyer, I'm the only colored face they see in court—other than family. And there's not enough of me to go around."

We paused outside a house—it was sunk lower than the other houses, like it was inviting all the rainwater into its front parlor. We stepped carefully down the front path, still slick though it was a sunny day. Some of the Bottom never dried out.

"We all thought we were going places twenty years ago. But the white folks didn't like it. White folks never like it. Your Mamma thinks the only place we've been going is backwards. Can't say I think she's wrong." He looked at me and smiled. "What year you born? 1879? Been going downhill since you were born. You the opposite of Jesus, boy. The star started to set when you were birthed."

"My Mamma don't think so," I said, and he laughed. "But what about the governor? He seems like he doing something."

I wished I hadn't said that. Governor Bradley was a sore subject to Mr. Benjamin. Governor Bradley was the first Republican governor the state had ever had. Looked like he might be the last one, too. Hadn't gone down well in the Commonwealth, the few Negroes he'd appointed, including Judge Harper. But it had only been a few, a real few. Mr. Benjamin hadn't been one of them. The Governor wouldn't even answer Mr. Benjamin's letters. Not personally. Had his secretary scribble something. We were halfway up the next block before Mr. Benjamin answered.

"He is a good man. Trying to get the Legislature to repeal the Separate Coach Law. A man 'should be judged according to his conduct, decency and good citizenship rather than his color.' I appreciate him saying that. But that's about all he does: say it.

"But I do not want to be unfair. Getting repeal through that group of would-be-plantation owners would be like getting old Bessie," he pointed to a pony tethered behind one of the shotgun houses who looked like she was having a hard time even standing up, "to win the Derby. Bradley's just nodding to us. Telling us, 'See? Your vote wasn't wasted.' It's a gesture. But we need more than gestures."

A lady answered the door. A colored lady. "My man's not home but would you come in and rest a bit? I've got some sweet tea made."

Mr. Benjamin made his courtliest bow and declined. His gait got some of its bounce back.

"Of course, some people call *me* a gesture. They say this whole run for Congress is a gesture." I looked at him. He felt me staring at him and he gave me a wink. "But sometimes gestures is all we got."

That was the last time we tried to walk the precinct. And when I asked for more handbills to put out, though people had hardly waited until I was out of sight before they crumbled them, Mr. Benjamin told me that was over for now. "Just not the right time," he said, and I thought about all those "about times" people had thrown at him just a couple weeks before.

It wasn't just people like Mamma saying he didn't have a chance. It being Kentucky, there was almost always a horse in the telling: "Not in the running…. Can't go the distance…. A two-horse race and he ain't one of the two." Jake, the bartender at George Thomas, put it best. "Your man might have been first over the starting line, Noah, but he'll be last at the post. Hell, boy, he won't even make it to the post."

That was pretty straight. Might as well run that Bessie in the Derby as run Robert Charles O'Hara Benjamin in the Seventh Congressional District.

But it was more than him not having much of a chance. A lot of people—good colored citizens—didn't like the idea of him running in the first place. Who was Mr. Benjamin? He hadn't been living here twenty years and most of them had lived here all their lives. They were good church-going people. Mr. Benjamin went to church only when his wife, Maria Lulu, persuaded him to it. Or when he was preaching. He's a preacher, too. Just didn't cotton to church much.

And when he went, folks thought he came looking more for votes than salvation.

Then some whispered scandal. They didn't whisper it around me much, but I still heard. Wondering if he hadn't left a wife or two up North. Clergymen whispering. The Reverend Pickering the worst of them.

I don't think he ever got over Mamma shutting the door on him. Missed those chicken dinners maybe. Surely missed Mamma staring at him like he Saint Paul preaching to the Corinthians. He know I work for Mr. Benjamin, know I look at Mr. Benjamin like Mamma used to look at him. Didn't take him long to figure out that Mr. Benjamin the source of all that wicked restlessness he seen in me. All the wicked restlessness infecting coloreds all over town. Especially the young.

Reverend Pickering thought the world of Booker T. Washington. Thought we should all be learning a trade and forget all that other stuff. Like voting. Like any kind of civil rights. Just keep your head down except when you had to lift it to bob it back down, nodding at what the white man was saying. "Yes sir, yes sir. You sure got that right, sir."

Reverend Pickering got half the "good" colored people in town upset with Mr. Benjamin. Even Mamma's new church. I tell Mamma she might as well save herself the walk over to Short Street. But one change is one change too many for Mamma. She ain't gonna make two.

Of course, Mr. Benjamin got a lot of support among the so-called "bad" coloreds, but they don't count for much. That mean they don't vote except when he drags them to the poll. That mean they too busy just trying to survive to think about voting or politics or anything that don't help them survive right now. Tell them that it will help them in the long run and they just shake their heads. "What long run you talking about, boy? Next week? Next rent check? Because if I find a way to make the next rent check, that be long-run enough for me."

Mr. Benjamin say that I shouldn't get so mad at them. That's just the way things are for colored people. "They come along slow," he says. "But they coming."

I want to say he didn't sound like he was bringing them along slow with that column. "Fight and fight. Curse and curse." But I don't say it. That column the only thing you ever knew about him, you'd think he was all shout. But he mostly quiet. He mostly real quiet. He talk in his writing. But sometimes, he'd say, you got to erupt. Mount Vesuvius quiet a long time before it explode, he told me once and I knew what he meant after he explained to me what Mount Vesuvius was. Mr. Benjamin just like that mountain.

All our people just like that mountain. Pressure building up. Every day. Every time they get abused. Every time they got to be quiet when people insulting them. Colored boys got to learn to speak in their heads and not with their tongues. But that's the way it is with all colored folks. Even folks like the Reverend Pickering. Every bob of that head. "Yes sir. Yes sir." It all pressure. It gonna let out one day. One day.

I tell Mamma just a little of what I think and she say I talking nonsense, but she don't say it hard. I can tell she thinking about it. I know she miss the Reverend Pickering. She can't look at him the same way now, and she miss the way she looked at him. Mamma need someone she think Jesus walking the earth. Sure can't see Jesus in me for all she love me. And she don't see it in Mr. Benjamin. Don't think he wicked. Don't think he Satan stirring up evil. But he not the Savior in her eyes. He not the one to lead us out of Egypt.

I don't think he Jesus neither. But I ain't religious. Mamma drag me to church like Miz Maria Lulu drag Mr. Benjamin. But if he ain't Moses, he the next thing to him that we got. At least here in Lexington. And if he pull back from running for Congress, that don't mean he pull back from the fight. He gonna erupt one of these days—just like Mount Vesuvius.

He gonna erupt and I gonna erupt with him. The whole of colored Lexington is gonna erupt.

It'd be about time.

CHAPTER 5

Jake the bartender, October 10, 1898, Yellmantown, Lexington, Kentucky

"Jake, Jake, fill'er up, Man!" The Mayor of Yellmantown is shouting his orders.

You don't have to be the Mayor to boss the bartender. Every fellow with a jingle in his breeches wants you to bring his beer at the double and don't forget the cheese and crackers. A man don't shell out nickels just to wet his whistle. The Mayor's a blowhard by the name of George Broadus. Of course he keeps his nickels in his pockets. He's the mayor. I put the beer down and he gives me that mournful look that say he starving and I run back for the food. When I set it down, he intones, "A man don't live on beer alone, Jake. No sir, not on beer alone." And all the men crowded 'round him hoot and holler like they ain't heard him say that ten times an evening.

He the local point man for the Democrats. Last election he deliver almost forty votes to Billy Klair. Billy Klair give him some walking-around money, though from the looks of him—he as wide as he is tall—he don't do much walking. That why we call him the mayor. He pass around some of that money and the few jobs Billy Klair give to the coloreds. Chop the grass around the courthouse in the summer, clear the ice in the winter. Not much more than that.

Colored Democrats. Noah think there something unnatural about being colored and being Democrat, but Noah young. He don't understand how things work. Democrats always been in power around here. Looks like they gonna stay in power. And people got to live. Noah thinks being colored and Democrat must make you a crook. I tell him it all depends on who you call a crook. Some of them nickels fellows pass over the bar never make it to the till. George Thomas know they don't. But enough of them do. That okay with George Thomas. That make me a crook?

Maybe.

But George Thomas know I got to live, and I can't live on what he pay me. We got an agreement we don't need to talk about: I steal what I need, but I don't get greedy. Sometimes a real job come up—working in a school, cleaning or fixing things. Maybe even teaching if it a colored school, Mr. Green Pinckney Russell got a lock on that. Unless Billy Klair ask as a special favor.

It don't really need to be a special favor if Billy Klair ask. Mr. Russell gonna do it. He got his own agreement with Billy Klair. They don't need to talk about it, either.

Mr. Russell another colored Democrat. He doing real good for himself. Runs all the colored schools in the county. Couldn't do that as a Republican. Course he don't come to Yellmantown much. Surely won't see him in George Thomas. He too respectable for that. But I see him sometimes near the courthouse. A fine-looking man.

Puffed up a bit. It like he bring his own wind with him. Don't even need to move his feet. The Mayor just small change when you look at Mr. Russell. Just nickel beer. Like me.

Maybe Noah right. Maybe we are all crooks. But a man got to live. And it ain't easy.

The Mayor be giving Noah a hard time tonight.

"I was looking forward to voting for your man, Noah. But I read the ballot in *The Morning Herald* and I ain't seen him. *The Herald* must have messed up, I'm thinking. Damn Democratic rag. But then I look in *The Leader* and his name ain't there either. And that the Republican paper. They never mess up."

Noah keep his head down like I tell him to do, but I know he ain't keeping it down for long.

"I read in *The Leader* when your man say there's sixty-five thousand colored Republican votes in the Commonwealth of Kentucky and they all gonna line up behind him. Sixty-five thousand colored Republicans! I think I'm doing good rounding up one hundred votes just here in Yellmantown. I think sixty-five thousand votes and he shouldn't be running for congressman, he should be thinking of being governor. But maybe he right, maybe he should start with Congress. But then I don't see his name nowhere. He decide to skip the little offices, Noah, leap right to the presidency?"

By this time he's almost off his chair, he laughing so hard. And his chorus crowded 'round him yessing and shouting and laughing so loud, I think they all end up on the floor.

I look hard at Noah. He's across the tavern and so much racket he wouldn't hear me if I was standing next to him, but he glance over to me and see my face. He know what I thinking. *Just walk away. Don't say nothing. Just walk away.*

But that's not Noah's way. He turn his face from me and walk up to the Mayor. He wait until the Mayor catch his breath. He just stand there. Finally, the Mayor stop laughing. Then all the men around him chug to a stop. For a moment, everybody stop. For a moment it quiet.

The only time it quiet in George Thomas are the moments when we finish cleaning up at night, with the glasses all washed and the floor clean, when Noah and I are the last ones standing and we don't need to talk. Sometimes I close my eyes, just for a moment, almost too tired to walk the few blocks over to the little house I rent in Davis Bottom. I try to slip Noah a few of those nickels I've gathered over the night. They don't jingle in my pocket. They too sticky with men's sweat and spilt beer. I try to pass some over to Noah, but he almost never take them. Maybe he know where those nickels come from. He just smile and shake his head. I worry about Noah. How he gonna live in this world? How he gonna survive?

The Mayor look up at Noah. He break the quiet. "You got something to say, boy?"

"I just got a couple questions, Mayor. You right about Mr. Benjamin withdrawing his name from the race. People just didn't think he could win and I guess they were right. But what I want to ask you is why he couldn't win? Everybody know he's the best man in town, white or colored. But nobody wanted to vote for him. Or almost nobody. Now you a politician, Mayor, though you ain't run for office you get the votes where they need to go. You say a hundred votes; I hear more like forty but it ain't no matter. Why your hundred votes or your forty votes go to your boss, Billy Klair? Why not to Mr. Benjamin?"

He just let the question hang there. One of the worse yessers, Hiram, start to laugh but one look from the Mayor just choke that off. It kind of gurgle into a fake cough. Hiram look like he swallowed a slew of those nickels he's always paying for the mayor's beers. It make me want to laugh myself. The Mayor look at him a second then turn to Noah.

"Maybe, boy, them men don't want to vote for Mr. Benjamin. You say he the best man in town. Maybe them men don't think so. Lots of good men in this town. Lots of good colored men."

"There sure are," Noah nodded. "Sure are," he said again like he was amening the Mayor. "But it don't matter. Those men gonna vote for who you tell them to. And you gonna tell them to vote for who Billy Klair tell you to. It don't matter if there lots of good colored men in this town, you ain't gonna vote for them. Don't have to be Mr. Benjamin. Could be Mr. Green Pinckney Russell. And everybody knows, *he* a good colored man. But if Billy Klair don't say vote, it won't happen. Why's that, Mayor?"

Noah had gone and done it now. Broke the first rule. The last rule, too. Never say the truth out loud—not a truth like that. Of course it weren't a secret that Billy Klair was running things. But it made everybody feel good, even me, to pretend it was the Mayor in charge. Made us feel less small. A black mayor even if we just kidding ourselves, even if it was just a joke we all were in on.

The yessir men around the Mayor looked as shocked as if the local school teacher had sidled up to the bar and asked me to slide her a beer. All we know she might be inside her room drinking a beer some admirer brought her. That okay. It private. Just some things you don't do in public; some things you don't say.

The Mayor was shamed. The whole bar ringed his table, staring like it the last ten seconds of the Derby. The only thing that could have turned their heads away would be shooting a pistol in the air. I don't even know if that would of worked.

I dropped a keg instead. It cracked and split, and the beer rushed out like it was one of them oil geysers in Pennsylvania. Everybody rushed to fill their mugs before the beer all soaked into the sawdust. Noah rushed over to help. I grabbed him by the head.

"Get on home, now, Noah. Now." He gave me just a glance and went on out the door. George Thomas ain't gonna be happy. I gonna have let a whole bunch of his nickels find their way to the till to make up for all that beer—maybe two three weeks of nickels. But that okay.

A man gotta live.

But it can't just be all about nickels—nickels sticking. Nickels jingling in your pocket. Nickels clanging in your mind like you on some chain gang. Noah telling us that. He saying that we chained to them nickels. That we selling our souls—selling our manhood—for them nickels.

The Mayor and his men come out of their daze. They know Noah telling them that, too. Some of them men born slaves. The Mayor born a slave. He don't tell that. I don't tell that. None of us tell that like it our fault we born slaves. Noah telling us we still slaves. Only they pay us nickels now. And that be our fault.

The Mayor and his men ain't gonna like that when they think of it. They won't like the man who tell them that. There a rage just underneath that ready to shoot up like that Pennsylvania gusher. A rage that cover us all with black sludge. A rage that would beat that boy to a oozing mess, put him on a stick and run him out of town. If he make it out of town. Colored rage that might even lynch one of its own. That would prove they ain't slaves. That would prove they still men. A man gotta live.

But Noah right. Sometime a man need more than nickels to live. And even when he make them nickels dollars, sometimes he gotta do something more than just live.

CHAPTER 6

Maria Lulu Benjamin, October 15, 1898, Lexington, Kentucky

Snow in the Bluegrass doesn't put people in shock as it does in Alabama. One time we woke to an inch in Birmingham. We kept the children in, not sure what it would do to their skin. So much whiteness might hurt the eyes. A blessing it melted by noon or we would have starved to death—we didn't dare go out in it.

But snow in October was a surprise, even the half-inch that was still flaking its way slowly over us at eight in the morning as we huddled like refugees on the wide lawn at Ashland. The little dusting barely covered the tips of the grass, but it was enough to soak my shoes— silly shoes, I saw now, meant to impress the lady of Ashland. Ladies Welt Buttoned, velvety boots already falling apart. I hoped they wouldn't disintegrate entirely before the visit was over. *That* would be impressive.

Of course, Miss Emma Bisou, whose footprints I tried to follow up to the door, showed no surprise at the snow. Her shoes, sturdy brogans, could have plowed through a foot of the white menace with no trouble at all. Her black face, so much darker than mine, was like a black exclamation point above the shimmering blue-white of Ashland's turf. No October's feeble attempt at winter would impede her progress. She looked down at me impatiently as I knelt and attempted to pat my shoes dry—my dainty handkerchief no more use than my footwear.

Miss Bisou was an old time Kentuckian. She said nothing, but I knew she thought me a soft Alabamian, not quite ready for winter. Or life, either, I thought. I was Robert's young wife, though, and I needed to play my role.

Miss Emma Bisou is impressed with Robert.

"Girl, you need to be headed that way," an old porter had just rounded the corner of the west wing. He was carrying a broom near as bent as he was and pointing to the rear of the sprawling estate. He meant it kindly, not wanting us to make a wasted trip. The two wings to Ashland lengthened the way to the rear entrance considerably. He looked down at my footwear dubiously.

"You just wait a moment, I'll clear a path for you." He smiled as he spoke, and started to brush at the snow, widening a green trail with each sweep of the broom.

"Please don't trouble yourself," Emma pulled herself up to her full five foot one. "We are using the front door." The old man stopped mid-sweep, his mouth opened wide. I smiled at Emma nervously as we waited for the door to open. Her mouth pulled tighter.

"You are not afraid, I hope," she said. "Madeline McDowell is a gracious hostess and we are here at her invitation. There is nothing to be fearful about."

The maid who opened the door could have used the same speech. She surely had been alerted to our coming—to the front door—but her eyes still registered a sort of shock. And something else. A sort of affront, as if our visit wasn't fitting. Emma Bisou brushed by her as if she wasn't there. Like a white person would, I imagined. I smiled at the girl—my daddy had worked so hard to make sure I wasn't that girl. Emma Bisou had been that girl when she was young. I had heard that from others. Emma never referred to her past herself.

My smile was a nervous smile again, I feared. The girl made a sort of gurgle in her throat and scrambled to show us the way, but Miss Bisou knew the way to the side parlor. She was already there when the maid finally finished taking my coat. I saw that she was puzzled as to where to put it—did it go with the white folks' coats? *That* would hardly be fitting. Emma had kept hers on. As chilly as the front hall was, I wondered if that wasn't the better choice. But the maid had finally found a place for my coat and I didn't want to make any more disturbance.

I had read the letter:

> Can you come to morning tea, Miss Bisou, tomorrow? We must make final arrangements concerning the school board election. And please do bring any other ladies whom you feel might add to our efforts.
>
> Very truly yours,
> Madeline McDowell

Only one other lady was at the tea, a tall rather gaunt-looking woman in her mid-thirties.

"Do you know my soon to be sister-in-law, Sophonisba Breckinridge?" Madeline McDowell asked. Her words made it sound as if it was the most natural thing in the world for black and white ladies to meet, but she herself had a pinched look about her face. The lady nodded at us but did not approach.

"She is paying us an autumn visit from Chicago, though unfortunately she has brought Chicago weather with her. She has kindly consented to advise us on our undertaking as she is a lawyer, though of course she is not allowed to practice. None of us ladies are allowed to practice. We are too delicate."

She gave a small ironic smile at the word delicate but blanched when she spotted my shoes.

"Oh, your poor boots! Uncle Hector is so slow in clearing the walk. May I get you some slippers to wear while you are here? You don't want to catch a cold?"

"Uncle" Hector looked twenty years too old to be clearing any walks, fast or slow, but the thought of borrowing Miss McDowell's slippers made me blush. I saw that even Miss Bisou's eyes widened. Everyone knew Miss McDowell's condition, the loss of her foot to tuberculosis. Did she have a slipper for the false foot? I smiled and assured her I would be fine.

Miss McDowell looked a bit relieved. Sometimes Kentuckians, especially the ladies, are swept away by what Daddy says is a too polite tongue. They say more than they mean, offer more than they intend to deliver.

I hoped that wasn't the case today.

Emma Bisou had had enough of my shoes. "Her shoes are fine. And if they're not, it's not because Uncle Hector didn't clear the walks in a timely basis. Maria Lulu is not accustomed to uncles clearing her path and should have worn sensible footwear. You called us here to discuss the upcoming school board election and our part in it. One thing you might do is persuade ladies of your acquaintance to provide two hours off for our ladies on election day—since so many of our ladies are your employees, it would be a benefit."

The girl who had opened the door for us was carrying in a large tea tray while Emma spoke. Of course, a good servant never hears the conversation, but it was beyond her capacity to pretend she didn't hear this one. She visibly shook with surprise at the brisk tone Miss Bisou had taken with Miss McDowell. The tea cups clanged together. I saw Miss McDowell look at her in concern. The china looked delicate, if we were not. Delicate and expensive.

"What is your name, young woman?" Emma had noticed her as she had not at the door. The young woman looked frightened: she had broken two rules—hearing the conversation and becoming visible. She didn't answer for a second.

"Answer her, Sally." Miss Sophonisba Breckinridge had started to pour the tea. She kept her head down as she poured. I could not read her expression.

"Sally. Sally Johnson."

"And are you twenty-one, Miss Johnson?"

The girl's eyes widened at the *Miss* Johnson. "Yes. Twenty-one since May."

"Good. Will you make arrangements to enable her to vote, Madeline?"

"Madeline" did not answer at first. She nodded at Sally who scurried out the parlor door. Only when the door was closed did Miss McDowell turn to Miss Bisou.

"I had no idea Sally might be interested in voting. I will certainly look into it. But that is not why I asked you here today."

Miss Bisou raised her eyebrows. "I thought we were here to discuss how to increase participation by colored ladies in the school-board elections."

"We are. I had hoped that you through your church affiliations and Mrs. Benjamin through *The Standard* might do more to encourage colored women to vote. We were sorely disappointed to see how few voted in the last election. We women have only this limited enfranchisement—are only able to vote in a school board election. Gentlemen are already making the claim that women have no interest in voting at all. If we do not increase our participation, we will have proven their case."

Emma shook her head vigorously. "It does little good if they want but they can't get. Maria Lulu might want an uncle of her own fussing over her but all she got is Mr. Benjamin and he doesn't fuss. Those women might want to vote, but if your folks don't give them time off and a way to get to the voting booth, it *ain't* gonna happen."

The "ain't" surprised us all—almost rattling the tea cups. Miss McDowell jumped a bit in her seat, one of her feet—the one?—started a little tap. I made a small sound. All three looked at me—as startled as if Sally had decided to volunteer her viewpoint, not just been forced to speak. Robert sometimes gives me the same quizzical look when I add an opinion. Daddy had been different. He said I was too quiet.

"Do you have something to say, Maria Lulu?" Miss Bisou looked vexed. She certainly had more to say—good things to say. Almost always. But Emma did not like interruptions.

"Only that we might prove another part of the gentlemen's case if we—we colored ladies, I mean—participated in much larger numbers." They waited. I felt as if each word was a pebble I had to dislodge from beneath my tongue. Miss Sophonisba had raised her head. She was giving me particular interest. I felt myself flush with the attention. But I plunged on. "They already claim that the school-board elections have been dominated by ignorant, illiterate, colored women." I took a breath. "Sometimes they claim that these women are not only ignorant but..." I could not believe I was saying this aloud in Miss McDowell's front parlor, in the midst of Ashland's elegance... "immoral women."

Silence. The faint brush of Uncle Hector's broom sounded in the distance.

"Immoral women!" Emma almost looked embarrassed. We were both guests of Miss McDowell's. But I was her responsibility. Was I about to shame her? I looked down at my embarrassed shoes. I was one of those women—no not immoral, I am too timid for that. But ignorant and if not illiterate, the next thing to it. Daddy had been my only real teacher, but he had been so busy that my lessons had been few. I had only to listen to Robert who was so well-read, who knew so much. I knew so little and that so ill. I would have liked to run—barefoot if necessary—through the snows of Ashland back to my home.

"Of course, they do." Miss Sophonisba had spoken, the first time since she had told Sally to speak her name. "Women who claim their rights, or attempt to, are not real women. Real women know they have no rights—or only the rights gentlemen feel free to allow them. Ladies certainly understand that. If they do not, they are, of course, not ladies. And if not ladies, probably..." and Miss Sophonisba herself hesitated... "immoral."

Miss McDowell looked flushed. "I have been pressing for my rights since I was a young girl and nobody, I believe, has questioned my morality."

Miss Sophonisba gave her a gentle look, shaking her head. "Of course not, Madeline. And I don't think anyone has questioned my morality. At least not to my knowledge. But we have other protections afforded us, you and I. I need not spell them out. Mrs. Benjamin does not have those safeguards. Neither does Miss Bisou for that matter—though a certain age might buffer one if nothing else."

Emma had gotten over her embarrassment, if that's what it was. She nodded throughout Miss Sophonisba's speech. "Maria Lulu has a point," and I felt as elated hearing that as I did when Robert wrote down something I said to use in *The Standard*, as elated as when Daddy smiled at me for finally getting the words out. "We need the ladies' point of view, too," Robert would say, which only deflated me a bit. Emma continued.

"Maria Lulu thinks they might discredit the whole vote by women if too many colored women vote—and they will try. The point is what will you do when they do try? Run away?"

I hope that I was the only one who thought of that foot again when Emma asked, "run away." But Miss McDowell paused before she answered. The look on her face said that this definitely was not the way she had expected this meeting to go, transporting her parlor maid to the election polls, defending immoral women and their right to vote. Her foot—or her foot-substitute—kept on tapping impatiently throughout our tea.

Finally she stopped tapping, a veteran of too many meetings, too many coalitions not to know when to go with the unexpected. Indeed, to claim the unexpected—to make it part of the agenda whether it had been or not—was one of her strengths. I do not think she had considered all the ramifications of colored women voting in the Bluegrass, certainly not her Sally voting. But she would consider it now. I felt a moment's urge to mention Uncle Hector. Would she help him get to the polls? Certainly our male supporters were an important part of our coalition. Robert might have asked that question. But Robert could not be here. Asking a colored man to tea—even though a morning tea is more or less hidden from the world—was beyond even Mrs. Madeline McDowell's powers.

I suppressed the urge. I had done enough for the day. Besides, who knew if Uncle Hector was even a supporter.

"We women must take care of one another," Miss McDowell declared stoutly. "We are women first, colored or white. Of course there are many circumstances where we will be separate. That is the world that we live in and those circumstances will not change quickly. Perhaps they will never change. But in this struggle for the dignity of women, we must stand together."

Miss Emma Bisou walked briskly through the lawns of Ashland and I followed, almost as briskly. One has to almost run to keep up with Emma. "Uncle" Hector waved at us. I waved gaily back, and he smiled. I was sure he would support us if he had the opportunity. I was afraid his sweeping efforts had been wasted. October had become October again and the snow had faded to a wet dew. The dew still soaked through my sorry shoes which had begun to dry in Miss McDowell's snug and welcoming parlor, but I did not care. Miss Johnson had brought me my coat and smiled shyly at me as if she had gotten used to the idea of Emma and me sipping tea with the white folks. Perhaps in time she would even get used to the idea of voting.

Miss Sophonisba Breckinridge had walked us to the door and almost taken my arm in camaraderie before she remembered herself. She burst into a small giggle at the sight of my shoes and then apologized. But I waved my hand in dismissal and giggled in return. What did it matter?

We must stand together. It was more than Kentucky politeness going too far, promising too much. This time the promise was meant. This time we really would stand together.

CHAPTER 7

Noah Webster, November 8, 1898, Lexington, Kentucky

Miss Maria Lulu just left. Mr. Benjamin is mad again:

> The Fayette County school board election ballot is an obscene docu-
> ment, one that has been besmirched, distorted, and manipulated by the
> Democratic machine. These political hacks have kept the non-partisan
> ticket off the ballot. The ladies of this city have been granted the right to
> vote for their children's education. But what is the value of a hollow right
> that exists only on paper, our ladies ask? Colored men have been asking
> that question for almost thirty years.

For a sweet lady who don't seem to ever raise her voice, Miss Maria Lulu sure has the knack of getting others to raise theirs. Her tough-sweetness has got us in the school board fight. Miss Maria Lulu talk to me like I her much younger brother though there's only five years between us. She come down to the office maybe once, twice a week. Not really the place for a lady. Office so small it hard to move around. Especially when she was carrying. I thought for sure she stay away then. I didn't know where to put my eyes. I think women should stay home in that state. I tell Mamma that. Mamma shake her head at me.

"Ain't Miz Benjamin a colored lady? You think she something special and maybe she is, but colored ladies don't get to hide out nine months." Mamma look at me a little worried. But just a little. She know I don't think of Miss Maria Lulu like that. And Miss Maria Lulu sure don't think of me as nothing more than the nice boy who works for her husband. "Old days, you lucky you don't have to finish chopping the tobacco row. My Mamma almost birthed me in the fields."

"We're not in slavery days now. Things are different."

Mamma just look at me. "Things ain't that different," is all she say.

At least Miss Maria Lulu's time didn't come to pass in the office. It just about as dirty as any tobacco row though Lincoln and me do our best. Lincoln an orphan boy who run the errands I don't get to. He more or less live with Mr. Benjamin and Miss Lulu, though he got other homes he go to. Sometimes I think Miss Maria Lulu think I'm just another Lincoln.

I don't really see why we getting in this school board fight. Bigger things going on than deciding who gets to run the grubby schools in this county, especially the no-account colored schools. Miss Maria Lulu all upset about how the women don't get to see their vote count. A whole bunch of colored men don't ever see their vote count. Why we worrying about the women?

And school board fights are the worst there is. I ask Mr. Benjamin why that is. He shake his head.

"Jobs mostly. Lots of jobs in schools. But more than that. You get to choose the fu-ture—get to shape it at least. Everybody's got an opinion. Everybody thinks they know what's right."

Miss Maria Lulu just put it straight.

"Who runs the schools may be the most important issue in the Commonwealth."

I didn't see it at first but Mr. Benjamin did, especially after Maria Lulu's visit. And when the brick come crashing through *The Standard*'s window the day after the school board column come out, I begin to think maybe she right. We didn't even get a brick through the window when Mr. Benjamin run that column on that boy in Alabama.

But Alabama a long ways off. Our schools right here.

I run out the door and I see a man running away. It was early, just light. Nobody else on the street yet. He looked familiar. I recognized him from somewhere, I couldn't place where at the moment and then it come to me: a lumpy red-faced Mick by the name of Mike Moynahan. I about to run after him when Mr. Benjamin grab me by the arm. I tug but his hand grip my arm like an iron bit in a stallion's teeth.

"Let him go. You recognize him. Send Lincoln to fetch the police."

"The police? They ain't gonna do anything. Hell, they probably sent him."

Mr. Benjamin looked stern at my "hell." He weren't much different than the Reverend Pickering when it come to cussing. "You have to allow people the opportunity to do their jobs. If they fail to do so, that's another story."

Mr. Benjamin wouldn't let me clean the shards or even cover the broken window with a blanket. He wanted the scene to stay the same. The wind just whipped through that open window. Mr. Benjamin finally went on home. My fingers got so stiff trying to set the type, I just gave up after awhile. Huddled under the blanket Mr. Benjamin wouldn't let me use on the window.

It was mid-afternoon before Patrolman Luke Doyle strolled on up, though the police station wasn't three blocks away. He was smiling when he inspected the window.

"You know they got something called screens now. If you fellows want some fresh air, you might want to investigate getting some of them. A whole lot less expensive than replacing the glass. Of course maybe you colored know better."

The thing to do would be to laugh, bob my head a bit, and then ease into my story. The "colored" polite thing to do. But I wasn't up to it. Now I remembered where I'd seen Mike Moynahan—he'd be one of the Micks huddling in the white corner at George Thomas, looking over at the colored men like they were animals in some zoo.

"Why they come here to drink?" I'd ask Jake. "The town's crawling with Mick pubs."

Jake just looked at me. "Why you think?" is all he answered.

Patrolman Doyle'd be there, too, sometimes. I don't know if George Thomas was on his rounds or not, but the free beer brought him back if nothing else. He kept smiling at me now, like I was just too slow to get the joke.

"You should tell your friend, Mike Moynahan, that. I seen him running away after he threw the brick through our window."

Doyle stopped smiling at that. "A friend of mine, you say. Maybe. You want to be careful in what you say. You see him yourself tossing that brick?"

"I seen him running away."

"You seen him running away. The back of him then. And it barely light out. But you didn't see him throw the rock. For all you know he could have just been running for the joy of it. Some people do that, I hear. I saw some boys running over at the college so maybe that's what he was doing, though he'd be the first Irishman I'd heard of doing so. Most of them got more sense. You coloreds do a lot of running. Though I don't know that you do it for the sport of it the same way them college boys do. Mostly you do it just to get away from fellows chasing you."

He was smiling again, almost laughing. He didn't seem to mind that I wasn't joining in. Lincoln wasn't laughing, either. He had taken the blanket and was huddled in the corner. I wanted to tell him not to be scared, that Doyle was just a bully in uniform. That he couldn't hurt him none if he stood up to him.

Of course, that weren't true. He could hurt him a lot. But I was more mad than scared.

"I saw him. He was the only man on the street. You gonna arrest him?"

"Arrest him?" He stopped laughing. He got serious, as if the question perplexed him. "For going for a morning run? I might take him for a silly bloke, running when a nice walk will get you there just as well, but I'm not about to arrest him. If it was him. You only saw the back of him. How do I know you didn't throw the rock yourself?"

"Why would I do that?"

"I can't answer that. Maybe to cause trouble for *friends* of mine." He paused as if he was considering that. "Or maybe," and he was smiling again, "maybe you was just in a hurry to get some fresh air."

When Mr. Benjamin returned to the office about an hour later, I had cleaned the glass away and had blocked the window as well as I could. It was still cold, but the wind had stopped blowing the papers around.

"Well, you gave them the chance to do their job," I said. He listened gravely to my story of Patrolman Doyle. "What you gonna to do now?"

My question came out harsh. Mr. Benjamin looked startled. I was always respectful to him, always deferred. Mamma wondered why I couldn't be respectful like that to other colored men, to the Reverend Pickering or the deacons. *They didn't earn it,* I wanted to tell her.

But I still felt his hand on my arm holding me back. I felt just like that stallion with the bit in his mouth. I was gonna run, I was gonna break free, bit or no bit. He paused before he answered.

"We are going to do our job. Our job's not running after hooligans in the street. That's for other hooligans. Our job is to tell the truth—or the truth we see—in print."

I felt my muscles relaxing. Mr. Benjamin was going to get mad again.

"I'll stay the night, Sir. You give me the words, I'll set them in type. I ain't even cold anymore."

"Me? No, son. You give me the words. I think you graduated away from writing about ladies' chamois. I think it's time for you to do some truth-telling of your own. Maybe you could start with a column about how the police respond to complaints from colored businesses. Maybe you could tell a tale about Patrolman Doyle and his friend."

I was running free now. I was a twenty-year-old colored boy. Miss Maria Lulu was right about our schools. They needed to be better and nobody but us could make them so. The kind of schooling I got almost made me more ignorant than if I didn't have no schooling at all.

But my words sprang out past the starting flag just the same, like they'd been tensed up behind that flag for hours. For years. And Mr. Benjamin let me have my head, no bit tugging at my jaw. Just touching at me with a light rein now and then, just pulling in my spelling when he needed to, and calming my words when they looked like they was going to jump the fence. But mostly he let me have my head. Mostly he let me run down that track and kick up all the dirt I could. Mostly he let me run full out and tell my truth. I told it as well as I could. The third time I told it, it got better. I was just a half-educated twenty-year old, but my words came out and they didn't shame me. I thought Maria Lulu might even be proud when she read them.

Mr. Benjamin said it was a good truth. Said it did more than a fist in the face could ever do, did more to choke back Patrolman Doyle's laughter than a squeeze-hold 'round his fat Mick neck ever could.

"That's your job, boy," Mr. Benjamin told me smiling, leaning over to see what I'd written. He didn't pat me like some proud trainer pats a young horse who's done him proud. Mr. Benjamin held himself too stiff for patting. But I felt patted.

"That's your job, boy."

CHAPTER 8

Jake the bartender, November 14, 1898, Yellmantown, Lexington, Kentucky

The Mayor wasn't happy. He'd been digging into his own breeches for beer change and he didn't like it one bit. He be scowling like the judge told him he the proud daddy of one of them babies the ladies in the back room pop out every now and then.

But the beer money ain't the real reason he scowling. He ain't got the jobs he'd been promised—even those scraggly things chopping grass 'round the courthouse ain't coming his way. He usually surrounded by a dozen sad fellows who need them jobs, sorry as they is. Only two, three fellows even come near the Mayor now, like they embarrassed to leave him on his own. But they all look away when I tote his beer to him. I wait. He wait. Then he dig down and find a nickel.

But he ain't happy.

Comes from too much winning. The Democrats just swept through the town and county like there was nothing in front of them—got almost every office from mayor to alderman to school board. If it'd been close, those forty votes the Mayor collected for them would of been a big deal.

Of course those are forty colored votes, and the Democrats never wanted colored votes in the first place. Now they feel like they don't need them.

That mean they don't need the Mayor. Billy Klair used to let the Mayor shake his hand. He weren't happy about it—stuck his hand out there like it belonged to somebody else, but he put it out there. Tonight, though, he walked right by the Mayor on his way to the white corner. The Mayor nodded. If Billy Klair nodded back, I didn't see.

I thought things'd calm down after the election, but they just got worse. Noah's writing about Luke Doyle didn't help any. Doyle over in the white corner now, jabbing at George Thomas. He want Noah gone. I told Noah he crazy to write all that in the newspaper.

"I thought we got free speech in this country. Freedom of the press."

I look at him. Can't hardly speak myself. Sometimes I wonder what country he grew up in. Or maybe he ain't growed up. I know ten-year-olds got more street smarts than Noah. Maybe it because he lose his daddy so young. A daddy would teach a colored boy what's what. Wouldn't be no silliness about free speech.

"Ain't nothing free in this country, son. You pay for everything. Especially that speech you talking about. You better be looking for another job. Doyle won't rest easy till you gone."

Noah make a face like he didn't want to hear it. *Ain't my speech free, too?* I almost asked him. I wonder why George Thomas ain't fire him already. I think he like having a colored boy working for him who write for a newspaper, too. And he don't like the police telling him what to do. He'd like to tell Doyle that he's his own man and that he hire or fire whoever he please. That it ain't no business of Doyle's.

But he can't. That kind of free speech would close that back room and that's where half the money come from. That free speech would cost too much.

I don't know where Noah's gonna find another job. Can't be anywhere Doyle patrols. New job sure won't pay as much.

Not that I don't think he better off gone from here. Usually George Thomas an alright place to work. Heads got to be knocked now and then, but nobody really get too upset about it—even the fellows whose heads get knocked come back around in a day or two. I give them a look when they return but there ain't really no hard feelings. Sometimes a white man stumbles in for a drink—a man traveling from out of town who don't know no better—but I shake my head. He look around, maybe laugh, and leave right quick with a story he can tell his friends, how he stumbled into a colored saloon.

Of course, if he a friend of George Thomas, he go to the white corner. But no more than four or five George Thomas cronies at a time. All he can afford since I never collect any money from them.

But the day after the election, the white corner start to grow like mushrooms sprouting after a rain. I see two, three aldermen crowding 'round Billy Klair, laughing and slapping him on the back. "Just call me, Billy."

If you white. I call him Mr. Klair.

I don't know why they don't all go to a white saloon. The town is full of them—I counted fifteen on one block around the courthouse. Celebrate their victory in one of them. But I think colored folks be part of the show—or part of the audience. Wouldn't be half as much fun for them if we weren't there.

The white corner keeps growing. Like a neighborhood pushing on out. Ain't like Davis Bottom, though, where I live. Mountain whites keep coming—almost as many whites as coloreds live there now. But they ain't all in one place. They light where there's a house free or a lot where they can build. But the white corner just keeps pushing out. I'm having to take tables and chairs from the colored section and tell folks to give up their seat and squeeze on over.

I look over at George Thomas. He ain't happy, either. Not just because he pushing out his paying customers for so-called friends of his who ain't paying a dime. Because he a saloon man like me. He see trouble coming. But he think it just drinking man trouble—fists going out when a whiskey word cross the line. But it ain't a whiskey line that's being crossed.

Colored men being squeezed—colored men being pushed further and further into a corner. Colored men told to give up what's theirs and make way for the white man. And I the man making them move over. Always a colored man helping a white man have his way.

Tommy Davis first one to say it to my face when I tell him he have to give up his chair, that I need it for the white corner which ain't a corner no more—like half a block now.

"Here comes the colored overseer. Ain't we picking fast enough, boss?"

Me and Tommy grew up side by side though I older by a couple years. His mamma more mamma to me than my own. Half the time my mamma look at me startled—especially when I got older—like she can't quite figure who I be. That's what happen when you one of thirteen. But Tommy's mamma welcome me like I one of hers, feed me when there's food in the house which there weren't always. But I ain't always come for the food.

I ain't one for looking back and wishing things been different—ain't one for thinking I should of done things better—or not said something. What I said I'm ready to back up with a fist or a club. But I wish I had that moment back. I might of said, "Hey, Tommy. You know me, man. You know I got to do this job. It's a lousy job, but it's all I got." And Tommy might of nodded his head and shut his mouth. 'Cause a colored man knows what a colored man got to do sometimes.

Instead I told him "Get your sorry old ass out of that chair. Better yet, move your sorry old ass out into the street. Or I'll move it for you." And I grabbed hold the truncheon I always kept nearby, like I ready to slam the head of a man more brother to me than my own.

And maybe I was.

But I turn away before he get a chance to answer, carrying both their chairs. The Mayor look like the world coming to an end when I tell him he got to get on up, too. But he don't say nothing, just look at me like he grieving. That hurt worst than Tommy's words.

Next thing I know, one of our mugs is sailing past my head trailing a fountain-spray of beer behind it. Tommy never could throw worth a damn. Those mugs almost an inch thick. Drop them they crack the floor before they crack themselves. Hit a head and that crack, too.

So maybe Tommy just meant to give me a beer-shower, his way of telling me he weren't happy with me. I like to think so. Never got the chance to ask him.

Tommy's mug landed on a huckster named Charlie Downing, a neighbor of George Thomas, way over in Forest Hill. A long way to come for a free beer. He go down when that mug hit him. I thought, *Oh Jesus, Tommy done kill him.* But Downing up in a second, sputtering, and every white man in the place is throwing their mugs, full or empty back at the coloreds. I'm lying flat on the floor. It like a beer waterfall overhead. I see a couple colored men go down, but there's more of us so when they started throwing mugs, three or four white men hit the floor and don't come up.

Soon everybody out of mugs. Everybody shouting and cussing but I'm thinking maybe that's it. Only the Mayor take that moment to charge right at the white men. I know he ain't charging. The Mayor never charged *at* anyone in his life. He lead the backward charge. I know he headed for the door.

Only the door is by the white corner and that ain't a place a colored man needed to be headed. That huckster Downing picked out his gun and shot the Mayor right through his head. "Blasted his brains out" is the way *The Herald* put it next day. I don't know if it was brains that came out when his head split. I just know it was the end of the Mayor. Voted out of office, shot out of life.

Poor Mayor. He weren't much of a man. Maybe I ain't either. Still, I wish I hadn't made him pay for that last beer. Wished I hadn't looked hard when he fished for that nickel. Wished I'd let him stay mayor just a while longer.

Of course, I didn't think that then. We all just stood there—froze—white and colored. Lot of coloreds got down flat when the Mayor was shot—like they'd been shot, too. I looked around and didn't see Noah. He was behind the bar, keeping his head down.

A couple of colored men began to pull themselves up, but then dropped down real quick. I turned to see what they were looking at. Patrolman Luke Doyle was standing two feet ahead of the white corner, holding his police gun in front of him like he just following it. He kept searching the crowd of colored men like he's looking for someone. Looking for Noah.

I almost shout out, "Stay down, Noah. Stay down." But I kept quiet. Didn't want to tell Doyle where Noah was.

So I pray. I ain't much for praying, but Tommy's mamma taught me how. She weren't a preacher. She didn't yell about Jesus. She didn't shout amen like she's beating a drum. She told me, "Jesus ain't hard of hearing. You just need to ask him real soft and he'll hear you."

So I ask real soft, *Jesus, keep Noah's head down behind that bar. Jesus, give that boy some sense and keep him lying flat.*

Doyle looked around a little bit more and seem to give it up. He shrug his shoulders a bit. Then he see Tommy standing there. Tommy hadn't bent down like the others. Tommy kept looking at the Mayor, shaking his head. Then he turned to Doyle. He look Doyle straight in the eye. He know better than that. We grew up on the street together. Tommy know better than that.

"You gonna arrest that man?" Tommy asked, pointing to the rounder who shot the Mayor.

"Don't tell me who to arrest, boy," Doyle said and looked around the bar again.

"You police. You need to arrest him."

"You interfering with the police, boy?"

Doyle straightened out his pistol arm and shot Tommy through the heart.

"Jesus," I heard someone say. "Jesus."

Jesus.

He answer me, I guess. Just like Tommy's mamma said he would.

Chapter 9

Judge Frank Bullock, November 20, 1898, Lexington, Kentucky

Billy Klair was in my courtroom again. This time as a witness. He did not look happy. We had seen each other last at the Democrat headquarters, election night. He looked happy that night. A celebration. We had won overwhelmingly in almost all the races. Many races with no opposition.

I had harried Billy a little.

"All that worry about Benjamin. He didn't even make the ballot. The Republicans are a sad lot in this town."

"They are this election, Judge. But you got to look ahead in politics. And Benjamin is somebody we got to keep an eye on. He's out there rousing up colored votes almost every day. He's in it for the long term. We got to be, too."

He was smiling as he lectured me. The long haul. I wondered what the son of a drunken German immigrant knew about the long haul. Mrs. Klair, a Katy Slavin, daughter of Irish immigrants, held his arm. She was one of only two women at the gathering. A tall woman, taller than Billy, who did not seem to mind. Grace was a good two inches shorter than I am, the right height. Katy Slavin, towering above us all, did not look that different than the Irish wenches who appeared almost daily before me. But I did not have to socialize with those women.

The celebration had been a boisterous affair—several saloons had sent over beer as if the day's closing had left them with an excess they had to disperse with as quickly as possible.

"I hope we do not get too loud for you, Mrs. Klair," I said to her as the noise reached a new height. She looked blank for a moment as if she did not understand, then threw her red head back and laughed uproariously at my wonderful joke. Billy laughed with her.

"I might get too loud for them, Judge," she shouted—kindly, I imagine, so that I might hear over the din. "Where's Mrs. Bullock? She's missing all the fun."

Missing all the fun. I gave a weak smile. Attending such a gathering was part of my public duty. Or at least a portion of my party duty. Besides, I knew that Billy loved to prod at me, loved to see me stand on my dignity, as he put it.

"Oh, I fear Mrs. Bullock's idea of fun does not stretch much beyond the opera house. And the First Presbyterian Church, of course."

This time Katy Slavin's blank stare did not turn into a laugh. My humor, such as it were, eluded her. But she was not dumb. She gave a small shrug and turned away.

Billy looked at me, laughing. "Good thing women don't have the franchise, Judge. Think you might have just lost Katy's vote."

He was not laughing now in the courtroom. He was a witness to two killings. Actually, if truth be told, more than a witness: a participant in what seemed to have been a brawl. But some truths do not need to be told. I owe that much to the party. Billy Klair would stay a witness.

The preliminary hearing would determine whether or not a grand jury needed to be summoned. In other words, I would decide. The courtroom was packed, the first row with the two defendants, Patrolman Doyle and Charles Downing, and their two lawyers. Doyle's friends occupied almost the whole courtroom—so many policemen that I wondered who was patrolling our streets. And Katy Slavin's father, Alderman Patrick Slavin, sat among a group of aldermen. A gang of aldermen. I shuddered. I once suggested to Billy that we try to upgrade the caliber of our candidates.

"That's a good idea, Judge. You know lots of fine people. How about asking some of those fellows from the Iroquois Hunt Club? See if they'd like to be aldermen."

The Iroquois Hunt Club represented all that was uplifting and good in our aristocracy. Its founder, Colonel Roger Williams, did serve in the legislature. But it was well known Billy was angling for his seat. I did not dare bring Billy even as a guest, though he had hinted once or twice. I declined Billy's proposal.

"Well, there you go, Judge. If fine upstanding men won't run, we gotta go with what we got."

What we "got" filled the first seven rows. The next three rows of the court room were occupied with white men I did not recognize—friends of Downing, I imagined. The saloon keeper, George Thomas, sat among them, looking quite glum. His saloon had been closed for the time-being, standard practice after a shooting—shootings—but costly nevertheless.

But the back four rows of the courthouse surprised me: all colored men. Digni-fied-looking men, not the sort I usually see in my courtroom. Not the sort whom I would imagine would be friends of ruffians killed in a saloon brawl. In the middle of the men sat an older woman with a much younger woman on her left side who was clutching the older woman's arm. The older woman sat quiet and calm. She kept a steady gaze towards the front of the courtroom. I could not tell if she was staring at me or at Patrolman Doyle who sat directly in front.

I did recognize the man sitting on the woman's right side. Benjamin—the erstwhile Republican candidate for Congress, the lawyer and radical newspaperman. The one Billy said we needed to keep an eye on. Benjamin seemed to be here keeping an eye on us. I did not have to wonder at whom he was staring. It was as if I was the only one in the room.

I questioned Billy myself.

"What started the ruckus?"

Billy looked genuinely puzzled. "I don't know, Your Honor. We were all having a peaceful, good time, celebrating our party's big win. Everybody happy. Not a Republican in the place as far as I could tell."

The crowd, the first seven rows at least, broke into loud guffaws. I gave a sharp gavel rap. "I will not tolerate disturbance in this courtroom." I stared intently at those in the back of the room, who stared as intently back. They had not laughed. Their silence felt more menacing than noise, but it was not something I could gavel away.

Billy continued. "Then all of a sudden, a mug comes out of nowhere and knocks poor Charlie flat. Charlie Downing."

"A mug?"

"Oh, those mugs are like cannon balls, Judge. Crack your head wide open. Kill you maybe."

"But Mr. Downing was not killed."

"Nope. Charlie jumped right back up. Threw his mug at the fellow who had thrown the first one. Missed him. Then we all started throwing mugs at the coloreds. They threw their mugs back at us. It was pouring beer and mugs. But it wasn't a fair fight. Whole bunch more colored than white men in the place so we were getting hit left and right. Quite a few of ours went down groaning. But we got a few hits. Got me one big buck in the side of his face. I bet it loosened a few teeth."

He smiled at the recollection and paused. I had to prompt him.

"Then what happened?"

"Then we ran out of mugs."

The crowd laughed again, all but the back rows. The rest quieted quickly at my look.

"Well, that's not quite true," Billy amended. "We ran out of mugs in hand, but there were plenty around that the coloreds had thrown. Almost none of them had broke—I tell you, they're that thick—but when we were looking around to chuck them back at them, the Mayor decides to charge us."

"The Mayor?"

"Oh, that's what we called him: George Broadus. The Mayor. Mayor of Yellmantown. He thought he ran things." You couldn't tell sometimes if Billy was smiling or not—almost like a masculine Mona Lisa. He had that look on him now.

"What do you mean charge?"

"Well, he ran right at us, Your Honor. There we were, heads down, scrambling for mugs when the Mayor comes charging right at us. Charlie didn't have a mug in hand. So he pulled out his pistol and he shot him before he got to us. I told you there was a whole bunch more colored than white men. If the Mayor was leading the charge, somebody had to stop him. And Charlie had just about been brained already. He was the man to do it."

I looked through my notes. "I see some witnesses have claimed that the so-called Mayor wasn't charging anyone but was simply trying to run out the front door."

Billy just shrugged. "Yeah, I've heard that. I tell you it did surprise me when the Mayor came running at us. I expected him to run the opposite direction in a fight. Always had before. But it did look like he was coming at us. If he was just trying to make it to the front door, well, he chose a bad time to do it. Kind of like a soldier trying to skedaddle out of a fight and heading right into the cannon fire. Bad sense of direction. Come to think of it, that might have been the Mayor's case. Never did know which direction to head. And bad timing. Some fellows are like that. Got bad timing. The way things turned out, the Mayor might have had just about the worst timing in the world."

Billy smiled that half smile. He got fresh laughter for his troubles, but my gavel cut it short. "A man's death is not cause for amusement," I pronounced. The back of the courtroom nodded their heads at that but stayed silent. It was their first reaction to anything.

I turned back to Billy. "What of the other shooting?"

Billy's grin faded. He stiffened. "I didn't see that."

"How could you not see the shooting? You were right there."

"I was looking at the Mayor. I kept my eyes on him. He was a sight. I didn't turn my head from the Mayor till I heard the other shot."

"So you didn't see Patrolman Doyle with his gun."

Billy looked at me as grimly as I've ever seen him look. His eyes narrowed. "Nope, Your Honor."

Jake Winslow, the colored bartender, had a different story. It wasn't a new thing, coloreds allowed to testify against a white man, a big fight twenty years ago. But I could tell from the looks in the courtroom the fight wasn't done yet. If they'd had beer mugs, I think they would have tossed them. The idea was too much for them—too unnatural—that a colored man's word was as good as theirs, his oath the same. We'd been just a half-dozen years from slavery when we fought this fight. Been more than twenty years, but some hadn't come 'round yet.

"They'll be selling us south next."

That's how those speeches went, as if the war hadn't happened—as if all that blood was just rain sunk into a dry land. And the land was dry again. It was time for us to move on, I told people. They listened to me. I was the judge, after all. But they did not hear me.

I could hardly hear Jake Winslow at first, his voice so low. It wouldn't do much good if a colored man testified and we could not hear him. "Speak up, Mr. Winslow," I told him.

Billy has indicated that some people aren't happy that I use titles for coloreds. Nonsense. It is part of the order of my courtroom.

Mr. Winslow almost shouted his next words.

"Everybody who knew the Mayor knew he was just running for the door. The man didn't need to shoot him."

"But you yourself have said that it looked as if he were charging the crowd."

"Just that first moment. Then I knew he was headed for the door."

I had heard enough of the Mayor. "What of Thomas Davis?"

He looked confused for a second. "Oh, you mean Tommy." The bartender didn't answer for a second. He hung his head as if he were praying. Just as I was about to speak sharply to him—I am not used to being kept waiting in my courtroom, not by white men and certainly not by colored—he raised his head. I expected to see sorrow on his face.

But I saw anger.

"That man, Patrolman Doyle," and he pointed to Doyle in the front row, "killed Tommy in cold blood. He shot him down for no reason. No reason at all."

The rear of the courtroom was heard from at last. Shouts of "in cold blood" and "no good reason" erupted from the back rows. I slammed the gavel down.

"I will clear the courtroom at the next outburst." I looked particularly at Benjamin, but I could not see that he had opened his mouth. He looked particularly back at me. I cannot hold a man in contempt for a stare or I would have.

I admonished the bartender. "You are here to tell the court what you saw, not your conclusions. The court will come to its own conclusions."

The man looked defiant. I did not like it. Even white men lowered their eyes when I chastened them. But he took a breath and continued.

"What this colored man saw, Judge, was that man hold his gun out. Steady. Not pointing it at anybody in particular at first. Just holding it out in front of him. Nobody else in the place was doing anything after the Mayor got shot. No shouting, no nothing. We all kind of just froze there—white and colored just the same. The Mayor was a bloody mess. His brains just oozing out his head. We couldn't move, none of us could. Then Patrolman Doyle step forward and he looking. Waving that gun, looking. He looking for somebody to shoot. Only he don't find the man he want to shoot so he shoot Tommy."

"What do you mean looking for somebody? Who was he looking for?"

The bartender lowered his head again as if he were thinking. Then he shook his head as if he'd decided. I did not like that. Withheld testimony is perjury, too, but one I can often do little about.

"I don't know, Judge. But it weren't Tommy. Tommy weren't charging nobody."

Patrolman Doyle's lawyer had stood up and began demanding to be heard. I did not usually allow lawyers to question in preliminary hearings, but I felt it only proper after the barman's damning testimony against Doyle. And perhaps the lawyer could get all the testimony.

"Weren't you flat on the floor, boy? Face hugging the floorboards when all the ruckus was going on? Tell me how you saw anything, let alone how Patrolman Doyle had to shoot that buck to keep him from trying to brain another man."

"I lifted my head enough. I saw Doyle standing there, looking. Looking to shoot somebody."

The lawyer flushed at the disrespectful omission of Doyle's title. "Patrolman Doyle," I cautioned Winslow. He just looked back at me as if he hadn't heard. I nodded to the lawyer to continue.

"And did you look backwards, too? Did you see what that buck was aiming to do? He was the one who tried to kill Charlie Downing with that mug, wasn't he? How do you know he wasn't aiming to knock off Patrolman Doyle with his next toss? Or maybe you can see in both directions?"

The lawyer smiled. I did not like sarcastic questioning of this type, but before I could admonish him, the bartender responded. He did not seem intimidated.

"Tommy wasn't aiming to kill nobody. Sure not Charlie Downing. He didn't know Charlie Downing. He was aiming the mug at me." We waited as he hung his head once again. We would run all day at this pace. When he raised it, he did look sad this time. "He was mad at me. Tossed that mug at me just to let me know it. Meant to miss me. Tommy wouldn't hurt anybody. Hit Charlie Downing by accident."

The lawyer took a second. This was news to everyone.

"So, according to you, he was aiming that mug at you. But he hit Charlie Downing and nigh on killed him. Now what's to say he wasn't about to aim another mug at you and maybe brain Patrolman Doyle in the process? You're still only looking in one direction—still staring at Patrolman Doyle. You're facedown on the bar room floor, I don't see how you can see him, but you sure don't know what that buck was aiming to do."

With that the lawyer made a gesture of contemptuous dismissal as if there was nothing else to say. The bartender did not agree, however. I should have been quicker, should have dismissed the bartender before he spoke again. It would have prevented the turmoil that followed.

"My eyes was on Doyle but other eyes saw what happened. White eyes turn blind when a colored man gets shot, but colored eyes keep seeing. They saw Tommy just standing there. Doing nothing but standing there with nothing in his hands. Call them up, Judge. Let them tell you what they seen. All them colored eyes saw Doyle just steady and calm shoot that man in his heart, shoot that man in his big heart and take him from us. Take him from his mamma sitting back there, listening to that man call him a buck, like he some wild animal off in the woods. Tommy weren't no animal though that man shot him like a dog. Only he wouldn't shoot a dog like that. Only shoot a colored man like that. 'Cause a colored man matter less than a dog. 'Cause a colored man don't matter to a white man like that. Don't none of us matter."

I had been gaveling from the beginning of his speech, for that's what the bartender's testimony sounded like. Like a rabble-rousing speech. As much of a rant as I've read in that man Benjamin's paper. I looked sharply at Benjamin, but he stood in the back of the room just nodding. Not saying a word though all around him shouts of "Like a dog" and "Wouldn't shoot a dog like that, just a colored man" rang out. The back rows had been silent through almost all of the proceedings, but now they would not be silent for all of my gaveling. The first ten rows of the courtroom looked increasingly uneasy.

For a few moments as I banged my gavel, I felt as if my courtroom had been transformed into George Thomas' saloon, that I had lost control. The colored bartender had actually told me whom to call to the stand, told me I needed more colored voices testifying. I looked at my normally ordered courtroom in near chaos as if only the flying mugs were missing. The dozen policemen present had their hands on their side arms. I was not certain they would not be needed.

But Benjamin and the old woman beside him sat quiet. Benjamin held the woman's arm. He kept staring at me as if he were waiting. The colored around him kept looking at him and gradually they began to settle back into their seats. They looked to him and quieted. Not to me.

But I knew what I had to do. My job was order—order in the courtroom, order in the city. Order. Tradition, the natural hierarchy, respect for the social verities of our culture and society. We were being threatened. White and black. Disorder threatened us all.

The white men in the courtroom had settled down, too. They looked up at me and expected that I would repel the threat. Billy Klair was among them, waiting for me to do my job—the job that he had helped elect me to. I glanced at the policemen who tensed in readiness at my look.

I once heard an actor say that he always chose one member of the audience to stare at when he orated a monologue. I chose Benjamin, who returned my stare.

"The court has heard enough to conclude that both defendants had ample reason to fear for their lives. If the threats were not real, both defendants could not, reasonably under the circumstances, have determined that. The court therefore concludes that the killings were justifiable homicides for reasons of self-defense and that there is no reason for the Commonwealth to go to the trouble and expense of summoning a grand jury."

The eruption from the back of the court was immense. If nothing else, it justified me further in my ruling. Screams and shouts of anger. I had never in my life seen such a response from the colored community of Lexington, a community that had always—with few exceptions—been a respectful and respected one. They had degenerated into a near rabble.

Benjamin and the old woman were quiet, however. Benjamin kept looking at me. I waited for him to join the din, but he did not. One move, one shout, and I would have had the court guards lift him out of that mob and into a jail cell. It would have been a very long time before his words, or his gaze, incited anyone again.

But he stayed mute—mute with that silent stare that streaked across the courtroom like sunlight off a glass and into my eyes. I felt my face flush with its heat and with my own anger. I saw more danger in that look than in the loudest scream of the feckless people around him.

Benjamin's quiet stillness seeped like a slow flood oozing dampness and decay, leached like rain water that trickled into the cellars of our Bottom neighborhoods, rising gradually into the bedrooms of the poor and into their kitchens, cracking the foundations, collapsing the shabby shotgun houses at last into themselves.

But Benjamin's gaze, Benjamin's words, threatened more. They threatened our tranquility. His gaze said that none of us are safe, no matter how solid the ground. I know that change is upon us, but it must come gradually like a soft spring.

Billy was right. Mr. Benjamin is a menace to the well-being of Lexington, a hazard greater than any creek overrunning its bank. He is a sinkhole opening wide, sending fissures through the ancient limestone foundations of our city. Our gazes locked. He finally nodded to me, the slightest movement of his head. I did not return his bow.

Mr. Benjamin needs to learn what cannot be changed. He needs to be stopped.

CHAPTER 10

Noah Webster, January 2, 1899, Lexington, Kentucky

Mamma made me quit George Thomas. I'm twenty-year-old last September—a grown man and then some. I don't need my mamma's permission to work anywhere. But I didn't tell her that. She just would have given me that look of hers and told me to save my breath to cool my porridge.

"You gonna quit that job, boy, right now. If George Thomas don't give you the money he owe, you still gonna walk away. Better to walk away with nothing in your pockets than be carried away with a hole where your brain used to be. Sometimes I think ain't much brain there, but it worth keeping in your head."

George Thomas gave me my money and a little extra. I think he grateful I go so easy. Of course I know he about to fire me—another reason not to argue with Mamma. They let him reopen a week or so after the trial, but business is bad. He even lower his prices which got a few people back, but most of his regulars ain't returned. It's like they still see the Mayor with the top of his head blown off. Still see that boy, Tommy, shot in the heart.

I think they still hear that judge, too, saying it was self-defense. Bullets against beer mugs. Even *The Morning Herald*—the Democrat paper—almost call the judge out on it. It don't say it plain, it don't go that far: "The ruling of self-defense by Judge Bullock in the shooting of the so-called 'Mayor of Yellmantown' certainly raised troubling questions. But the claim of self-defense by Patrolman Doyle in the shooting of Tommy Davis perplexed much of the court and this paper's observers as well."

Mr. Benjamin wasn't perplexed any. I set the headline:

PERPLEXITY AT THE MORNING HERALD

The Morning Herald says it is "perplexed" by Judge Bullock's rulings concerning Patrolman Doyle. What mystifies *The Morning Herald?* Judge Bullock is a high official of the Democratic party in Lexington. Billy Klair—its unofficial chief—was seated ten feet from Judge Bullock. Though I, along with the rest of the colored community, was placed in the rear of the courtroom, I had a clear view and saw no notes passed between the two. But then Judge Bullock is too astute to need written instructions. He knew how his bosses wished him to rule and did so accordingly.

Do you think the law blind? Do you not realize Dred Scott's infamous dictum—that the black man has no rights that the white man is bound to respect—is still the governing rule of Kentucky's courts? If so, I would suggest to *The Morning Herald* that it is not the law that is blind, rather it is *The Morning Herald* that cannot see. Or perhaps its esteemed editor, Mr. Desha Breckinridge, chooses not to see.

I wished I could see Mr. Breckinridge's face when he read that. Hope he's not the type to come 'round toting a billy club. Mr. Benjamin just smile when I say that to him.

"Oh, Mr. Desha Breckinridge has better weapons than truncheons. So do I."

I don't tell Mamma what Jake told me—that I was the one supposed to be shot, not Tommy. I don't know how he knows that. Jake came over to tell me that again when I left.

"Steer clear of Doyle. Hang low."

"For writing a few words in a newspaper only coloreds read? He got me fired; he's not gonna shoot me."

Jake just give that look—kind of like Mamma. They both think I'm about ten.

"Steer clear of Doyle," is all he said again.

I'm wondering if he thinks he better steer clear, too, after his testimony—not that it did any good. Still, him pointing at the man in court got to be more serious than my making fun of him in a newspaper nobody much reads or remember a day after it's written. They gonna remember Jake pointing at Doyle their whole lives.

But I'm not about to tell Jake what to do though. He one tough fellow. Doyle take a shot at him, he might get one headed back at him. Besides, if business don't pick up at George Thomas, Jake probably head out anyway. Maybe head to Louisville. I hear things are better for coloreds in Louisville. I tell Jake that, but he just shake his head again.

"Lexington the best place for coloreds in Kentucky. It ain't no good, but it the best place we got."

Of course I steer clear of Doyle. If I can. But Lexington not that big a town. Maybe *I* should head to Louisville.

I'm surprised to see a crowd the last time I leave George Thomas. Not inside the saloon—out on the sidewalk. They just standing around, not saying much. Maybe a dozen men all together. A couple fellows my age, but mostly older. A few of them nod to me. I tell them I just quit and they almost amen me like it a street church and not a saloon they milling around. One fellow—Old Luke, we call him—give me a pat on the shoulders like he the granddaddy I never knowed.

But I ain't never paid him much attention. He was just one those fellows who hung out regular—sometimes half the day—but couldn't afford to get too drunk. Sat in a corner, mostly, off to himself. I hear him talking sometimes. I think he talking to me once or twice, but he just talking to himself, Jake told me. The men around him usually give him a breathing space when he talk too loud. I ask Jake what his story was, but he wouldn't tell me.

"Old, poor, colored, and Kentucky. You need to know more?"

Jake roused the old man a couple times, told him the space was for paying customers. But mostly he let him be.

Now the old man looked at me like he wanted to tell his story. I waited.

"That's right, boy. No place for a fine young man to be working. Don't know why your mamma let you stay this long."

I didn't even know he knew I had a mamma.

"Ain't no place for a man to be drinking. If a man got to drink—and sometimes he do—he better find a place that treat him like a man. Not shoot him down like a dog. Worse than a dog."

And the crowd around him grumbled louder, like it did in the courtroom. But this crowd hadn't been in the courtroom. Only time they go to a courtroom, they be dragged there.

"I read what your man, Benjamin, wrote." I was surprised again. The old man could read? He smiled at me. "Read you, too. And what you wrote about that policeman." He chuckled a little bit. But then he pulled his mouth from its smile. "But what Benjamin said, about the white man not respecting black man rights. He telling the truth. White man don't want the black man to have no rights. No respect. White man think we got no rights—and if we scrape out a few, they bound to scrape them right back."

The old fellow had everybody looking at him now, like maybe he never had before in his whole life. They were nodding their heads, murmuring, "He got that right." "He telling it like it is." The old man knew he had the crowd listening. But he kept his eyes on me.

"I wasn't much older than you when I got my freedom. It a hard freedom, but it freedom. I fight all my life to keep that freedom, but it seem like it get harder and harder to do. They shoot you down like a dog and call it self-defense. I call it murder."

The crowd shouted at that. The old man's eyes opened wide. I saw two policemen round the corner. Their eyes opened, too. A dozen colored men gathered around some old man in the middle of the day. It didn't look good.

The old man stood tall for a few seconds, then began to sag. I wanted him to keep his head up high. I grabbed his arm and squeezed it. I wished I listened to him when he talked to himself off in his corner. I didn't think he had anything to say worth listening to. Just an old drunk, full of old stories.

He straightened up when I grabbed his arm. "I'm an old man and can't do too much about all that. But I know one thing. I got enough freedom to pick where I want to drink and where I don't want to drink. And I don't care if they lower the price of beer in this joint till they almost paying you to drink it. I ain't gonna drink it here."

And I swear he could have been charging up San Juan Hill when he said, "I ain't gonna drink it here." The rest of the men came in close, patting him so hard on the back I thought he might fall over, but he didn't. They cheered him—me, too—like he was Teddy Roosevelt himself. But Teddy Roosevelt had all them Rough Riders behind him. That old man didn't have nobody. Except us. And we weren't much.

But maybe we were enough. He made us feel like that.

Jake had come to the door with all the fuss. I caught his eye when the old man finished. He shrugged. I guess the old man wasn't the only one who'd be searching for another saloon.

I saw the policemen looking nervous, not sure what to do. There were just two of them—one of them fresh on the beat, but the other one old. Too old to be on the street. But I caught a sight of his eyes. He wasn't long sober if he was sober yet. They moved slow towards us, wary.

But cops almost can't resist troubling colored men. They started to push in. "Move on," they said, soft first, then louder. "Break this up."

The men moved over a bit—like a horse will when you shove on it but it doesn't want to move. They didn't look at the policemen, just shuffled over a foot or two, then closed back in when the cop moved to the next man. I saw the younger one reach for his stick, but the older one shook his head. He lowered his voice, got friendly. Started urging the men into the saloon. "Go on, boys, now. Have a nice cool beer and get off the street now." Soothing. Like it was for their own good.

But the men weren't drinking. And the younger cop started to get mad. Even a Lexington Mick can't arrest you for not drinking.

That's about the only thing he won't arrest you for. The young one, about my age, with a nose looked like he got his police teaching in bar fights, shoved a young guy named Bruce toward George Thomas. Wouldn't be a man I'd pick to shove. Bruce—he a rod-rider with a nose to match the cop's—shoved back so hard the young cop almost hit the ground. The cop sprang back up swinging, aimed his truncheon right at Bruce's temple. Only I was standing right there, the cop's arm passing right in front of me and I shoved my fist into it before it was half-way down. The club went flying. The cop turned to me, his right arm dangling like I broke it. I saw him reaching over with his left hand for his gun—saw it slow motion like I was just a bystander, waiting to be shot—when Bruce knocked him flat.

The old cop found himself standing alone in the middle of us. I don't know what we would have done to him. I felt like stomping on the young cop's face, mashing that smashed nose of his right through to the other side of his head, taking that billy club of his that he was so ready to use on colored heads and rain it on him like a summer hail storm I got caught in once with hail as big as small rocks. Time I'd run through that storm it looked like Daddy finally lost patience with my shenanigans and been beating at me for an hour or more. Only Mamma never let him beat me like that. Made him stop after a few minutes, when I knew he was just getting started. I was just getting started with that young cop.

And when we finished with him, I'd turn to that old rheumy police and kick him all the way down that street he didn't think we had a right to stand on. Knock out the five teeth he had left in his mouth. Take that cold beer he thought we should be passing the afternoon drinking, pour it over his body sleeping on the sidewalk.

I ain't never been in a mob before, but it felt good. I could see all the others felt like me. We just stood there when they blasted the poor old Mayor's brains away, just watched when they shot Tommy. We shouted when that Judge lied in the courtroom but that's all we did. We made some noise and then got quiet again. Like we always did. Grumble and shut up. Move on. Move on.

But we had these two policemen now and at least they wouldn't be shooting any more coloreds, at least they wouldn't be walking the colored beat and telling us to move on. Move on.

These two policemen would be lucky if they moved on anywhere. These two policemen be lucky if they walked anywhere again.

I could taste that vengeance and it tasted good. But it weren't to be. Old Luke was on top of that young cop and we couldn't get to him. We yelled at Old Luke to move away but he just shook his head. Bruce looked mad enough to punch right through Old Luke, but he didn't.

The old cop stood right behind Old Luke, like I used to hide behind Mamma when I tried Daddy's patience to the last nerve. Luke didn't move like, he was standing at attention. His eyes wild but he was sober now. All the way. "You know there'll be trouble, boys, if you beat this young police. Feel good now, but trouble later. Too much trouble."

We stopped shouting after a bit. The young cop opened his eyes but had enough sense to stay down when Luke told him to. The men drifted off. I stayed until Luke told me I better move on, too.

"Don't go home," Luke told me. "Tell your mamma you need to lay low for a few days. Let me know where you'll be and I'll tell her. Now move on before the other police get here. Move on."

We all moved on. Just Old Luke stay holding that young cop's head like he his son. His white son. I don't know how he do that. Just that old cop standing stiff as Lot's wife—as white, too. Not looking at me, not looking at anybody. We all move on except for them three.

Least none of us moved on to George Thomas.

I run home to Mamma's and grab some clothes. She don't even ask what's going on, like she everyday expecting her son to have to be hiding from the police. She just grab some food to put in my satchel. "Send word when you can," she say. I start to tell her I'm sorry for the trouble I brought and she look mad.

"What you sorry about? You might as well be sorry for being born colored. Now hurry up. I'll send anything else you need. Wait." And she run in her room and come back with her Bible. It a big, tattered book, the pages rubbed smooth with her reading. I look at her. She can't want me to tote that big book with me. But I see she just want to read a passage over me. Time racing and the policemen looking to pound my head into mush, but Mamma wanting me to listen to some book two-thousand-year-old. But there weren't no help for it. I bowed my head and waited while she rustled through the pages.

But she couldn't find what she was looking for though she know her Bible better than a farmer know his fields. She put the Bible down finally and placed her hands on my head. She closed her eyes and said the words she'd been looking for:

"Though we walk through the shadow of death, I won't fear no evil for you're with me, Lord, and with my boy. You're my rod, Lord, and my staff. You're all the strength we got, and you will comfort us. Yes, Lord, you will comfort us. Jesus' name."

I don't know if the two-thousand-year-old book had done some magic or if it was just Mamma's hands on my head and the sound of her voice.

But I felt comforted.

CHAPTER 11

Maria Lulu Benjamin, February 2, 1899, Lexington, Kentucky

Noah and Lincoln are sharing the upstairs room, my sewing room though Sheila does the sewing. Does most everything and "don't need a whole room just to sew." It's a small room but Lincoln's not there much. I urge him to treat our house like his own, but he knows better. Makes me sad. Robert tells me Lincoln is a beaten dog and will take a very long time to heal if he ever does.

"We all have our pasts," Robert says. "Lincoln just needs more time to row away from his."

Row away. His island accent makes it all one word: roooaway. Robert thinks we can all roooaway when we need to. His island childhood.

"We lived in North Alabama, Robert, hill country. No getting away by boat."

"I was your boat," he says and I laugh, for boat comes out as boot. "I was your boot." He was. He is. My boot.

I ran from Alabama, but Noah has run from Lexington. He's found our island. Noah is here almost all the time except when he is working at another job—something with horses from the way he smells when he returns. He slinks to the back and pours as much water over himself as he can without drowning, but still he smells.

The children love him, whatever his smell. I have to keep them from climbing all over him when he comes in soaked from his washing. Robert Jr.—we call him Charlie—especially feels the need to grab at Noah. He loves his daddy, but Robert does not invite that kind of contact, even from his three-year-old-son. I wish it were different.

Sometimes Robert's dignity seems so fragile, as thin as the Northern accent he's stuck on top of his island lilt. As thin as Lincoln's believing this is his home, too.

Even Lillian is held apart. She is too young to crawl to Noah herself but she yearns for his touch, for a man's touch. She strains in my arms. Robert holds her like she's a delicate doll he might break. He gives her back to me as quickly as he can.

But young Noah swoops her up and presses her to him, sweeps Charlie off his feet and tosses him into the air until I catch my own breath.

Daddy would do that. He'd bring the street in with him and cover our Sunday best with his smell and his sweat. Mamma would despair at the state of our clothes.

"Your daddy loves you too much," she'd say to us, but it wasn't a complaint.

Robert loves his children, too. I know he does his best in this strange world he's landed in. Kentucky. As inland a place as you can get. Even Alabama had its gulf.

It doesn't matter.

His boot is there for them.

Of course, Mamma didn't have my Sheila to do the extra work that comes with Noah. Sheila doesn't approve of the roughhousing, says she knows when Noah's been around. "I can't keep these children clean. Even the bath water ends up smelling like a horse trough."

Noah goes to *The Standard's* office in the early evening, sets the type and does the other chores that he must do there. At least he can do some writing here. Robert does not think it safe for him to be at the office in the daylight. Not for awhile. I didn't ask. "Being young and colored is not a healthy combination in this town," is all he said.

I nodded. "I am colored, too, Robert. And many still consider me young."

He laughed. I loved to see Robert laugh, even if he is laughing at me.

"Well, male, too, then. Young, colored, and male." But then he stopped laughing. Sudden. He looked pained. "That's not true. Young, colored, and female can bring even more trouble." He took my hand. "You are spared much of that trouble, Lulu. Thank your God for that."

Spared? Where did Robert think I grew up? He won't talk about St. Kitts. A hard childhood, he tells me. "Sugar," is all he'd say. "You had cotton in Alabama. We had sugar. And our slavery ended thirty years before yours did. That's all."

That's not all but all that I can get from him. He is strange and distant, my boot. How could he think that a colored girl from Alabama, even a colored girl from a good family, would be spared such troubles?

I have been lucky—just pestered. Pestered until I have wanted to scratch deep rivets into the faces of my tormentors but never the worst. Though I have come near. I am fair, the fairest in my family and pretty. Very, very pretty, I'm told.

I am not bragging. It is a curse being pretty and fair. And colored. A plague. I look over at pretty Lilly and I tremble for her.

How could Robert not know that?

He is a man, my grandma would have said. No man could understand.

And a foreigner. Robert knows about Alabama. But he knows it like an outsider, a foreigner. He shudders when he talks of it, but he doesn't know. He thinks I've been spared.

"Thank your Christian God," he says, half teasing.

I say nothing. It's part of his strength, not really knowing. As bad as St. Kitts might have been, he kept his confidence. I saw too many in Alabama lose theirs. I see Noah holding onto his, but fighting. Always ready to fight.

I saw Daddy, gentle Daddy, get sadder and sadder.

We fled to this near North country though they still call it South. Not the South that I knew, that I know. But South enough.

Robert thinks he knows that South, too. Robert Littlefield and Mississippi, the boy who shot back, who fought back. *Kill and kill. Shoot and shoot*, letting others see what I had already seen: the rage beneath all that dignity, rage like a bullet ready to blow up all that politeness.

I remember how people were shocked at that column. How could Mr. Benjamin write like that? He who is so distinguished, so careful with his words. Even Sheila who says she is never surprised at anything.

But Daddy wasn't surprised when he read it. I wasn't surprised. Daddy knows about rage and putting on a mask. Knows about smiling when you got an anger inside you that works at you like Alabama's fire ants crawling in your clothes. It makes you want to claw deep ruts in your own skin.

Daddy knew when he brought Robert home to meet his daughter that he had that kind of anger. "Gentle him, daughter," he said to me that first night and I knew then that he wanted Robert for my husband—knew it before Robert knew it himself.

Daddy saw me as a gentle woman. But daddy is a man. He thinks all women who are not crazy are gentle. Men don't think we share that anger. Or have our own.

It is our job to have them think so. White or colored. It does not matter.

The sisters taught us about Catholic saints who turned their rage upon their own faces. The sisters did not mention rage. The women ripped their faces with their own nails so men would not want them, the sisters told us.

But we girls understood, we pretty girls. Robert says those women were sick and perhaps they were. Perhaps we are all sick. Not just women. Not just black women. I look at Robert, at Daddy. We cannot get at the face we wish to rake. Our rage needs somewhere to go.

Robert thinks I have been spared that kind of anger. Because I am a lady. Because I am pretty. I thank God that Robert thinks so.

Hide. Hide.

I tell you, I am so tired of this hiding.

I am a foreigner, too, here in Kentucky. Miss Emma Bisou says that I have grown in confidence lately, ever since our meeting at Madeline McDowell's mansion. She thinks that meeting has given me confidence. Maybe.

Or maybe I have simply rooowed far enough away from my past.

Robert has hurried off to the office, leaving me with young Noah. He is smiling at me, now, shyly. I can see the signs. Men have smiled at me all my life. My prettiness is always present, a throb, like the pain I sometimes get around my temples, the pain Robert tells me makes me look as if I were trying to remember something that I simply cannot recall. I nod to Noah, but do not smile.

"I am going out," I tell him. "Please tell Sheila. Tell her not to save me any food—that I will eat something."

He does not seem to hear my curtness. He bobs his head and smiles again. He does not ask where in Lexington a colored lady can eat if not in her home or the homes of her friends. I do not tell him that food has become an enemy lately. He is young and healthy and male. He would not understand. I close the door behind me.

Mr. Benjamin and I have been arguing about Noah. Not the flirtatious smiles—Robert would never notice something of that sort and I would never bother him with such nonsense. They are not flirtatious in any case, just revealing. I don't think he knows what he's doing when he smiles at me. Or ducks his head. We argue about Robert pointing to Noah as a Tuskegee example.

Robert's no Professor Russell, who says our schools ought to stop teaching so much book learning and train the children how to work. Imagine, telling that to our farm boys who spend twelve hours in the fields. But Robert does think it almost criminal—he's used that word—to fill our boys with Latin and Greek when they don't know how to make a living. He points to Noah.

"The boy's learned more from reading a hundred and more publications every week than he ever learned in school. Noah's learned to typeset, proofread, and someday he might even learn to spell. He's learned the practical world. Thank the Lord he was such a poor student in school and was spared being filled up with nonsensical Latin and Greek."

"But you were filled with Latin and Greek. So was Daddy. And both of you found how to make a living."

Robert pulled his head up. I knew what he thought: that he was not an example. He was the exception.

"Your father and I are lawyers. Four practicing colored lawyers in this town with enough full-time work for about two. Actually, that is not true. There is plenty of work, but enough money for about two. So where shall all that Latin lore find employment? Our boys need to learn a trade, need to learn how to survive. Save the Greek for their tombstones."

Lincoln, I think, would make his point better than Noah. Why would one attempt to teach Latin to Lincoln when he needs so much else? Robert has asked around for a job for Lincoln—perhaps at one of the stables. But Lincoln is so young, so frail. Carpentry or stone masonry might be a better route. Greek would not help him, even if he could learn it. It would be criminal.

"But we are not just 'hewers of wood and drawers of water'. We must have something more." Robert flushed. Booker Washington's white supporters love to cite that Biblical passage.

"Must have missed it when you hewed the wood. And far as I know, Sheila does all the water hauling in this house."

I know I am a silly woman, that there's not a colored woman in Lexington who does not envy me. Perhaps even many of the white ladies think I have everything I could want. So why do I feel as if I were locked in a small room with my two babies and only Robert allowed entry? He wants me to take my freedom.

But it is such a small freedom. Four lawyers. We need more. Our boys. Our girls. They need more. Perhaps they don't need Latin or Greek, but they need more.

I made my way to the Ladies Hall school committee. How Emma Bisou persuaded them to accept me is a mystery. I am fifteen years younger than anyone. And a foreigner. But I am Robert's wife. Emma helped start the Chandler Normal School over on Georgetown Street, a school all our younger colored teachers come from. Professor Russell took the school over when it moved from Fourth Street, persuaded the city to make it our first colored high school.

I must remember that Professor Russell has done much good.

We are meeting in the small auditorium of the school. It does not feel like a high school. I do not smell the air of learning in its halls as we always could with the nuns. Robert would say that what I smelled was incense and stale Catholic piety. He is unfair. The nuns wanted us to learn. They expected us to learn.

I do not feel that in our colored high school. The boys in the shop, the girls sewing. Useful trades, Professor Russell claims. It is his school now: the Russell School.

Miss Sophonisba Breckinridge is waiting to talk to us, a small surprise. We had not seen each other since our tea. We have not seen Mrs. Madeline McDowell—now Breckinridge—since the disastrous election, though she had sent a note to Emma saying she was appreciative of Robert's editorials, more than her new husband, Desha, had seen fit to print.

"Why a note to you? Why not to me? Or Robert?"

Emma rolled her eyes at the thought of Madeline Breckinridge writing to Robert. As for me, "Oh, Madeline is a believer in hierarchy."

I greeted Miss Sophonisba with a nod and a smile. She did not smile in return. Not unfriendly: she is simply a lady who does not smile. Neither of us offered our hands.

"I have been reading the school articles in *The Morning Herald*. They do not sound like your brother. Are they by your father?"

She looked pleased and a bit surprised. "How astute you are. Yes, Father has very strong views on colored education. He is a great friend to your race. I have read similar sentiments expressed by your husband. And by Professor Russell, even though he is not a favorite of ours, Madeline and me, in other respects."

"No. Too close to the Democrats in so many ways." We left unspoken what those ways entailed. We were ladies after all. "But I have misgivings concerning his views."

"But are they not your husband's?"

I did not answer at first. Miss Sophonisba was looking at me with renewed interest. She waited as only the daughter of a congressman and the sister of an editor knew how to wait..

"They are in part, but Robert is not so extreme." It would be news to many that Robert was not extreme, but I could not explain. Miss Emma Bisou was frowning at me. The meeting was about to begin. I smiled again at Miss Sophonisba and took my seat.

Miss Sophonisba stared out at us for so long we began to feel uneasy. She is just a few years older than I am. I can see the girl she was, awkward, shy. Not pretty. Her long thin face is too earnest, too anxious. She finally speaks, her voice a thin arrow sent wavering over our heads.

"The most important thing that we can do as women is to make sure our children receive the education they require."

The arrow lands with a thump among us. She pauses. *Our children.* It feels like an accusation somehow. She speaks as if all women are mothers to all children, for she has none. Our children. Are our colored children hers too? I have read her articles where she railed against the evils of truancy—as if it was just a failure of dedication, as if most of our children were off playing baseball or lolling about fishing, not in the fields before dawn, not in the factories until dark. We are prosperous ladies here, of course. Our children are not in the fields or in the factories. But around the rims of our lives are all the others—the Lincolns.

And what of my own two children? Babies still. Cloistered. They do not even know yet that they are colored. That knowledge has not sunk in yet. I dread the moment when I will see it in their eyes. *I am colored. This small world is all I have.*

They will know that soon enough. Perhaps without even Robert or me telling them. Had anyone told me in Alabama? I had been sent away so young to the Sisters. To keep me away from understanding or to train me to it? Our children. What is the education they require?

It was as if our thoughts were arrows shooting back at her, for her face became less stern as she looked at us and she was a girl again. She started again and her voice now was less a challenge, less an accusation than a confession.

"I am not a mother myself. I do not face the daily difficulties you face. As mothers. As mothers of colored children." She paused again. "But I want to share those difficulties as much as I can, help alleviate them if I can…" She stopped again. It moved me. The stopping. The looking for words. I am always looking for words.

A flurry at the door distracted us, Madeline McDowell Breckinridge entering in a rush. She looked at us in surprise as if we were the intruders. For a moment it seemed as if she were about to rush back out again when Miss Sophonisba appeared by her side, having quickly left the podium to greet her. Sophonisba looked relieved. Two white faces in a swirl of black ones. Madeline McDowell Breckinridge smiled at her sister-in-law. She took her arm and smiled as if she, too, had been rescued. Emma waved them both to the front of the room.

"What a pleasant surprise, Mrs. Breckinridge." I had never seen Emma smiling so. "Do you have something you'd like to share with the Ladies Hall committee?" No one seemed to wonder if Miss Sophonisba Breckinridge was finished speaking. Madeline McDowell Breckinridge had arrived.

Madeline moved so quickly that I feared for her steadiness. But she stood firm.

"I do, Miss Bisou. Thank you." She looked out at the room filled with colored ladies. She believed in hierarchy, Emma had said. All sorts of hierarchy—racial, social. And of course, that special niche reserved for McDowells and Breckinridges.

But she was here to challenge one of those hierarchies: the male one.

I blushed at my own unfairness. How much did I challenge?

"The next school board election we *will* be on the ballot, ladies. You have done such good work—the Chandler Normal School, and the valiant labors to bring quality education to colored youth. But so much of your efforts have come to naught."

She did not pause. She had our attention though her words stung. We had not expected such mixed praise. We had done good work but it had come to naught. We did not think it had come to nothing but Madeline McDowell Breckinridge plowed ahead, telling us why that was so.

"Just as the Fourth Street Colored School has been renamed the Russell School, so have your well-earned gains been corrupted and diverted to benefit the Democratic Party machine led by Mr. Billy Klair. Certain prominent colored citizens have reaped the gains of this corruption while your children—our children—have been robbed."

Robbed. I felt myself flush. Lady or not, she had said the word. I hadn't dared. We looked at each other. We wondered what Mr. Green Pinckney Russell, who ruled the colored schools in Lexington like a tawny czar, would think to hear his name used so in one of his schools.

"Some have written that it is criminal to waste time teaching young coloreds Latin or Greek." She searched the audience until she found my eye. She held it for a second. I felt myself grow rigid. "I will not get into that debate tonight." I looked down with relief. "I will reserve the word criminal for the real thing: the pilfering of the resources of our schools for the benefit of the few. We need to stop this. We need, as women, to rise up and take back our children's schools."

She paused finally. She, too, was not a mother, but she did not apologize for the "our children." I looked around me. The ladies sat, faces firm and stern. She had called the most prominent colored man in Lexington a thief, a party stooge. She was telling us what we knew but what we had not said aloud. She was telling us that if we wanted to change anything we needed to stop being respectable colored ladies. If we wanted our children to have a chance, we needed to stop being quiet, discreet. To show ourselves. To stop doing what we did best. Defer. Demur.

Hide.

Mrs. Madeline McDowell Breckinridge did not hide. She came into our den of colored women, hobbled with her false foot, and stood there and told us one of our own race was a bandit in respectable garb. It hurt us to hear that, though we knew it in our hearts. So few colored men made it to the top or near the top. Green Pinkney Russell had been praised by the mayor, had earned a Bachelor of Arts from Berea College when so many colored men still struggled to sign their name. We had no other school named for a colored man. He may have plastered his name like a school boy's scrawl on a playground, still it was there. He was there. But he had got there by climbing over everybody who counted, by telling white people what they wanted to hear. By listening to Billy Klair and the Democrats. He did not listen to us.

He had gotten there by selling his dignity and our dignity. Madeline McDowell Breckinridge said he was a thief. It hurt to hear a white woman tell us this. It hurt, but we knew it was so. What did it matter if he had gained our little world and lost his little soul?

Madeline McDowell Breckinridge was not surprised by a colored man's corruption. Just one more piece of flotsam who had bubbled up from the dirty immigrant stew of Lexington's politics. Irish, German, Polish, Italian, colored. She was here to tell us what we must do. It was her natural place. As a McDowell, as a Breckinridge.

Her daddy-in-law wrote editorials about how the coloreds should be educated, thoughtful columns that even Robert listened to, almost repeated in his own columns. A Breckinridge. It did not matter that five years ago all the nation talked of was his love nest—that he finally had to resign his seat in Congress. He is still a Breckinridge. He knows what is best for colored minds.

I was new to Lexington then, new to Robert. I've heard the whispers about Robert. A man near forty. Never married. Whom had he left behind. In Philadelphia? In St. Kitts?

But the white world did not care. Thank God. *The Standard* did not care. Madeline McDowell Breckinridge would not be shocked, would not notice. Robert was just a colored man doing what colored men did.

He was not a Breckinridge.

I care, but I do not know. And I do not ask.

Rumors abound about Desha, though they are married just a year. His daddy's boy, people say.

Are they all their daddies' boys?

I do not think we will read about Desha in the newspapers. At least not in his.

It does not matter. A man's past gets to stay hidden. And Robert has been true to me. I am certain of it. In our five years, he's come to me fresh every night. He comes to me naked, stripped clean. New. I have never smelt another woman on him. I have never seen him look at me and see someone else. He has come to me, eager, grateful.

And our children. He lifts them in his arms, receives them like gifts he never hoped to receive.

I do not know if there is a woman somewhere he has not been true to, another woman he has left behind. *Please Jesus*—that is what I ask the God Robert sees me praying to—*do not let a woman be out there crying for Robert. Let there be no children looking for their daddy.*

I ask this of Jesus as if even Jesus could make what was, not. As if Jesus could make it all right just by whispering a small breath on history and it would all disappear. All be made right.

We ask so much of Jesus. Colored folk. Women.

We had stirred with Madeline's last words. Take back our schools. From the politicians. From the thieves. Madeline McDowell Breckinridge waited for us to order ourselves, her face a picture of calm and impatience. She took little care for our hurt feelings. She is not our friend. She is offering us alliance. She would never sit across a table from us. Never share a meal.

I listened to Madeline McDowell Breckinridge, who barely keeps herself from shivering in distaste when we get too close to her, a startled look on her face like the one she wore at our tea. But she is doing her job. She soldiers on. Our captain leading us into the battle. For education. For the rights of women.

"You educated colored ladies must be in the forefront of this fight," she told us and I winced at her words. I saw some frowns. Emma Bisou pulled her shoulders back and I thought for a moment she might say something in response. Educated was code. Madeline McDowell Breckinridge's cousin Laura Clay used it to soothe those who worried that colored women would overwhelm whites. Emma looked at me. She understood but shook her head.

"Not the time, Maria. Not the time."

Not the time. Emma was right. Emma let her shoulders relax too. We were polite Southern ladies, all the way through. Duty governed us, too. And manners. The right way to do things. The right time to say things. It settled over us like a giant mesh veil. Our world. Their world.

Madeline McDowell Breckinridge's world. I did not care if I ever had tea at Ashland again. Eating eggs with ill-educated Sheila—and whose fault was that?—gave me more pleasure. We did not need to like each other to tell each other hard truths. It came over me that I did not like her, Madeline McDowell Breckinridge.

Sophonisba…I wish. But she remained of that world, too. Just visiting ours.

It didn't matter. I would follow Madeline McDowell Breckinridge. For women. And for my children. For Charlie and Lillian. For everybody's children, I would ape her limp all the way to the voting booth. We all were limping, all wounded. But it didn't matter. With her help we would make it. She couldn't help the contempt she barely veiled when she looked at us. She couldn't sweep away all the clinging hierarchy that crippled her much more than her missing foot. But she didn't have to eat with me. I didn't have to eat with her. I might have a hard time swallowing, too. None of it mattered. Or it did not matter enough.

For she had come out of hiding, had left cloistered, safe Ashland. She had come to lead. And for the children, I would follow her. For myself, I, too, would come out of hiding.

Part 2

Handicapping

CHAPTER 12

Noah Webster, March 1899, Lexington, Kentucky

Mr. Benjamin gave me more work since I left George Thomas. He might not think a Negro in the South should spend his days worrying about being shot, but he don't think a fellow should set up house in a shooting range, which is what George Thomas was starting to feel like. Actually, Mr. Benjamin didn't give me more work—I always had plenty of that. He just paid me a bit more for the work I was doing. Three dollars a week which is about a dollar less than a hostler makes full-time in this town, but it still ain't enough. Mamma sews and cleans houses and sometimes helps to cook when one of the big houses has a party and needs somebody extra. If she brings in four dollars, it's a good week. So we got six, seven dollars a week coming in and it just ain't enough. Especially with Mamma putting fifty cents in the collection box.

The Reverend Pickering's collection box. She back to him, says we all misspeak now and then.

Sometimes after setting the type, printing, hawking the newspaper everywhere I can think of, and maybe writing a column or two if Mr. Benjamin let me, I head over to Healey's stables. They sometimes have a few hours mucking for me and I might even pick up that fifty cents Mamma give to the poor Reverend Pickering. Most nights if I get three dimes out of all that muck, I'm lucky. Mamma says it ain't worth it, that she spend more than that on soap trying to get the smell out of my clothes. I'd rather be smelly than hungry, I tell her, and she look hurt. Like I still ten years old and it her job to feed me. I'm back living at home now. Mr. Benjamin thinks things with Doyle have calmed down. I don't know about that but I can't be hiding in his spare room forever.

At fourteen, Lincoln got more freedom than I do.

Besides I don't know that Maria like it much, me being there. She never said anything, but it can't be comfortable having a near stranger so close. Mr. Benjamin off in his books don't even know I'm there. Don't know Maria there half the time. Maria might want her home to herself. I glance at her and I feel her shucking off my look.

But being home got its problems, too. I see how Mamma look. We're both working ourselves to death, but Mamma ain't young. I look at her getting more and more tired every day. I can't stand it. I tell Mamma I'm thinking of looking for another saloon job.

"You can't hardly drag yourself to your chair. George Thomas at least give me enough money so we eat three meals a day without you killing yourself." Mamma had plopped herself down. She'd been cleaning all day in one of those big houses over on Sixth Street. She went regular to two houses there and two on Fayette Park. They brought her in for the heavy work. Forty years old and she still doing the heavy work. That mean she going all day—if she take five minutes to catch her breath they look at her like she stealing. When I work at George Thomas, she only do that once or twice a week. I want her to quit it altogether but she never would.

When I tell her about looking for a saloon job, she say, "Don't do that, Noah. I'm just a little weary. I go to my bed, I wake up rested, ready to work again. But all that time you working at George Thomas, I stay tired. Tired to the bone. Tired of worrying that you'd come home shot. Or not come home at all. Going to my bed just make me more tired. Don't do that, Noah."

It don't much matter if I'm grown or not. If Mamma says, "Don't do it, Noah," I don't do it.

But I got to get more money somehow. The old fellow at Healey's who gave me the mucking work told me about some races they scratched up out in the old race track. He used to be a jockey himself but he got too big. He don't seem that big, a little black fellow who has a right leg that don't seem to bend much. "Least you still get to work around horses," I say to him and wish I had shoved some of that muck in my mouth before I opened it. But he was a nice fellow. Just gave me a look that told me I was an idiot and went back to grooming. He was pulling a bristle brush down the back of an old mare and the way she quivered with every stroke you knew that fellow was the center of her world. That mare had come in from ten hours hacking, but fifteen minutes brushing she looked ready to hit the streets again. The fellow murmured something to the mare and nodded to me.

"That's right. Leastways I still get to work around horses. This mare's a whole lot better company than a lot of folks I know."

They closed the racetrack over on Third Street—went bust with the depression a couple years ago. They closed the racetrack but it's still there. The fellow says they put on about three races a week start in April and they need help. They sneak everything in—horses, jockeys, hooch.

"People with money just itching to slide some out of their breeches. People need to bet. Gamble on the weather if they have to, but they rather lose their money on a horse. You good with numbers. Mike's the chief bookmaker. Tell him Buster sent you. Good money. Better than mucking."

I scrambled over to Third Street first chance. Daddy used to take me—the first time I was about five or so. He'd come in from the country when John Fielding had a couple horses running. Wanted Daddy just to keep an eye out. Biggest crowds I ever been in. Sunny April afternoon, though it'd been raining that morning and most of the night. I almost fell in a mud hole deep as me. Daddy swooped me up on his shoulders.

"Your mamma kill me if I let you drown. Or get crushed to death." I remember how that felt, going from banging up against all knees and legs like you was in the middle of a bramble patch, then going up high in one jump to the top of the mountain onto Daddy's shoulders. I could see the whole world up there. The crowd pushed itself up against the rails down on the grounds. Colored and white men standing side by side, arguing over horses. Some fellows—colored mostly but a couple white men—wandered through the crowd writing. "Bookies" Daddy called them. He just waved them on when they came to him.

"Know too much about horses to be betting on them."

But then he called to a fellow he knew. "Third Belle, straight," he said and handed over a silver dollar. I hadn't seen a silver dollar but once before. The sun sparkled off it before it disappeared into the fellow's breeches.

Daddy smiled at the look on my face. "Belle's a good horse. Isaac won't let me down."

There was a few women down where we were. They weren't with any men though, and except for two who held each other's arms, they wandered alone through the crowd of men. I never seen ladies dressed in such bright dresses. One lady was all in pink with a green hat that stretched so wide fellows had to duck to keep from being hit by it. She gave me a wave when she saw me staring at her from high up on Daddy's shoulders and a loud howdy, too. Didn't know what to do. A white lady had never howdied me before. I didn't say anything. Daddy told me, "You just howdy that lady back."

I whispered a real small howdy. She laughed, pulled my head down, and smacked a loud kiss on my forehead.

"Always howdy folks back," Daddy said, spitting on his kerchief and wiping off the lipstick. "Just don't tell your Mamma who you've been howdying this time."

More ladies sat in the stands, but their dresses weren't nearly as pretty. Their white parasols shadowed their faces. About three, four men surrounded each lady, like she was a little island they were trying to get onto. Sometimes all I could see was the parasol sticking out.

I didn't see any colored folks in the stands. I waved at all those white folks thinking maybe this was a new thing you could do, but nobody waved back. I yelled howdy but nobody howdied.

"We too far away," Daddy said.

The jockeys were all colored men. I didn't think anything about that. Nobody else seemed to either. Daddy's voice took on some special feel when he pointed them out.

"That Billy Walker," he whispered to me. "Derby winner and he showed up that Mabel Mare from California. A good filly but ain't nothing like Kentucky bred."

He waved and Billy Walker waved back. Even howdied him though he was further away than those ladies in the stands. Almost all the jockeys knew Daddy.

Daddy's shoulders jerked forward so hard I almost fell off them when a man Daddy called the Prince came over. He reached down and shook Daddy's hand and gave my head a tussle. Isaac Murphy—people almost whispered his name. Then they were off and everybody stopped talking. It always like that the first few seconds after a race start, everybody freeze—the men surrounding the ladies just turned their backs to them and the ladies didn't mind. Everybody's eyes just locked on the horses. And it quiet—for a moment. For a moment it all possible.

Then the yelling starts. Yelling at the horses, yelling at the jockeys. Yelling just 'cause it a horse race. You might be quiet the rest of your life, but you yell at a horse race. All the men were shouting. Even Daddy, jumping up and down so hard I thought I'd go flying except he gripped hold of my feet and pulled me down even as he bounced me up. "Come on Isaac, come on Belle!" The horses ran so close I could see the steam snorting out their noses, the whips beating horses' flanks as fast as a gallop, the jockeys' heads bent to the horses' ears yelling as loud as the men on the side. "Come on Isaac," I yelled, too. "Come on, Belle!"

Our ladies didn't yell, but they squealed when the horses ran right by us and sprayed a fountain of brown mud on top of us. Hard to tell who was colored or who was white when they were past.

Then it was over. Done. All that slow dance to the starting line, all that fiddling. Then that blaze down the track. Then done.

"Oh," Daddy said, when he set me down and tried to wipe me off, "I should have just let you play in the mud hole." He crumpled up the paper the man had written for him and threw it down. Two fellows were whooping but most of the men just stood there, shaking their heads and grumbling. "Should have stayed home and played in the mud hole myself." He shrugged. "Belle didn't seem to like the mud much, though. Not a mudder."

I looked confused, I guess, because Daddy laughed. Laughed even after losing that shiny silver dollar, so I know losing couldn't be too bad. "Not like your mamma—just a horse who likes to run in the mud."

"Mamma don't like mud," I said, and he laughed again.

"Neither do Belle. Or my man Isaac. Even the Prince lose sometimes. Not a mudder." And he dipped his fingers in the mud and streaked them right across my cheek, the cheek he had just finished wiping. "But you be. You run in all sorts of weather. Don't much matter if it muddy or not." And he started clearing off the mud he had just put on. Daddy wasn't making much sense.

"You a winner every time."

I don't know if Daddy would still think me a winner. Twenty years old and hoping to get on with a bookie. Track looked about the same but the crowd was small. Surprised it ain't burnt down since it went broke. Nobody knows who owns it anymore. Been the biggest thing in town. Standing there empty, it was a big hole in the town. I shook off thinking of Daddy.

That was another big hole.

Three, four hundred people, straddled around the rails, filling that hole at least half ways. The stands were empty, waiting for the real owners to show up. No parasols. Still some ladies—women—making their way through the men on the rail. But not a fancy green hat among them. Just working girls, about half of them colored.

I finally found Mike, an Irish guy about forty. His face had that red flush Irish guys get when they drinking. Or they're mad.

He wasn't drinking far as I could tell. Couldn't hardly get him to look at me until I told him Buster sent me.

"Buster said to tell you I was good with figures."

"Buster?" He looked at me hard for a second then shoved me a page of figures. "Add these up."

The adding wasn't hard. Trying to read what he scribbled was the challenge. But I guess I did a good enough job of it. He kept shoving me pages of numbers to add up. He didn't even bother double-checking after the first couple. Then he went running through the crowd. I say running because that's what it took for me to keep up with him. But I kept up. Men kept shouting horses' names and numbers at him. He kept shoving papers at me to add up.

He had a white boy doing the same job when I showed up—looked a couple years older than me. But the boy couldn't add. Or add fast enough to suit Mike.

"Goddamnit Shane. Who you working for? Me or them?" Mike grabbed the sheet from him and thrust it at me. I handed it back in about half a minute. Mike nodded. Shane just glared at me.

After about ten minutes of us both following him around, Mike sent Shane off to talk to a man about a dog. Took me a moment to figure out a dog was a horse that didn't have a snowball's chance in hell of winning but padded up the tab nicely. Sometimes Mike had me write those bets on a different ticket. But not in front of the bottom feeders—that's what we called the fellows always looking for the long shot. They long shots for a reason. Mike didn't care about sparing their feelings—he didn't think much of none of the marks. But he didn't want to discourage them.

Before he left, Shane tried his best to discourage me. He sidled up close so Mike couldn't hear, not that he'd care.

"Real good with them numbers, nigger, ain't you? But you need more than figuring to keep a white man's job." Then he jabbed me real sharp and hard, but sneaky so Mike couldn't see. It took me a couple minutes to catch my breath. Mike looked disgusted when I fell back.

"What's wrong with you, boy? I'm twice your age, and you don't see me panting like a dog at the end of a rout."

I knew my line. "Sorry, boss. I'm coming." And I just ripped through that pain like it wasn't there. Colored boys know how to do that. I wasn't a dog. I was gonna win this race.

I was a nigger who knew how to add.

But Shane was right. I needed to know more than figuring to keep that job. I learned about touts and wise guys. I found out about thickums and bankers. I had to watch out for welshers and learn what tipsters really had the inside track. There a whole sign language bookies used called Tic-Tac that Mike thought I should have learned at my mamma's knees. He'd show me once, and man if I didn't get it then, he'd cuss me out in language I had learned early on—not at my mamma's knees, though. Mamma spent her life trying to keep me from that language. But I learned. After Shane's sucker punch, I ain't never fell behind again.

Bookies and handicappers got to move quick—sometimes a rumor would float out onto the track like a cloud of smoke and change a lock into a dog or at least a roughie. Most times, it weren't that big a change but you kept your nose to the air all the time, sniffing for trouble. About half the bookies were colored—they had the contacts with the big stables, knew more about what horses were ready and which had a ways to go. Ex-jockeys were the best wise guys. You gave and you got. "Go ask Soup," Mike might tell me, wondering about a maiden. Soup just shook his head and the odds went up. "Tell Soup to steer clear," Mike told me about a gelding two races on, paying Soup back. Soup didn't flicker an eye letting on that he heard me. But he had. All day go on like that. I close my eyes at night and numbers float by like they tails on a kite.

Less than half the jockeys colored. Times tough for all the jockeys since the track went bust, but worse for colored. When a race only had one colored jockey, he was riding a dog or a lock. They might put Willy Simms on a lock—he won the Derby last year and he hot. Owners still more interested in green than black. Beside Willy pull out so quick the white jockeys don't have time to do nothing. But you young and colored you probably get a dog, riding for spit and change.

White jockeys don't care if you ride a dog.

But you don't want to ride something in-between if you the only colored jockey. You might be "pocketed," squeezed like an apple in a cider press, only it won't be apple jack that spill on the track. Or shoved so close to the rail you almost riding it. Or crashing through it.

Can't jam a man if he got three, four other coloreds riding beside him. But more and more races only a couple coloreds riding. Only two coloreds riding, nobody betting them anymore. Owners don't like it either. Horses worth a lot more than jockeys, colored or white.

Crowds betting mostly white—always were. Not too many silver dollars in colored breeches. But crowds getting whiter. Don't see colored and white men arguing anymore. Not over horses anyway. They always quarreling with me. I'd turned into that real scary fellow, that person all the newspapers warn about—a young colored man.

"Nigger, get out of my way," or "Nigger, you write that down right?" Or when they come back with a loser, "Nigger, I didn't bet that. You deaf?"

Mike would growl them off if they pressed too hard, trying to crush me like a colored jockey out there on the track all by himself. After awhile they backed off some. I wanted to smack them hard, but I couldn't do that. Bad for business.

"Boy," Mike said, one of the few times I think he even looked at me, "you're good with numbers but you're not real good with people. White people at least. You don't think they can tell you want to slap them around? Need to smile more, boy."

"Like you do, boss?"

He actually laughed at that. Only other time he laughed was when a lock lost and he cleaned up.

"Oh, I don't need to smile, boy. I'm white. You do."

Time went by and I'm not sure I even heard "nigger," anymore. Like people say you stop hearing the railroad if you live right next to it. Or maybe you hear it but you don't pay it any mind. If you pay it mind you go crazy. Mamma say that about her arthritis pain. Always there.

But worse if you pay it mind.

Mike was paying me not to pay it mind. Good money. Real good money. The first day—a long day I'd thought he'd fire me more than once when I messed up on the Tic-Tac—he had me add all the totals and then grunted. He peeled off a five dollar bill and I couldn't hardly believe it. More than I made a whole week at *The Standard*.

"Be more when you learn," he growled. And it was. Five dollars a low day, ten dollars a good one. And one long stretch of an afternoon, when the Kentucky April softened the air with the locust trees blowing a cloud of white petals over everyone, and the money-losing crowd happy with dozens of new marks choosing the funny-named dogs, and even a few ladies spiking the blue sky with their parasols so if you squinted it was the old days, Mike made a bundle and he spotted me a twenty. Twenty dollars. Mamma might work a month for that.

It was worth it not to mind.

Except when it wasn't.

Mr. Benjamin was good about me working at the racetrack. Even let me write about Jimmy Walker once, growing up dirt-poor in Chilesburg—that's country-Lexington—and making it big. Started out racing for eight dollars a month. Made over a thousand dollars just on the colt he won the Derby on last year.

I didn't write about him just hanging on now, how he has to scramble just to get a decent mount. How he's talking about going to Russia because he ain't riding for eight dollars a month. His boots cost more than eight dollars. Of course I told Mr. Benjamin all about that. Told him about the way the white jockeys were out for blood. He took notes. Nodded his head. I could tell he was getting mad—could see his neck muscles tightening, just like they did when he talked about Wilmington, just like they did when he talked about that boy in Mississippi killing that deputy. Just like he did when he had to write about the boy being caught and lynched.

But a man can't run a newspaper mad all the time. You can't run a colt start to finish all out. You'd kill him. Kill yourself.

Finally, Mr. Benjamin let out a breath and said that was a column for another day. Just to keep bringing him what I saw and he'd be thinking about it. First we'd write about how good Jimmy Walker was doing—just like the late, esteemed Isaac Murphy—one more colored triumph.

Tomorrow maybe we'd write about him maybe moving onto Russia: home of the free.

"Credit to the Race" stories we called them. The race just needed a few more folks like Jimmy Walker and we'd be all be hauled along, be recognized as full-fledged Americans by everyone.

Everyone being white folks.

The next day we might tell about a few white folks being mean. Real mean. Some of them trying to kill us.

Couldn't write like that every day. Couldn't slap our readers around like that. Bad for business.

I worked nights if I had to be at the track during the day, or got up real early. The police were gonna shut the track down soon. Of course, they getting their cut to look the other way and whoever owned it—if anyone did—was getting their cut, too. But a whole bunch of people didn't like horse racing, thought it immoral. Lots of things immoral. Sometimes I even felt bad for the marks, but they were gonna lose their money to somebody. The world is full of sharpies.

Mamma says that's just excusing wickedness. But you got to excuse wickedness. No living in the world if you don't.

Had to make money while I could. Even Mamma seemed to agree. I handed her that twenty-dollar-bill and her eyes got wide. "Wages of sin," I teased her. One of Mamma's favorite quotes: "The wages of sin is death but the gift of God is eternal life." Mamma held that twenty in her hands for a good couple minutes, like she was trying to decide whether to throw it away or not.

Of course, Mamma'd never do something so foolish. She put it in the bank with all the rest of the money I gave her. She say we got more than a hundred dollars in the bank now, drawing interest. We rich. The wages of sin might keep us going for a few months at least.

Mr. Benjamin said he'd like to come see the races before they closed down. Liked to bring Mrs. Benjamin, too. I didn't know about that. He saw my look.

"Colored ladies not at the track?"

I squirmed a little. "Some. Some other women I might not call ladies. Last big day I saw a few white ladies, but they off in the stands. I don't know where Maria—Mrs. Benjamin—might sit."

He looked impatient. Where his wife might sit wasn't something he worried about. Mr. Benjamin wasn't what you call a woman's man. He treated women the same as he treated men. He didn't worry about men getting a place to sit, either. But sometimes he didn't see things.

"It's not really about where she might sit." I didn't know how to go on. But he finally got it.

"It's about her not being respected. Or treated like one of those ladies you might not call ladies."

He thought about it a moment. "I'll bring a chair. She'll have a place to sit."

CHAPTER 13

Noah Webster, Saturday, May 13, 1899, Lexington, Kentucky

Some people go to the races like they going to work. It's about money and money ain't about fun. I ain't even talking about the crooks—racetrack full of crooks, trying to fix it so it certain they win and you lose—maybe that's fun for them. No, I'm talking about people who show up like it's a regular job. I ain't never overbroke a bet for Mike—pay out more than we took in—and I hope to Jesus I never do. It'd be my last bet. Sometimes I wonder if Mike even know they running horses. I doubt he cares. Could be kangaroos circling the track: kangaroo #8 six to one; kangaroo #4 paying off even money. And what's going on with kangaroo #6? He's supposed to be a dog.

Most bookies like that, but not all. Bookies like Ollie Lewis—ex-jockeys mainly—are up there on the horse every time the starter drops the flag. Didn't matter that Ollie hadn't raced in years and weighed as much as some of the ponies now. I've seen Ollie cheer on a horse that was gonna lose him money, or at least make him a lot less. Mike would just shake his head. Who cared what kangaroo won? But bookies like Ollie are in it for the religion. They got to have faith in something.

Mamma say folks like that got faith-hearts, doesn't matter if they go to church or not.

"You got a faith-heart," Mamma says. I was missing church again—the weekends was all racing. She was disappointed about church, but she didn't press it. Made it almost worse that she didn't press it.

"I figured you put me down as a heathen by now."

"I hope you're not a heathen, but even if you are, you got a faith-bound heart."

I had too much of Daddy in me just to be a money-man, too much seeing Mamma slaving for a dime not to pay attention to business. Still, I'd put a dollar into my own pool every once in a while. I kept away from the dogs—and when the word came down that a fix was in, I steered clear of that, too. The fix is almost never fixed when ten horses are running. Somebody didn't get the word or somebody didn't get paid. Sure way to go broke is to bet a sure thing.

But I did about the next worst thing: I bet the jockey more than the horse. That's a losing bet, ask anyone. And I didn't stop there. I bet the jockey based on the color of his skin. Mike didn't know I was doing that. He'd say just hand the money over, not to bother putting it in the pool.

A boy named Eddie Buford was my favorite. Lost a fortune on that boy. Not even full-growed yet, he was just sixteen years old and a little fella. Ollie would of made three of him—but he was all muscle. I've seen him bring a dog up to almost winning, Mike cussing him out more than once having to pay out show money on a horse that had no business showing up anywhere. Eddie'd slip out of the pocket the white jockeys tried to put him in like loose change through a hole. He'd be ahead of the pack and it was almost a steeple chase, like he'd just leaped over everybody. It didn't matter that some white jockeys used their whips more on him than they did their own horses. He was Isaac Murphy come back to lead us to the Promised Land.

Only thing: to get to the Promised Land, you got to go through a lot of desert.

Most of the owners weren't pure money-men—horses a way to spend their money, not make it. Still they tried to keep from going broke too fast. They knew that the odds were against Eddie. And it wasn't like they had any liking for colored jockeys, though I don't think they much cared one way or the other. Not like the jockeys. But Eddie was making them money and as long as he was, some of them was willing to take a chance on him.

I was gonna take my chance, too. Mamma was right: I got a faith-bound heart.

The day everyone showed up was the second Saturday in May—the week after the Derby—like Lexington was trying to send a message to Louisville, even if they had to send it from a track that really wasn't open. Track didn't look closed. Somebody had spruced up the stands like they were expecting the ladies, for word had spread to the gentry, the horse people, and then some. Mr. Benjamin wasn't the only editor come to see the excitement, semi-legal or not. *The Morning Herald* editor—Mr. Desha Breckinridge—was sitting by a lady in those cleaned-up stands. People kept coming up to them, but more to her than to him. She was a strange-looking lady—no hat, no parasol even. She just sat there looking over the race track, kind of like she owned it.

We weren't legal, but you wouldn't have known it from the crowd. The Mayor and the police chief. Half the lawyers who hung around the courthouse. I even spotted Judge Bullock, law and order himself. I nodded at him, knowing he wouldn't remember me from Adam though I spent about the worst fifteen minutes of my life testifying three feet from him. I think he did something with his head back, maybe a nod. Probably didn't recognize me having to look up at me rather than down. You wouldn't know how short he was sitting high up on his podium. About as tall as Eddie, though a whole lot rounder.

Billy Klair passed the other way about the same time. He was headed over to a group of touts. I saw Shane with them. He'd quit Mike in disgust after about the second day I started working. Quit just about five minutes before Mike fired him. Mike didn't even look up. Peeled off two dollars and waved him off.

The touts greeted Billy like an old friend. They was up to something. Touts always up to something.

Billy stopped when he saw the judge, like he wanted to tell him something. But the judge turned away after he nodded to him—a real nod, a whole bend of his head, not like the one he gave me—and Billy just went on. Looked kind of disgusted. Billy gave me a wave, though. Billy always friendly like that. For all he knew I was a voter. I don't think he much liked colored voters, but he'd wave to them.

The judge's lady was with him, but she didn't look at me. She looked in my direction but somehow did that white lady thing and didn't see me. You think white ladies just don't know you're there until they hand you something to tote. They see "uncles." It's okay to see uncles.

The sun was blazing, August jumping into May. I felt half-sorry for the fancy folk—the men in full suits and vests, and the ladies dragging so much clothes on their backs it was a wonder they didn't break down, like some old hackney horse dragging a wagon full of people. The ladies all wore large hats, one larger than another, to show off a bit, and they shaded them some. And they had their parasols. They worked their fans as hard as they could. All that did was cool the sweat running down their faces.

I was down to shirt sleeves myself and would of stripped off more if I could of. But Mike wouldn't like that. All that mucking horse stalls made me pretty strong looking. Could of showed off some muscles for the ladies—the colored ladies that is. And if a white lady sneaked a peek, I wouldn't much mind.

But some others might. I kept my shirt on.

Maria didn't wear as much clothes as the white ladies, and what she wore didn't look like she had pulled it in with ropes to fit her body. She was just six months off from baby Lilly and there was still something soft about the way her dress just lay on her, not a white dress like almost all the white ladies wore. Some kind of purple, I don't know. She wore a little pink hat with just a tiny brim that didn't give her much shade from the sun, just dimmed her forehead a bit and made you have to look for her eyes a second in the sunlight. No parasol. Maybe her brown freckled face didn't need as much shade as the white ladies did.

Mr. Benjamin was carrying a small wooden chair. I took it from him quick and set it up on a little knoll about a hundred feet from the track. He looked puzzled that I chose a spot so far from the horses. He looked over at the stands. He was a good distance from them but he gave a nod to someone. I looked and saw Mr. Desha Breckinridge nod back. I hoped Mr. Benjamin wasn't gonna try to sit in the stands.

"Don't want to get too close," I said. "Mud and dust."

"Mud and dust," he repeated, and pulled the chair out for Maria to sit. "Appropriate. A bit of the Bible and Darwin combined." Sometimes I didn't know what Mr. Benjamin was talking about. He looked around at the crowd, mostly white even near the rail, but with a good number of colored. A mixed crowd and I don't mean race only. There was touts and Bluegrass upper class, ladies who just glided over the grass—had to look down to be sure they had feet, never too sure about their legs—and some "ladies" who might slide down into that same grass for a price. At least you knew for certain they had legs. Guess those shady ladies thought a sunny day in May was the place to show off their charms. Lexington not that big a town, but it weren't often females so different come within shouting distance of each other. Men might meet at the courthouse, might even holler howdy. Women did not.

Of course, if you was Judge Bullock, you didn't need shouting distance, and you never hollered howdy. You just gaveled the rabble on to jail.

Mr. Benjamin shook his head.

"Not certain how far we've crawled from the ocean shore."

I didn't have time to figure what he meant, for Mike was looking mighty impatient though we was forty-five minutes from the first race. One thing about being a bookie is that the world comes to you. Mostly they talked to Mike. They only noticed me when he'd jerk his head in my direction for them to pay me, or for me to pay them if they won. I jotted down names and figures. Mike talked horses to them and wrangled the odds. The only time I talked odds was when I was betting. And the only time I bet was on Eddie. Then I said the bet out loud to Mike and he had me write it down. It'd be out of my pay or on top of it at the end of the day.

Didn't always lose. Pay got topped a couple times. One big bet and I might even break even. That's about every better's dream: ending up where he began.

Folks always asking us for tips, but Mike didn't give out tips and I didn't have any to give. Mike just thought it bad business telling people how to lose their money especially when they were losing it with us. Hard feelings. So when Mr. Benjamin and Maria wandered over and wondered if I had any advice, I didn't know what to say at first. Eddie was running on a colt named Bluegrass Funeral in the big race. He was supposed to be a killer—that was the word—so big a three-year-old it was hard to imagine he had a year or two more growth in him. John Fielding, Daddy's old boss, had a half-interest in him. John Fielding was an owner but he was almost a pure money-man. All about the money. He passed by me more than once and looked puzzled when he saw me, as if he ought to know who I was but couldn't quite place me.

That's all right. I could place him.

All sorts of rumors as to why they hadn't run Bluegrass Funeral in the Derby. The one that seemed to stick was that he tossed his jockey on an exercise run the day before, an old white jockey named Skip Garrison. A couple broken ribs—just a day's toll for a jockey. But Garrison seemed to take it personal. I already heard what he said a half dozen times: "Bluegrass's gonna be somebody's funeral, just not mine. I won't ride him for love or money."

That's all there is, love or money. You got to be in it for one of them.

People listened to Garrison, a big name jockey who raced head on against Isaac in the eighties. Jockeys listened to him leastways. John Fielding couldn't get another rider, even for the Derby.

But they got Eddie for today. Weren't calling the race The Bluegrass Stakes, but that's what it was really. All the big horses, all the big jockeys. Except Eddie. But they got him cheap probably. And maybe they didn't have much choice. It was his chance. Didn't know how I thought about it. It was a chance, alright. Didn't know if he was riding for love or money. Hoped it was both.

Wasn't really a tip telling Mr. Benjamin about Bluegrass Funeral, just the common talk of the track. I looked over at Mike. He flicked an eye at me. That meant go on, he didn't care.

"Eddie Buford—he's that boy I told you about—and Bluegrass Funeral in the fifth. The big race. Only we just paying even money. He the favorite."

"The colored jockey? He's on the favorite? They going to let him run his race?"

I couldn't hardly answer that question with Mike about a foot away so I just shrugged. "Bluegrass Funeral's almost a lock. They gonna have to let him run it."

He handed me a five dollar bill—two more than he paid me in a week. Maria raised her eyebrows at the amount but she didn't say anything. She hadn't said anything but a soft hello the whole time. She almost never looked at me, either. I could have stripped off shirt—pants, too—and she wouldn't a given me a glance. I felt she didn't care for me looking at her, either. I tried not to. At least I tried not to linger.

"Boy, are you taking bets?" I looked up to see Judge Bullock looking up at me. I guess he'd been standing there for a few seconds. He wasn't the kind used to waiting. He held out a five dollar bill himself. "Bluegrass Funeral. To win."

"Well, Judge," said Mr. Benjamin, "we share the same horse. Do you think that is good luck? Or bad?"

Judge Bullock turned to the colored man who came up to him like he had a right to, like he was just another fellow. Too much even for the race track. Hard to explain the color line. Whites and coloreds still discussing horses, arguing sometimes. But the line was there and everybody knew it. Mr. Benjamin ain't said nothing much different. It just the way he said it, like he didn't see the color line. But that can't be right. Everybody see that color line.

Judge Bullock pulled himself up—as far as he could go—but so far, I thought he might fall over. But his look changed when he saw who was talking to him. He was still mad, but his look changed. He took a moment, but his voice was soft—almost polite—when he spoke.

"Supposed to be a sure thing, Mr. Benjamin. I do not bet long shots. I am surprised that with your propensity for long shots, yourself—your run for Congress comes to mind—that you have chosen such a horse."

"I'd say my run for Congress—my non-run—was more of a scratch. But I've chosen Bluegrass Funeral because of young Noah here. You remember Noah? He testified in your court about that killing you ruled a self-defense."

I nodded to the judge. The way he stared at me, I felt a bit like I was back on the stand.

"Difficult to follow your logic there," Mr. Benjamin continued, "but you seemed to hold fast to it. Anyway young Noah recommended Bluegrass and the young colored jockey riding him. I always follow young Noah's testimony. Especially testimony he has firsthand knowledge about."

The judge's mouth tightened. His voice got louder. "Firsthand knowledge is not always reliable—in fact, sometimes it's an impediment. Somewhat like eyewitness testimony. If we're talking about horse racing still. If not, I believe I already read your opinion of my 'logic' as you put it, in *The Standard.*"

"You read *The Standard*? I am surprised. But it is good to know. I like to hold the audience in my mind when I write. But I did not expect my audience to include you, Judge."

"You have a much wider audience than you might know, Mr. Benjamin. An audience who pays attention to your words and to the actions your words might generate. Perhaps with that in mind, you might take more care. You have been in my courtroom, both as visitor and as lawyer. I would not want to see you there in any other capacity."

"I hope not, either, Judge. A black man in your courtroom has as much chance as a dog running the big race. Even with a fine young colored jockey riding him."

Judge Bullock flushed red. I was thinking he might like the chance to get a certain black man in his court.

"The colored community has always known me as a particular friend. I resent your allegation."

"Resent? Oh, Judge, you do not know what resentment is. Be a colored man in Lexington. Or a colored woman," and he looked over at Maria.

Neither man said anything more. Maria took Mr. Benjamin's arm and pulled him towards the knoll I'd set her chair on. The men had inched real close during their conversation, so Maria needed to come real close to the judge to steer Mr. Benjamin away, but he didn't even look at her. I'm not sure he even saw her. Reminded me of how the judge's wife never looked at me.

Of course, plenty of white men staring at Maria all the time. Sometimes I wanted to kick them in their faces the way they stared at her. They wouldn't look at a white whore like that. But not white men like Judge Bullock. His kind just couldn't figure her out. Where she fit. They wouldn't call her missus and didn't feel right calling her anything else. A woman like Maria confused him.

Wouldn't even sneak a peek.

I was so busy writing down figures I didn't look up again till the big race was about to begin. I got a breath, though, and I called out to Mike.

"Ten to win on Bluegrass Funeral."

"Who's betting?"

"Me."

He looked at me hard. "I don't like my boys going broke. Can't concentrate right. Don't like 'em tempted, either. Mashes their brains. Makes them think they can pull one over."

Wasn't likely I'd try to pull one over on Mike. Not if I wanted to go on breathing.

"I could ask Ollie. He'd take my bet."

He didn't like that. "Suit yourself." I wrote my ten dollars down in the book—about three week's pay at *The Standard*.

Eddie wasn't the only colored jockey in the race. Two others in a field of twelve, made me feel a little better. The other two coloreds weren't riding dogs, either—too much money upfront to put a dog in. But they were on long odds, stuck on the outside even though one of them was Willy Simms and he just won the Derby last year. Now he was scrambling for mounts. Eddie and Bluegrass were right in the middle of the pack. They say the jockeys pull cards to see who's placed where but if John Fielding pulled anything, it was strings. Got Bluegrass right where he needed to be. Daddy never called John Fielding a crook—just said he was an angle man.

Angled Daddy out of this world. Figured John Fielding could help angle me a horse race.

It was a good distance for three-year-olds—a mile and a half—but Bluegrass Funeral was a router. He already shown he could run that far and more. The horse was huge—sixteen hands high—all leg and muscle. Usually you hold a horse like that back in a long race, don't want to go to the front and wear him out. But I was afraid the white boys would try to pocket

Eddie in, push him to the rail, or something. I didn't think Bluegrass was the kind of horse you could pocket. I didn't know what would happen if you tried. And Bluegrass was such a steam engine, I just didn't see him being worn out if he went to the front.

So, I was happy when he went out like a shot—the flagman dropped his arm and Bluegrass Funeral was two lengths ahead of the pack and stretching a lead. It was gonna be a blowout.

"Whooeee!" I shouted. Mike don't like me to show partiality towards any horse—don't want the losing marks to feel like we got a stake in their losing—but just about everybody was shouting. Even Mr. Benjamin. Maria wasn't, but she had leaped up from her chair and was doing a little dance and clapping her hands.

Then it was all confusion. The flagman's assistant—about a hundred yards down the track—was waving his own flag. Half the horses pulled over right away, the others kind of dribbled to a stop. But Bluegrass Funeral was still running, almost ran the assistant down when he jumped onto the track. Assistant kept waving his flag and shouting something.

The crowd had got quiet—as quiet as a thousand people can get.

"What's he saying?" I asked Mike, pointing to the assistant.

"False start," he answered. "They're going to have to start over."

Eddie finally managed to pull Bluegrass over. You could tell the horse wasn't happy—reared up his front hoofs and almost bucked Eddie off—but Eddie got him stopped. Don't know how. That horse weighed more than half a ton, Eddie maybe a hundred.

Bluegrass Funeral was a router, but heck, he'd already run a half mile before the race began. A two-mile race even for a three year old router is a long race. Bluegrass was the heavy favorite and the marks around weren't happy. They smelled something and it weren't horse muck.

"What do they mean, false start?" One of our regular marks, an old man, was shouting at me like I was the one waving the flag. He usually bet long shots but had put down heavy on Bluegrass—fifty dollars. Marks try to make up all their losses in one shot by going heavy on a lock. Hell, I did that. The old man kept yelling. "Those horses all started the same—as soon as the man lowered his flag. Did you see anything? What are they pulling?"

I didn't see anything. Nobody but the flagman seen anything. Or said he did. They were pulling something. I could of told that old man I was in the same boat—my ten probably more to me than his fifty to him. But Mike didn't like the marks to know that kind of stuff.

Eddie had gotten Bluegrass back to the starting line. He was leaning over the horse, talking to him. I hoped Bluegrass was listening. I saw him panting, almost like he'd run his race already.

But Bluegrass had a lot of race in him still. He didn't get out ahead this time around but he was in the first group of horses, six of them grouped together with the other six falling behind. They rode 'round the first bend, Bluegrass edging ahead steadily. He still had a lot in him, only not the burst of speed he had the first time out. But before he could break free, the horses on either side of Bluegrass gave their own burst of speed and pulled right in front of him, then the next two horses in the bunch of six pulled right next to him. They had him pocketed, boxed in front and side. The third favorite, Fair Chance—a colt ridden by Skip Garrison, Bluegrass's old jockey, was the sixth horse in the bunch. He pulled ahead of everyone. I hadn't thought Fair Chance had a chance in hell, but the money had come on heavy in the last minutes before the race ended. His odds had gone down to three to one. One of Billy Klair's buddies had put down a hundred a minute before we closed out. I looked over to Mike. It bothered me some. But Mike just nodded. I should of known something.

I looked at Fair Chance pulling ahead of the rest of the field and I started cussing. Mike didn't even notice—or he didn't pay it any mind. Everybody was cussing, shouting, screaming. White marks yelling at colored jockeys a regular thing, telling them to go back to riding zebras, leave the horses for the white boys. But this time most of them had bet on the colored boy, and money didn't pay no mind to color. The marks were yelling at the white jockeys, seeing that pocket, knowing what was going on. "Let the nigger go!" they shouted. "Let the nigger go!"

But they weren't letting him go. That pocket rode down that track like a closed carriage, not like anything you ever seen. "It's all over," I said to Mike. "It's all over."

Except it wasn't. Maybe it should have been, the way things turned out. It would have been a lot better. But it wasn't over.

Bluegrass Funeral was just too much horse to let a pocket keep him in. They could of sewn that pocket shut with steel thread, he was gonna rip it free. Or maybe those white jockeys all around him just overplayed their hand. They put Bluegrass under punishment, whipping him more than they whipped their own mounts. Whipping Eddie, too. And both of them seemed like they'd had enough. The jockey on Eddie's right side was flailing with his whip so hard he hit the horse placed right in front of Bluegrass—which made him startle and run to the rail. That left a space and that was all Eddie and Bluegrass needed. They through it in a flash, squeezing through those two horses in front like Moses parting the Red Sea. Fair Chance was five lengths ahead but Bluegrass was closing fast.

The crowd was shouting louder now and that must of told Skip Garrison something was up. He turned his head and saw Bluegrass bearing down on him, coming up the rail side fast. They were a quarter mile from the finish line. Bluegrass Funeral was going to catch him. Maybe old Skip remembered how Isaac beat him head on in a match race back in the eighties—settled once and for all who the best jockey was. Probably seemed like it was happening again. Or maybe Skip just put down a lot of money on Fair Chance— we found out later the whole court house crowd had—and he just didn't want to face them. But he just wasn't gonna let it happen. He just wasn't gonna let that colored boy beat him.

He moved Fair Chance right in front of Bluegrass when Bluegrass was just a length behind and pulling up like a freight train. Eddie didn't have time or space to go around him. He'd have to pull him up short and break his stride. Even a monster horse like Bluegrass Funeral didn't have three starts in him in a race. It was all over. Didn't much matter if it was fair or not, Fair Chance was gonna win.

Only Eddie didn't pull him up. Or couldn't. I'm thinking couldn't. Bluegrass Funeral been made to start over once, he weren't gonna let it happen again. He plowed right into Fair Chance who must of thought he was being ripped at by wolves. He went sideways, trying to keep his feet, and veered to the mob pressed against the rails who scattered in panic as he headed towards them. But Bluegrass hadn't just nudged him, he had rammed him so hard Fair Chance couldn't keep his footing. He landed with a crack—I swear you could hear it in all that din. Fair Chance lay there in the middle of the track, his back broken, his hoofs flailing in the air.

The four pocket horses were on top of Fair Chance in a moment's run. One of them crashed into the mess, his jockey shooting over him like a circus cannon shot. Two of the pocket horses headed for the stands—you could tell the jockeys didn't have any say in any of it—as if they was chasing the few spectators who hadn't run away yet. One horse crashed right into the rail, throwing his jockey into the infield before he tumbled over into the track. His front hoofs bent in front of him, like he some parade horse kneeling. But I didn't think he was gonna get up from that kneel.

Skip Garrison been thrown when Bluegrass ran into him. Somehow all those horses joining his catastrophe missed him. He sat in the middle of the track like he'd bought a front row seat and watched it all pass by. One of them passing was Willy Simms on a long shot— fifty to one. Colt named Evening Breeze. Just breezed on by them all.

But Eddie didn't have that kind of luck. Not even-money. Not fifty to one. Bluegrass Funeral plowed right through the rail and took Eddie with him. Only Eddie didn't make it through the rail, just halfway through and lay there spread out waiting for the last pocket horse to choose that very same spot in the rail to try to crash through, too. A whole mile and a half of rail. You'd think that horse could a chose a different spot. What was the odds?

The pocket horse didn't make it all the way through. Just mashed up poor Eddie before he mashed up himself. Bluegrass Funeral made it through. Ran around the infield free and clear. Took them half an hour to catch that horse. Only caught him because he finally wore out. Seemed fine otherwise. A couple scrapes, a couple bruises. It'd take a shotgun to hurt that horse.

Two of the white jockeys got a couple of broken ribs out of it. Not Skip—just like Bluegrass Funeral. A scrape or two. Hurt pride.

Only I don't think Bluegrass Funeral's pride was hurt.

Eddie was the only one paid the real price. Oh, I guess Fair Chance and those other horses paid some, too. You wouldn't of known that listening to the marks. All the money they lost. Not just the marks. Billy Klair was shouting at a group of his courthouse pals. Smiling Billy. He weren't smiling now. I saw John Fielding over in the infield with a group of fellows trying to catch Bluegrass. He weren't smiling, either.

Mike didn't much care. Evening Breeze wasn't a dog so Mike had put him in the pool. He just took his cut. Didn't much matter if a long shot or a favorite came in. Actually made more money with the long shot. Don't know if we had more than two people bet Evening Breeze. A lady sent her beau over from the stands—fellow looked embarrassed when he bet for her. Told us she liked the name.

I liked the name, too. Evening Breeze. We could of used a little cooling. The sun was halfway down but it was still hot.

The crowd was leaving fast. Supposed to be a couple more races but that wasn't gonna happen. They were dragging off the dead horses. Nobody had dragged off Eddie yet. Hadn't even covered him till Mr. Benjamin walked over and started yelling at John Fielding. Finally got him to stop chasing Bluegrass long enough for him to cover Eddie with a horse blanket. Didn't mean no disrespect. Only covering they could find.

Mike slipped me five even with my ten dollar bet. And we ain't had a whole day. Surprised me some, but Mike always was a generous fellow and he'd done good even without the last two races. I told him I wasn't coming back. That surprised him.

"Why's that? Thought you were doing good."

"Thank you, Boss. But I just don't feel the race track the right place for colored anymore. Just don't seem welcoming."

He was mad. Would of snatched that five back if I'd given him half a chance. But I was out of chances. Blown all my chances with Eddie.

I passed Judge Bullock. He was moving fast. Would of run me down if I got in his way. He looked mad, too. Everybody looked mad. I saw Mr. Desha Breckinridge escorting his lady out as fast as he could, too. But she limped some so he had to wait on her. It was a day for limping. Seemed like half the horses left standing was limping. I don't know to get out of a place, but something holds you back. I felt that way myself.

I went over to stand by Maria while she waited on Mr. Benjamin to return from seeing about Eddie. Mr. Benjamin wanted to know about Eddie's family—kin, friends. He wasn't getting many answers from John Fielding. All John Fielding knew was that Eddie could ride. All he was interested in. And that was all done. John Fielding was done. But Mr. Benjamin kept pestering him, and didn't seem to understand that a very valuable piece of property was still running free in the infield. Nothing to do about Eddie. Nothing anyone could do about Eddie. Bluegrass Funeral needed to be caught.

Maria stared out at Mr. Benjamin and I could tell she was frightened. Not for herself. I don't think she was ever frightened for herself. I heard her whisper—not to me, just whispering—"Oh, Robert, Robert." She put her hand on my shoulder to steady herself as she whispered. That hand was like a heat that sank through my shoulder and into my chest, that caught on something tight in my breast until I needed steadying myself.

"Robert, Robert," she kept whispering. *Maria*, I wanted to whisper back.

They finally caught Bluegrass Funeral so John Fielding could turn his attention to Eddie and get Mr. Benjamin off his back. John Fielding waved two big colored fellows over from dealing with Bluegrass. Bluegrass was almost settled. Didn't need ten grooms pulling on him. The two fellows grabbed the two ends of the blanket covering Eddie and wrapped him in it. They were moving fast and maybe they expected Eddie to weigh more because they jerked him into the air like they were going to toss him and he almost went flying. They was big fellows. One of them could have slung Eddie over his shoulders with no trouble. Eddie'd never been any trouble, except maybe to some white jockeys. Wouldn't be no trouble anymore.

Maria's eyes strayed from Mr. Benjamin. She stopped whispering his name. "Oh," she said as she saw them carrying Eddie. "Oh," she said again and tears filled her eyes. The sun had passed behind some clouds; the little pink brim didn't shade her face anymore. You could see her eyes now.

Nobody had cried for Eddie yet. She was the first. The marks had yelled and cussed the other riders, even the ones who tumbled over horses. Cussed them when they were carried off the field. Cussed Willy Simms when he walked 'round on Evening Breeze as if he'd been part of it all. Even cussed and looked slant at Billy Klair. They loved "Call Me Billy." He usually got a cheer when he showed up. But they weren't cheering now. The rumor went 'round quick, almost beat Evening Breeze to the paddock. Billy was messed up in it somehow. Would of been worse if he collected. But he was a loser, too. Everybody a loser except that lady with the shamed-faced beau. Everybody cussing.

They cussed Eddie, too. Cussed him when they had him boxed in, cussed him for not getting out. Cussed him when he got out and crashed into the rail.

They didn't cuss him lying there under his horse blanket. Limits to what even a mark will do, even a mark that's been cheated.

But they didn't cry for him, either. Not even the colored marks cried for him. Marks are a tough bunch; it's a tough game. They got quiet when Eddie got covered with the blanket. Stood uneasy when they carried him off the field. They might of felt bad for a moment but they shook it off. They didn't let that bad feeling reach their brains. They weren't boys wailing skinned knees. They were men. Bets got lost. Jockeys got mashed.

But I looked at those tears in Maria's eyes and something ripped in my chest. At first I thought I was gonna be sick, thought I might vomit that whole miserable day out on that pretty green turf in the middle of all them fancy people. Make them sick, too, watching me throw up.

But it was something rough and loud that poured out my throat, not sickness. Something cracking. Men scattered away from me like I was another runaway horse. Looked more shocked than they did when Bluegrass Funeral plowed into Evening Breeze. A grown man crying. It wasn't right. It wasn't proper.

Maria took her arm from my shoulder and looked at me wondering, her eyes widening at first as if she was afraid of me, too. She stared a second. And then her shoulders started to rock. Soft and then harder. Her grief mellow next to my loud rumble, a faint fiddle that grew till it grew almost as loud as my moan.

I grew stronger as I heard her. Her cry weaved through my sobbing like a stitch that kept the wound from tearing all apart. She gave me comfort. That sadness would of swallowed me whole without her sharing it. She took my shoulder again and pressed my arm in her hand. And it comforted me.

"Eddie," I whispered to her when I caught a breath, "Eddie."

"Eddie," she whispered back.

CHAPTER 14

Noah Webster, Tuesday, May 16, 1899, Lexington, Kentucky

A good thing I quit when I did, because Mr. Benjamin tapped me on the way out and said he needed me next day, that he was making some changes to *The Standard*. The paper came out on Tuesday but we'd been ahead of the game. I'd been looking forward to a light Monday's work.

But that all changed. Mr. Benjamin just ripped out the front page and most of the second. Couldn't afford to print more than four pages usually, but we was going to six this time. Two long days and it be pretty close. But he said there'd be more money in my pocket. Help fill up that money hole Eddie left.

Only nothing fill that hole.

Mr. Benjamin lead the new front page with a headline:

MURDER AT THE TRACK

The aristocracy of the Bluegrass was gathered en masse on Saturday at the grounds of the bankrupt Kentucky Racing Association, a thousand people perhaps. Not all aristocrats: touts, bookies, and men and women whose sense of decorum might not be ours. But we will direct our attention to the leaders of our community: *The Morning Herald* editor, Mr. Desha Breckinridge, and his lady, Mrs. Madeline McDowell Breckinridge, the noted women's leader, Judge Frank Bullock—chief judge in our courts and a prominent counsel to the Democratic party—and Mr. Billy Klair, the leader of that party. Mr. Klair—Billy as he likes to be called—was surrounded by many of his informal courthouse advisers. These are men who receive no official remuneration but are handsomely rewarded in other ways.

A hot May afternoon, our ladies shaded by wonderful hats and parasols, the bookies doing a brisk business—some of which was mine. A young, very young, colored jockey—Eddie Buford—caught my eye. The rich color of his skin, perhaps, influenced me more than the speed of his horse.

The years since the great Freedom War have been difficult for the colored race, a continuous fight to maintain our rights: our vote, our ability to compete in the workplace, our farm land, our dignity, and even, in many cases, our very lives. Colored jockeys in this struggle have been a bubble of prosperity and hope. Isaac Murphy is the best known, perhaps, but there are many others: Oliver Lewis, the first winner of the Derby; Billy Walker, born a slave in nearby Versailles but a Belmont Stakes winner and now a prosperous trainer; and more recently, Soup Perkins, Willy Simms, and Jimmy Winkfield—well known in Kentucky and in the nation.

But Jimmy Winkfield and Willy Simms, for all their success, have had difficulty acquiring good horses of late, for white owners are increasingly reluctant to let even the finest colored jockeys ride their best horses. White jockeys are against it. They resent colored jockeys winning. Coloreds winning anything is not normal, they claim. In this, they are right.

Many white jockeys refuse to mount beside colored jockeys. When they do ride, they push colored jockeys into pockets, shove them against the rails, use their whips more on the colored jockeys than on their own mounts. White owners rightly fear injury of their very valuable horses.

Jimmy Winkfield did mount on Saturday, on a fifty-to-one colt named Evening Breeze. But Eddie Buford, a slight sixteen-year-old, was placed on the heavy favorite, Bluegrass Funeral—a giant of a horse. Why? Perhaps because Eddie was young, eager, and cheap. Perhaps because no one else would ride the horse. Skip Harrison, his previous jockey, thought him too dangerous to ride. I, however, want to believe they chose Eddie because Eddie was so good—as good as Isaac Murphy in his prime.

Bluegrass Funeral is a dangerous horse, but the horse did not kill Eddie Buford. His fellow jockeys did. They are the murderers. That is not too harsh a word. They boxed him in; they pushed him to the rail. Perhaps they did not mean for the tangle of hoofs to result in death; perhaps they only meant to steal the race. But the law is clear. Even an unintended crime committed in the middle of a felony is still a crime. Judge Bullock, who I believe had placed a bet on Bluegrass Funeral, will attest to that.

Behind the murderers on the track was a cabal of criminals led by Billy Klair. They had their money on Fair Chance and Skip Harrison and had arranged to make a bet of chance a certainty. Fair Chance was put down, too, in the catastrophe of fallen horses on Saturday; Billy Klair and his courthouse cronies did not collect their crooked monies. But a failed bank robbery is still a crime. And since a person was killed in this failed robbery, they too, are murderers. Again, ask Judge Bullock. The winner of the race was Jimmy Winkfield on Evening Breeze. In his entire racing career, Jimmy was surely never more surprised.

But what will the leaders of our city do about it? They were witness to the crime. Will Judge Bullock convene a grand jury to investigate? Will Mr. Desha Breckinridge print an editorial demanding justice? Will his lady arouse the indignity of our women to protest this heinous offense? I do not expect Billy Klair—as a party to the felony—to step up.

Eddie Buford's murder is part of a larger crime, the crime that tries to take from colored jockeys their earned place, their well-deserved winnings. *The Morning Herald* so often references the "Negro Problem" in our land. Here is the Negro Problem: our race's continual persecution. Harriet Tubman says never wound a snake; kill it. The snake of racism was wounded in the Freedom War, but its venom lives with us and grows more deadly as the years pass. Thirty-three years since Emancipation, thirty-three years—Christ's life-span—since slavery ended. And each year's passing since has tightened the Negro's bondage.

I lay those type side by side, the letters adding up to sorts, then lines, then meshed it all into a form. I made sure all the letter faces was the same height so the surface of the paper would be smooth and even. You could glide your hand over the page and you wouldn't feel a thing. It was only when you read the words that you felt any friction. I knew this column would cause more trouble than Willy Littlefield, the Mississippi boy who shot the deputy. That ruckus calmed down after a bit. What did it matter to folks around here if Mr. Benjamin went on about a colored boy killing a couple white police in Mississippi? But Mr. Benjamin was calling out the chief judge of the city, taking on *The Morning Herald* editor, and even challenging his lady. I didn't know who was gonna be madder.

Actually, I did. Billy Klair. Mr. Benjamin called the man who really ran the city a murderer. Billy Klair, the man who whispered in the Mayor's ear and the Mayor made a speech. Billy Klair who halfway ran the state. He'd end up running it before he was done. *Call me, Billy.* All smiles and friendly waves. But mean. As mean as any Mississippi sheriff.

I looked at that column as I lay it out. I wanted to let out a whooee like I did when Bluegrass Funeral shot down the track first time out. *Keep on running, Mr. Benjamin. Keep on kicking mud-dirt in their faces. Whooee!*

But then I remembered the second run, the tangled mess of hoofs, the twisted legs and the mashed heads. That horse blanket on the infield. My fingers hovered over those typed words like they wanted to snatch them back. Or rearrange all the sorts, mold different forms. Run the words together and blur them, like a newspaper does when it's caught in the rain. So the sounds they make would fall gentle, like a spring shower. But Mr. Benjamin's words cut: like a summer hail. Mamma said you didn't use words like they knives slashing at people. But truth too hard for Mamma sometimes. She lullaby words to me as a child when I cried about some meanness. "I'm here, child. Don't fret, child. It's gonna be all right."

But it ain't all right. And I don't know that it's ever gonna be right. I don't blame Mamma. The world's too hard to face sometimes. And you got to protect the young plants from the hail. They be bruised to death. Mamma still tries to lullaby me. Pretty words. Uplifting words. Lying words.

But I ain't no child anymore. Happy words don't soothe like they used to. Words that tell us we making good progress, Negro coming up in the world. Words telling about all the colored ladies club news, all the good work they doing. All the colored winners—George Washington Carver, Booker T. Washington, Isaac Murphy. Might need to go back to the Freedom War, drag poor ol' William Carney from his grave to show off his Medal of Honor. Can't even let Frederick Douglass rest easy in his grave. We need heroes. Need proof that coloreds can make it.

Too many stretching their necks in Kentucky, let alone Mississippi. Too many like Eddie trying their best but ending up mashed, smashed like a June bug that ain't even had a whole summer's living. That's what Mr. Benjamin's words telling us. I pushed those words down and they hurt. They hurt setting them. They hurt reading them. I was afraid. Afraid of what those words said. Afraid of what they would do. They already making it hard to believe in anything, in anyone. What if I ain't got no future? What if Mr. Benjamin leading the charge down the track only to end up boxed in like Eddie? What if we all end up smashed into the rail? Shattered, cracked, mangled. What if we all just headed for the final box?

Mr. Benjamin sent those words out. He charging down the track like Bluegrass Funeral. But maybe it Billy Klair on the winning horse.

John Fielding paid for the burial plot. Or at least he contributed fifty dollars and that paid for the plot with a little left over for the stone. Probably afraid of what Mr. Benjamin might write if he didn't. Mr. Benjamin wanted a funeral New Orleans might put on, not Lexington. Fifty dollars was something but it wasn't enough. Then just about every colored jockey still riding and even a couple white boys put in some dollar bills. And some colored trainers stepped up and some bookies like Ollie Lewis. Added up to more than three hundred dollars, Mr. Benjamin told me. Said Mike threw a couple dollars in the hat. That surprised me some. Three hundred dollars was lots more than we needed even for a fancy funeral. Would of given the leftover to kin, but if Eddie had any, we didn't know them. Came up on his own, somewhere deep South. Probably thought he be safe up here in the near North. I asked Mr. Benjamin about the extra money. He said Eddie was gonna get a statue.

"Young colored teacher does sculpture on the side—Isaac Scott Hathaway. I've seen his work. He's going places. He took a death mask. Said Eddie will look wonderful cast in bronze in his jockey suit. First one of its kind, he thinks."

Mr. Benjamin's face lit up when he talked about the statue, like a splendid statue made up for everything. Like Eddie, if he was around, might think so even. But I can't blame Mr. Benjamin. I felt the same way. Not just about the statue, though that was something. A statue of a black jockey. We felt that way about the whole funeral. We was celebrating instead of mourning.

Ain't no way around it. The funeral was fun.

We started with the carriage. A grand carriage. Four black beauties tied up to a shiny black coach paneled in glass that sparkled in the sunlight. Everything draped in flowers—the horses, too, like Derby winners. And Eddie laying inside that glass house on satin pillows dressed all in white with a red hat on his head and shiny black boots on his feet. *Whooee, Eddie. Whooee.*

The band in front wasn't any New Orleans noise—a church band—ten brass strong and two drummers on either side. The horses looked like they were keeping time, stepping high. The band must of used some of Eddie's money for their high-collared red cloaks with shiny gold chains clipping them 'round their necks. They and the drummers clip-clop beat down the street and we clip-clopped with them, singing out the song they blared. An old song, a sad song, but one that just filled us up with glory and sadness. A sadness we couldn't tell from joy. I don't know why that is, but it is. Glory and sadness. It made us feel so good.

> Were you there when they crucified my Lord? Were you there?
> Were you there when they crucified my Lord?
> O! Sometimes it causes me to tremble! Tremble! Tremble!
> Were you there when they crucified my Lord?

And when we sang the "tremble, tremble," we just shook with the joy of it all. Mamma was walking by me, holding my arm. I felt her shake with the words.

> Were you there when they nailed him to the cross? Were you there?
> Were you there when they nailed him to the cross?
> O! Sometimes it causes me to tremble! Tremble! Tremble!
> Were you there when they nailed him to the cross?

We were there. We were there then and we here now. For all Mamma's trying, I wasn't no Christian. I didn't believe. I didn't want anything to do with the churches and the preachers. But it didn't matter what I believed. We felt the nail together. And we trembled together. It was nine a.m. and another day full of May glory—just like Eddie's race day. But it could of been Calvary's dark afternoon when we shouted the last verse to the sky:

> Were you there when the sun refused to shine? Were you there?
> Were you there when the sun refused to shine?

O! Sometimes it causes me to tremble! Tremble! Tremble!
Were you there when the sun refused to shine?

It was our time. Weren't gonna need the weather to shine our sun. We was colored folks together, singing of misery but joyous, marching our way up Limestone over to Seventh Street and the new colored cemetery.

I was wrong about us going down. Wrong about making fun of all those happy words. Happy words. That how Mamma survived. That how we all survived. Even Mr. Benjamin up in front of the line, walking arm in arm practically with Reverend Pickering, singing that song out like he wasn't the half-heathen I knew him to be. Didn't matter. We was colored folk together and we were going make it. Down was where they pushed us, but we was gonna rise again—three days, three years, three hundred years. We was gonna rise again.

Half the colored population of Lexington followed that coach. Oh, it was fun. Mamma would of smacked me up the head if I told her that, twenty years old or not. Disrespectful to call a funeral fun. But Mamma was right there by me, swaying and singing. The glory and the happiness. We needed Mr. Benjamin's hard words, too, but he was wrong about us being enslaved again. This wasn't a slave people marching up Limestone. This was a people saying you might try putting those chains on us, but we gonna break those bonds just like we did before. You might kill some of us—you killed this boy—but we full of life for all the death you throw at us. We wound that snake. We gonna kill it one day. We gonna smash its head one day. That sun gonna shine. That sun gonna shine. Lord, Lord. Shine that sun.

"Were you there? Are you here?"

That's all that matters. That's all that counts.

CHAPTER 15

Judge Frank Bullock, May 17, 1899, Lexington, Kentucky

"Well, Judge, when you calling the grand jury that nigger Benjamin demanded? I might have some suggestions for names if you need them. Of course I don't suppose you could make me head seeing as how I'm the murderer."

Billy was waiting for me before I even opened the office. He was smiling. Seemed like he was always smiling, but this smile was so tight it looked like it had been carved in the stone of his face—Billy at his angriest, his most dangerous. The column in *The Standard* had come out late the previous night. I had just finished reading it myself.

I did not return his smile. "Is it true, Billy, that you had an interest in the horse? Blue-grass Funeral? An interest in seeing he did not win?"

Billy's smile grew wider, more real.

"Now, Judge, I tried to steer you in the right direction, but you brushed me away like I was some pesky courthouse job-seeker. You didn't bet on that colt, did you?"

"I did. As things turned out, it was better that I did. At least I am not being accused of murder. Perhaps I *should* convene that grand jury?"

Billy gave me a quick glance and saw I was not serious. In truth, that suggestion by Mr. Benjamin to summon a grand jury had infuriated me. The man knew no boundaries. Or ignored them as if they weren't there. But they were there. Ancient boundaries that served us well, a solid wall of boundaries that protected everyone. And he was about to crash into them just as surely as that boy had crashed into the rails.

Perhaps Benjamin thought of himself as a colored Morgan, disregarding tradition in the name of some higher cause, a cause that perversely justified disregarding tradition or any rules that governed civilized behavior. The Major would sometimes defend himself, though no one in his presence ever dared allude to the murderous raids he participated in. But he needed no allusion. Once—in the middle of one of Mother's Sunday afternoon receptions, with no prelude, no context, he started talking about a man named Davis. A Union man, he told us. From Scott County.

"We called him. But he wouldn't come to the door. Hid behind it like we couldn't see him there. But wood doors don't stop bullets. Four of us took aim and that door dissolved like it was all glass, him with it. Shame his wife and daughter died, too. But his fault. If he had come to the door like a man, we would have just shot him. Burnt that place to warn other Union traitors." He looked around at the shushed faces, not a few of whom had been Union traitors. "That's war."

Mother had not tried to shush him. She knew better, though some of her guests looked aghast, their punch glasses rattling in their hands. Legends of the glorious Morgan cavaliers were already half-gospel in Lexington. And here was my father: an apostate to the tales.

I do not defend my father, or any of the near-outlaws riding with him. But that was war. And the cause they fought for—the upholding of certain standards, the natural formation of certain elites—did not disintegrate with the war. We needed to rebuild some of them, just as I imagine that man Davis's family—what was left of it—had to rebuild. We cannot let new raiders, whatever their imagined justification, spray wild bullets into our midst, hitting whomever is nearby.

I imagine Benjamin thought our doors were wood, too, or glass that would shatter. But he will discover that they are doors made of cast iron and he is about to crash into them.

Actually, I think he might have crashed into them already. Certainly Billy Klair thought so. He sat down uninvited. He had ceased smiling. His face looked naked without his smile.

"What about a grand jury investigating slander, Judge? I'm thinking this town's got one too many nigger newspapers. A big fine for the paper. They won't be able to pay it but that's alright. Then some jail time for the editor. Should get things right in line. What do you think, Judge?"

I thought Billy usually more astute than he was showing himself. The murder charge must have upset him more than I would have guessed.

"Billy, did you see the funeral procession for that boy yesterday? It clogged the main part of the city for hours. This is not the time to shut down the most prominent colored paper in town, or jail the editor for writing an angry editorial about that boy's death. If you were involved in any way in that whole fiasco, Billy, I have to say it was poorly planned."

Billy flushed red at my comments, actually looked like he might lash out at me before he controlled himself. He did not get where he had gotten without controlling himself. Still, I felt pleased. He was always prodding me. It felt good to prod him back a bit, if a bit unnerving.

"So we wait a little," Billy said, "I got time. We wait a month and then we hit him for slander. Maybe even contempt of court."

"Slander? It's only slander if it is not true." Billy flushed again at my words. I held my hand up. "I am not calling you a murderer. But do you really want the issue discussed in court which, of course, it would have to be if you accused him of slander. And as for contempt of court, asking me to convene a grand jury is not contempt. If it were, both *The Leader* and *The Herald* would be in constant contempt."

Billy sat there quiet for a few moments. He was a very clever man. My logic had convinced him. But Billy always found another way if you blocked him.

"So there's nothing legal to do about this. But we have to do something, Judge, before he gets too big. Half the coloreds in this town already think him some kind of Moses leading them. We can't have all of them thinking that."

He looked at me then and let his silence envelop us both. I did not feel comfortable with the conversation—the unspoken one. I had already told him there was nothing legal he or I could do about Mr. Benjamin's writing. I had nothing else to say. Nothing I could say. I was not the Major. I stayed within the law.

Billy had started smiling again. "So you think we should leave things alone, Judge. Leave Benjamin alone?"

My clerk had come to the edge of the office, a cramped dank, dark place, able only to wave at me. My cramped office could not hold more than two men, even two men of such short stature as Billy and me. I longed for the opening of the new courthouse, a magnificent structure rising daily. Granite and marble. It would withstand a siege if needed, cannon fire let alone mere bullets. But its completion was at least six months away.

My clerk held the day's agenda, a full day's docket I had already glanced at the previous evening—the usual drunks, assaults, questionable women—poor women of the lowest kind who had neither the brothel's nor the police's protection. The women had spent the night waiting in cramped cells, cells where no one slept. I would fine them and send them back out to make their fines. Hopefully, they would have a few days' earnings before they returned. I felt the Major's scornful glance in my mind's eye. But I shook it off. This, too, was the work of civilization.

In the afternoon, a change of pace. Ten vote challenges, all by Billy's friends. All the challenged were Republicans and all were colored save one. The one white man was a fine touch by Billy. Half of the challenged would not show—unable to take the loss of a day's wages. They would be marked "doubtful" and have a difficult time voting. The rest I would ertify as voters. Billy accepted that. The law—at least the facts—were all on the side of the challenged. At least I did not feel the Major's glance as I went through the names. The whole issue would have eluded him. Colored voters?

I grew irritated only when the voter challenges became too blatant: several of those challenged had lived at the same address for twenty years. It made the court look ridiculous. Billy accepted that irritation and my admonishment as well. It was all part of the game.

"What you do politically is up to you, Billy. I'm simply saying there is nothing I can do in court."

"Oh, Judge, you can do lots of things in court. When the time comes." He jumped up like he'd forgotten some errand and was at my doorway in a second, brushing past my clerk. "I'll let you know when the time comes, Judge. Won't be like that horse, Bluegrass Funeral. I'll make sure you're listening." He nodded and smiled at me. The smile chilled me. A smile should be friendly. A smile should come with a joke. But Billy did not joke. Not about the business of power. He was like the Major in that regard, though neither would recognize the other. But neither of them joked about power. He waved a final goodbye over his shoulder, his face already turned away. Done with me for the moment.

"When the time comes, Judge. When the time comes."

When the time comes. Sometimes I wondered about the times we are in and the part I have in these times. The Major knew his part—it was a brutal part. And then he was done. Still a young man, but done. He had no place afterwards—certainly not telling romantic lies at Mother's receptions. No one dared tell them around him. One or two gushing ladies had learned that the hard way. He was not brutal. He just told the truth as he remembered it. That was brutal enough. But my part? Shuffling poor women out of sight, keeping everyone in their place. I am not allowed to tell the truth in the way the Major could. Though my truth is as brutal.

Grace tells me that my conscience is tender. And she does not say it tenderly. I sometime thinks she would have preferred the Major in his day. Perhaps even now.

Holding on. The times comes. The time goes.

As dark as my poor office is, it does have a view of the rising new courthouse. *How the law mounts over our Bluegrass plain*, I thought and shook off my malaise. I thought of my new office. The plans for it were among the most magnificent of the whole glorious edifice. When the time came, I would take my place there. When the time came, I would ride as high as the Major galloping by the side of Morgan. We would speed along as fast as any Bluegrass Funeral.

The Major was mistaken. One's height did not matter when you were on top.

And I would be certain to keep my seat steady, unlike that poor colored jockey. Unlike even Morgan who did not survive his bravura, who did not live to hear his legend. Whatever it took.

Benjamin was riding high, too. A new Moses. He thought he was leading a colored charge up Main Street. Perhaps onward to Frankfort. But he might be wise to look to his own saddle, to make sure he was riding firm. That colored boy he eulogized yesterday was a splendid rider. And he ended in the dust.

PART 3

TEACHING THE COUNTY

CHAPTER 16

Noah Webster, May 20, 1899, Lexington, Kentucky

Seems like I've been closing work places left and right. George Thomas saloon and now the race track. Closing their doors right behind me. Leaving black bodies behind, too. First poor Tommy Davis and then Eddie. I say that to Mr. Benjamin—like maybe I'm some dark cloud blocking out the sun. Blocking out black lives. Mr. Benjamin don't give it much truck.

"You're not the grim reaper; you're just a colored boy living a colored boy's life in Lexington, Kentucky at the end of the nineteenth century." The way he said nineteenth century, it was like he was cussing. But Mr. Benjamin didn't cuss. "Have to hope and pray the millennium will be better. Doesn't look promising."

When Mr. Benjamin says 'let us pray' he ain't just passing words. He bow his head and we—Lincoln and me—got to bow our heads, too. Didn't matter what you was doing, when Mr. Benjamin became Reverend Benjamin, you bowed your head. He might keep us all bowed two, three minutes. Sometimes I feel Lincoln trying to catch my eye so he can roll his. Lincoln ain't one for religion, but I don't dare even look at him. I ain't too religious, either—ask Mamma—but I'll pray with Mr. Benjamin when he want me to.

He don't pray often. Sometimes a month might pass by and he ain't pulled the reverend once and I'd forget all over again about him being a minister, too. It just one of four or five degrees he got. Every few months a church invite him in to preach and he might do it. He good at it. But most time he don't want anything to do with the churches. Most time he think the churches—or at least the colored ministers who run the churches—just part of the problem. "One more set of piglets feeding off the sow. The poor sow has only so many teats."

Mr. Benjamin's says those things out loud, sometimes prints them in *The Standard*. Most ministers hate him. Reverend Pickering think he's the devil incarnate. I tell Mamma it's because Mr. Benjamin tries to be a Christian, not just make his living as one. Mamma pull her lips tight when I say that. Means she thinks I'm right but she's not saying it.

Meantime I got to find one more way to make a living, something that will let me keep working at *The Standard*. Working and looking for work, that's a colored boy's life. White boy's life, too, I reckon, but they got more teats to suck on. I can always go back to mucking horses, but it's not something I look forward to.

Maria Lulu came to the rescue. She on some school committee with club ladies. Club ladies, colored and white, run this town as far as I can tell. I saw some of them at Benjamin's house when I live there—even some white club ladies one time—though one white lady didn't actually go to the house. She wait in her carriage and make Maria Lulu come to the curb to talk to her. It the same lady I see at the track that last day, the one with the limp. Desha Breckinridge's lady. I thought that she had some nerve, making Maria go to the street like that, but Maria came to that closed cab door and listened to that lady for five minutes, then just nodded. Even when it started to drizzle, Maria stood by that carriage. I don't imagine the lady sitting down minded much. She wasn't getting wet.

But I guess Maria getting wet worked out for me. All those ladies deep into school business—white and colored schools—and Maria hear of an opening way out in the county.

"I'm not trained as a teacher," I tell her. She's so excited, it's like it's her job. "I hear Superintendent Cassidy wants everybody trained, even in the colored schools."

"He does. And that's a good thing. But this is just for the May term and they really have nobody else. It pays 28 dollars a month for three months, until the middle of August. But it's only for four days—well, three and a half days—so you'll be able to keep working at *The Standard.*"

She look shy, like she's asking me a great favor instead of doing one for me. She's always like that. I'm always trying not to look at her too much. But I sneak in glances. She's tired. Got dark spots under her eyes. Ain't looked right since she birthed her youngest last January. Sure didn't need to be standing in any rain. I wonder if Mr. Benjamin see how tired she be. He's a great man but he don't notice things like that. He don't ever get tired himself that I can tell so I don't think it come into his mind that others might wear out. I don't care if he wear me out, I'm young. Supposed to be used down to the nub.

But Maria Lulu look like she could sleep for a week. I wish she could.

Mamma's so happy with my new job, you'd think Bluegrass Funeral had come in a hundred to one shot with Eddie riding high. Only Mamma don't go with gambling. No drinking, either.

"You choose your jobs to plague me?" she said to me after I started at the track. "First helping drinking men flush their money into the gutter along with the few brains they got. Now you taking working men's wages to chase some horse around the track. You know most of them got as much chance of winning as they got of catching those horses."

"What about my newspaper work?" I say to her. She close her mouth at that. She proud of me, I think, especially when Mr. Benjamin let me write something. Only she don't know what to think of Mr. Benjamin. It's not just Reverend Pickering whispering in her ear. She knows Mr. Benjamin is the biggest target in town. Makes me the second biggest target working next to him.

All in all my *Standard* job don't bring Mamma much comfort.

But school teaching make her sing.

"A school teacher!" And she glow so, her smile takes up her whole face. Make me feel mean I ain't tried harder to put that smile there.

"Your daddy and I had to sneak our lessons in. The white folks didn't care, only there weren't no time. One old man, a carpenter, taught any children willing to try. He could only teach us when the tobacco was drying. Or a hour or two some rainy afternoons when we couldn't work in the fields and we weren't needed somewhere else. Took us forever to learn that simple half torn book we got to share between us. Your daddy never did get comfortable. And here you be a school teacher. I'm sorry he gone. Your daddy be so proud."

I'm sorry he gone, too, but don't know if I could take both of them being so proud. Didn't matter to Mamma that it was just the May term they hiring me for and that they desperate. Didn't matter that it a county colored school open just three and a half days a week to August. None of that mattered to Mamma. I was a school teacher.

Didn't matter to her, either, that the position was way up near Briar Hill Pike, and that it took two hours walking after I take the trolley to Loudon Street. Five cents for two miles sitting in the center of the car when there was a seat.

Mr. Benjamin says I shouldn't go on the trolley since the Separate Coach Law. And he right. But I already got seven miles walk after Loudon and I just don't think I can add two more. So I give them my nickel. I don't tell Mr. Benjamin. The front of the car was for whites, the center for coloreds. Sometimes in town, I was the only colored in the whole section, the whites so crowded up front they almost sitting on each other. Sometimes they try to sneak into the colored section but the conductor strict. Jim Crow trains, white men always lounging in the colored section—white children, too, with their colored nurses. But the Separate Coach Law too new. Conductor probably worried some important man report him. He shoo the whites back to their section.

No coloreds in the white section. Don't matter how crowded we get.

The back of the car for smokers. I guess it don't much matter what color you are when you covered in smoke. Mamma and Daddy both hated smoking, so it never seemed worth it to me to jangle them one more way. "Filthy weed," Mamma say when I was small and we come in from the tobacco fields just covered in stickiness and smelling so musty a bath wouldn't hardly do the job. But I sat with the smokers that day—seemed like the friendliest group. Almost all of them colored

It was five o'clock of a morning, so dark we could hardly see our neighbor, though we could smell him. Like we all just come from the tobacco fields instead of headed to them. So dark you didn't know if white folks had snuck in among us. They'd jump in the same farm wagon once we got to the country, anyway. That early nobody paid it much mind. The conductor more or less gave up once we left downtown.

Just a waste of time separating white from colored anyway. Smell don't know no boundary—it float on past the colored line. Some people got fine nostrils and know which smell is white smell and which is colored. They tell who smells worse, too. But I can't. And tobacco all one smell.

It was still dark when I left the trolley and started my trek up North Broadway. Then somewhere it become Paris Pike, though there weren't any signs. Walk another two miles and then veer off to Briar Hill Pike. It's all country once you pass Loudon. Some coloreds from the street car kept me company the first mile or so, joshing me about being a school teacher. They was nice about it, happy for me. "Better than working for old Stonewall, I reckon," one fellow told me, giving my arm a friendly poke. He was about my age. They almost all got off at a country lane. Stonewall's Place.

One old fellow kept with me another mile or so—a white fellow, but then he stopped at the Campbell Place. He looked worn. Said he worked with the Campbell horses. I hoped it wasn't mucking. Looked too old to be mucking for a living.

"Where you going?" When I told him, he just shook his head.

"You got a ways, young fellow. A school teacher." And he looked at me strange like he ain't ever seen a colored school teacher. I felt my shoulders go tense, waiting for him to say something ornery. But then he smiled. Didn't poke me in the arm, but it was a friendly smile.

"Well, teach them young'uns good. Wished I'd gotten an education."

After that I was by myself on the Pike. I don't know what I might of felt if it'd been stormy or cold, but if you ain't cheered by a Kentucky May, Mamma says, you might as well ask the Lord to call you home. I didn't bow my head like Mr. Benjamin had us do, but seeing the sun peeking its way up over the meadows that first walk, watching the young colts stretching their legs trying to keep up with their mammas—one came racing down to the fence line to check me out—feeling the strength in my own legs and back after all that bending over typeset, after all that quibbling figures at the track, feeling my muscles stretch like I was one of them colts—all that made me feel like I was praying.

Only I didn't have any words. I didn't feel like I needed words, though words is what I lived by, what Mr. Benjamin lived by. I was a young strong colored man right on the edge of the start of a new century. A new century that was gonna shuck the old misery of slavery. I strode that road like I owned it. For the first time, Mamma's joy just seeped into my bones. I was a school teacher. I didn't know anything about it, but I was gonna learn and I was gonna teach.

The seven miles stretched before me like the board slide some white folks built by their new school when I was real small. Four giant boards they sanded so smooth you could rub your face up and down it and not get splintered. Then they covered it with so many buckets of white paint, you could of almost painted half a barn. They slanted those boards on a

93

hillside, and watched their tiny children slide down, squealing and laughing all the way. Mamma and Daddy paused a bit from their work to watch.

"White folks sure love their children," is all Mamma said before she went back to her washing. Daddy just shook his head.

Must have been ten colored children at the edge of that lot staring at those children, and I don't know that we would of given everything we had just to do one slide. It looked more fun than tumbling down a snowy hill, without the cold or the wet. I would of snuck over at night, but Mamma would of had my hide if I tried it. And anyway they was just boards on a hillside at nighttime—you needed folks squealing and shouting to make it fun.

But I felt like I was going down that slide now. And it was fun. Seven mile walk in the most beautiful country God ever made. "A slide into Kentucky heaven," Mamma might say. "Whooee," I squealed, and startled some colts two fields over. I saw their mammas give me a look, then turn back to their grazing like it didn't take them long to decide that I was okay. "Whooee," I shouted, like I hadn't shouted since Eddie broke free from the pack. I felt just like that: like I had broke free. *Here I come, young'uns. Your brand new, untrained, know-nothing school teacher. I don't know what I'm doing, but I'm gonna give it all I've got.*

"Whooeee."

Stopped a white boy for directions when I thought I was getting near to the school. It was just past eight—the sun getting hot even for May. Or maybe just because I'd been half running the last mile or so. I promised them I'd be there in the morning. The white boy looked at me strange but pointed the way—said I'd see it on the right coming up. He was behind a mule plowing, probably been doing so since first light. Maybe earlier. Fourteen or so—too old for the May term. Farm boys his age come winter term when there's not much going on. He might show up at the white school May term on rainy days when the fields too wet to work in. Might not. Mamma always made me go. When they could spare me.

The school was on the right when I rounded the bend and it surprised me. Looked brand new or not more than a couple years old. And two rooms when I thought I heard just one described. Solid roof and strong sides. You can tell a well-built building, one made with pride and thinking about who was gonna use it. Not just thrown up like an after-thought, the kind that says don't-fall-down-till-I-turn-my-head. This school was meant to last a few years. I counted four windows and two chimneys. Cassidy, the superintendent, had condemned just about every county school in Fayette County, but he hadn't got around to half of them yet. I was surprised Maria hadn't thought to tell me he got to Briar Hill. This was a good omen. I wished Mamma could see this school. Maybe I could get her out here somehow—borrow a wagon.

Nobody was in front of the school waiting for me, which I thought a bit strange, but maybe they'd heard I might be late. I went up to the main building and swung the door open. About twenty white children—from about five to maybe nine—swung 'round to stare at the strange black man. A white lady teacher gave a small yelp. She froze with her pointer aimed at a word on the black board. We stared at each other about five seconds or so. Then a small boy—I'm thinking six—spoke up.

"What you want here, nigger?"

My mind couldn't come together for a moment. I stared at the boy.

"I'm the new school teacher."

The class broke into laughter.

"Not here you ain't, nigger," said the boy, and the class laughed harder.

The woman teacher started to bang on her desk with the pointer. I was afraid she'd break it. The class gradually calmed down. She turned to me.

"You want the colored school, Briar Hill. This is the white school, Briar Hill #7. Your school is another quarter mile or so. Turn left at the Post Office. It's not on the road."

She smiled at me as if to make up for her class's behavior. She smiled but she didn't say sorry. Probably didn't even think she needed to. I glanced back at the boy. He looked pleased with himself, certain he got a story to entertain his friends with for a long time. "Not here you ain't, nigger." I would of liked to take that small white body and break it in two over my knee.

"Suffer the little children." One of Mamma's favorite Bible quotes. I'd suffer him if I could of. Thank Mamma's God she wasn't here to see this. But I just nodded to the lady teacher and closed the door.

Briar Hill Colored was all I heard it was and less. The walls did make it to the roof—just. Big gaps in the rough wood chinking. Good thing, I reckoned, for fresh air might be scarce since I spotted only one tiny window. One chimney, too, waiting for the next strong wind. Heck, the way it was leaning, a big breeze might blow it all over. The straggliest bunch of colored children you ever seen was gathered out front. Same age as the white children only there seemed more little ones. Two older children—a boy and a girl—looked about twelve. I wondered at that.

I wondered at everything. They did, too, I guess. They didn't make a sound as I approached them. I found out later they'd been waiting more than two hours. Waited way more than that really. Hadn't had a teacher since half a month before winter term ended—more than six weeks. Maria never told me why the teacher left. Looking at the sorry scene in front of me, I guess the real question was why she came in the first place.

Why I came.

Whooee. I am a school teacher.

Finally, the older boy left the group and approached me, as quiet and gentle as if I was a spooky colt. "Are you the new school teacher?"

I pulled myself up and tried to look the part.

"I am. I'm Mr. Webster—like the dictionary. I hope you have one. We'll be using it a lot. Spelling's the sign of an educated person. You all are gonna be educated when we're finished."

Oh, that was a long opening speech. Their eyes just widened, the littlest ones so wide their eyes about crowded out their cheeks. Back of my brain I heard a voice starting in to mock: *when you learn to spell?* But I shushed it. I'd learn to spell right along with them, I reckoned. Mr. Webster would help us all. My speech froze them. I took off my hat and wiped my brow. I smiled at the older boy. I tossed him my hat. He caught it in one grasp with the soft ease of a natural-born ball player. I'd remember that.

"Before we get to Mr. Webster, I'm real thirsty. Think somebody might fetch me a cup of water?"

And they all—even the tiniest of them—scrambled to quench my thirst. I must of drunk four or five cups to satisfy them all till I felt I might just float away. They crowded around me and watched me drink like it was one of the Seven Wonders. I sat on a stump in the yard and the littlest ones just jostled each other for leg space. I felt the peace of May come back into my spirit every drop I drank. The peace of Jesus, Mamma would of said. I don't know about that.

But at least I knew now what He meant when He said, "Suffer the little children." The line always half confused me. They suffered enough, maybe even that little white boy I wanted to break in half.

I reached out and stuck my fingers in the tangled wool of one of the smallest fighting to keep his place on my knee. He was a tough one, I could tell. I smiled at him. He smiled back. I remembered why I came. I wondered how that other teacher could of left.

I was set to board with a family—name of Chiles—pay them a dollar for three nights of bed and board. Mamma says I could hardly eat that cheap in town, but I'm just making seven dollars for the week as is. For that I'm janitor, and handyman, and teacher only after a list of chores that might make those field hands think twice when they teased me about being a school teacher. Thursday after dinner time, I start my trek on back to Lexington. Somebody usually headed in that direction—save shoe leather in the back of somebody's farm wagon—sometimes the same fellows I travel out on the trolley with. Nobody talking then. Too worn out.

I need to make it in time to set the type for *The Standard* and maybe write a story or two. Spend Thursday night and Friday doing all those things Mr. Benjamin's been saving for me. Sunday I rest. After I finish all the chores Mamma's been saving for me.

None of that matter to Mamma.

"You a young man. Supposed to work hard."

She say that and wait for me to give her some kind of answer. I could of told her young men supposed to have fun, too. I could of said this young man getting old real quick with all the work he got to do. I could of said there's working hard and there's working yourself to death.

I got a half-dozen things pop into my head but I kept my mouth shut. Truth was, I was having fun. The kind of fun that brings sore muscles and a tired brain, the kind of fun that got me worried all the time and when I ain't worried, afraid. Afraid I'm doing it wrong, afraid I ain't doing enough, afraid I'm gonna mess up my best chance. Afraid I'm gonna mess up the *only* chance these children got. Still I feel like waving my arms like Mamma does in church when the spirit catch her. *Thank you, Jesus, oh thank you, Jesus. The spirit's caught me.*

I'm having fun.

Mr. Benjamin wants me to write about the school but I tell him I need a little time yet. I don't know enough yet. He has all sorts of ideas about what I should do.

"Practical education is what they need," he tells me. "They need to learn a trade. Poetry and literature are a waste of time for colored children in their condition. They need to earn their living. Who's going to pay them for poetry? Teach them Greek, teach them how to starve."

Of course, I know he's right. But the only decent trade I really know is typesetting and I can't show them how to cast metal sorts out in Briar Hill without the presses. I could show them horse mucking. But I think they might know all about that. I could show them how to handle a mean drunk or how to treat him so he don't turn mean. If you work in a saloon that's real practical knowledge. Knowledge that might keep you alive. Their parents might not like that though.

Still I couldn't teach them to typeset even if I dragged the presses out to Briar Hill. They couldn't separate the sorts into words because they didn't have the words. Got about a hundred words they circle around and around. I see where the lady-teacher before me work them hard and she made good progress before she left. But they got so much more they need. They a well that don't seem to have no bottom. You throw your pebbles down and you wait and you wait for the sound to hit bottom.

Maybe that why she left. Didn't know where to start. Didn't know what pebbles to throw.

"Start with what they need most," Mamma tells me.

"They need so much. They need everything."

"Start with what they need most," Mamma says again. "When you was little, you wanted everything. We couldn't give you everything. We didn't have it to give. You needed everything, too, and we couldn't even give you everything you needed. Me and your daddy had to figure out what you needed most."

"How'd you do that?"

She thought awhile. "We gave you the things that made you happy."

"Happy? I don't remember too much happy giving. I remember getting all the chores I could handle. And then some. I remember the back of your hand when I sassed you. When was all that happy giving?"

She looked a tiny hurt, though Mamma knew I was just jostling her. But she shuck it off.

"I give you the back of my hand now you keep talking like that. I ain't saying we handed out happy like slices of peach pie—though you ate enough of my peach pies to fill an orchard. That ain't the kind of happy I'm talking about. I'm talking about the happy you needed to grow. The happy you needed so you think you knew more than your daddy—or me. We wanted you to know more. We needed you to. That kind of happy. We tried to give you that. Give them children that kind of happy. Find out what kind of happy they need most."

What they needed most. Mr. Benjamin thought he knew what the children needed. He and Booker T. But he and Booker T. weren't out in Briar Hill in a school half-fallen down with children who got three and a half day's schooling from a man ain't half educated himself. What did they need the most?

What would make them happy?

I found an old poem of Mr. Benjamin's. His poetry book was with his others, but he didn't talk about his poetry. I don't think he'd written any poetry for years. Nobody paying anybody for poetry. The poem I read he wrote almost twenty years ago during some political campaign. I didn't know how good a poem it was but I needed something. I thought maybe Mr. Benjamin wouldn't mind so much if I taught the children poetry if it was his poetry.

I started with the first stanza and we worked on it most of a week.

> Colored heroes, seek your Standard,
> Know you not the foeman's near,
> Know you not how they'll enslave you,
> You and yours who are so dear,
> Gather then, combine for freedom,
> Fight for that and bravely die,
> Only cowards turn their faces,
> Cowards then who turn and fly.

The children knew colored but they never heard the word heroes. When I explained it to them, and it took some explaining, they couldn't get past the two words joined together. "Colored heroes?"

"Yes," I told them. "Lots of colored heroes." I told them about Frederick Douglas and Harriet Tubman, how they escaped slavery themselves and then helped others. Harriet Tubman sneaking back across the slavery lines.

"My own parents was born into slavery," I told them and they nodded. They knew about that. Some of their folks and all their grandfolks had told them tales.

I told them about Sojourner Truth and her fighting not just for colored freedom, but for women. One little girl, Luella, perked right up.

"Women? Why she'd have to fight special for women?"

"Ain't I a woman?" I told her and her eyes grew so wide at the crazy man asking such a question, I almost had to kick my leg from laughing. I explained how that was a famous speech Sojourner gave. "Some men said women were delicate, couldn't do what a man did. But Sojourner Truth told them all the hard things she done. And she'd always come back with 'Ain't I a woman?'"

I needed to do a lot of explaining, spent two days talking about colored heroes. *Lord help me,* I thought. *Not even through the first line in the first verse.*

They didn't know what seek meant, either, but they got that soon enough till I confused it. "What you're looking for," I told them.

"What you looking for?" I asked them.

"I'm looking for the ball my daddy made me," said Clay. He was the little fighter on my knee that first day. "I think somebody took it."

"Ain't nobody take your raggedy ol' ball," said his sister. That was Luella, two years older and about a foot taller than him. "You always losing that ball and thinking somebody took it."

"No, no," I interrupted quick. They could square off faster at each other than grays and blues in the wilderness. "I don't mean that kind of looking. I mean what you looking for in life. What you want to be?"

Now the whole class just stared at me. Lost again. They could of been in the wilderness. They thought they knew what I was talking about, but seems they were mistaken. We spent a long time with that one. It wasn't just that they didn't know what they were looking for. They didn't know they were supposed to be looking. They were gonna farm like their daddies and their mammas did. They were gonna clean houses. They were gonna strip tobacco. They were gonna live in raggedy old shacks and make their children raggedy old toys.

I had to slow myself down. I wanted to race through that poem of Mr. Benjamin's like I was leading a cavalry charge. But I would of been the only one charging.

The last morning of the first week, we finally got to "Standard." We made our own standard out of some cotton rag strips Mamma gave me. The whole class sewed on it, even the boys. I started to tell them the bigger meaning of the standard, how it meant what we valued. But I could see their brains just melting in the May-time heat so I let it be. "Sufficient unto the day," Mamma would tell me. It was the standard of freedom, I just told them, and they nodded at that.

When we got the standard put together finally—Mamma's cotton strips were a strange motley of blues and yellows with just a bit of red—I let them run all over the playground waving that standard and yelling out the names of colored heroes: "Frederick Douglas," the boys screamed, with the girls streaming behind them. And then the girls. "Sojourner Truth," they yelled and the boys followed. "Sojourner Truth!"

What about Harriet Tubman? I wanted to ask, but the playground's their territory as long as nobody's killing anybody. And I saw a group later on, sneaking off someone to freedom and being chased by a slave master so Harriet made it to the playground after all, though sometimes I knew they were confusing Sojourner and Harriet. I wanted to step in again, but I didn't want to stop the game.

"Part of being a teacher is keeping your mouth shut," I said to Mamma later.

She just looked at me. Didn't say nothing.

One thing I certain of: Briar Hill playground never had such names echo off it ever before. We made so much noise I hoped Briar Hill #7 could hear it. The way the children said Sojourner's name, I could tell she was their favorite, even the boys. They always said the full name: Sojourner Truth. Harriet Tubman just didn't have the same ring, I reckon. When they were playing on their own before school or during lunch time, they'd fuss about who got to be Sojourner. At first the girls wouldn't let a boy play her, but the boys said the girls could play Douglass so they compromised. I watched them negotiate like they were Grant and Lee, only there weren't no surrendering. Most of the time they let the oldest boy, Willy—Willy Chiles, the family I was staying with—play Sojourner anyway. He was everybody's favorite. He'd charge across the field waving the standard. The standard of freedom.

"Ain't you a woman?" I yelled at him once 'cause I just couldn't help it. Mamma says I got more mouth than sense. He looked at me strange but kept on running, all his freed slaves running close behind him.

Standard. The last word of the first line of the first verse. The word Mr. Benjamin took to name our paper. It was slow going. I was hoping we wouldn't spend the whole May term on the one poem. I don't know if that'd be the right thing to do. I don't know if the children were getting what they needed.

But it was fun. And they looked happy.

I'd stay confused and halfway lost the whole time I was teaching, but that first day I was looking through a glass darkly—only it wasn't dark but full of colors like a church window. Willy Chiles and I walked to his house together that first day. I could tell he was anxious to leave me behind and run on, but he was too country-polite to hurry me and I was too done in to do more than one foot in front of the other or tend to any directions. I'd be sure to get lost though it was just over a mile of land dipping and gently climbing but mostly flat. We cut across tobacco fields colored that new green that makes me happy just looking at it. Like it gonna turn into something that don't make you cough, or smell up the house. Made sure we didn't step on any vegetation. Tobacco farmers get right mean when you step on their plants.

Could go by road, Willy said, but that was twice as long. Not sure I'd want to be a strange colored man traipsing through somebody's land—folks might get mean—even being careful where you put your feet. But it was okay with Willy. Only one man—a white man—even looked at us. But he waved when he saw Willy. I could tell he was curious about me, but I was with Willy.

"Tell him I'm the new colored teacher coming to board with your folks," I told Willy. He looked at me strange, but yelled it out. The man nodded. I wanted him to remember me when Willy wasn't there escorting me.

Nobody was home when we got there—a nice built cabin, three rooms down and a loft up above. I'd be sleeping in the loft, Willy told me. A pot was simmering beans and ham hock, and a couple of thick slices of corn bread been laid on the table. A pitcher of buttermilk stood waiting for us. Willy filled two bowls, poured us drinks and was through his meal almost before I sat down. He ran out the door, mumbling, "Chores. Make yourself to home. Nobody be in from the fields before dark."

Dark was four hours off. And I knew Willy got in a couple hours' chores before school, too. Way before light. But that whole long day of light, his folks set him free. All those hours in the field, when a strong twelve-year-old boy like Willy might begin to pay back all them beans and ham hock, all that rich buttermilk. But they let him free to get some schooling. From me. Maybe the most ignorant teacher you could think of.

Made me scared.

I sat down on the cabin steps and looked in the direction Willy had disappeared to. A little hill blocked the straight view but far as I could reckon, we weren't too far from Briar Hill #7, the white school that plowing white boy had steered me wrong to. He was working out there, still. I wondered if it ever entered that boy's mind to want to go to school. Probably wasn't that different than the children I was teaching—not knowing enough to want anything. His folks hadn't found their way to sending him to school—not in planting season.

I didn't blame them. I don't blame poor people, white or colored, for the choices they got to make. Life was hard and planting season short. Just made me think of Mamma and Daddy—all those days they sent me to school when they could of used me. But they didn't think like that. They were the ones supposed to be used.

I put some more beans in my bowl—the pot was a good half full—and poured me just a little bit more buttermilk. Mamma always said I was greedy for buttermilk, but I didn't want to drink them clean. The ladder to the loft was good and solid—I hate a rickety one. Up above was a chair and straw bed covered with two quilts. Everything clean, everything in place. I felt like I knew Willy's folks, even before I met them. The loft had two openings on both ends. The breeze just passed through like ten church ladies waving their fans at you. I lay back that first night after my first day teaching, intending to keep my eyes open till I met Willy's parents who done that little miracle of keeping him out of the fields. Mamma would of been right mad if I weren't there to welcome them back to their home and thank them. For the beans and ham hock. For the clean quilts and the well-built ladder. For the buttermilk I couldn't help taking a froth more up the ladder with me.

Thank them for Willy.

Didn't even get to meet his folks the next morning. Gone before I opened my eyes. Willy woke me. He'd been doing chores for hours. Said some corn pone and grits was waiting for me. Coffee, too. Told me his mamma was sorry but they'd run short of buttermilk. It'd be waiting for me when I came back that evening.

I didn't meet them proper till the third day. His mamma first. She came in early from the fields—more than an hour left to sundown. Three other ladies were with her, all come to meet the teacher. Didn't take me long to figure out it was more than a greeting.

"Call me Noah," I told them when they first came in. If they heard what I said, they were too polite to let on. I stayed Mr. Webster. "Like the dictionary," one of the ladies commented. "Must be a good speller." I just smiled and nodded.

That was Miz Groves talking about my spelling, mamma to my little fighter, Clay, and his sister, Luella. "My girl, Luella, tells me you teaching them poetry. You think that what they need?"

All four women waited for me to respond. I couldn't smile and nod this one out. Miz Chiles took the coffee from the stove and poured me a cup. Miz Groves sliced a large wedge of apple cake and smiled as I plunged my fork in. I was the only one eating or drinking. That's not why they were here. They waited while I chewed. I couldn't chew forever.

I spent a good hour talking about the poem, how I wasn't just teaching them poetry but how to read. Word by word. How I was teaching them history. Our history. Not just George Washington and Abe Lincoln. How I was showing them how to think. Miz Chiles picked her head up at that. She was a big woman, tall, with arms fleshed with muscles. She clenched her mouth.

"I'm not telling them *what* to think—well, I am some—but *how* to figure things out on their own."

"Figure things out on their own?" She settled her mouth like I seen Mamma do when something don't set right. She pulled her arms in front of her and clenched her hands about her elbows. "Why we need a teacher if they gonna do it on their own? How much training you got? You got any training? Mr. Green Pinckney Russell sent us a no-account teacher this spring. Knew nothing. Taught nothing. We needed to ask her to leave."

Asked her to leave? Nobody told me about that. Nobody told me I'd be answering a school board of mammas. I saw that teacher in my mind's eye leaving in the middle of the week. I hoped the children didn't see that. I hoped they wouldn't see me leave.

Willy's daddy came in just when his woman asked me about doing it on their own. Still light outside. A farmer comes in from the field with the sun in the sky, it got to be serious. He nodded to me but waved his hand to tell me to go on. Answer the question. Which question? About my training? Maybe they'd let me stay the night. Or the question as to why they needed a teacher if they were gonna have to do it on their own?

Especially why they needed another flunky from Green Pinckney Russell? At least that weren't true. I might be a flunky but Green Pinckney Russell ain't sent me.

"You teach Willy how to hunt?" I asked his daddy. The man pulled his head back like a skittish colt. I don't imagine he expected to be called on, like *he* was in the school house. But he nodded yes.

"He a good hunter?"

"Better than I was at his age."

"Don't surprise me. I just known him a couple days, but I can see that and I've never seen him hunting. He looks about him and he pays real close attention. He sniffs the air. He understands things I bet you never told him. He learned how to learn on his own. Ain't just aiming a gun and shooting. Whole lot more to it than that.

"You all taught your children to look and listen, to figure things out. That's all I'm trying to do, too. But with books. I want them to figure out books and all that world." I turned to Miz Chiles.

"You ask me how much training I got? I don't got much. Most of what I know I learned from reading books on my own and from working at the newspaper. From Mr. Benjamin. If I keep at this teaching, if you ladies allow me to keep at it, I'm gonna have to learn a whole lot more. And some of that learning is gonna be on your children. They gonna suffer for my ignorance. That's the truth of it. All I can tell you is that I'm gonna work real hard at learning."

I read them the whole poem then and I tried to show them again what I was doing. The second time 'round seemed easier. I told them about the newspaper and Mr. Benjamin. I didn't know if I was making any sense, but I led the charge. Just like Willy as Sojourner.

I looked at those ladies set to turn me out if they got a mind to. I thought of my yelling at Willy: "Ain't you a woman?" They were all Sojourners, though only Miz Chiles was as tall as Sojourner. The other three ladies small, tough like briar bushes that never toppled over, that let the wind pass over them, right through them and all around them, but stood even after the meanest storm. They just stared at me, not even nodding much. Willy's daddy stood off to one side. It was the ladies gonna do the deciding. He was just here to back it up.

Finally I trailed off. Everybody was silent for a moment. Miz Chiles cleared her throat.

"You teaching the children numbers, too? They need their numbers."

"Yes, Ma'am, I'm teaching numbers. We start the day with numbers. Not just poetry."

Miz Chiles nodded. They all nodded, even Willy's daddy. He looked relieved. Wouldn't of been pleasant walking me off the place. Miz Groves reached for her apple cake.

"You need another slice, a young man like you."

I tried to refuse, but not too hard. Wouldn't of been polite. Felt good eating that second slice of apple cake. Felt like I'd passed the test. Wished I had a mug of buttermilk to wash it down with, but wishing ain't fishing, Mamma always told me.

And the coffee was good.

CHAPTER 17

Maria Lulu Benjamin, May 27, 1899, Lexington, Kentucky

I have been so tired lately. Tired since Lillian's birth, though it was an easy birth. Robert got Doctor Hunter to check on me—the first colored doctor to operate at St. Joe's. He doesn't really do babies. But Robert asked him. My tiredness makes Robert impatient, though he tries to be kind. He does not understand fatigue.

Now Miss Emma Bisou has called another meeting. Everyone expects that since I am Mrs. Robert Benjamin, I will be his equal in temperament. But I am not.

The meeting is about the school situation in the county. The Democrats—how Robert hates the Democrats—are trying to fill the colored schools with their cronies. The Democrats. Sometimes I think of them as the enemy of the colored race. Robert agrees.

"Republicans aren't much better but the worst are colored Democrats. Green Pinckney Russell. Green. A good name for him, the only color he adheres to."

Green Pinckney Russell has forced his new teachers into the schools. It is not fair, perhaps, to call all of his teachers venal and ignorant. But they are all beholden to him. To Billy Klair. "The colored mothers in the county are gathering. We must support them," Emma says.

I have had two letters from young Noah. He thanks me for his employment. We should have let him know what he was getting into, but events have moved so quickly. He writes me funny stories of his children, especially one young Willy, who is his oldest pupil. Willy as Sojourner Truth. I laugh so hard, Sheila comes in to ask if I am alright. She sees my eyes.

"Glad to see you laughing, Missus. You been drooping lately."

Noah's admiration for me is balm. He is so gentle, so respectful. It may be wrong of me to look forward so to his letters. But Robert does not mind. He would not think to mind. He raised his eyebrow slightly once when Noah almost ran to open the door for me. He looked at me and smiled slightly.

"Of course," he said.

It comforts me, that "Of course."

I wonder briefly if I am different than Mr. Russell in securing young Noah this job, for I know he lacks training. But I tell myself it is only for the May term—the children would have had no one. And he will learn. The job will train him, for he is not ignorant, simply unlearned.

A fine difference. But a difference.

Robert says there are rumors of real trouble in the further reaches of the county. I hope that I have not placed young Noah into turmoil.

Emma is at the door. "Have you eaten? Ask Sheila to give me something that I might carry. I have been running the morning and feel a hollowness inside. Do you know what that scallion Russell is doing in the county? Good heavens, Maria, are you not dressed? Oh, my goodness, child, what do you do with your morning? Hurry. There you are, Sheila. Food, Sheila, give me something I might eat on the run for I am faint, faint with hunger."

She did not look faint. She looked ready to take on the world. Anyone in her wake feels compelled to take on that world, too. Even Sheila ran to gather her food, and Sheila runs for no one.

I felt a bit faint but dared not admit it. I rushed as quickly as I could to finish my dress. I wanted to throw a sack over my head and be done with it. But colored ladies have to be vigilant in how they present themselves. Low class and slatternly was one color too bright. Proud and stuffy was a coat too fine or even the lace Mamma went almost blind sewing for me.

Robert would watch me dress with a mild contempt as if I took such care because I was vain. I am not vain. I wish I had a cloak of vanity which could buffer me from all the slights and bruises I feel. When I tried to explain all this to Robert, his eyes withdrew.

We live in different worlds, men and women. Sometimes I understand Madeline Mc-Dowell Breckinridge in her high white world better than I do Robert. I know the hurt in her eyes when people openly and carelessly notice her limp. The world has a sharp glance for women.

Emma waited impatiently for me at the door, chomping some meat and bread Sheila had mustered together. Emma ignores dress. She is respectful. Her suit compresses her round and ample bosom like a uniform. I wonder if she chose anything frilly as a girl.

The thought rose, gurgled in my throat, and erupted into a giggle. I twisted it to a cough. Emma's look of impatience turned to concern.

"Are you alright, girl?"

"Yes, I am fine. Just a scratch. Please sit, Emma. Take a moment to eat. Sheila, get some tea."

"No tea, no time. We are late, Maria." And with that we were off.

The club was full of colored ladies, club ladies, all like Emma in their energy. Indignant. The energy of indignation. Our ladies needed no tonic to rejuvenate their blood. I reached for some indignation and felt myself revive. Emma was behind our small lectern and started speaking. She needed no gavel to quiet the room.

"Ladies, our colored sisters in the county are doing their very best to make sure that their schools, our schools, do not become dumping grounds for Mr. Russell's leftovers."

She smiled at our puzzlement of the word "leftovers." "It is a term I heard recently for food that has not all been eaten the first time and is served on another day. You need a good icebox to preserve it. Unless you are like most of us and change the food into something else—such as soup or stew and keep it cooking. But Mr. Russell has not changed the food. It is the same stale food that got left in the first place. And I am sorry to say Mr. Russell seems to lack a good icebox, too. His leftovers are starting to smell."

The ladies laughed hard and loud. "Oh, Emma," I heard several ladies say from around the room.

"I say that we begin our meeting with a resolution supporting our country sisters. It has been passed among you so you are all familiar with it. Somebody propose it? Good, Mrs. Bennett. Maria, will you second? Good. Now a show of hands. Fine. We have passed the resolution. Now let's get to business."

One did not fall asleep when Emma led a meeting. We raised fifty dollars to help our sisters cover some of their expenses, the expenses of the very poor. The lost wages they endured for meetings, the fines they might face. The extra meals they would make. Fifty dollars might not seem much, but in truth, we were not much richer. Most of us barely covered our own expenses. For all of Robert's multiple jobs, we saved almost nothing. Sometimes in the night, I would wake worrying about our children and how I would manage if something happened to Robert.

The worry could pry me out of the deepest sleep like a walnut popped from a tree. I could feel my pulse beating as if I'd been running. Running and getting nowhere. Someone was behind me. The children would be there, clinging to me and crying. Lillian in my arms and Charlie begging to be carried. "Your father will carry you," I'd tell him. But Robert was not there. Was he behind me? Was he ahead?

Robert would wake me, gently pushing at my shoulders. Sweat would cover me, soaking the sheets.

I tried to calm myself. Robert is strong and healthy. And though he is sixteen years my senior, I am more likely to leave first. If I do, he will care for the children. My children are safe, as safe as any colored children can be in this world.

"Money always helps," Emma was congratulating us. "But what they also need is advice, legal advice." She turned to me. I understood. Robert was going to be asked to do another job, another unpaid job. They waited.

"Mr. Benjamin is busy. I do not know what time he can spare."

Emma tossed her head. I had not answered the right way.

"We appreciate the many jobs Mr. Benjamin does for the community. But surely he can make time to help our children. Surely their education needs to come first. We must make every effort to prevent the Democratic machine—Billy Klair and his instrument, Green Pinckney Russell—from converting our colored schools into sinecures for his political hacks."

The energy of indignation was being directed to me and to my husband. I flushed. How dare Emma suggest that if Robert did not make Emma's priorities his, he would have betrayed our children, left them to the mercies of the Democratic devils?

"Mr. Benjamin cares very much for our children—all of our children, not just the ones we share as parents." I said, "He cares very much for colored dignity and for our rights as citizens. How Mr. Benjamin continues his fight for colored rights is a matter he chooses. Neither I nor this group, as well meaning as it is, has the right, the ability, or the wisdom to choose for him."

A silence followed my speech. Emma looked taken aback, as did several other ladies. I do not believe I had ever spoken so to her. I remembered my speech at Ashland. That lady of energy seemed long gone. I felt exhausted—as exhausted as I did when I woke in a sweat.

Finally, Mrs. Jackson arose. So calm, she keeps us from turning our indignation onto each other. She stood shyly waiting for Emma to call on her. Emma finally nodded in her direction.

She turned to me and smiled before she began.

"Of course, Maria is right," she said so gently we all got quieter in order to hear. "Mr. Benjamin must decide his own priorities. We are grateful for all he has done. But perhaps Maria could broach a suggestion to him?" She waited until I nodded. "Perhaps Mr. Benjamin could advise his young assistant, already teaching in the county, as to how to counsel the county ladies? Perhaps this young man could come into town to gather that advice and we could help finance his traveling. The ladies would receive Mr. Benjamin's guidance without putting another terrible strain on his time."

It still seemed a strain to me—on Robert and Noah—but everyone else thought it a marvelous compromise. I could see by their smiles and nods that they were relieved. Mrs. Jackson still looked apologetic, as if she alone understood how much she was asking. Emma's charge could be repulsed, but Mrs. Jackson's sweet language could not be resisted. Of course I would relay the suggestions, the requests. The commands. For our children. For our race. Of course I would ask Robert to do one more thing. And Noah as well.

They would sleep when they could. Sheila complained when Noah lived with us that pulling him from a sleep was like hauling a full-bucket from a deep well. Robert sleeps almost as soundly. The sleep of the virtuous.

The sleep of the healthy.

Dreams trouble me. Dreams keep me always with one foot in the waking world. What child needs me? What colored child needs me? "You look more tired now than when you went to bed," Sheila would sometimes accuse me in the morning.

"I will ask Robert, Mr. Benjamin," I told the ladies. For the colored children of Fayette County needed us. "I will ask Noah, Mr. Webster, too. I'm sure they will do their best."

We would all do our best and the ladies smiled at me. Emma, at the lectern, beamed at me as if I were her favorite student. I had been the nuns' favorite, too. I was a pretty, light-skinned colored girl. I knew how to please.

CHAPTER 18

Noah Webster, June 10, 1899, Briar Hill, Kentucky

They charge me forty-five cents on the Lexington and Eastern Railroad. Start from the depot back of the Phoenix Hotel to Fenwick Station—almost nine miles, though it's less than half-way to Winchester and that only cost fifty-five cents. I complain to the stationmaster, but he says I'm lucky they let me ride at all. They wouldn't stop in Fenwick Station, not even to pick up the mail, if it weren't for me. Coming back, a conductor needs to flag them down. Doesn't half want to do it, either. So I reckon I am lucky. Colored lucky.

For that I stand in the back of the coach—the Separate Coach Law won't let me sit down. No call for a separate coach since I'm the only colored riding most days. Sitting be good after a full day teaching—standing forty-five minutes—a penny a minute. Forty-five cents! First class fare.

But money don't buy you first class if you're colored.

Still, it beats walking. And sometimes when the cab's empty, or near empty, I do sit down. The conductor don't seem to mind. I fall asleep as soon as my back touches leather. The club ladies are paying my train fare so I shouldn't be complaining. And it's less than a mile to Briar Hill from the station. If I'd known that the first day I could of saved myself a long walk.

But I didn't know that the first day. Seems I didn't know lots of things that first day. I thought I'd be training as a teacher. Come to it, I was starting my legal training, too.

Mr. Benjamin says he don't have time to put me through law school, but he gives me books to read and points out passages I should know. Then we go through all sorts of things the ladies might face in their protest—what's public property and what isn't. The right to protest. He gives me a whole section on that. Who can keep you off property and who can't. Who has the legal right to appoint a teacher. What to do if any of them get arrested. What to do when they do get arrested.

"That's our friend Judge Bullock's territory. He's mighty touchy about anything that disturbs the order in his jurisdiction. His order, that is. He doesn't much mind our order being disrupted."

Ever since the trouble started over in Cadentown, I make the trip to town and back four times a week now—that's costing the ladies three dollars and sixty cents—which would be about half my salary for the week. I spend an hour with Mr. Benjamin—all he can spare he tells me—then swing around to see Mamma. I wish I could see Maria—Mrs. Benjamin—too. But I don't have time and it's not likely she'd see me anyway. Though she write me a little. Real little. I ask Mr. Benjamin how she doing. He look at me strange, smiling and not smiling.

"Poorly. Tired all the time. Don't understand it. Sheila does all the heavy work."

Mr. Benjamin's a wonderful man, but sometimes he just don't see things. What he sees though, he see all the way. I couldn't make head nor tails about the trouble or why the parents in my school cared much about what happened over in Cadentown—that's three, four miles over—near Todds Road. Mr. Benjamin just shook his head at my ignorance.

"The Democrats are moving in—electing trustees to take over all the colored schools in the county. Then they're moving out the old teachers who just happen to be Republican and planting new men—or ladies—who just happen to be beholden to the Democrats. Green Pinckney Russell is the man they say is in charge, but really it's Superintendent Cassidy and our friend, Judge Bullock."

"I thought Cassidy was a reformer?"

Mr. Benjamin's face got hard—I had crossed the line, said something almost good about the enemy. "He says he is. But he's a Democrat first and foremost. The most important thing for a Democrat is to keep the colored race down. Only they've done such a good job, it's become inconvenient. Embarrassing. Mostly expensive. Cost them too much money keeping us ignorant so Superintendent Cassidy has to bring us back up a little bit. Just a little bit. Doesn't want us to get too much above our raising. Doesn't want us to start making decisions on our own."

He reached for another book from his shelf. I groaned, but not out loud. I tried to look as eager as I could at the notion of a hundred more pages of law to read. He flipped open to a passage, read for few seconds, and put it back. Saved for the moment.

"That's Judge Frank Bullock, too. Know what he said? Said Lexington had a school board but Fayette County lacked one. 'So I just resolved myself into a Board of Education.' Imagine that. Resolved himself into a Board of Education. That way we don't have to bother none with all those parents, colored parents especially. Voters who don't know the first thing about voting—which is that you vote Democrat or you don't vote at all. Mostly being colored, you don't vote."

Mr. Benjamin had commenced to almost shouting as if he forgot that I was the only one there and that I was on his side. "Those women know that Cadentown is their business—even three, four miles over. A hundred miles. Doesn't matter if the teacher they want is the better teacher or not. They're the ones who should decide. That's how Superintendent Cassidy and Judge Bullock are 'progressives.' They do 'good' by taking that decision away, taking decisions away from poor, ignorant, colored women. How would those women know what's best for their children?"

He calmed down some after that. Found another passage. This time I wasn't so lucky. He handed me the book and indicated a chapter—a long chapter. He sat down and sighed. Maybe he did get tired. I sure did and I was twenty years younger. He patted my arm. That startled me. Mr. Benjamin wasn't one to show much affection.

"But they do know what's best. And I'm going to help them fight to get it." He smiled at me—a whole smile this time, "Well, it's going to have to be you doing most of the fighting. Be sure to read those chapters. The law doesn't much care if you're right or wrong. But it sure doesn't like ignorant."

After seeing Mamma, I catch the last night train to Winchester and they let me off in Fenwick Station. Mamma had a sack of food for me like she afraid I'm gonna starve that long trek to the edge of the county. Nobody, not even the stationmaster, around when the train stop. I walk that mile to Briar Hill in the dark. A looping kind of road, up and down, the moon giving me the only light I got. Cloudy night so dark, I follow Mamma's caution. "Watch your feet," she tells me. "Make sure they touch the ground."

Miz Chiles is waiting up for me though I tell her not to. She has some buttermilk ready. I try not to drink any because I know it cost her. If she see a dime left over from the board money I give her, she doing well. But the buttermilk's there. I tell myself it'd hurt her feelings to turn it down.

Miz Chiles wants to know everything Mr. Benjamin's told me.

"What about this new group of trustees the Democrats put in? Nobody elect them."

"Superintendent Cassidy and Judge Bullock put them in. Bullock says he needs to bring order to the county. Made himself a school board of one."

She pull her head back at that, but didn't say anything more for a few moments. Watched me drink my buttermilk like I was just another child she was put in the world to take care of. A grown up Willy, not his teacher. Sure not the "lawyer" meant to guide her and keep her and her friends out of jail if I could. She lifted herself up from the table.

107

"Need to get a few hours' sleep. You, too. Don't be reading those books tonight. Suffice the day. Let the morrow take care of the morrow."

She turned before she entered the small room off the kitchen she shared with Mr. Chiles.

"A school board of one? He can do that? Lord, ain't nothing a white man think he can't do." Miz Chiles stood tall in the doorway, like a female Martin Luther.

"Well, I'm not a school board of one. I'm a whole bunch of people: Briar Hill, Athens, Bracktown, Chilesburg, Colestown. Every county colored school in Fayette standing by Cadentown. Judge Bullock want order? Won't get it taking away our teachers and putting in turncoat colored Democrats. He a school board of one? We one, too. He gonna find that out."

The children must of sensed something was up. I couldn't get them to concentrate on anything. I started the day with numbers just as I promised Miz Chiles, but the numbers just didn't add up. I was as bad as they were.

"Mr. Webster, nine plus thirteen ain't twenty-one." Luella looked indignant. I brought myself back to the slate her brother Clay had just finished.

"Sure isn't. Why didn't the rest of you catch that? Good job, Luella."

She looked pleased at the praise but not convinced. Numbers weren't the only thing not adding up. The meeting was that night—we were all leaving as soon as school was done. Wagons of women and a few men. The rumor was that a fellow named Graves—Professor Graves they called him—was going to show up at Cadentown. He was one of Green Pinckney Russell's teachers. The women were gonna intercept him. Peaceably. Just block his way.

We could just see the road from the school's playground. Not much of a playground, just a flat area the men kept hacked down so the children could run around. Two swings hung from two tall oaks at the edge of the property. The children swung them high. I half-expected broken bones by the end of May term. I should have calmed them when they got wild, but I loved watching them. *Swing high*, I'd sing in my mind, *sweet chariot. Swirl through the air. Point those toes out, children. Stretch those legs. Soon enough, the taut rope will reach its end and bring you home.*

I let recess go on longer than usual. Thought it might calm the children down. Calm me down. Luella brought me back to business again. She was the taut rope.

"Mr. Webster, we gonna play outside all day?"

The road below us wasn't traveled much, perhaps a wagon an hour. Farm trucks just passing from field to field. But today we seen a whole parade of vehicles—once, two even had to back up to let another one pass. I felt Willy's eyes on me. Luella's, too. But they didn't ask. Well-behaved colored children don't ask hard questions.

With all that traffic, I didn't notice at first the brougham pull off the road and attempt the cow path that led up to the school. Not fair to call it a cow path—the men had banked it and lay down stone. But it didn't get enough traffic to keep the weeds down, and the summer's work didn't leave the men time to do it themselves. Miz Chiles says nobody tried the road in snow and ice—spun wagon wheels and twisted horses' legs. And spring was mud.

But the brougham pushed through the tall grass fine enough. I told Willy and Luella to gather the children into two groups. Luella lit up. She loved leading a group. Willy just nodded—like I'd told him to carry in some sacks of feed. Straightened his shoulders and got to it.

I waited for my visitor.

A hundred yards off I began to admire the brougham. More like a courting vehicle than something that would attempt a country road. Its bright red roof was sharply squared. It rode high—black and white painted wheels like two giant ears on each side of the coach. The colored man directing the gray-dappled mare high-stepping through the black-eyed Susans wore a top hat and black shiny suit, as if he didn't much notice the dust he trailed. I didn't for a moment think somebody was in the cabin behind him. He didn't look like anybody's coachman.

When he pulled the horse up, the dust swirled from behind the brougham and covered me. He sat high up and seated in front of the cabin. I coughed. He waited for me to finish.

"You're the May term teacher I heard they hired. Didn't agree with that. What's your name?"

I looked up to talk to him. He didn't seem like he was going to get down. I felt the children staring through the two windows. I turned before I answered him. "Luella, Willy. Bring the children back to their tables." I waited as one by one, the children were unstuck from the windows, the last one Willy, who looked hard at me before he turned away. I heard the man above me tap his riding whip impatiently against his boot.

"You should have more control of the children than that. I've asked your name."

I felt myself flush but I kept my voice steady. "My name is Noah Webster. I have been hired for the May term. May I ask who I'm speaking to?"

"*To whom* you're speaking to. Learn good English if you're going to teach it. I am Green Pinckney Russell, the superintendent of colored schools in Lexington, Kentucky, and your superior."

I'd begun to suspect as much though I'd never met him. Saw him at a public meeting once. All I remember was him waving his arms and intoning some big public truth. My superior? I didn't think his title carried authority out in the county, but I decided not to dispute it. A cat can be queen of the barn if it wants to call itself that. Don't mean the mice got to call it that.

But they need to take heed. All the mice need to take heed of a cat in the barn.

"Won't you step down, Mr. Russell? Our well gives cool, clean water." He looked disgruntled as if I'd said something improper. But he put his reins down. It was a ways to the ground and I wondered if I should offer him a hand. He wasn't old—maybe mid-thirties. Held himself stiff like an old man. But he placed one hand on a wheel and leaped to the ground like a twenty-year-old.

Once eye-level, he relaxed a little. "Yes. Cool water would be welcome."

I pulled the bucket up slow and rinsed the tin cup before I handed it to him. He sipped slowly and looked over the fields surrounding the school.

"I was a country school teacher. Over in Chilesburg, not too far from here. Straight from Berea College to Chilesburg." He looked at me. "Green as you probably. But better educated."

I'd already taken Mr. Russell for a man who dropped insults without noticing—a just-stating-the-truth kind of insulter. Only I've noticed that a colored man who does that almost never brings that kind of truth-telling to white folks. Saves hard truths for coloreds. I felt a little raw but I couldn't argue. He was better educated than I was. Just about everybody was.

"You received your appointment through the local trustees, though they are not legally entitled to that power. Nor is the so-called Kentucky Negro Education Association to whom they turn to for advice on hiring, advice that obviously included your name." He shook his head. Disgusted and offended. He handed me the cup and waved it off. He looked at me silently for a second.

"Noah Webster. You're Robert Benjamin's assistant at *The Standard*. I knew I had heard your name. Well, that's interesting. He's a remarkable man, your boss. He has sound views on education—much aligned with mine and Dr. Washington's. I hope you at least try to apply his principles to your teaching here, as brief as that tenure might be."

Somehow, at the top of a rutted country road in the far reaches of obscurity, I'd managed to come to the attention of the most powerful colored man in Fayette County education. It didn't look good for my career. I parsed my words carefully.

"I always listen to Mr. Benjamin. I pay close attention to what he says about every-thing."

He looked at me carefully. Like he was wondering if a country school teacher—a brand new, green, poorly educated school teacher—might be trying to put something over on him.

"Good. See that you do. That way you won't do too much damage. Let me talk to the children."

I gave Willy and Luella a smile as we entered our ramshackle school. The children were all bent over their books. I couldn't of done better. But a public man, especially a large colored man in shiny black clothes, was more than they could bear. They scrambled 'round him like he was the ice man, coming to offer them cool slivers soaked in syrup. Green Pinck-ney Russell let out a harrumph that sent them scurrying back to their tables. He came 'round then and looked over their bent shoulders.

He picked up a list of vocabulary words from in front of Luella. I held my breath. She didn't tell him the words came from a poem. He didn't ask.

"An unusual list of words. Do you know their meanings?" He looked down the list. "Tell me the meaning of prejudice."

"Prejudice: it's when you against somebody on account of them being different some way."

Mr. Russell waited. A good teacher waits. Luella continued.

"You don't like people because you think they something before you even meet them. Just by looking at them. But you don't even know them. So it ain't them you don't like, it's something they can't help. Mr. Webster explain it. He said like you decide all Catholics drink too much. We don't know no Catholics so we don't do that. Mamma says she knew some Catholics and they didn't drink no more than the colored men she knew. Or not liking coloreds because they colored. Just about everybody we know is colored so we don't do that neither. We wouldn't not like nobody. But some white folks do. Some white people got prejudice against coloreds for no reason 'cept they colored. 'Course some coloreds got prejudice against white folk. But mostly coloreds got reason to not like the white people, so I don't know if that's prejudice. And I sure like Mr. Calley at the store. He a white man but he always real nice. And Miz Calley give us candy sometime and we don't even have to pay for it. She a real nice white lady. I don't have no prejudice against Miz Calley. Mr. Calley, either."

Mr. Russell nodded all the way through Luella's ramble. Getting Luella to start wasn't that difficult. Stopping her was another story.

"You want me to do another word?"

"No, no, that's sufficient for now. A good job, but try not to use the word 'ain't'. Have a prejudice against the word 'ain't'." He smiled at his joke. Luella and the other children looked blank. Explain too much and it all goes out the window. A good teacher knows when to keep his mouth shut. "It's not a proper word," he continued, looking over at me sternly. "Mr. Web-ster should not allow its use in the school room. Or even in the play area."

The play area? I kept my head down. Mr. Webster had other things on his plate be-sides "ain't."

He spent a few more minutes circling the two large tables, but I could tell he'd some-thing else on his mind. Didn't come all the way out here to Briar Hill to look at vocabulary lists. I waited.

A good teacher waits.

"Mr. Webster, might I speak with you outside for a few minutes? The children seem settled."

The children weren't settled, but they would hold for awhile. We closed the door be-hind us. I gave Willy and Luella a look and they took over. Sometimes I wondered how much they needed me. It was bright outside. May term had turned to June and it was hot. My throat was parched. I pulled up the well bucket and filled the cup. Mr. Russell waved it away.

"I know that you have heard of the meeting at Cadentown."

Ah, I thought. *Here it comes.*

"Yes. I plan to attend."

"In what role?" His tone was sharp.

"Witness, mostly."

"Witness? What else? Legal advisor?"

Mr. Russell smiled at my surprise. "Lexington's a small place. Word gets around."

"Legal advisor's too big a term. I'm just there to try to keep things calm. And legal."

"That's good. Good. What I want, too. We're on the same page."

He changed his mind about the water and pointed to the cup. That shiny black suit couldn't be comfortable. I waited for him to explain himself.

"Some women have taken it in their heads that they run the schools. We are plagued with their efforts—from the high and mighty Madeline McDowell Breckinridge to more lowly contenders such as your employer's wife and her friend Emma Bisou. It is very difficult to accomplish anything when a committee of women is looking over your shoulder, second-guessing every decision you make. Now this female contagion has spread to the country and colored women—near illiterate women—have decided they know how to judge the credentials of the teachers selected for the county schools. The *county's* schools. Not *their* schools as they call them."

Uppity colored women. I looked at him wondering if he remembered that he was colored, too. He had worked himself into a froth and needed a pause to gulp some water. He drank so quickly it dribbled out the corners of his mouth and slouched its way to his collar. The collar was pretty limp, though I imagine it had started the morning proud, white, and stiff.

"Like deciding about me." I startled him. He pulled his chin from the cup like he'd almost forgot I was part of the conversation. "Judging whether I was the right teacher for *their* school. A group of ladies questioned me hard. Wondered if I'd last my first week. But here I am into my second month already."

He looked at me steady for a moment. "The question is will you last past your third month?"

"Depends on the ladies, I reckon."

He shook his head. "No, son." He was maybe a dozen years older than me—not enough years to make him my daddy. "No, son," he repeated. "Whether you last past the May term or not depends on what you do tonight. On what kind of 'legal advice' you hand those ladies. The best advice you might give them is to not show up at all—to let people who know better choose the teachers who will help their children become useful and productive citizens of this community."

Useful and productive citizens. The four words rolled out of his mouth like one big one. Booker T. Washington used that term all the time. Even Mr. Benjamin's been known to reach for them. *Useful and productive citizens.* I bet white folks in their minds' eyes saw happy, contented coloreds when they heard those words: bent over in endless tobacco rows. Saw smiling mammies cooking and fussing at white babies who fussed right back at them, their own babies bent over slates in nice little cabins. Ain't nobody saying "ain't" to nobody.

"Afraid I won't be able to keep the ladies from the meeting. Sort of like keeping the children from using the word 'ain't' when they chasing each other on the playground. They just don't seem to listen."

"You have to make them listen!" Mr. Russell looked like he was working himself into another froth. Like he could use a church fan to cool him down. I've seen ladies rush to the pulpit to fan a preacher about to boil over. Praise Jesus. Only I didn't think to bring one with me.

Mamma was never one of those ladies. Said if a preacher heated himself up, he could cool himself down. Mr. Russell cooled himself down.

"But I see your point. They wouldn't listen to a boy-teacher they just hired. Another reason to keep the hiring out of their hands. But you can help in other ways. Let us know what's going on, for one thing. I tell you, help like that will be rewarded." And if Mr. Russell been a winking-type fellow, I swear he would of winked at me. But he weren't. I just had to imagine the wink in the stare he gave me.

Felt kind of sad. I liked teaching. Maybe someday.

"I'll do my best, Mr. Russell. *Ain't* promising anything, but I'll do my best."

He looked puzzled at my ain't, like I was some sassy student. The teacher in him wanted to slap that word right out of my sentence. But Mr. Russell's a politician first and a teacher way down the line. He kept his mouth shut, hopped on his brougham seat and started back down the cow path.

"You won't regret your decision."

Oh, too late for that. Regret followed me like heartburn after fried turnip greens. I watched my teaching career wind its way down our pretty June countryside along with Mr. Russell's pretty red brougham. God's country. Only he gave it to some sorry people.

Mamma says be patient in tribulation. Well, she should know. Tribulations been most of her life.

I waited to give Mr. Russell a final wave. Country folk wouldn't think it fitting if they didn't wave a final goodbye as you turned the bend. But he didn't look back.

Fellows like Mr. Russell never do.

CHAPTER 19

Noah Webster, June 10, 1899, Cadentown, Kentucky

It took us two hours to do about five miles cross-county. Cross-country it could have been. The county didn't really plan for county folk to visit each other—at least not those neighbors who weren't right next door. Come to Lexington or stay home. Athens sure shouldn't be moseying on over to Avon. Bracktown and Jim Town should just see each other on maps. And Briar Hill sure has no business in Cadentown. Still, folks got around, even on paths that were more rut than road. They knew people in hamlets clear cross the county, knew them like they visited each other as neighbors back on Upper Street. Mamma says the way people pop into other homes on Upper, you might as well leave the door wide open.

"You the first to invite them in," I tell her.

"Well, you got to be neighborly. Just being Christian."

Of course that's where a lot of county folk meet—in church. Some of their churches a good distance away, though they might have a different one fifty yards away.

It was still light when we got to Cadentown. I wasn't looking forward to the trip back in the dark. I offered to take the reins—I was the only male in the wagon—but Miz Chiles looked at me like I was Willy, smiled and shook her head. I had to admit she knew more about handling that old mare of hers than I ever would. She clipped her the tiniest of nips and that mare stepped around boulders and rolled crevices as dainty as a dancer, though she was a big clod-hopping work horse. The three other ladies sat in the bed of the wagon in straight-backed chairs that they kept steady, tilting them like rocking chairs when they needed to. I wondered why no men but me came but I didn't ask. Like I told Mr. Russell, I was mainly here as a witness.

We pulled up rein right in front of Cadentown school, a big bungalow, twice and more the size of Briar Hill. About as big as Briar Hill #7, the white school. They were both brand new. Superintendent Cassidy hadn't just been building white schools. He'd been tearing down old colored schools—tearing them down just before they fell down on their own mostly. Preached to white folks in *The Morning Herald*, told them colored county schools "were a disgrace and a danger" and they needed to put some money into the pot. Telling white people they needed to pay for colored schools. That was something.

None of that money had got to Briar Hill yet. Put together with "spit and prayer" is how Mr. Chiles put it. I take the children outside if it's blowing hard, even if it's raining. Better wet than crushed.

Superintendent Cassidy and Judge Bullock been raising colored teacher pay, too. Not much. But the raises maybe give a year or two stretch before starvation set in. That's real progress in Fayette County. "Raising standards and bringing order" is how Mr. Cassidy put it in the same article.

Right next to the school was the prettiest little teacher cottage, right out of a picture. Mr. Cassidy's doing. A teacher wouldn't have to board.

I liked boarding myself. Maybe 'cause my cooking's been known to confuse people.

"Boy," Mamma asked me once, "is this an egg you fried or bacon you burnt?"

"Well, Mr. Cassidy's done some good," I said to Miz Chiles. She turned to me.

"Nobody denying that. He built some nice schools. Even got rid of some bad teachers. Some good teachers, too. But he thinks they're his schools. They ain't."

With that, she climbed down to join about a dozen women and just two men lined up in front of the school. I started to join them. Miz Chiles turned to me.

"No, this ain't your fight. You the teacher—a good teacher and we appreciate that. And you here to advise us some when we need it. But you stay in the wagon. Might be trouble. We need you here to help clean up that trouble, not get in it yourself."

"Miz Chiles, remember I read you where you can protest and you got a right to assemble. But you can't block the road. And you can't keep a person from entering a public building."

She nodded, the other women coming closer to listen. "If you mean this school building's a public building, then we gonna get trouble sooner than later. We hear they sending someone who calls himself Professor Graves to take the place of Mr. Martin, the teacher the Cadentown folks hired. Well, I tell you, kindly because I know you telling us what we need to hear, Professor Graves ain't passing into this public building."

It was a good twenty minutes waiting after that. I began to think nothing was gonna happen. The chatting died down and it was quiet, so quiet we all heard the trotting—pretty fast pacing for a country road full of ruts—like the rider knew the road real well. Or somebody who thought he could handle anything.

The pony and cart that rounded the bend was going so quick it almost plowed into the first line of women standing there. The colored man pulled up hard—started to yell at the women but broke off mid-word. He looked at the crowd. Didn't expect to find a crowd of people in the middle of Cadentown on a summer evening. His eyes opened wide.

"What are you all doing here? Blocking the road. Almost ran you over. Who are you?"

Miz Chiles stepped in front of the women. "The question is: who are you?"

The man stood in his seat. He would of towered over Miz Chiles, but she's a big woman. He barely had a head above her even standing up in his wagon. "I'm Hesiod William Graves, the new teacher and principal of this school, appointed by Superintendent Cassidy himself."

If he expected the waves to part when he said that, he was bound to disappointment.

"How do you do, Professor Graves. I'm sorry to tell you that you've been misinformed. We already got a teacher and a principal who we like right well. Seems you made a trip for no purpose. Turn back now before it turn dark. Take care, now."

I heard some of the women murmuring behind her, but Miz Chiles raised her hand just a little and it stopped. Professor Graves didn't say anything for a moment or so, his mouth gaping. Then he gripped his whip and raised it to his side. *Oh, don't do that* I prayed. *Don't do that. The Lord knows how it'll end if you do that.*

He lowered his arm. "Women, get out of my way. I have been appointed by Superintendent Cassidy. I do not want to hurt you. Move."

The whispers grew louder behind Miz Chiles and she didn't put her hand out to quiet them. She walked closer to the gig, put her hand on the gelding who was starting to pace. She murmured in his ear and he quieted some.

"Mister, you been told. Persons who hired you ain't got the right. We hope nobody gets hurt tonight because we don't want that either. But you got to leave. Now."

That *now* rang like a clapper on a bell. Professor Graves looked at her a second then sat down hard. The gelding jumped and stepped forward, but Miz Chiles' patting calmed him. She rejoined the women to give him room to turn. The road was narrow where he stopped the gig, with a large oak on one side and a creek on the other. Twenty yards further the road widened to a turn-around, but Professor Chiles had got as far down that road as he was getting that night. He tried to turn the gelding but the horse was already half-spooked and just kept trying to push forward. Then he tried backing the horse up, but that's a trick the best horseman got a hard time doing. I don't know what Professor Graves was like when he was calm but he wasn't much of a horseman when his nerves was up.

We watched him twisting and turning for fifteen minutes, begging and cussing that horse. The wheels on his rig sometimes jammed, sometimes looked like they might break in two. Miz Chiles could of turned that wagon in two minutes. I might of done it in five. Neither of us offered to help. We figured to leave the man with that much dignity.

Only his dignity started to leak when one of the woman let out of a snort of a laugh that set us all going. Some of us could hardly stand we was laughing so hard. Professor Graves sweated and shouted and cursed. He was a fine-looking, upstanding man when he first trotted 'round the road's curve, but he was a cheese left out in the sun now. He cursed us now, not just the gelding. Just made us laugh harder.

Finally Miz Chiles stepped forward again. She was the only one not laughing. She grabbed the gelding's harness and talked to him. He quieted. So did Professor Graves. Our laughter trailed off to a couple of hiccups, then stopped. Miz Chiles curved the gelding into a circle and pointed the rig the other way, the way the professor had come in, the way he was headed out. He had dropped the reins when Miz Chiles stepped forward. She picked them up and handed them to him.

He rode off without another word.

We all went into the school for our meeting then. Mr. Martin, the teacher and principal came out of the cottage. I guess he thought it best to hide out while the women handled the difficulties. He was all smiles, like he'd done something. A Mr. Johnson, one of the two men there, told the women he and the other fellow was Cadentown School trustees, elected by Cadentown folk, and that Mr. Martin—he waved to us all and we cheered—was the man they chose to be both teacher and principal. He thanked us all for our support like he was a congressman, like the women could vote. Well, they could vote for trustee so I guess he knew what he was doing.

That was the end of the meeting. It was all done.

Only we knew it weren't. I didn't understand why Green Pinckney Russell hadn't shown up or why he sent Professor Graves into a group of riled-up pilgrims without so much as a heads up. That didn't make sense to me. It'd been all too easy turning back Professor Graves. I knew Superintendent Cassidy wasn't gonna put up with us leaving his man behind like he was some sorry also-ran at the race-meet. Knew it wouldn't suit Judge Bullock's notion of order. I'd seen him in his courtroom get a man took out for the look on his face.

But I didn't say nothing. People were in too good a mood, laughing and talking loud. If there'd been any music, we would of started dancing—us four men run ragged by all those women, though women don't need men to dance. Folks told the story about Professor Graves and his gelding over and over again—the tale getting bigger, sillier, each time they told it. But nobody corrected anybody—just added on. Could see the legend growing. Folks do that, make what happened even more outlandish. Making Professor Graves even more ridiculous. Poor man didn't need our help to do that but we gave it to him anyway. "Professor Graves," they'd stretch his name and we'd all just wipe our eyes.

But I knew something was up. So did Miz Chiles. She'd smile when people congratulated her, shake her head when they had her leaping up and practically carrying that gelding over the side ditch, but she didn't laugh. And when they turned away from her, that polite smile faded. She looked down the road she had pointed Professor Graves and just stared.

I know she was wondering who was coming up that road next. I know she was wondering when. I was, too.

CHAPTER 20

Judge Frank Bullock, June 12, 1899, Lexington, Kentucky

What did that miscreant, Oscar Wilde, say? "No good deed goes unpunished." His deeds—his unspeakable crimes—were justly punished, but I think of his words as I look at this school war. For that is what it has come down to: a school war, though bullets have not yet flown. Massillon Cassidy and I have put our money, our labor, our very beings into rescuing the county colored schools and what is our payment? Abuse, and worse than abuse: slander and cries of tyranny. Tyranny? How many colored schools have we built? How many teachers have we rescued from penury? We are strange tyrants indeed.

And how many times have I testified before indifferent white committees and told them that they must—not should, *must*—procure monies for the colored schools. People hostile to the whole idea of colored education. Hostile even to education for poor white children. "Education is a private affair," my fellow Brahmins tell me. If one cannot afford to educate one's children, let them go happily into the fields or the factories. One doesn't need Shakespeare to strip a tobacco plant.

"Father could bring Colonel Morgan to one of these meetings," I said to Grace. "If he removed his spurs, his views on the colored would fit in perfectly." Grace frowned. She is proud that Father was one of Morgain's Raiders. Proud that one's closest connection had once been an outlaw.

Grace is too discreet to share her own ideas on colored education. I do not press her for them.

But what does one say to such ideas? Are they ideas? They are too cloistered from the world, a luxury I do not have. If they sat in my seat, if they saw the parade of ignorance that led to misery—white and colored misery that could have been prevented by a little education, the smallest bit of education—they would see the benefit to themselves.

But perhaps not. Massillon and I left together in near despair after talking to the Iroquois Hunt Club, a club I have belonged to all my life and one I felt represented the highest standards of our society. Colonel Roger Williams—e he was the presiding officer that night—was particularly adamant. "Money for colored schools? Might as well teach our horses how to ride us!"

I remember regretting to the point of grief when Billy Klair took the Colonel's seat in the legislature. The Colonel is one of us after all. I believe we're even cousins of some sort, though distant ones. I hoped he could not see the disgust on my face, but Grace tells me I am not good at hiding what I feel.

Teach our horses to ride us? Our horses—our Billy Klairs—have already learned to ride us. What you need to learn is how to be ridden.

"Well," Massillon said, "perhaps they have a point. Education does not seem to have done much for them."

But we did raise the money finally, or at least the beginning of the money that is needed. And this is our thanks. Disorder. Rebellion. Ingratitude. My personal feelings do not matter, but I will have order. I have sent Deputy Sheriffs Freckman and Siebrecht with a commodious four-horse wagon, large enough for a good dozen of the ringleaders. I have instructed the constable, George Rose, to clear his lockup of common drunks and riffraff, to prepare to receive a more elevated kind of riffraff. I will put the whole colored community of Cadentown—or at least their so-called leaders—in the local jail if I have to.

Men and women together if need be, for it is mostly women who are leading this disgraceful action. Women who so forget the reserve their gender demands should not expect any special consideration for their sex. I believe few men are silly enough to suppose that women have no opinions on the issues of the day. But the barrage of women sharing those views in the public sphere has become unbearable. And it is led by ladies from the highest spheres of our society—Madeline McDowell Breckinridge, Laura Clay. Cousins of mine, also, of some sort. They claim education as a subject peculiar to their sensibilities and talents. Nonsense. Once the child leaves the home, he is in the public sphere and that sphere is still one where men govern. Men understand what is needed to survive in the world. This franchise which allows women the vote in school board elections is a terrible idea. It will lead to endless trouble. Billy agrees with me.

"We're getting rid of it next session, Judge. Just got to get through one more election."

My cousins are, at least, ladies. The colored women who emulate them cannot claim that status. They lack even the pretense of gentility. I know such women. Rough women who use their fists, on men and on each other. I see them in my courtroom, though the women in my courts have at least the excuse of drink or dire necessity. These Cadentown women are not starving. Most of them—though not all—can look to males to protect them and their children. Yet they choose to loudly impose themselves and their views on the world.

So, let them pay the world's price for their audacity.

As for their choosing trustees for every little colored school, nonsense. If trustees are needed to care for daily trivialities, I will appoint them. There is such a thing as paying too much attention to local sensibilities. And then there is chaos. As the elected County Judge, I am the only school board they need. Superintendent Cassidy and I have proven our good will. If people do not trust us, it must be traced to the deficiencies of their character, not to any defect in ours. I deal with such defects on a daily basis.

Oscar Wilde notwithstanding, bad deeds as well as good are punished in my court.

Grace is a proud woman who knows how to keep her own counsel. Even her pride for the outlaw Morgan's connection to my family, is expressed only by a passing look. We never quarrel. I would find it distasteful, humiliating, to quarrel with a woman. Grace knows this. Any true woman would know this.

"Kentucky women are not idiots," my cousin, Madeline, has been quoted as saying, "though closely related to Kentucky men." Amusing. Madeline is correct. So many Kentucky males are idiots.

Kentucky women should take care not to join their ranks.

Chapter 21

Noah Webster, June 13, 1899, Cadentown, Kentucky

We got word late and had to scramble. Professor Graves was coming back and this time he might not be alone. Miz Chiles showed up at the school—told me to hop in the wagon if I wanted to join them. Her mare was straight from the field, half covered in mud. So much rain lately. Miz Chiles' farm dress had a wet line halfway up it, like a flood's high water mark. Surprised me. Miz Chiles always clean and neat. But there weren't no time for cleanup.

I sent the children on home though we had two hours left in the school day. First I thought to try and save some of the day by telling Luella and Willy to put the children in two groups, see if they could get some studying done. But it didn't take me a moment to see nothing much would come of it. We like to think we can wall off the world inside the schoolhouse, even a schoolhouse about to fall down on our heads like Briar Hill. But you can't do that though you might be in the far out ends of Fayette County.

The world's just too much with us. At least it's too much with us lately, too much to expect a child to do much studying.

Only one other lady, Miz Beatty, was in the wagon. Somehow she'd time enough to clean up. Her old-timey dress looked good enough for a church supper. I told her she looked real nice. She just smiled at me.

"We picking up the others?"

"We're all there is," Miz Chiles said and nipped the air above her mare's back with her whip. Might not be in the fields, that nip said, but it still a work day.

Miz Beatty explained.

"Can't leave the fields. One more day gone, Alice Lawson say, and you might as well give the whole crop over to weeds and beetles. I told her to plant more corn like I do—beetles don't bother corn much and the weeds don't knock them over. But I know what she mean. Don't feel like I can leave myself, but some things more important. 'You want your children fighting weeds and beetles all their lives, too?' I say to Alice, but she just give me that stare she give folks who ask her things she can't answer. Well, I don't blame her. Can't answer most questions myself. But letting the bugs go free range one more day ain't gonna starve us."

We hoped there'd be others waiting for us when we got to Cadentown. We didn't expect a crowd like before, but it disappointed us some to see only six other women. Another rig pulled us behind us with two young gals—one with a long single braid down her back that made my arm kind of itch to pull like I was ten years old. Neither of them looked old enough to have children in the schools but one did, Miz Beatty whispered to me.

"Five-year-old twins. They sisters. The other one, Lizzie Price," pointing to the tan colored one with the braid, "ain't married. Pretty, ain't she?"

That made ten women.

And me. I was the only man. Mr. Martin, the Cadentown teacher, had let his children go early, too. I don't know if he was hiding in the teacher-cottage. We didn't see any sign of him. No sign of the two trustees, neither. A speech don't do much good most times, but a speech about then could of cheered us some. Could of been a comfort.

But there weren't any words. No sounds. Sometimes a June afternoon is as quiet as a empty church. The women moved silent, almost like they were in a church. No laughing. No shouting. Not like the other night. Not yet at least. The fields around the school looked like they didn't have a thing stirring in them. The birds and other critters are hid that time of day. And the crickets don't start their chirping till twilight. If the beetles were chomping, they were doing it quiet.

The fields stretched out green with just a little yellow edging its way in. Like a painting I saw in Cincinnati. Mr. Benjamin took me with him. He went up with the colored sculptor, the one who made that bust of Frederick Douglass, Isaac Hathaway. Next time I see Mr. Hathaway, I'll have to tell him about the children running the school ground, fighting to play Frederick Douglass. He'd like that. Should do a bust of Sojourner, too. I might tell him if I build up the nerve.

I was along to do the heavy lifting on that trip, but I didn't mind. Mr. Benjamin said it'd be an education. Not just looking but listening to Isaac. Not ten years older than me, but his eyes seen ten times more than mine. The paintings I seen before just dead people in white people's houses. Ancestors. I guess colored people don't have ancestors—none we put on the wall at least.

Colors in some of those Cincinnati paintings didn't look like real life. But I didn't mind. Like a dream, some of them. A different kind of dream.

I said that to Isaac when I could find my voice. Afraid he'd laugh at me. But he nodded and told me I was right. If I looked real close, though, he said the paintings got more real, even with their strange colors. And if we looked real close to real life, those same colors would pop right up in front of us.

A daytime dream. A dream with your eyes open.

The field in front of me now was like a picture where the painter tries one green— hard and deep—and then another, so soft you could rest on it like a pillow. Off to the side he splashed some gold, like a sunbeam coming in from a morning half-night still. Like Mamma when I was a boy, dribbling cold drops of water on my closed eyelids till I opened them.

"Get on out of bed, you sleeping beauty," she'd whisper and my waking would be as smooth as the cheek she patted. When she see my eyes open, she might pour the whole cup and I'd squeal and jump out of bed. That squeal was the whole gold, the full sun risen.

I looked at that field, trying to decide which color the painter was gonna settle on. But I couldn't decide. My eye just couldn't figure out where to look.

But I feared it wasn't gonna be any easy waking.

Miz Chiles decided for me. She weren't as gentle as Mamma, but she was just as quick. I left that dream on the double.

"Nail the school doors shut. The window awnings, too." Nobody thought to ask who put Miz Chiles in charge, we just got to it. Some boards were found in back of the school, left over from building the teacher cottage. The women let me do some of the first pounding, but I was taking too long and they joined in. The two young women especially went at it like it was personal.

"Sister, you pound that board like you a preacher pounding drink out of a sinner." I smiled my prettiest at the braid girl, Lizzie.

She didn't pause but a half-second to look at the fool who was spouting off and went back to hammering. Like I was one of those horses with feet going every which way. I saw Miz Beatty look at me and shake her head. Thank the Lord Miz Chiles was out of hearing.

We knew boarding up the school wouldn't keep anyone out forever, but it would slow them down. Like fighting beetles in a tomato patch. Can't keep them from eating, but you can slow their appetite some. Miz Chiles divided the women into two groups of five and set them on the two roads that branched into Cadentown. She joined the group on the main road, the one Professor Graves came in on two nights past. Just two nights. Seemed more than that.

"Which group you want me in?" I asked her. I was the odd number, the odd man. Miz Chiles shook her head.

"I want you in the wagon, Mr. Webster. Like I told you the other night. You our witness. If we get in trouble, you tell others the kind of trouble we facing. You the nearest thing we got to a lawyer. Thank you kindly for the help with the hammering, but I need you to stand off now."

When Miz Chiles tells you to stand off, I know there ain't no arguing, but it was hard. "I'm just to sit here in the wagon like some child you want to set out of trouble—the only man here—and watch while you women face what's coming? Whatever that is."

Miz Chiles looked at me kindly. Even the pretty gal who knew me for a fool gave me a small smile. Miz Chiles might look kind, but she weren't budging.

"You ain't no child, Mr. Webster. You a grown man and a good teacher. But I need you in that wagon and that's all there is to it."

We waited then. The women by the two roads. Me in the wagon. Waited in the June heat and in the silence that took on sounds as time passed. A chirping of a few stray birds. A rustling in the grass, maybe wind or maybe small creatures moving around, eager to start their night, hoping the dark would hide them, keep them safe. Just wishful thinking, Mamma would say. None of us know what the night brings. The grass only hides so much. The owls are high above, just hovering, with keen eyes and ears that hear the smallest tremble. Ready to swoop.

Colored folks in the country ain't afraid of owls. They put their chickens inside their coops, they safe enough. But other things hiding in the hills with talons a lot sharper than owls.

We all heard the wagon about the same time. Probably more than a mile off, that first rumbling. A big wagon, you could tell without seeing. Nobody said anything. All the small sounds going away, all the small creatures diving back into their holes. Just that rumbling, that roll of metal wheels scraping over rock.

It was coming from the same road Professor Graves had traveled. We listened for a few minutes, then Miz Chiles gestured to the other group. They all joined together into a body of ten. I saw the sister who was mamma to the twins start to tremble but she made no sound. Miz Chiles patted her, just like she done with the professor's gelding. The gal stopped trembling. Her sister with the braid stood still beside her. All the women did.

I was fifty yards back alone in my wagon, standing up so I spotted them first. Four men, one driving, two other sitting on either side of him, long rifles in hand, battle-ready. A fourth man—a colored man—sat on a little hutch in back.

It was too far away to see their faces, but I recognized one just by the fancy kind of top hat he sported. That was a famous hat in Yellmantown. Fellows joked about it. He'd come rouse drinkers at George Thomas—sometimes just for meanness—they not doing anything but being happy and colored. I guess he figured that weren't natural. One top hat among a sea of derbies. Like he just dropped in from the Hunt Club.

I reached for his name. Deputy Sheriff Siebrecht. German. Worse than the Micks sometimes. Hated coloreds. At least he didn't much care for me.

Not a funny fellow even with his top hat.

For a big wagon it was moving fast, two giant geldings clipping along like that road was a racetrack instead of the back-breaker it was. Miz Beatty weren't gonna stop those two horses with a soft whisper. The pace they were coming at, I didn't know if they were gonna stop at all. I started to yell out to the women, tell them to jump clear, but the look on Miz Chiles' face stopped me.

Oh, Jesus, I thought. *They gonna plow through those women like a truncheon mashing through a drunk's skull.*

But the wagon stopped—don't know how but it did. A swirl of dust swooped from the back and covered the riders. When the dust finally passed, I saw the four men clear. Deputy Sheriff Freckman—another German—was sitting by Siebrecht who was doing the driving.

Constable George Rose flanked him on the other side. He was another regular over at George Thomas. Not as mean, though. Real polite fellow. As long as you did what he told you.

Professor Graves was on the hutch seat. Come to claim his place. White guns in tow.

Siebrecht hadn't pulled up more than two feet from Miz Chiles, who stood in front of the group. He steadied his top hat with his left hand, grabbed his rifle with his left. He let the reins dangle.

"Goddamnit, woman. You want your nigger head smashed to pieces? What in damnation are you nigger bitches doing standing in the middle of the road? Get the hell out of the way before I let these geldings roll right over your sorry carcasses."

Miz Chiles stood still. I swear she looked taller even than her six feet. I don't know that she ever heard language like that, not words thrown at her like stones, meant to cut. She a church woman—they all church women. A man learned early on not to even cuss in front of whores. Of course I ain't been around white whores much, but Jake'd throw a man out into the street if he started to abuse the ladies doing their business at George Thomas. "Ain't no call for language like that," Jake'd say, as if the women were young gals at a church picnic. Jake was right. Even those ladies got some dignity. Needed to protect that.

Miz Chiles waited, like she waited for the dust the geldings roused up to settle. Waited for those cuss words to fall to the ground. Then she spoke softly, but her voice carried.

"We here to protest. We got a right. We stand here to protest the teacher we choose being fired. We here to protest the new teacher—that Graves man sitting behind you—a fellow we told two nights ago we don't want—coming in his place. Ain't no place for him here. Told him that once. We here to tell him again."

Miz Chiles' soft words. Her standing there in front of that wagon and those huge geldings as if they couldn't squash her in a moment made the veins in Siebrecht's neck bulge till I thought they might burst.

"That nigger teacher been hired by Superintendent Cassidy himself. Judge Bullock sent us to make sure he ain't intimidated by no mob of women. I don't give a pig's shit if you got teachers or not. Judge Bullock ordered us to come and we here. Can't think of a surer way, myself, to waste white money than trying to learn a bunch of ignorant niggers. Have better luck with these damn geldings. But the trick with geldings is that you don't try to reason with them, you just show them the whip. Which is what I'm about to do with you, woman, you keep standing there."

With that he lay down his rifle and picked up a large bull whip—a whip long enough to cover the backs of six horses instead of the two in front of him, as big as they were. True to word, the geldings snorted when he pulled the whip out. Just the sight of that whip enough to bring religion to them. Or the memory of it. Siebrecht didn't look like the kind of man to spare horse flesh if it suited him. I wondered how those horses saw that whip, they staring straight ahead and it in back of them. But they did. Ripples passed up their legs and over their backs, like wind blowing waves on a river before a storm.

But the women gathered closer around Miz Chiles, just bunched in. Women do that. I seen ladies at George Thomas gather 'round a sister who some fellow threatened, turn on even a big man if he hit a girl. Gathered 'round before Jake even noticed sometimes. I know these were church ladies circling Miz Chiles—Christian ladies and it wrong to put them in the same thought with those other women—but the way they stood tall, even little Miz Beatty, they reminded me of it. Only thing moving was that pretty girl's braid, swaying back and forth behind her like a gallows rope.

Miz Chiles didn't move. Not even a mean German sheriff who hated coloreds would whip a woman. He might not spare horse flesh, but he knew better than to hurt a woman. At least not in public. At least not with people looking on.

The whip didn't snap when it came down on Miz Chiles—it lay like some giant black snake circling her head. It carved into her face like a branding fork. When it pulled back up it sucked spurts of blood with it. The women around her started to scream in a keen I ain't heard outside a funeral. Miz Beatty on one side of her and the young pretty braid gal on the other side tried to hold her up, but Miz Chile's six feet was too big for them and she crashed to the ground like a poplar struck by lightning. The whip came down again and again and the women started to fall like tall grass cut clean by a scythe.

The geldings startled and reared. The whip was meant for them as far as they knew and they pulled forward, trying to escape. Constable George Rose grabbed the reins and leaned his whole body back, trying to keep the horses from running over the fallen women. Siebrecht kept whipping. Freckman, the other deputy, finally grabbed Siebrecht's arm, struggling with him to stop.

"You're gonna kill them," he yelled, but it was just one more yell among the others. "Stop."

All ten women lay sprawled on the ground when Freckman finally pulled Siebrecht's whip down. Like they'd been shot. Screaming and shouting and crying. The geldings' whinnying was tortured and strangled. Constable George Rose sat down heavy. He had held them.

I had to pull on Miz Chiles' mare some. "Whoa," I whispered to her, "Whoa. Everything's all right."

Everything's all right. I stood there frozen, stood there and let that man beat those women. My women. Beat Miz Chiles, who like my own mamma. Like I still a little boy whose mamma needed to protect him, not a man needing to protect his mamma.

I jumped out of the wagon and ran to the women. I moved the young braid gal—she was laying across of Miz Chiles like she was trying to protect her. I picked up Miz Chiles like she didn't weigh more than Luella and carried her back to the wagon. She was breathing, but her face kept oozing blood, the gashes the whip made crisscrossing each other like some road laid out in hell.

"Where you going with that woman, boy?" Siebrecht looked beat, like he'd done a full day's work. "Leave that nigger woman laying there. We'll pick her up and throw her in the wagon. Drop that woman, boy. You hear me?"

Siebrecht tried to raise his whip hand but Freckman still held onto it. George Rose pulled back on the geldings again, new roused by the shouting. He yelled at them the way you yell at horses when you need their attention but don't want to spook them.

Too late for that. They was already spooked. We all was. George Rose's face was whiter than I ever seen a white man's.

Professor Graves had ducked down low in back. I couldn't see how white his face looked.

Women were picking themselves up—the screaming trailing off. Miz Chiles was the only one who got the whip full force. Didn't see it coming. None of us did. Miz Beatty and the others got time to put their hands up. Duck their heads. They were hurting, but not like Miz Chiles.

The braid gal found some water. "Lizzie," I heard her sister call out to her and Lizzie went searching for her.

I took my shirt off and ripped it in rough squares and dipped the pieces in the water. I wished it was cleaner. I pressed the pieces against Miz Chiles' face and bosom where the whip had left slanted gashes, ripping her dress. The gashes crisscrossed when Siebrecht changed directions, lifting his whip first one way into the air and then another. One of Miz Chiles' bosoms lay open where the cloth had split, the lashes making a giant X. I wanted to close my eyes to the sight. You should not look on your parents' nakedness. But I needed to keep my eyes open, needed to find the deepest wounds and set the strips, needed to press the patches down to sop the blood oozing like a wet weather spring when the ground is full of life and underground streams push their way to the surface. I needed to see what the man had done to my mother.

I placed the patches in the same crisscross direction as the gashes so like I was piece-making a quilt on Miz Chiles' face and bosom. A crazy quilt. A drunkard's path. Each ragged square first white. Then red. I pressed harder, trying to stem the red.

"Easy now, boy," Miz Beatty cautioned. "Easy."

Miz Chiles stopped bleeding. Ain't but so much blood in the face and the wounds in her bosom closed quick. Like her milk had dried up. She made soft moans as she came near to waking, but her eyes kept closed. She weren't ready for the world. Not just yet.

She opened them finally a little, a crack—just about when Siebrecht leaped down from the wagon. Maybe she heard his boots hit the ground, crushing the pebbles as he landed. George Rose and Freckman followed him, toting their guns. Professor Graves stayed back.

"You're all under arrest. Get in the back of the wagon. All of you. Get your colored asses up there." And with that Siebrecht started shoving the women, like they working girls back at George Thomas and he'd been told to clean up the place. They did that every once in awhile. Siebrecht'd cuss those ladies—nothing Jake could do about that. But it was the way you cussed a horse that was moving too slow or a rainy day. Siebrecht never poked at them with the butt of his rifle, never kicked them with his boots like he was doing now. He knew those ladies at George Thomas. Just doing his job, they just doing theirs.

But these were different colored women—colored women he ain't never seen before. And they stood there and faced him like they was his equal. More than equal. He couldn't stand it.

He grabbed the braided gal by her braid, pulled at her like a horse groom might pull a filly's tale to keep her from kicking. She let out a fighting scream and tried to swing 'round to hit him, but he had her off-balance and her fists swung wide. "Jesus!" she yelled. Not like a prayer. Like a angry mamma giving last notice to a child that he better show up or face real trouble. "You see this, Jesus!"

Her screams opened Miz Chiles eyes all the way.

"Leave those women be!" I shouted. The three men startled. Like they'd forgotten about me among all those women. Another man.

"What are you arresting them for? Where's your warrants?"

Nobody said anything for a second. *Warrants?* Sounded silly even to me. Women bleeding and sprawled all over the Lord's creation and I asking for warrants, like it a word I just learned from Mr. Benjamin's law books and this the first time I got to use it.

But if I thought my big word might do the trick, it didn't.

"Who the hell are you?" Siebrecht pulled his gun around and pointed it at me. A whip might not do. Needed a gun for an unarmed black man.

"I'm these women's lawyer!"

The three white men looked at me again like they was considering whether I was crazy or not. Or just a fool colored boy. Would of shot me if they thought I was crazy. So I reckon I was lucky.

"Their lawyer? Think their lawyer'd be able to afford a shirt!"

I felt shame cover me. Standing there half naked—like some buck in a slave pen. That's how they saw me. I stood there shaming while those three men about doubled over laughing, like there weren't ten women straggling on the road in front of them, bleeding and moaning, and it their doing. I stood there and hated those men more than I ever hated anybody before in my life. More than I ever hope—on my mamma's soul—to hate anybody like that again.

"I'm their lawyer whether I got a shirt or not. And I want to know what you charging them with. Being whipped ain't a crime yet—even for coloreds."

They stopped laughing at that. Siebrecht shouted their answer.

"They blocking a public road. Standing so nobody can pass."

"Standing in a country road? And you sure this a public road? This ain't the middle of Lexington. I don't see no street cars backing up."

Siebrecht turned to Constable Rose. He had his gun pointed at me, too. Never know what a shirtless colored boy might do. Rose whispered something to Siebrecht. They both smiled.

"They're being arrested under Kentucky Statute 1241."

"Kentucky Statute 1241? What's that?"

Constable Rose kept solemn, but Freckman started laughing. Siebrecht looked like he wanted to join in. Not friendly laughter, the kind of laughter that sound more like yelling.

"Not been used much lately so it don't surprise me that you ain't heard of it—you being a lawyer just starting out. The Ku Klux law. Law meant to keep the Ku Klux Klan from running roughshod over people. Keeps people from gathering together to intimidate another person." He let that sink in a bit—let it sink into the shirtless colored lawyer staring up at him like a fool. "Professor Graves who's hiding in the back of the wagon. You all done intimidated him."

The Ku Klux law. I heard of that law. I ain't ever heard anybody being arrested with it. No white men. I felt a roaring in my ears and a dizziness. The sun was setting behind the jail wagon, all the colors I seen in those paintings stabbing at me. Only this wasn't no painting. Wasn't any dream. This was a nighttime dream I was living wide awake. I felt myself swaying, the white men in front of me looking at me strange.

Somebody grabbed my arm firm. It was Miz Beatty. Her pretty old-timey dress was torn now and muddy. Probably had that dress forty years. Ruined now. One of her sleeves was the same rust color as my torn shirt. I thought maybe she grabbed my arm to keep herself steady, but that weren't it. She held onto my arm like she was holding me up.

"Get back in Miz Chiles' wagon like she told you."

I looked at her like she was crazy. Maybe we was all going crazy.

"I ain't getting back in no wagon. You see what these men did? You see how they beat her?" I pointed to Miz Chiles who was sitting, not all herself yet. "Pulled that gal's braid till it almost yanked out of her head. Beat you, too! And you want me to get back in the wagon?"

"So you getting killed gonna help? Or getting arrested like us if you ain't killed?" She looked mad, like a teacher who's mad because she gotta explain the first lesson all over again. But then her face soften, like a teacher who remembers what she has to do: explain that first lesson all over again.

"You say to Miz Chiles that you ain't a child, you a man. Well, here's the test. A boy—a child—would fight just like I see you wanting to. A boy would let his fists shoot out from his body and joy when the bullets came shooting back. That's what a boy would do. A man's gonna get back into that wagon."

The three white men laughed when I turned and walked back to Miz Chiles' mare. "Better get back to them law books," Siebrecht yelled, "look up Kentucky Statute 1241."

And then Freckman—I hadn't heard him before. His voice was like a high whine.

"Next time, get paid up front. That way you can come to court full dressed."

Just two of them started a long laugh—I don't think Constable Rose joined in. But that laugh lasted all the way around the curve in the road until they was out of sight. Even then I'd hear it rouse up, like dogs barking at night. A few moment's silence and then commencing again. "Go to sleep," Mamma'd tell me. "Put them out of your mind.

The mare was glad to see me. I had left the reins dangling. She was a good old mare, hadn't wandered more than a foot or so but she'd got nervous. I pulled her up. I watched them pile all the women into the back of that big old wagon. Two women—Lizzie one of them, the gal with the pretty braid that'd almost been pulled out of her head—helped Miz Chiles. She looked like she coming to, but she was shaky still. Lizzie turned to help Miz Beatty—it was a long climb up that wagon and no one wanted any of those men to help, but Miz Beatty just waved her off. Gathered up her old-timey dress and jumped in that wagon like she was a young girl. I felt bad about that old-timey dress. Wished I could of seen her when she was fifteen and that dress was new. But she'd bring it back. Sewing and soap, that dress be good as new.

I followed that wagon all the way to the jail in Athens. No jail in Cadentown. No need for one up to now. Stopped an old colored man walking on his way. Don't know where he was walking to and I sure didn't want company, but I was headed his way and you don't let folks walk when they can ride in the country. Fellow looked too old to be working the fields but folks work till they drop in the country. But he didn't look dropping, just old. Had a lot of vigor in his walk, still. Didn't half need that walking stick.

Got in and rode with me awhile. Didn't say nothing about how I looked though I must of looked mighty strange. I told him the whole story or as much of it as I could in the two miles or so he rode with me. Told him what I was gonna do. Told him I wasn't even half a lawyer but I was gonna do all I could to get those women out of jail.

He didn't say much, just those sounds old people make when they hearing a tale they can't half believe. When they soothing you.

He looked me over when I stopped my story. All of a sudden I feared he was gonna joke like those white men about a bare-backed lawyer. But the old man got too much dignity to joke like that. Got too much respect for other folks' dignity to even think it. He held up his hand when we reached a small walking path leading up a gentle hill. I pulled up. Would of liked to help him down—Miz Chile's wagon built high—but didn't want him to think I thought he was old.

"You need a shirt, son," he said and started to take his off when he finally made it down to the ground.

"No, no," I said. "Don't do that." He looked a little hurt.

"Ain't the best shirt," he said as if that were the reason I told him no. "But my wife made it. She used good cloth."

It was a lot better shirt than the one I ripped off for Miz Chiles. A good strong cotton blue. Blue was probably dark when it was new. Robin egg blue now and the cloth so soft you could of wrapped a baby in it.

The man took the shirt right off his back and handed it to me. He waited while I pulled it over my head. It was a tight fit. I didn't dare move my arms much, but it would do. Might be better keeping my arms to my sides—just like Miz Beatty warned me. The old man smiled like it was Christmas when he saw me put it on—stood there skinny ribs showing in the June twilight like it was Christmas. Then hiked on up to his cabin.

Wondered what he tell his woman when he came in bare-backed.

"You see," Mamma would say to me when I told her that story. "God's grace is all around us." She'd store the rest of that terrible day in her heart like all the other pain she's stored in her life—a barn filled with grief. Wouldn't even hear those men laughing. What men laughing? What dogs barking?

But she'd take to her grave the image of that man taking off his shirt.

"Imagine a poor man doing that. Probably didn't have more than three shirts in the world. That's Jesus walking the earth."

"That's right, Mamma," I'd say right back. Because she's my mamma and if she can keep hope in this world, if she can see Jesus when the rest of us just see white men trying to tear us down, white men trying to keep us from seeing anything, white men with whips in their hands that don't spare nobody—not women, not children, not Jesus—I ain't the one to tell her no.

"That's right, Mamma. You just got to be patient. All's right with the world. God's in His Heaven. Jesus on the highway. And He's handing out shirts."

CHAPTER 22

Jake the bartender, June 14, 1899, Yellmantown, Lexington, Kentucky

It took me a good month to find another bartending job after George Thomas closed. George Thomas himself stay low for a while. I figured he open up a new bar in a week or so but he got more bad name with them killings than he expected. Don't imagine he expected much. Just a couple colored men shot down in a saloon—happens every day. White men killing each other, too. It's Lexington. Even white men killing don't get much more notice except it something unusual. Or if a black man kill them.

People talked when those two big-shot Republicans shot each other down in the Post Office. Friend of mine said the ladies and gents were diving under cover. Bullets flying in a saloon is one thing, Post Office another. But this town getting bloodier by the day. Even a lot of ladies got guns in their purses.

Two colored men caught in the crossfire? That's yesterday's news before it yesterday.

Yet somehow shooting down the "Mayor" of Yellmantown just put a sour taste in people's mouths, like drinking a whiskey that ain't had time to settle or eating some pork meat left sitting in the sun. Nobody liked George Broadus much, but he was the man who handed out jobs—the ones the Democrats let us coloreds have. Wasn't half greedy about it. Only a little worse than folks expected, though expectations was about as low as they could be.

Only they got lower. The poor Mayor getting himself shot just when the Democrats won so big told us the Democrats felt they didn't much need the colored vote. That lowered the going price considerable. Man willing to sell his vote for a beer and nobody buying. Folks held it against George Thomas. Not fair, maybe. But then the Mayor getting shot weren't fair. Or Tommy.

I hear Tommy's mamma had a spell after the shooting. Now that really ain't fair.

But the Democrats coming 'round again: saw the last vote number. They hate the colored voting, pull every kind of trick there is to keep us the from voting booth. But we still voting. So they figure the next best thing is to make sure we vote Democrat. Vote price climb back up to $2.00. Good times. Buy a lot of beers with that kind of money. I ain't sold my vote yet. Not claiming to be better than other folks. Just waiting for a better price.

"Don't make no difference one way or another," a fellow says to me. "They all crooked. Do what they want and get paid for it. I'm just getting a little piece of it."

I'm the one paying him, so I don't know why he got to justify what he doing to me, but he does. Like preachers I know come in the saloon of a morning when they don't think nobody around. *Ain't Jesus watching you?* I want to ask but I never did. A bartender keep his mouth shut.

But this fellow roused me some. I gave him twenty-eight dollars for all his family vote, just two silver dollars shy of thirty.

"You right," I tell him. "They all crooked and now you crooked, too."

I smiled big at him. Why not? I was getting a whole lot more than he was. He didn't know whether to nod back or to slug me.

But I'm a big fellow. He decided to nod.

I paying him in the new bar George Thomas finally got around to opening. Heart of Yellmantown. Called it Timmy's Place. Don't know who the hell Timmy is. Everybody knows it George Thomas only he don't sit in the corner anymore. Remind people too much. But folks set on forgetting gonna forget.

We the new headquarters for colored Democrats in Yellmantown. Funny how George Thomas hire me back. Think I'd be part of that bad memory, but he don't trust too many people. I ain't saying I one of them. It just he trust others less. Especially he don't distrust me as much as the Micks he got working for him though he's Irish himself.

I feel the same way about some colored men—wouldn't let them pass the collection plate in a church pew without they dipping in some.

Of course, some colored men I life-trust. Maybe young Noah. Maybe Tommy.

Don't think George Thomas life-trust anybody.

What he do trust me with is vote collect. Almost don't got time to bartend. Doing the same thing the old Mayor did only nobody calling me the Mayor. Two dollars a vote. Two dollars almost as much as some men make in a week. A bonus if you get your whole family signed. I paid one old man thirty dollars for his four sons, himself, and a brother. I tell him to keep that quiet—can't be paying that to everybody. But he bring in his whole block on Upper—that worth it.

Sometimes I wonder what young Noah think of what I'm doing. I might tell him I still vote free but he'd just look at me. "Just getting my piece," I'd tell him, like that old fellow said to me. That the way the world is. Always gonna be George Thomases. Don't matter what they call themselves.

Oh, I know what Noah'd say. Say the world that way because we let it be like that. The world like that because we selling it off piece by piece. Two dollars and we get to rent that freedom we all talk about. It's Timmy's Place, now.

Whoever the hell Timmy is.

One thing I know: Timmy ain't no colored man. Ain't never knowed a colored man named Timmy. But he ain't greedy, Timmy. Just like the Mayor. He always leave something in the collection basket—got to take care of the minister.

Of course, that don't leave much for the church. "But that's the world we live in," I'd tell young Noah again. Boy got to realize that. Got to get his own. Hold out for more than two dollars. But don't wait too long. Collection plate be empty if you wait too long.

I'd smile big when I told him that—like he just one of us.

But he ain't one of us. I pray Jesus—that Jesus looking down over them beer guzzling ministers—he don't never become one of us.

If Noah become one of us, ain't no hope nowhere.

The old man I give thirty dollar to come back for more. I tell him I already paid for his whole family. His whole dang block.

"I ain't paying for no vote twice. You can vote twice if you can get away with it, but you only get paid one vote, one man. That's democracy."

"What about my woman? You ain't paid for her vote."

"Your woman?" I had heard about women voting in the school board elections, but I ain't never seen it. They needed a special voting booth and Yellmantown didn't have one. Irishtown did, finally. Last election Judge Bullock said it wasn't necessary—too expensive to make separate booths for women. But then the white women didn't come out and the colored women did. Changed his mind quick when the Democrats almost lost the school board.

Bullock should of known better. Maybe he did. Couldn't have women voting with the men. Ain't an election I've seen yet without five fights breaking out. Some of them bloody. They close the saloons on voting day, but it don't seem to damper the drinking much. Women voting. What next? Women climbing into the prize-fight ring? I just shook my head at the old man.

"Don't know anything about buying your woman's vote. Just for school board anyway. Wouldn't be worth more than a dollar."

"Dollar? The school board's the ones who decide on most of the jobs the city got to hand out. Should be worth twice the rate for a man's. Or at least three dollars each. You get me three dollars and I'll sign you up a dozen women. Keep them school jobs Democrat."

"Keep them school jobs Democrat." The old man's heart was in the right place, folded right into his wallet along with the rest of our hearts. But he was right, too. Most of the jobs the city got was school jobs.

"So your woman's vote worth more than yours? How I know she'd vote the right way? How you know? All alone in that voting booth—they don't even let men near them booths if they ain't working them."

He pull his head back at that, the idea of his woman voting on her own. The old man shook his head. "She wouldn't do that. Vote like I tell her to vote."

But I see the idea disturb him some. I told the old man I'd check with George Thomas, see what we could do. He went off shaking his head still. Almost wouldn't be worth it, even at three dollars, maybe giving his woman some ideas. Maybe even a taste of freedom.

But freedom ain't cheap. Ain't never cheap. Made me proud to be an American. Our people moving up and bringing their women with them. What young Noah yell when he get excited? Whooee! I didn't know the old man's woman. She probably do what she was told to do, vote like her old man said.

Then again she might decide to climb in the prize ring after all. Take her gloves off. Strike a blow for freedom.

Whooee!

CHAPTER 23

Noah Webster, June 15, 1899, Athens, Kentucky

Judge Bullock set the bond high for the ladies. Two thousand dollars. Don't know that there's two thousand dollars in all of Briar Hill and Cadentown together. They spent the night in jail. Next day the judge lowered it to one hundred peace bond for each of them—just had to pledge it, not actually pay it. Miz Chiles asked me what that meant, a peace bond. I told her it meant if she protested any more, she'd have to pay it. A hundred dollars cash would just about soak all their savings up like an August dry spell sucking up a spring pond. Some of those ladies and their men owned their own land. Or at least they owned a few acres and tenant farmed the rest. Miz Chiles was one of them. They'd have to sell some to pay a hundred dollars bond. They'd be all tenant farm.

Sell land. Last thing a colored farmer and his woman ever want to do.

I see Miz Chiles sitting on the one bed that jail cell had, thinking about that, the other ladies waiting on her. She shared that bed with Miz Beatty but only after fussing. Lizzie, my braid gal, was the loudest, out-shouting even Miz Beatty.

"I don't want to hear any more about it. You and Miz Chiles take that bed. We're young. Floor won't hurt us."

That floor sure didn't seem to hurt her. She looked feather-bed fresh, the black plait hanging down her back as shiny and smooth as if her momma had spent a morning braiding it. I felt a couple kinks I got from sleeping in Miz Chiles' wagon but I just shook it off. Mamma says aches pass through young folks like water from a warm weather pitcher.

"But it's January water for old folks. Freeze up and stay stiff till you ease some warmth into it."

"Old folks? You talk like you ninety year old. You ain't even fifty." I hate it when she act like she gonna die before the first frost hits.

She smile sad when I complain. "Don't know no ninety year old. Fifty old for a colored woman. But don't fret. I ain't leaving anytime soon."

Lizzie waiting for Miz Chiles to talk before she move. Miz Beatty, too. Miz Chiles look at me. Her X scab on her face still look raw, puffed up and runny. I wonder if it will scar white, a white X on a black face her whole life. If she lived to be ninety. Or fifty. Sitting in that jail cell, her eyes on each side of that X look like they in another jail cell with bars bent sideways. Looking for a way out.

"None of us can afford that kind of money. We'd have to sell and move to Lexington. Other folks, too." She paused. "Don't want to move to Lexington. Don't want any of our neighbors to move, either. What'd that be like? Have our school but no folks and no children to send to the school." She turned and helped Miz Beatty up from the bed. Bed didn't look any more comfortable than Miz Chiles' wagon bed but I could see Miz Beatty trying to pretend she didn't hurt. Miz Chiles waited before she went on. "Guess we need to figure how to fight different."

Lizzie and her sister, Suzie, were shaking their heads. I could of told Lizzie to give it up, but it be like arguing with Mamma once she set her heels in. Lizzie said her Jesus wouldn't of backed down.

"Jesus was a fighter," she said before Suzie shushed her.

First I ever heard that: Jesus a fighter. Thought the way he fought was turn the other cheek. Maybe when he ran out of cheeks, he started to fight.

"We're not giving up," Miz Chiles soothed them. "Just gonna figure how to fight different."

Only it felt like giving up. Just Miz Chiles and Miz Beatty in the wagon on the way back to Briar Hill. Lizzie and her sister's daddy came to pick them up in his own rig. First he had to trek over to Cadentown to pick the rig up. He didn't look friendly when I shook his hand, like I was the fellow who gotten his girls in trouble. But Lizzie smiled at me—first smile she gave me. Didn't seem like a smile you give a fool just to hustle him on his way. Sister smiled at me, too, the mamma of the twins. Whole family real nice. Except for the daddy, maybe.

Made me feel good. Almost like we'd won.

But we'd lost.

The children knew we was in trouble. I tried to cover, but the closer we got to August the harder it was getting. They know I'm leaving, know they gonna get some teacher Lexington send them. "Gonna be a good teacher," I tell them. "Know more than I do. Trained special for teaching. Not just picking it up like somebody looking for loose change under some bleachers."

They look blank when I say that about the change and the bleachers, like they look blank at half of what I say. But then Willy pipes up.

"I still gonna get to be Sojourner Truth?" he asked me. This was a day or two after we got back from Athens, when the cuts on his mamma's face still needed a bandage that crisscrossed her face. His mamma had told him about the jail night. His daddy didn't want to—I heard them discussing it in low murmurs outside below my window. His daddy thought it'd shock the child into sickness. Willy was strong, only got a frailness in his eyes. But Miz Chiles thought he should know.

"Needs to know what has to be done in this world. You taught him farming—how to plow straight—how not to break the plow on rocks. What if you never told him about them rocks? What kind of farmer you think he'd be?"

Could of told Mr. Chiles just to give it up. But I guess he knew that already. He didn't say much more.

"And how I gonna explain this X on my face? Willy too smart a child not to know the truth, whether we the ones to tell him or somebody else."

I don't mean to say Mr. Chiles was wrong. That frail look got wider in Willy's eyes once he heard about his mamma's jailing—I could see it spreading like thin cracks in old glass every time he looked at his mamma's face.

But Miz Chiles right, too. At least Willy know about the rocks now. Colored parents got to tell their children about the rocks. Can't be pretending the world's a pretty place. Maybe white folks can fool their children for a bit, although there's plenty of rocks waiting for white children, too. But coloreds can't wait. And at least they the ones to tell him.

The other children stopped like they was frozen when Willy asked about playing Sojourner Truth. Didn't even take the chance to tell him he probably meant Harriet Tubman. She was the one leading the slaves across the freedom-river at night, their favorite game. But it didn't much matter, the children confusing the two women. They knew who they were even if they got the names mixed up.

Colored heroes.

Didn't answer him at first, because I didn't know what the new teacher was gonna think about any of it, let alone what they'd say about a boy being proud to play a woman. I don't know that I could of done that as a boy, too boy-proud to even look at girls let alone pretend to be one. But my Briar Hill young'uns just switched back and forth between Frederick Douglass and Sojourner Truth with Harriet Tubman sometimes trailing up behind. Didn't think twice who led them, whoever grabbed the standard first.

"Of course you will!" I said real loud, more loud than sure Mamma would of said. "Just explain to the teacher what you're doing. He—or maybe she—will sure understand. Just explain."

None of them looked sure for all my loudness. Somebody had told them about the rocks. This sure looked like a rock to them.

That's when the idea for the 4th of July pageant came to me. Looking at their faces, I knew we needed to do something to cheer them up. Cheer me up, too. I thought about it a whole night. Came in next day just brimming. Made myself hold it in till we took our morning break, but the children knew something was up. I waved for a morning circle and they was formed up before I even got to my place.

"I told Willy he could still play Sojourner Truth, but that's not right. I don't know what your new teacher think about all that. But I know one thing—we gonna put on a whole show this July 4th for your folks and anybody else who want to come. You gonna get to play not just Sojourner and Frederick Douglass but Eliza and little Harry from a book called *Uncle Tom's Cabin* which I'm gonna tell you about. One of you might even play an evil man called Simon Legree, only we're gonna call him Sheriff Siebrecht. This is gonna be the best 4th of July you ever seen."

A lot of colored folks don't celebrate the 4th that much, especially country coloreds. Especially when it fall on a Tuesday like it do this year. Too much work to do. Not independent enough to take off Independence Day.

Besides. Whose independence we celebrating? Coloreds sure didn't get independent. Mr. Benjamin said the British promised freedom to anybody fighting for them, but after they lost they left most of their colored behind in Charleston. Or took them to places like St. Kitts where he grew up. Slaves there, too. Another fifty years. And George Washington? Hated the whole idea of colored fighting, let alone giving them freedom.

"Left them free in his will, didn't he?"

Mr. Benjamin looked at me like I was his slowest student. Sometimes I felt like that. "Some of them. And what's that do? Slaves no good to you when you're dead. Might as well free them."

Of course town-colored celebrate the 4th, usually get the day off. Wave their flags, yell about freedom. All men created equal. Bet Jefferson wish he'd bit his tongue that day. Wondered how he looked his slaves in the eyes. "Oh, I didn't mean you. I meant men. White men. Rich white men."

Maria say he didn't mean women, either. Sure not Miz Chiles, that scar on her face like a brand.

Sure didn't mean me.

Don't know if Jefferson freed his slaves when he died. Got to ask Mr. Benjamin.

I was one of those town-colored waving my flag. Colored footraces all over town. Won my share of them. Daddy and Mamma relaxing. Well Daddy relaxing. Mamma cooking up a storm. Another reason I liked the 4th. Fried chicken, corn bread, pies. Peach pie, just like Mamma say, but apple, too, and huckleberry.

But even as a boy I came in all mad one day. Found out Patrick Henry owned slaves.

"What's he mean? Give me liberty or give me death? How about his slaves? How'd he say that and own slaves?"

Mamma looked at me worried. "Give them death probably. Hope you didn't say that to your teacher."

"Sure did. Said it was different times. What's that mean, different times? Coloreds didn't want to be free just like him?"

Mamma shook her head. "Got to choose your fights, boy. Don't need to be fighting 1776 all over again. 1893 hard enough to fight."

1899, too. But we was gonna celebrate this 4th. Maybe even quote Patrick Henry.

Mamma started sewing soon as I got word to her. Miz Chiles, too, and Miz Beatty. Funny how you ask somebody to do something who work a twelve hour day and somehow they find time.

"What kind of clothes Sojourner Truth wear?" Miz Beatty asked me. "Or Harriet Tubman? Each child I ask gives me a different name." I just stared at her.

"Clothes that helped her escape slaves. Doesn't matter about the name. Got a lot of territory to cover. Swamps and woods. Rivers to cross."

"Men clothes," she nodded her head. "Can't be dragging petticoats over no swamps."

Men clothes. Good. Less explaining to do to the audience if Willy played her.

I thought I'd be Frederick Douglass himself only the children raised a fuss about that. Luella looked so put out I had to settle for Abe Lincoln. Mamma said she'd make me the stove pipe hat.

Didn't think anybody'd want to play ol' Simon Legree or Sheriff Siebrecht after I explained who he, was but half the class fought for the role. Had to divide it up. Two Simon Legrees. Lord have mercy. A whole slew of blood hounds, too. I'm afraid we mixed up the plots some. Sometimes Simon Legree was chasing Sojourner over swamps—sometimes over ice floes—we colored some paper patches blue and green. Had to yell out things like "This ice floe sure is slippery. Hope my child and me can keep on it till we get to the other side!"

"Get to the other side." We'd all shout. "Hurry, child! Hurry." "Fall, Simon, fall!" And one of our two Simons would take such a leap I know their real mammas were holding their breath lest they break their real necks. But everybody else was cheering and jeering.

I know the crowd got confused some when Willy said he was Sojourner Truth, but the man clothes helped ease that. Wouldn't let him yell "Ain't I a woman" which he'd been yelling ever since that first time I shouted it. Thought I might lose the audience. Did let him pick another line from the speech. I told him to stop and look at his mamma when he said it.

"If the first woman God ever made was strong enough to turn the world upside down all alone, these women together ought to be able to turn it back, and get it right-side up again!"

Willy said it slow. His mamma didn't flinch but everybody else just broke down sobbing. Began to look more like a funeral than a 4th of July celebration.

Crowd got a tiny bit perplexed when Luella gave a speech as Frederick Douglass but they cheered her. Especially when she turned on one of the Simons who was chasing her and intoned a speech about freedom. She memorized almost the whole speech Douglass gave on the 4th of July, 1852, forty-seven years ago. She wanted to give the whole speech but I wouldn't let her. Just do a couple lines, I told her. Pick the ones.

She picked a couple lines alright. She put them in her words a little. They were Douglass' thoughts but Luella's words. I looked at them.

"Sure you want these?" I asked. I was hoping she choose something not so hard.

"You said I could choose, Mr. Webster." Luella had that look on her face she got when she felt she was being done wrong. Like *her* independence was being taken from her.

"No, no. You say it out."

She did. She flung her arms out. The crowd was spellbound.

"What to the American slave is your 4th of July? I think it's the day that shows him how free he ain't, how much he the victim of gross injustice and cruelty. Ain't no other people treat their people worse."

That calmed the cheering down for a second. I see women nodding their heads, turning to look at Miz Chiles again. Feeling that X scar like it was on their own faces. Like it wasn't just slavery times we was talking about.

But the cheering started right up again when Luella tripped the Simon chasing her.

They knew me as ol' Abe right away, especially when I intoned the Gettysburg Address at them. Lizzie and her sister had showed up along with her sister's twins. Lizzie had a blue and red ribbon wrapped 'round her braid. Right patriotic. She smiled at me before I started. Almost smiled back before I remembered I was the President and needed to be solemn. I was solemn as could be, but she bent over laughing so I had to smile.

"Four score and seven years ago," I started, and the crowd straightened up like I was the real thing, Father Abraham himself come out to Briar Hill colored school. Promising them a new freedom. "Of the people. For the people. By the people."

Only it wasn't really so. They knew I'd be leaving in a few weeks. Knew they didn't have much to say about it. They were the people but other people were deciding.

Only that was tomorrow's troubles. "Today's worries sufficient unto the day," Mamma would tell me when I'd fret too much about what was coming.

And some days are just fun. The bloodhounds wouldn't stop chasing Little Eva even when the ice-floes got tore to pieces. And Luella got a chance to do a whole lot more of her speech off-stage to a whole little crowd of ladies. One man, too, off to the edge. Don't know if that was her daddy.

"My goodness, child. How you remember that whole speech?" one lady said. She kept urging her on. They all did. Ain't just pie our mammas feed us. Sometimes they feed us what makes us happy. I don't know how they know that, but they do.

Nobody gathered around Willy, but I see his mamma lay a soft hand on his shoulder, then take it back real quick. But it was enough. Seemed like he looked less fragile. Didn't know about the morrow, but today he looked strong. And that was something.

Nobody knew about the morrow. But the people were happy today. And that was something. Lizzie strolled by, without her sister in tow. She lay a hand on my arm like the promise of a new day.

A new day. Sufficient unto the day are the troubles thereof. Maybe the day's happiness is sufficient, too. At least it felt that way in Briar Hills, Kentucky, on the best July 4th I ever celebrated.

"Lizzie!" her sister, Suzie called, and Lizzie went off to join her. But she turned her head to look at me halfway there and she caught me looking at her.

A new day.

CHAPTER 24

Lizzie Price , July 4,1899, Fayette County, Kentucky

I won't deny it. I thought him a fool the first time I saw him—the first time I heard him—chatting me up because I knew how to hammer a nail. What did he think country girls did? Of course those with brothers might not do as much hammering as Suzie and me did, but even they did their share. And everything else there was to do. Letting a mule drag you through the fields. Mucking a stable full of cow droppings. Putting the chicken coop back up when the wind knocks down the one your daddy must have put up when he wasn't minding business. When his mind was off in his books. After you do all that, you do the women's chores, which is everything else as far as I can tell. Suzie could tell I wasn't going to give him the time of day or even the back of my hand.

"He's a nice-looking boy," she whispered to me. "Give him a chance."

I just looked at her. She was never what I called strong-minded when it came to men—hence the twins. Well, at least she waited until they were married.

Or near enough.

Suzie probably thinks it was the sight of him, shirtless, shouting at the deputies. But it wasn't that. I didn't mind looking at him—like I don't mind looking at anything pretty—and he was pretty. But him standing there shirtless, shouting at those terrible men, just showed he had courage, that he was a fine-looking boy with fine shoulders.

But getting back into the wagon after Miz Beatty talked to him showed he was a man.

That must have been hard. Suzie says I sounded mad not scared when that man Sie-brecht grabbed my braid. I would have shot him if I could have, but nobody expects a girl to face down a gun. They expect it from a man though it doesn't make any sense. Nothing made any sense. I remember that moment: Noah was going to die and Miz Chiles was bleeding to death with her head in my lap. Suzie heard my yell, though I don't know that anybody else did.

"Jesus! Damn it all. Are you looking at this? Are you seeing this?"

Suzie says I talk to Jesus like He's one of our mules, the simple-minded one who keeps dragging us into rocks.

"That's the way He acts," I tell her and her mouth just opens wide in shock, like I'm blaspheming.

I'm not blaspheming. Jesus knows what I mean. That's the way we talk to each other.

Anyway, I guess He heard me that time. Miz Chiles didn't bleed to death. Noah got back in that wagon. Even that mule steers us clear of the rocks after you bash him a few times on his head.

Only Jesus didn't clear the rocks. He just didn't let the rocks crush us to death.

This time.

Suzie thought Noah looked silly showing up at the jail wearing that blue shirt that old man gave him. Couldn't even move his arms practically. Every time he'd raise one of them, that shirt would start to split like pants on a fat man. I looked at Suzie hard. I knew she was two seconds away from bending over double laughing, but I thought that would tatter Noah's dignity worse than any torn shirt. She pulled herself in—guess being a mother has given her some self-control. And I liked the way Noah had to keep his arms to his side. Taught him to use his mouth.

His mouth might get him shot, too. A colored man has all sorts of ways to get shot in Kentucky. But raising his arms was just about a certain one.

"Thank you, Jesus," I said out loud and everybody but Suzie looked startled. She knows my ways with Jesus. When I'm mad at Him, I let Him know. But when I'm thankful, I don't need church to tell Him.

I didn't see Noah again till the 4th of July celebration. Suzie kept asking if he'd come to call, like any of us had time for calling. Like we were southern gentry living the life of leisure on our plantations. Only without the slaves doing the work. We the slaves.

Shouldn't be so hard on Suzie. She makes time to get herself arrested and she the mother of two and the wife of a man who makes Daddy look practical. Daddy asks about Noah, too. Jesus. Give me strength!

But it was fine seeing him on the 4th, seeing him with his children. Oh, my goodness. I'd rather see him with his children than shirtless any day, fine-looking shoulders or not. Seeing him dancing and reciting and carrying on just lifted the heart like you were part of a choir carrying a hundred sinners to heaven and you one of them. I know it was so much foolishness, but it all seemed like it had more dignity than a funeral with a hundred top hats and a team of white horses. Noah in his own top hat made Suzie just bend over—I couldn't stop her this time but it didn't matter. Folks were laughing and shouting all around us. I had to laugh myself. But I wasn't laughing at him. He knew that. It was joy that made me laugh. Joy. He laughed himself.

"Thank you, Jesus!" I said, as I heard Suzie call me to come help her with the children. I turned to smile at Noah and he was there smiling at me. "Thank you, Jesus," I said again. I don't know that anybody heard me in all that noise.

Well, Jesus did. He was trying to make up for those rocks He let us crash into. I didn't forget those rocks, but I thanked Him anyway.

PART 4

THE FIFTEENTH AMENDMENT

CHAPTER 25

Maria Lulu Benjamin, July 5, 1899, Lexington, Kentucky

Robert was quite upset with *The Morning Herald's* headline last week and the story they ran:

NEGRO SCHOOLS SCENES OF RIOTS IN THE COUNTY
Teachers Locked Out and Threatened. Twelve Made Prisoners.

"*Ten* were made prisoners. And the only riot perpetrated on them was by those hoodlum deputies sent by Judge Bullock."

When Robert gets angry, his West Indian lilt comes out in full sing-song. It is hoodlum deputies and Judge Bullock. I sit back and wait for him to calm down into a regular English. Of course, what I call regular English, he calls Alabama slow-talk.

He gave me the editorial he's started for the next week's edition of *The Standard*.

> ## *ARREST DEPUTY SHERIFF SIEBRECHT!*
> ## *IMPEACH JUDGE BULLOCK!*
> The brutal whipping of wives and mothers in Cadentown, Fayette County, because they had the audacity to stand in a country lane and attempt to delay the hostile takeover of their school by a corrupt and overbearing Democratic machine employing criminals, is an affront against decency that even the complacent and racist authorities of Fayette County cannot allow.

"Robert. Breathe." Robert, upset, will forget the point of a pause, let alone a period.

> The whipping of Mrs. Chiles, an upstanding leader of the Briar Hill community, put a scar in the shape of an X on her face, like a cracker's signature.

"Robert? Criminals? Cracker signature?"

"What would you call them? They are criminals and crackers." But he took the paper back and scratched out the offending passages.

"And do you feel Miz Chiles would want her name in the paper?"

"She is a heroine. Her name should be shouted from the rooftops."

"Or from *The Standard*. I agree, Robert. But she is a country woman—she's been whipped and scarred. She would be shamed, Robert."

He took the paper back more slowly this time. He scratched out the name. "Southern gentility even among the coloreds. What good will that do anyone?"

I continued reading.

> Scarcely conscious after her assault, the lady was then dragged from the lane and thrown unceremoniously into a prison wagon along with nine other exceptional women, members of the Briar Hill and Cadentown communities, as if they were degraded ladies rounded

up from a house of ill repute, rather than mothers and sisters and wives trying to protect the school teacher they had hired from being replaced by a Democratic hack, a so-called Professor Graves.

"Robert!"

"What now?"

"You cannot compare these ladies to ...." I was at a loss for a moment. But he grabbed the paper from me and scratched away.

> For this heinous crime, Deputy Sheriff Siebrecht must be arrested along with his fellow conspirators, Deputy Sheriff Freckman and Constable George Rose. And the man who sent these hoodlums, who authorized their crimes, Judge Frank Bullock—County Judge and one-man, self-appointed school board for Fayette County—must be impeached.

He watched me as I read. I read as slowly as I talk so that I can almost feel him repeating every word, every syllable in his own cadence. I take my southern Alabama time, as he would say.

"It is very strong," I tell him and he nodded. But he waited for me.

"I think those men should be arrested. I hope they will be. But who will order their arrests?"

He thought for a moment. "Nobody will order their arrests."

"But who could?"

He nodded again. "Judge Bullock. And he cannot order their arrests if he's impeached." He took the paper back once more. He spent a few minutes. I am always so surprised at his speed. He handed me the revised paper.

> Judge Frank Bullock ordered these criminals to arrest these good women who were exercising their Constitutional right to protest, a right the whole country celebrated yesterday. Judge Bullock has taken on so many powers as his prerogatives. Now he must order the arrest of these men, remove them at the very least from their ill-gotten and mishandled authority. If he does not, he himself should have his authority removed; he himself should be removed from all his power.

"Criminals again?"

"Criminals," he said, and I saw that he was through editing. He did revise the headline but there is a limit to my gentling, as Daddy would put it. Still Robert feels a need for it. Perhaps he still feels the outsider and needs my perspective. Which is funny. I am the ultimate outsider.

I was so young when Daddy first brought Robert home from his law office, Mamma still alive, though ailing. Grandmother my real mother—doing all the daily tasks a daughter needs. How Mamma and Grandmother so liked him—more than I did at first. Though Grandmother turned a quizzical eye on him. She was country-colored, suspicious of everything, everyone.

"So charming. But up in years to be single. Better find out if he got a wife hid."

I was shocked. He'd come as Daddy's guest, not my suitor.

Or so I thought. "Gentle him," Daddy told me. As if he were a horse I was to ride.

I was too Southern genteel to ask about another woman—or too colored shy. But how could I ask? "Do you have a wife hid?" Surely that was Daddy's job to find out.

Well, I am the un-hid wife, the mother of his children. Even an editor when he wants one. And his gentler when he feels the need of one.

He looked at me closely, looking for weariness. He is never tired. I smiled brightly.

"They need to be turned out of office—that whole school board. But from what I hear, the non-partisans haven't got it together enough to even get on the ballot. Or have they?"

I did not know the answer. Robert is not cruel, but he expected me to find the answer. I could not be tired.

"I will call on Emma Bisou. She will know. She is in touch with Madeline McDowell Breckinridge, working on the election together."

"Together?" He stretched the word out in his soft island cadence till the idea of Emma Bisou "together" with Ashland's mistress stretched to absurdity. But I had seen them together at Ashland. I had been at Ashland. Robert was suggesting that we were being used.

"Yes, together, Robert. It is not an absurd idea."

He waved his hand at me. "Of course, of course. But you know that her husband Desha is close to Superintendent Cassidy and Cassidy's close to Judge Bullock. They're a den of thieves and conspirators. You read *The Herald* story about the 'riot.' That's Desha's writing: all that nonsense straight from Bullock."

"They are not thieves, Robert. And perhaps Madeline's views are not shaped by her husband's. Perhaps his views might be shaped by hers."

Robert smiled. He liked it when I contradicted him, as long as I did not make it a habit. "They might not be thieves but they work with thieves. Billy Klair. Green Pinckney Russell. If he's not a thief, he's the next thing to it. But you go find out. See what your 'friend' Madeline is up to. Only they're running out of time for this election. Running out of time."

Running out of time. If we had time enough. No, that's not it. Had we but world enough and time. We have world enough. So much world crowding in upon us. Robert brings the world with him in every sentence he writes, every syllable he sing-songs in his West Indian lilt. I wanted that world. I knew when Daddy brought him home, that world would come with him. I welcomed that world in my slow Alabaman girlhood.

Robert almost ran out the door. Only his dignity kept him to a trot. I stood in the entry and watched him until he turned the corner of the block, then closed the door softly. Lilly was sleeping. Sometimes, I wish I could close the door to everyone, tell the world that I am just not accepting visitors this afternoon. Not any time this week. Perhaps come visit in the autumn?

I wonder at that hid wife if she exists. Is she resting in some quiet room? Does she have a Sheila who's shuttered the windows against the glare of a Lexington summer?

The July sun was not diluted by any slatted shutters as I walked the dusty streets—North Upper—with Emma Bisou. I kept my eyes down, avoiding the horse droppings that lay like small traps for one's shoes every few feet. We had started at the farthest reaches of Upper—almost to Loudon—or I had. Emma began a few blocks closer to town. Between us we hoped to contact every colored family on Upper, working our way, house by house. I stopped to catch my breath, being careful not to breathe too deeply. Clouds of flies hovered over the fresher droppings.

Emma Bisou had been only slightly surprised when I showed up at the meeting.

"Finished resting?" she asked, failing to sound solicitous.

I smiled, "Oh, I feel wonderfully rested. Robert wants to..."

"Robert!" Emma and Robert. She adored him. He infuriated her. I understood how she felt, but sometimes it exhausted me. Today was an angry day. "Mr. Benjamin has made our whole endeavor more difficult! Have you read his editorial on the ruckus out in Cadentown? Well, of course you have. Calling the sheriffs criminals. And his very disrespectful treatment of Judge Bullock who, I might add, is the very power we need in this election. He is the only one who throws out the vote-challengers almost en masse in his court. Another judge in his place would give us a great deal of trouble. We would not have half the colored voters in Fayette that we have if not for Judge Bullock. Yet Mr. Benjamin almost called for his impeachment, for heaven's sake."

She breathed heavily as if she'd been running. The world, and Robert especially, it seems, did their best to plague her.

"Those sheriffs were criminals, Emma. Did you not read how they whipped that woman?"

Emma Bisou pulled herself up, all five feet of her. "Of course, they're criminals. I've not had a protected childhood, Maria, unlike some people. I know all about such men. I've not been whipped but I've come close. Come close to other things I won't even mention. So I needn't be lectured. What happened is a horror and a tragedy. But Robert's language. So intemperate. You should try to calm it down, Maria."

I nodded. "I will do my best, Emma."

But the look I gave her made her blush. Mahogany-toned ladies such as Emma do not glow pink when they blush. If anything, their skin grows darker. Emma was shamed as her words became clear to both of us—a speech that almost defended the brutes who had attacked our own, attacking the one who called public witness to it.

But I understood, too. These were the people we worked with. We needed Judge Bullock.

"Robert wants to know," I continued, "the state of our school board election. He's heard a rumor that we may not get an independent slate on the ballot."

Emma's skin grew darker. I did not think it possible.

"Mr. Benjamin is a newspaper man. George Goebel and William Taylor almost have the state in a civil war. Fayette County's school board election is not the first thing on everyone's mind at present."

It was true. The governor's race was more like a war than an election. But what did we have to do with that? Emma must have had the same thought.

"We are certainly doing our best. Madeline's husband, Desha, has promised to print our list of names in the *Herald*. At the very least, people can cut out our list of independent names and pencil them in. They have to put the names right above the stamp but it's not difficult if they follow instructions."

I said nothing for a bit. *Follow instructions? Not difficult?*

"And we have the ballot initiative for the new schools—the two white and the colored—fifty thousand dollars."

Emma was relieved to have changed the subject. "It's actually wonderful that you've come in today. You can walk the precincts with me and help register. I have promised Madeline that we would canvass in the colored areas and concentrate on women. It is disgraceful how few colored women voted the last election. They're already claiming colored women are not interested."

"Miz Chiles was interested."

"Who?"

"The lady who was whipped."

Emma was quieted. For a second. "I imagine she's still interested. At any rate, you will appeal to the younger women. Some very timid souls, I am told, find me intimidating. Poppycock. But they can talk to you. And it is not so very hot. Well, for July. For those who are not registered, we will have to return in October. One day to register! Kentucky's way of keeping the vote low—even among white men."

Emma no longer wondered how rested I was as I followed her, first taking the trolley up Limestone, Emma getting off at Third Street, I continuing to Seventh. My area was new: new homes if you could call them that. Shanties mostly, but families filled every space. If you wanted space in Lexington, you needed to move out to the country. If you're colored, that is. Plenty of room in Briar Hill, Noah says.

Emma's neighborhood was older—the shotguns more tired, their walls leaning toward the center, only gravity and pressure holding them up. Sometimes the whole house shifted to the right or the left and a wooden beam would be planted against the leaning side, holding it up like a strong arm. Occasionally, not even the beam did its job, though the grumbling of the roof shifting usually warned people to get clear before it all collapsed. Emma knew almost all the old-timers who filled these homes, filled them sometimes ten to a room. They wouldn't hide when they saw her coming. Or they'd hear her rumbling down the block—giving plenty of warning just like their creaky roofs—and get clear quick.

No seats in the colored section of the trolley, though I counted three empty in the white area. I wished I dared. I looked at Emma's stalwart face. She'd spent years fighting the Separate Streetcar Law, but she was not one to break the law. She'd call it a distraction.

Like Robert's intemperate language.

Upper had no streetcars—just horses whose sweat dripped in puddles from their foreheads. Poor creatures. Their tails swished broadly but could not reach the flies which plagued their eyes. I waved the flies away from my own face. They were big and heavy, fat from their feasting.

We had written out the six names of the men running on the non-partisan slot and made several copies. "Write the names down," I told the bewildered ladies who came to the door wondering who on earth would be out in such a heat. They came to the doors carrying babies, chastising children, just trying to survive an airless July afternoon.

No, not airless. The air moved as slowly as the horseflies, but it was so humid it clammed about one's mouth like a wet rag, making it painful to breathe. My long dress clung to me, pinched me, my corset squeezing the last breath from my lungs. Ridiculous, but I had not known I would be walking the streets. I almost lost my footing as I leapt over a dry horse pile, the ends of my dress sweeping over it, catching only a dusty brown residue on the hem.

I explained why I was there to wondering eyes. I explained what non-partisan was. What partisan was. I had brought paper and pencils.

"What do I have to do?"

"You have to write in these names on the special ballot, the school board ballot. But you must write them above the official stamp or the vote will not count."

"I thought only men could vote," this from a girl with three children—none older than five—clinging in fear to her skirts. She was half-undressed as a mother of three—one nursing—almost had to be. I envied her her light clothing, but I could see that she was shamed to appear so in front of me. I was the one who should have been embarrassed, dressed as if I expected to be offered tea. The children, tugging at her, almost toppled her, as if she were some aging shotgun house. But she was a strong young mother. She kept her feet.

I smiled at the children, but I could see that they found a stranger—even a colored stranger—too fearful to be endured. Two of them—the three- and four-year-olds—started to wail. Only the baby stared calmly at me. Perhaps it wasn't fear of me. Perhaps it was just the heat. I pulled my dress away from my bosom where it clung like a wet towel. The baby took my gesture as a cue to pull at his mother's breasts.

143

I remember that pulling. It'd been only a few months since Lillian had grabbed at me night and day. Robert thought it unseemly. Oh, he never said anything, but I sometimes wondered if he thought Lillian should have pulled at me only at *her* dinner time. Robert did not seem like a man who had been around children.

"Are you twenty-one?"

"This month." The mother smiled at me proudly. I could see that she wanted to please me, wanted to vote though she had never, probably, ever thought of it before. For me.

"They all men. Women can't run?"

"They can. But for this election it was thought best…" I paused. I had no good answer. "Well, maybe next election."

She nodded. "Any colored men running?"

I shook my head no. She nodded again. "But you think this is a good thing?"

"I do," I told her. I did. And I took the baby from her though she made noises in protest about the baby drooling on my wonderful dress. "Let it drool," I told her, "let it drool." I held him as her mother printed the names of the six white men I had told her to vote for, men I didn't know from Adam. But Emma had approved them. Madeline trusted them. Desha and Robert would print their names in their newspapers. The baby's eyes widened but she did not wail as the strange overdressed lady held her. She even placed a small hand on my breast but took it back again quickly, my expensive crinoline not the soft cotton of her mother's. "No milk there," I wanted to tell her, and wished suddenly there was, wished I could rip that hot silly dress off my shoulders and offer that sweet baby a breast.

But it would not be seemly among the new homes of North Upper, their new wood belying their shanty construction. I handed the baby back, her mamma scanning my dress with concern. I explained again, as much as I understood, how to locate the names above the stamp.

"Above?" she asked.

"Above," I said once more though in the afternoon's wavering heat, I wondered *was it above?*

The next two ladies were too busy to stop and looked at me as if I were crazy when I asked them to copy the six names down. I told them to look in *The Herald* or *The Standard*, then, and to cut the names out when they printed them, and they nodded and murmured the words that you murmur to a foolish woman going up and down Upper Street on a July afternoon talking about independent school boards and how much good they'd be for colored children. "Miz Chiles got whipped," I wanted to shout at some who turned their backs, or who turned to a crying child or cooking that had to be stirred, stirred in this heat though nobody was going to be eating, not in this heat. "Miz Chiles got whipped because the wrong men were on the school board."

But they would have known I was insane then. Might have called for the sheriff to take me away, called the same sheriff who had whipped Miz Chiles.

Maybe I was crazy. Putting my small cache of energy into such work. Copying out names. Above the stamp. Below it. These women did the real work of the world, the soothing and feeding of babies, the cooking of dinners that may not get eaten.

Just the heat talking, Maria—Robert, or Emma, or even Madeline—would tell me if I dared speak aloud what I thought, if I dared grab one of those empty seats in the white section of the trolley car and sit and fan myself. Would they dare to arrest a woman just for sitting? For holding her fan high up against the slant of the July sun? Could they?

Madeline McDowell Breckinridge and I would sit together. Sophonisba will grab an empty seat in the colored section. All of us will have canvassed together—surprising white and colored women. Babies will be passed from woman to woman. Madeline would laugh as children dribbled onto her expensive silk dolman. "So silly of me to have worn something so impractical," she'd murmur. We would be white and colored together—urging our women to vote. United for our causes. Children and women. Robert was wrong. We were together.

I laughed at my daydream. I smiled brightly at the next woman who opened her door. My smile unnerved her for she listened to my whole speech and meekly copied down the names. I kept on smiling. I remembered our tea at Ashland. Madeline's husband Desha might even join us. He supported his wife. He let her write in his newspaper. Robert had never asked me to write.

But Madeline McDowell Breckinridge—like Emma Bisou—would never break the law: the empty seats across the color line—white and colored—would stay empty. She would continue to ride alone in her carriage, only her colored driver accompanying her. Separate. Not equal.

I drooped before the next door, but I climbed the steps. It was close to dinner time. In this heat, you corralled your children to stare at plates as you stared at yours. "Eat," you prompted your children. "Eat," you counseled your husband. You did not bother to tell yourself. But you cooked and you walked and you hoped. You did all that you could and you prayed it came to something.

You could not hide. You could not steal away from the world like a hid wife. You had to do something though it all might come to nothing.

I climbed up one more porch to greet one more surprised mother. My mind wandered again into daydream. What if one of Madeline's carriages came for me? We'd sit in the shade at her garden in Ashland. Cool punch would substitute for tea. 'Oh, Maria," she'd say, "all your canvassing and Emma's has made such a difference. Hundreds of women carried the names of the non-partisan slate into the special voting booths. They wrote them above the official stamp just as they needed to."

"It *is* above, then," I said to Madeline. "At the end of the day, I wasn't sure anymore."

Madeline's eyes grew wider. "Above, below. What does it matter?"

The trolley was full when Emma and I finally took it home, though Emma stern-stared a young man into standing up. He'd been sitting next to an old woman and Emma squeezed in so tightly next to her, the old woman almost popped from her seat. Emma gestured for me to take the empty space she'd created. It wasn't a cushioned recliner at Ashland, but my feet were sore.

"I hope we're not crowding you," I said to the old woman by the window seat.

"Oh, no, no, no," she protested. "Always room for one more."

Always room for one more. Ten to a shotgun room? Make it twelve. Just keep listening for the roof rumbling. Just make sure you get out before the whole thing collapses.

CHAPTER 26

Judge Frank Bullock, October 1, 1899, Lexington, Kentucky

I've told Billy Klair over and over again not to crowd my courtroom with vote challenges that make us all ridiculous. The whole day was taken up by thirty-five Negroes and one hapless white man—all registering Republican, of course. "No Democrats misrepresenting themselves?" I asked one of the complainants, but that subtlety was beyond him.

"The law that authorizes a voter the right to challenge any other voter has been pushed to the limit," I said in open court. Some of the men challenged have been living in their houses twenty years. One of them, George Jackson, used to work for my father—has been at his address on West Fifth Street since there's been a West Fifth Street.

"Hi, Judge," he waved when he entered the courtroom. "They say I need to prove who I am in order to vote. You know who I am, Judge. I worked for your daddy till he passed, God rest his soul."

I could hardly gavel silence to someone blessing my father's soul. Father's soul needs all the blessings he can gather. I just smiled at Mr. Jackson, nodding and putting my fingers to my lips. signaling him quiet. I felt like an idiot. Billy has made us all feel like idiots with his challenges.

"Well, Judge, you might feel both idiotic and unemployed if all those upstanding Negroes get to vote. A whole bunch of new registrants. A good many of them brought by your good friend, Mr. Robert Benjamin. He's the fellow who all but called for your impeachment a couple months back. It'd be something if you got voted out. Imagine you'd feel right ridiculous then."

Of course I remembered that *Standard* editorial, calling on me to remove the deputies I had sent to quell the Cadentown school riots. I did question the men closely. I imagine from their answers that things did get out of control. Deputy Sheriff Siebrecht, in particular, is a man who likes power a bit too much. Such men are dangerous. The other two, however, would not confirm that he had overstepped his bounds and, without their testimony, there was little I could do.

I wrote Mr. Benjamin a summary of my findings. The tone of his editorial did not deserve any notice whatsoever, but I have always prided myself in going the extra step, even when it goes against my better judgment. Grace was not in favor of my letter.

"Can you imagine your father, Major Bullock, communicating with a such a man as Benjamin?"

"My father could not imagine such a man as Mr. Benjamin. Coloreds were slaves and runaway slaves to him and his fellow Morgan's Raiders, not lawyers and journalists."

"Precisely," she replied as if I had agreed with her.

I received Benjamin's reply at breakfast the following day.

> Have you interviewed the women victims, Judge? Have you seen the whip slashes on their faces and backs? A young assistant of mine, a Mr. Noah Webster, saw the whole tragedy unfold. He would be willing to give you an eyewitness account. Of course, he is also colored, but it has been more than a decade since Kentucky courts have been required to receive testimony from colored, even when they are testifying against Caucasians.

I have often been in your court, Judge Bullock. I have never seen you simply take the word of the accused criminal without trying to verify their accounts. It would strike me as very odd that the first time you do so, it is the word of your own deputies you are taking—the very men who committed this atrocity. But perhaps you are too close to the crime, Judge. Perhaps you need to recuse yourself and let a more objective jurist preside.

"You see," Grace said to me. I was so upset with this reply I could hardly sip my coffee. I might have replied that my deputies were not criminals—surely they had the same right to presumption of innocence of any in my courtroom—and that I had had many reports of the severe troubles in Cadentown.

From what I have heard, also, his so-called assistant and would-be lawyer was very fortunate not to have been arrested himself. In fact, he came very close to being shot, Constable Rose has informed me. I do not need the testimony of someone who came very close to criminal conduct himself. I do not care if he is colored. He could be green. His testimony would still be worthless.

As for the suggestion that I could not exercise judicial objectivity, the idea put such a tremble in my hand that I spilled half my coffee onto one of Grace's finest damask table coverings. I saw the regret in her eyes as the brown stains spread even as she attempted to soothe me.

I wrote most of this in a letter in my first flush of agitation, but this time Grace prevailed. Silence is the only answer people like Robert Benjamin deserve.

I remembered those brown stains on Grace's table cloth as I answered Billy.

"People do not read *The Standard*. I would not have read the article but for people like you making certain that I saw it."

Billy's smile loped into a laugh. I seemed to always make Billy laugh for some reason.

"That's my job, Judge—pointing out things people don't want to see. Keeps us all on the payroll." He glanced around my new office, and sank into one of its several leather armchairs. He never fails to mention the office though it should be old news to him by now.

"Great setup you got here, Judge."

I am a bit embarrassed by its somewhat lavish furnishings, though it is not, as *The Herald* put it, "the most elegantly appointed room of the building." Still the two sets of chandeliers, the finish of deep red, and the clusters of roses in frescoes, are all of very high quality. I find it very soothing. Grace does, too. She finds every opportunity to visit my chambers with friends in tow. I do not recall her ever willingly coming to my old office.

"But you're wrong about people not reading *The Standard*," Billy continued, "especially the colored. That paper gets passed to every colored in town. And those coloreds ain't likely to think too kindly of you. Which don't much matter as long as they don't vote."

"You cannot challenge the whole colored population into not voting. At least not in my court. All thirty-five of your challenges—thirty-six including the one white Republican—had overwhelming proof of identity. You simply wasted their time and ours."

"Maybe. But twenty others never showed up for court—that means we get to challenge them when they try to vote. Which means they won't get to vote that day. And those thirty-five who showed up took a whole day doing it—lost a day's pay. How many people they tell that tale to are gonna want to do the same? I don't see it as a waste of time, Judge. We're not challenging the whole colored population of Lexington. For one thing, we got a good number voting Democrat. Green Pinckney Russell and his whole crew, and we got a few other things going on you'd be better off not knowing about. No, not a waste of time at all, Judge.

You did your job in court—came across as an upstanding Judge above all the nasty politics. People almost forget you're high up in the Democratic Party. Almost as high up as I am."

It was my time to smile—Billy reminding me that I might be the judge, but that he outranked me where it counted. Billy was usually more circumspect. He had sunk almost up to his neck in the leather chair he chosen, a chair much too large for him. He wasn't looking so high up. He saw my smile and broadened his own. Billy always let the other fellow get his point in.

"Anyway, Judge. You did your job in the courtroom. And we're doing ours."

We stared at each other for a few minutes. Billy kept smiling. I stopped. *Our jobs.* Billy and Benjamin—both of them suggesting that I'm a Democratic official before I'm a judge. How dare they? The insult crawled at my stomach, rose to my chest, shot angina pains through to my arms. A weakened heart, my childhood doctors had warned my mother. "A runt with a bad ticker," is how the Major put it when my mother told him, cautioning him not to expect too much from me.

He took her at her word and never expected anything from me.

I breathed deeply and calmly. Billy kept staring at me, aware of his insult.

"My job, as you put it, is to uphold the law—and the sanctified reputation of the law. We cannot have the courts clogged with spurious challenges."

"You're right. Don't look right. Thirty-five is too many. But that's okay. Got plenty of other things we can do. Hear what they did over in Paris? Hired a couple coloreds to rig up a crap game, bankrolled them and gave them a place to play. Police raided them and arrested more than forty fellows. Gonna keep them in jail until after the election."

Billy bent over. His laugh full, not forced. "That something, ain't it? Wished I had thought of it. What would you think if I brought in forty coloreds for shooting craps instead of vote challenging them? Would that be less or more ridiculous?"

My face must have told him my answer because he just waved at me, still chortling. "That's okay, Judge. Just fooling. Ain't got any crap games on board. Don't need them. Slow lines and early closings will do the same as a dozen games of chance."

Then he turned somber, his smile gone in an instant. "But I tell you, Judge, the things we do to keep order in this town might not always work. Your friend, Benjamin, keeps rounding up new colored to register—brings them down by the dozens. Coloreds who'd never find their way to a voting booth by themselves. Benjamin is rousing them. Who's that man who said he worked for your daddy? George Jackson? Must have been seventy years old, maybe older. Think he ever bothered with voting before Benjamin got to him? Probably never even thought of cashing in his vote, which would have been okay, and I'm sure he needs the money."

Billy pulled himself up in the chair, trying to sit straight in its leathery softness. But the leather was slippery, and sitting upright his feet didn't quite reach the floor. He kept slipping.

"Then Benjamin commences to drag him down to the 20th Precinct and make a whole lot of ruckus. That precinct's been solidly white forever and now it's about half colored. Benjamin keeps at it, it'll be most colored before too long. What would your daddy think about that? Think he'd like George Jackson deciding how the city should be run?"

He put his derby on. He always took his derby off in my chambers—a sign of respect, he said. Putting it on meant he was about to leave, but he took his time, the derby snug on his head.

"Judge, we can't let that happen—not in the 20th, not in the 30th, not out in the county where those women went wild. They can't even vote, those women, except for school board. But it don't matter. People get a taste of power and they don't want to let go. Your man had to whip them back into line. Ain't pleasant, Judge, but we do what we have to do."

Billy's smile became almost rueful, like he'd come to some reluctant conclusion. He made a leap for the floor from the chair, then gave it a backward glance as if it were some uppity woman trying to vote. Some uppity black woman.

"We can't let that happen here. And we can't whip them in downtown Lexington. Too many soft souls writing in the newspapers. Got to do other things. Legal things. Some not so legal. Some things we never gonna talk about."

He headed to the door then, a good fifteen feet away. I loved this space but it really was more than I needed.

"That's what I mean when I say we're doing our jobs. We'll do whatever it takes. You don't need to know too much about how we do our job."

He was by the door, but he turned before he left. He took his derby off his head as if he was saluting me. Or something. He smiled again but I heard his warning. "Just as long as you do yours."

CHAPTER 27

Mamma is real upset I've left teaching.

"Mamma, I didn't leave nothing. It left me. Only way I keep teaching was if I toadied up to Green Pinckney Russell. Even that wouldn't work, probably. I'm no good at being a toady. You want me to become part of that whole bunch?"

"Once you inside the classroom, you your own man. Those children loved you. Who they have now? Some half-count who don't know how to teach, probably. The problem is you too proud. You think you the only colored man in town who have to give and take some?"

I look at her. She knows she talking foolish, only she had her heart set on me being a teacher.

"Mamma, if I could of stayed, I would of. Best job I ever had. I loved those children. But I couldn't stay, Mamma. You know it as good as I do."

She pull her mouth in but don't say anything more. Mamma not saying anything means she thinks I'm right but she don't like it. I don't like it either.

Saying goodbye to those children was real hard. Luella clung to me like I was her third leg. About all the children did. Except Willy. He stood off—just stared at me, not saying anything. Never asked me why I was leaving like the others did. I wanted to tell him I'd stay if I could, but it wouldn't of done any good.

Willy reminds me of Mamma some.

We had a good six weeks of school after our July 4th celebration. The fall term don't start until after the main harvest's in—middle of September. I tried to make it as much fun as I could. I thought up new things all the time—not just history they didn't know about, but number games and word pictures. Maria and her club ladies sent over almost a whole library full of books—some of them new—and the children grabbed them up like I was handing out taffy. Even Willy took a book from me, one telling the whole Sojourner Truth story. "Ain't you a woman?" I teased him when I handed it to him, but he wouldn't even smile.

Mamma thinks I'm too proud. I ain't proud. If I could of made it happen and just kept a little dignity—maybe a loin-cloth's worth—I would of.

I waved the children goodbye that last day and went back in the schoolroom to give a final cleaning. I got my clothes and things from the Chiles' place that morning, carried it in to school with me. I hid my satchel behind the desk, but the children found it out—kept looking at it mournfully the whole day. Said goodbye to Lizzie, too—hiked over to her daddy's farm. They run a little country store. Or Lizzie runs it. Her daddy mostly got his face behind a book.

"You leaving the country?"

"No, just heading back to Lexington."

"Well, then I reckon we'll see each other again. Of course, it's up to Jesus, but I think that's what He's got in mind."

"He talking to you on a regular basis?"

Lizzie gave me the same look she gave me when I complimented her hammering.

"He talks to everybody, but I listen."

Mamma hasn't met Lizzie yet, but she'll like her.

I had started a long note to the new teacher, whoever he or she might be, telling about each child—what they needed help in, what they were good at. I'd spent a whole page just on Luella.

"She'd make a wonderful teacher," I wrote. "She's a wonderful teacher now. Let her help you. Get her to help the little ones. They'll listen to her more than they will you."

I doubted that the new teacher would listen to me. Why would he? She? They would of heard I was a troublemaker. Green Pinckney Russell would of told them.

I had to try, though. I stared at Willy's name next. William Chiles. I didn't know where to begin. He had so much. And so little. A boy like Willy—wanting to know everything—taking in everything you told him and asking for more. Like some colts I've seen tugging at their mamma's teats, never full. Making their mammas run from them to get some peace.

But where's Willy gonna run to in Fayette County? Fences everywhere you look. *Help him leap them fences*, I wanted to write to his new teacher. Help him get to those places people tell him he can't get to. A new century coming. Maybe even poor colored children—if they got the legs and Willy got the legs—can leap those fences. Help him, Teacher. Help him leap.

But I couldn't write that. New teacher wouldn't understand. Think I was a troublemaker. Think Willy a troublemaker, too.

I looked up and Willy was standing in front of my desk, holding out the Sojourner Truth book.

"Take it back. I don't want it."

He looked mad, real mad. The kind of mad a twelve-year-old looks when he'd rather take a beating than cry. I just nodded.

"Well, okay. I just thought you might like it."

"It's a bunch of lies, anyway. Just made up stories. Sojourner Truth didn't free no slaves. She just an old woman. Would of whipped her to death if she tried anything like that."

It was like he'd just showed me a picture of his mamma with that X scar across her face. We both stared at it in our minds' eyes for a moment.

"Ain't no lies, Willy, though you confusing her with Harriet Tubman again. Easy to do. Sojourner didn't sneak back into slave-land and free anybody. That was Harriet. But Sojourner freed herself and the child she could carry. Then went back and freed her boy. In court. Got a lawyer and argued her case. First colored woman to do something like that."

He picked his head up at that, his mouth a little less grim. "Like you lawyered for my mamma?"

"Oh, I didn't do much lawyering. But yeah, maybe a little. All sorts of ways to fight for freedom, Willy. Your mamma's a freedom fighter, just like Harriet Tubman. Just like Sojourner Truth."

"It just got her whipped and thrown in jail." His mouth was grim again, his lips trembling. I looked down before I answered. Last thing I wanted was him feeling shamed for crying in front of me. I waited till I thought he calmed a bit.

"Sometimes you get whipped. Get thrown in jail. But that ain't the whole story. It's what you do after. Your mamma's a freedom fighter. She's fighting for you, fighting for all the children. You got to be a freedom fighter, too, boy. First freedom you fight for is your own. First person Sojourner Truth free was herself. First person Frederick Douglass free was himself. You know how he did that? By learning. He free way before he escape. He freed himself, Willy, and that's what you got to do. I can't stay here. I know you mad at me. Everybody mad at me. I help you any way I can, Willy, but I can't stay here. You gonna have to help yourself—maybe more than's fair for a boy your age. But that's the way it is. Hope it ain't always gonna be like this, but that's the way it is now."

He didn't say anything, but I heard him breathing. Deep. We both breathed deep.

"One thing you got that a lot of folks don't is your mamma. And your daddy. He's a good man. You got that and a great big brain, too, a brain as hungry as a newborn piglet. About as greedy, too. You a piglet for learning." And I got a smile—just a little smile, but a real smile hearing me calling him a little pig. I would of told him he got a big heart, too, as big a heart as I ever knew. But I didn't want to shame him, didn't want to push those tears out that I knew were holding up behind his eyes.

Didn't want to shame myself, either. So I gave him a punch in his shoulder and made him take the book back. It didn't take much persuading. He hugged that book to him like you hug a long-lost friend. Or a friend you almost lost. He smiled at me and waved like we was gonna see each other the next day. Like it weren't goodbye. Well, maybe it weren't. Like Lizzie said, I ain't leaving the country, just coming in from the county.

"Ain't you a woman?" I wanted to yell out one more time but I didn't. See, Mamma? Sometimes I do got more sense than sound. Anyway, it weren't true. "Ain't you a man?" I could of yelled. Didn't matter that he was twelve years old.

Ain't you a man?

Had to free yourself first, I told Willy. But here I was, back considering mucking out stables again. Mr. Benjamin gave me a raise at *The Standard,* but it weren't enough. I needed something more. Free yourself, Willy, I told him, and here I was back at my Mamma's, watching her slave away to feed and house her twenty-year-old child.

Ain't I a man?

"You don't need to go back to them stables. I still got most of the teaching money you gave me. It'll last a good long time. You take that time to read them law books."

A good long time. That piddling little money I saved from the summer. Couldn't of been more than twenty dollars. Mamma'd have the first nickel she or Daddy ever made if we didn't need to eat. Never knew a woman who could make a dime do a dollar better than she could.

"Think I'd rather muck stables," I told her. "Stables smell a whole lot sweeter than the court rooms I been in."

"You like bacon, don't you?" I looked at her, waiting for one of her barnyard sayings. "You got to be around pigs if you want bacon. And they don't always smell so sweet."

"Telling me I'm too proud again, Mamma. Only trouble with your reasoning, Mamma, is figuring out who the pig is. Easy out on the farm. Not so easy in a courtroom. Then you got to find out where the bacon gonna come from. Or if you the bacon."

She looked disgusted, like I was a boy again trying to bamboozle her with some story. "That's what those law books are for. They'll tell you where to look for the bacon."

I shook my head back. No arguing with Mamma, my head shake said, but she wasn't done.

"What you tell that boy who so sad about you leaving? All sorts of ways of working for freedom. Harriet Tubman had hers, Sojourner Truth another. You tell me those stories and I get the names confused, too. But it don't matter much. All this talk about where to find the bacon or if you the bacon." She shook her head again like it was me who started the bacon talk. "What matters is how you gonna fight for that freedom you keep talking about if you don't know the law. How you gonna help that boy and them other children if all you know is mucking stables because you think you too big to take money from your mamma? Because you say the courtroom smell worse than a stable. Well, make it smell sweeter, boy. That's your job: make it smell sweeter."

Mr. Benjamin gave me a stack of law books and, when I wasn't setting type or writing or doing half of Lincoln's job, I would sit there reading, trying to make sense of Kentucky law. For a long time I felt like I couldn't do it. I'd try a sentence and it'd slip away like a wet fish. I'd waste time just looking for the verb in a sentence, only to find it at the end of a long paragraph.

"Backwards," I said to Mr. Benjamin, "like Kentucky."

"You're too hard on Kentucky. That's the way the whole country writes laws: first you put in a noun, then you meander around awhile till you figure out what you want to do with it. That's the action. But the law's afraid of action most times, unless property's involved. It's like a big ship docking. The big ship, the action, is surrounded by lots of little ships trying to steer it a certain way, trying to keep it off the rocks. Sometimes if the little ships don't like the action—the big ship—they might steer it onto the rocks. But nobody will say that out loud. Is that clear now?"

Mr. Benjamin looked stern but I could tell he was enjoying himself. I don't know why older folks like it so when young people got to sweat to learn something. Mamma's no better. I show her a sentence from a law book that go on for two pages, she just say that if I want to live in Mexico, I got to learn Mexican. "It's Spanish, not Mexican," I want to tell her but don't. I get her meaning. It's a foreign country, this law, and I'm going to have to learn the language. If I want to cross the border—leap those fences I keep talking about—I guess I'm going to have to learn Mexican.

I looked up the education law from back in '96.

> That every parent, guardian or other person in the State of Kentucky, having the control of any child or children between the ages of seven and fourteen years, shall be required to send such child or children, annually, at least eight weeks of which attendance shall be consecutive to some public or private day or night school for children.

In other words, after studying the dang thing for ten minutes, I understood that you had to send your child to a school at least eight weeks in a year.

"Why can't they just say that? In English," I railed at Mamma, but she just waved me off, like I was a child having a fit.

I started to learn Mexican. It helped me with the next sentence—eighteen lines long. But it was the one that let you off the hook. If you was too poor to clothe your child decent—"not able to clothe such child properly"—you didn't have to send him to school. Or if you taught him at home what he'd learn in school. Or if there just wasn't any school nearby, or a "proper" one. In other words, if there wasn't a "white school, in the case of white children, or colored school, in the case of colored children, taught within two miles by the nearest traveled road" then you were okay. Except if you was a colored child trying to get an education.

Well, at least that child's folks didn't have to worry about the fine up to fifty dollars for the second offense. Of course, if you could lay hands on fifty dollar, you could buy your child a whole closetful of decent clothes. Buy the whole school.

"Seems to me, Mr. Benjamin, that that big sentence is just full of little boats steering the big boat onto the rocks, just like you said. They aimed to sink that big ship, the one that says parents have to send their children to school."

He shook his head. "They meant to steer it, but they didn't mean to sink it. This is progress, Noah. A whole lot of folks in Kentucky think education is nobody's business but the parents', if they can afford it. White or colored. But here you have a law saying the Commonwealth thinks they *should* be in school. White and colored, Noah. That's progress. First time in Kentucky."

"Just eight weeks. And they don't have to send them if they can't afford decent clothes. Or if they live more than two miles from a public school. You know how many colored children live further than two miles away from a school?"

He held up his hand. "Progress, Noah. And the law doesn't say parents can't send their children to school if they live further than two miles. Just says they don't have to. The Chiles lived more than two miles away from your school out in Briar Hills. Or close to it."

"We didn't travel by road—had to make our own way through the fields. Don't know how far it was. Took close to an hour."

"Had to find your own way through the fields. That's the story of our people, Noah. We have to find our own way. You think Miz Chiles cares her boy's school is two miles or five miles? You think she, or his daddy, wouldn't rip their own clothes in shreds to make sure their boy was dressed decent?"

"You're right about that. But we not all heroes, Mr. Benjamin. Ordinary folks got children, too."

"Colored can't afford ordinary, Noah."

He told me this as I trailed with him through Yellmantown. An ordinary colored neighborhood with ordinary shacks trying to be pretend they were ordinary houses. When they weren't falling down. We were going door to door, trying to corral colored men down to the precincts to register. I didn't tell Mamma I was back in Yellmantown. She wouldn't like it.

I wanted to stop by the bar Jake was working in now, say howdy. But Mr. Benjamin didn't think that was a good idea.

"Your friend, Jake, is working for the machine, buying up votes fast as we register them."

"Jake wouldn't do that."

I almost had to trot to keep up with Mr. Benjamin, but he stopped suddenly and looked hard at me. "He's buying up whole blocks—whole families. Even women. And they only vote in the school board elections. Jake's just the broker, the man paying out the cash. But he's part of the reason things don't change. Your friend's part of the machine that's keeping this town down."

That explained the last fellow we'd cornered. "Already registered," he told us, trying to squeeze on by, but Mr. Benjamin stepped in front of him. He was a big man and could of run right over us, but he paused.

"I don't have you on my list? Where did you register? I want to make sure there's no mix-up with your name."

"Oh, ain't no mix-up. The saloon over by Fourth."

Mr. Benjamin just looked at him. He looked back.

"So I reckon you know who you're voting for."

He kept looking at Mr. Benjamin—didn't even seem to notice me. He gave a little shrug.

"I reckon I do."

Mr. Benjamin let him by.

Keeping the town down. Yellmantown looked like it was heading down—shotguns almost leaning against each other—you could barely walk between them there was so little space. Even the new ones. And there were new ones sprouting up every day. Seems like every place coloreds get to live in this town, we end up falling over each other.

The old man shuffling out of the saloon did fall over me. I reached down to pick him up and he smiled at me.

"That you, Noah? Heard you left off bartending? Your mamma know you come back?"

I had to think for a second—Old Luke—the fellow who wouldn't do his drinking at George Thomas after the killings.

"I'm not back bartending. I'm here helping Mr. Benjamin register voters."

He looked over at Mr. Benjamin. "That Mr. Benjamin?" I'd gotten him on his feet but he wasn't steady yet. He leaned hard on my arm. "I've read your writing, sir. Fine writing. Credit to the race."

Mr. Benjamin nodded. The old man continued. "I'm not much credit to the race. Your boy tell you that. A fine boy. You should be proud."

"No, I'm Mr. Benjamin's assistant, not his son." But the old man waved his hand.

"I know that. Knew your daddy. But we get our sons where we get them. Wish you mine, but you ain't." He looked sad for a moment but then lit up. "Your old friend, Jake, he's working here. Come on in with me. I told my woman I be home before dark, but this an occasion."

"No, Luke, we not drinking. I told you. Out trying to register voters. You registered, old man?"

The smile went quick. "I think so. Hard to recall. Your friend, Jake, signed me up. A while ago."

Mr. Benjamin turned to Old Luke. He'd been a slave, I remembered now. Gave that great speech about choosing where to drink. A proud day. But he didn't look proud now.

"How much did he pay you?" Mr. Benjamin said. "Or did he just take it off your tab?"

I think the old man would have slumped back to the ground only I was still holding on. "Don't …" I started to say to Mr. Benjamin, but he was pushing through the saloon doors by then, on a mission. "Don't say anymore," I wanted to tell him but he was gone. I needed to follow him quick only I couldn't let Old Luke go yet.

"He's right," Old Luke whispered to me. "Sold my vote and I ain't even know how much it went for. Took it off my bill. He's right."

It tore right at me. More things in the world than being right. "Remember that speech," I said, because I couldn't bear him feeling that way. "Got the whole crowd to move on from George Thomas. That was something."

I felt him grow steadier, like I could leave go of his arm finally. "That's right. That was something." And it like we were both watching the same kinetoscope—that picture machine the colored fair had on its grounds a summer ago. Folks lined up half a mile to peer it through it one at a time. Only Old Luke and me seeing the same picture at the same time. Him standing proud. Grown men listening to him.

"Well, I promised my woman," he said. "Better be going." I let go. He wobbled a little but didn't fall. I watched him go down the street. Slow walking but he kept upright.

That was something.

The saloon was smaller than George Thomas, but it had the same mean feel. At least in the afternoon. Night's different. You come in to see your friends when you done work. Maybe somebody even playing a little music. But you can't pretend that you came for anything but hard drink in the afternoon, can't pretend you got much of anything else in your life but that drink. Two groups of men sat in two corners of the saloon, like they fighters separated in a ring. One group, though, looked like they all done fighting—staring at their glasses, some of them empty.

Like their pockets.

The other group was shouting about something. Not fighting, just shouting. A big scary looking fellow named Zeke—I remember him from George Thomas—going on about a boxer named Johnson out of Texas. Zeke always on that line between being just loud and getting tossed. Jake took care of him in the old days. Wouldn't let me.

"Ain't ready for him," is all he'd say.

Zeke looked like he might need some handling today, hopped up about Johnson. Thought at first it was the black hope some fellows always rooting for. But it weren't that.

"Don't matter if he can fight. Soon as he knocks out some white man, they'll kick coloreds out of fighting. John L. Sullivan said he'd never fight a black man."

"Fat as he is, he ain't fighting white men, either."

"Wouldn't fight Johnson even when he weren't fat. 'Cause the black man whip his ass." Zeke tipped his beer back. Looked around the group like he wanted to kick some ass right there. Most of the men kept their eyes down.

"Look what they did with baseball. Fleet Walker the best catcher Toledo had. Too good. Let him play one season and then they ban all coloreds. Soup Perkins better get some wins in quick, before they get rid of all the colored jockeys."

Weren't any white men in this saloon, not like the old George Thomas. Didn't mean a white man didn't own the joint. It could be George Thomas himself far as anybody knew. Just knew better than to show up on a regular basis. Keep the overseers out of sight. Less chance of trouble that way, though the place still smelled of trouble. Men like Zeke got louder with no white men around.

I looked around for Mr. Benjamin. He wasn't shouting, but he was mad. At the bar, talking to Jake. Mr. Benjamin shoots his words out like bullets from a single gauge, one at a time, when he gets angry. Zeke shouting about black fighters, or colored baseball men, could of been in another county, for all Mr. Benjamin paid heed to him. He was aiming his fire at Jake, who didn't look happy.

"A man needs a drink. A man drinks more than he should, that's his choice. The ruin business is booming in this town. A man bent on ruin will do it without your help. But helping a thief—paying that thief for his stolen goods—you cannot excuse that. You steal a man's vote for pieces of silver, you're stealing from the community. Your community. You're a colored man stealing from colored schools and colored children. That so-called 'Mayor' of Yellmantown, George Broadus, who got himself killed in your bar. I don't pity him. He stole from us for years. But you are worse, Jake Winslow. He was a clown. But you understand. You are a thief, Jake Winslow, and you work for thieves."

I don't think anybody else heard but me, they too busy listening to Zeke. Good thing. Don't know what would of happened with an audience. Jake always kept a truncheon behind the bar. People knew it was there so he didn't need to use it much. A man went down when Jake swung that at his head. Didn't matter if the man three hundred pounds, didn't matter if he a foot taller than anyone in the bar, he went down. Touch and go whether he ever got back up again.

Mr. Benjamin wasn't no three hundred pounds. He turned his back on Jake when he finished shooting those word bullets. Done with him. I saw Jake reaching for that truncheon.

"Jake!" I yelled. He looked over at me. Jake always liked me. I don't know why. Mr. Benjamin turned to me, too—annoyed probably. He didn't like his preaching interrupted.

"Noah." Jake was breathing as heavy as if he run a race, like the day of the shooting. I'd been behind the bar that day, scrunching down for dear life. I was watching his arm now, watching it tense, watching it relax as he stared at me and let the truncheon go. I went over to the bar.

"How you doing, Jake," I said, greeting him like nothing had happened. Held out my hand. He let it stay there for a second.

"You don't want to shake hands with a thief, Noah."

"Oh, Mr. Benjamin, he…" I stopped. I kept my hand out. Jake shook it finally.

"Get him out of here, Noah."

"I will, I will."

"I'm no thief, Noah. These men come in ready to sell. I buy what they offer. That's all."

I nodded. Seemed friendly to nod, but I couldn't leave it there. "You're no thief, Jake. You a good man. Saved my life. But you're wrong. Mr. Benjamin put it too harsh, but he's right. The vote's the only thing we got and it's being stolen. Can't buy a colored vote in Alabama. Ain't none to buy. They've not stole them all yet in Kentucky, though they trying. Coloreds don't need to be helping them, Jake. Sure don't need to be doing that."

Jake had poured me a beer. Wasn't much past one in the afternoon, but I felt a power-ful thirst. It would of seemed too mean to turn it down. I gulped it quick while Mr. Benjamin had his back turned. He wouldn't of liked it.

"Seems to me you calling me a thief, too, Noah. You say it nice. But you still saying it. You the soft 'come to Jesus' parson. Your man there is the 'burn in hell' preacher I grew up listening to. Preaching hell to coloreds. Like they don't know all about hell already."

He poured himself a beer. Jake didn't do that too often, at least when I worked with him. Said he'd seen too many bartenders pour themselves down the drain.

"Only I don't agree with your sermon. That vote you talking about don't mean noth-ing, won't change nothing. Why shouldn't these men get something up front when they ain't gonna get nothing down the way? You believe we elect the right men, even the right colored men, and things get better? Well, Noah, maybe you better drink up and have some more. Need a whole lot of cheap beer to keep that pipedream going."

I finished the beer quick but waved away the second.

Mr. Benjamin had stopped at the tip of the triangle between the two corner groups so both groups turned toward him. He started talking, so soft I missed the first words. Everybody strained forward to hear him. They shushed each other to pick up his words. He got louder as he spoke.

"I know some of you men have already sold your votes to the Democrats. But it does not follow. A crooked contract will not stand up in court. And this was a crooked contract. Esau might sell his birthright for a mess of pottage, but you cannot sell yours for any amount of money. There is no honor among thieves and you may take your vote back—you have nev-er lost it. You may use your vote for the good of your community."

"You saying we thieves!" Zeke finally found his voice. Mr. Benjamin turned to him.

"I'm saying you're men, citizens, and that if you've made a crooked bargain, it means nothing. I'm saying that your vote is yours."

"If it's ours, I reckon we can do what we want with it. Sell it if we want to. Need to."

"No, you cannot. Your child is yours if you have one. You cannot sell the child."

"You saying selling a vote's like selling a child? First you say we thieves, now you say-ing we like slave-traders, selling our own children."

Zeke had got both corners murmuring. I don't think they thought they'd been insult-ed till Zeke explained it to them. I looked at Mr. Benjamin. I held my breath. *Don't speak to Zeke like you talked to Jake and Old Luke.* I would of called on Jesus if I thought He hung out in bars.

Mr. Benjamin was silent for a second. Then he smiled. "Weren't you the fellow talking about Johnson, the colored fighter out in Texas?" I didn't think Mr. Benjamin had heard him. I should of known better. Zeke still looked ready to charge, but he nodded. "How did you put it? That he'd 'kick white asses' if he got the chance." A few men tittered when Mr. Benjamin said that. It was like hearing your preacher say it: "kick white asses." Zeke didn't laugh, though. He kept tense, waiting to charge out of his corner. "All Johnson needs is a chance to fight, you said. But they're trying to keep him out of the ring. Just as they took Fleet Walker out of base-ball. Just as they're making it harder and harder for colored jockeys to find a horse—colored jockeys who started the sport. Who made the sport."

The murmurings stopped when Mr. Benjamin started speaking again. Now they be-gan to swell again. Men nodding in agreement. Nodding like they amening in a church and not a saloon. Like Jesus was hanging out here. Zeke had become the chief amener.

"Yes," Zeke shouted. "Yes."

Mr. Benjamin began to clip his words again, giving a space between each one that hit like a fist upon the chest. "I am not calling you thieves. I would never call any man a thief." I kept my eyes away from Jake. "I am saying you have been cheated. I am saying that they are trying to keep you out of the ring. Because they know that if you got in that ring, there would be a whole lot of white asses kicked."

"Kicked." He spit the word. Both corners converged like two creeks making a river, cheering and yelling, surrounding Mr. Benjamin. I worried they'd knock him off his feet. Zeke was the first to race forward, the first to grab Mr. Benjamin's hand. He shook it up and down so vigorous I thought he might wrench it off. He looked around fierce, challenging, waiting for someone to try to bother his man. Though two minutes earlier he'd been ready to knock Mr. Benjamin out of the ring himself.

I walked back to Jake at the bar who was shaking his head.

"Your man takes chances, Noah. One day he might take one too many chances."

"You live your life just trying not to be shot, it's not much of a life. Especially if you're a Negro in the South."

Jake looked puzzled.

"Something Mr. Benjamin says."

"Ain't much of a life when you get shot, either."

I stuck out my hand again to Jake, and he took it without hesitating this time. I reckon everybody's feelings been ruffled some. I gripped his hand and pulled him close so I could whisper my own sermon into his ear.

"You wrong, brother. Wrong. We gonna change things. And one day, brother, you gonna help us."

I turned my back on him and scooted after Mr. Benjamin. I knew better, but one part of me wondered if Jake's truncheon might land on my own head. Take the life he saved way back. But Jake wouldn't do that.

He was my brother. He was on the other side now, but he was my brother.

Chapter 28

Noah Webster, October 10, 1899, Yellmantown, Lexington, Kentucky

We kept walking Yellmantown.

"You sober enough or would you rather spend the afternoon drinking?"

I just nodded. Mr. Benjamin and Mamma. Nothing got by them.

We stopped by a church, built like two houses in that soft yellow brick you see all over town, the tall one in back spooning the little one in front. Only building like it in Yellmantown. The Quinn Chapel African Methodist Episcopal, the sign read.

"Churches in Yellmantown," I told Mamma, when she was going on about the place. "Not just saloons."

"Of course, they churches. You got that much sin, you need churches."

We stood on the sidewalk—about the only sidewalk in Yellmantown, the rest mud or dust depending on the day. The church was up on a little knoll. We looked down on the sorry sight that was the rest of Yellmantown.

"You know what I'd like to get?" Mr. Benjamin said. "I'd like to get Goodloetown, Branch Alley, and Chicago Bottoms rolled into one large ball and dumped into the Kentucky River for purification. And if it wouldn't pollute the river past saving, I'd dump in Yellmantown, too."

"Then where would we live?"

"We'd live where we wanted to." His face got stern. "We'd have to start with that wish first."

The Reverend W. C. Jones was the pastor, and lived right around the corner in a bungalow made of bricks the same color as the church, the most prosperous looking home for blocks. The sidewalk didn't stretch to the house, but solid wooden planks made their way to the Reverend's front door. *Anything to keep the polish on his shoes*, I thought, *the shine on his cassock*.

"Preachers the best-fed colored men in town," I say to Mamma. "Sure beats school teaching."

I don't know why I got to devil Mamma like that. She just nod. "You thinking of preaching? Because you sure ain't teaching."

"Wonder how Yellmantown support all this?" I say to Mr. Benjamin.

"We support what we need to."

I was surprised. Mr. Benjamin didn't usually pass up an opportunity to rail on preachers. He saw the look on my face. "If I were a church-going man this would be my church. Colored men started this church because they wanted their own place, away from the whites. Sued to be independent. Thirty, forty years before slavery ended." He pointed to the church. "When they're not preaching, they're teaching. Doubles as a school during the week. Let's look in."

See, Mamma, I said in my mind, *I could do both. Preach and teach.*

The Reverend W. C. Jones greeted us at the door. I thought he flinched a bit when he saw Mr. Benjamin, but he shouted out his greeting.

"Robert! You out politicking? I heard you were in the neighborhood." He grabbed his hand.

"I thought I'd show my assistant one of the un-bought churches. Hard to tell the difference from the outside, but the air has a different smell."

The flinch had turned into a full frown. "That's not fair, Robert, not fair at all. Only one minister's named. And he's not guilty till he's proven guilty."

"He's not guilty till Billy Klair says he's guilty. Until then we're all supposed to presume his innocence? That's why you're a church man, William. You have more faith than I do. Your man might not go to prison but he's guilty in the eyes of the people. The Lord, too, probably, but you'd know more about it than I do. On his way down, he's naming lots of names."

It was the biggest scandal in the black community though it hadn't even been mentioned in *The Morning Herald* or *The Leader*. Seemed like we were running a regular column about it in *The Standard*. The Reverend Elijah Hathaway charged with buying up votes en masse for the Democrats. Except his congregants didn't even get change in their pockets like Jake's customers did, or even money off their bar bill. The Reverend Hathaway used his influence to direct his people. Vote one way and get the use of a vacant lot for a church playground. Vote this man in—an upright Christian man—and there may be some city jobs for a few lucky parishioners. And what he didn't tell them: vote the way I tell you and there'll be money in the pocket. My pocket.

Everybody so mad at the Reverend Hathaway now he lucky to keep his pants, let alone his pockets. Billy Klair wants his money back so won't be anything in those pockets even if the Reverend keeps them.

"You're not suggesting I'm one of those names, are you Robert?"

Mr. Benjamin looked impatient. "I said I was bringing Noah to an un-bought church, William."

Reverend Jones seemed to remember his manners. He looked over Mr. Benjamin's shoulder at me, giving me a big smile, like he was running for office himself.

"You the young fellow helping Robert out? A school teacher yourself, right?"

"Not anymore."

"Oh, that's right, that's right."

I wasn't surprised he knew about me. Lexington remind me of Briar Hill in some ways. Nobody got any secrets. Of course, Mamma's been roving churches. If she'd been here, Reverend Jones knew my whole life.

About twenty children scattered in small groups around the main vestry of the church. They grouped the pews into little islands where about six children each were working on something. A young woman moving between the groups turned to us and the Reverend's voice lowered.

"That's Lizzie," he whispered. "She comes volunteering. We can't pay anybody yet but hope to." He turned to me. "We sure could use a man volunteer."

"I'm sure you could, Reverend. Only trouble is, my mamma sure could use some rent money. Now if you could get the landlord to volunteer the house, I be happy to help out."

He didn't take offense, let out a guffaw so loud all the children left off working. Lizzie hustled through the tables like a sheepdog rounding back strays. She turned and gave the Reverend a frown. Then she caught my eye. She caught my eye and then threw it back, like a fish not worth the catching.

I had recognized her immediately even from the back, even though she'd curled her long braid around the top of her head into a bun—like the schoolmarm she'd become. Only I never had a schoolmarm look like Lizzie. She didn't look surprised when she saw me. Just turned her back to me and her head down to the children.

"You know our Lizzie?"

"We met in Cadentown. I didn't know she'd come to Lexington."

"Just this month—a church lady knew her and thought she'd make a wonderful teacher. She is a great teacher. Pay her so little I call her a volunteer, but she live with us so she don't need to worry about that. Her daddy didn't want to let her go at first, but he knew there wasn't much out there in the country for her. She told him Jesus wants her here so he had to let her go."

No arguing with Lizzie's Jesus.

"So her landlord volunteer the house and feed her, too?"

He put his hand to his mouth to muffle his chuckling. He didn't want to get into more trouble with Lizzie. I could of told him he was right to worry. I saw her in my mind's eye: ready to slug Deputy Sheriff Siebrecht. She'd turned her back again, bent over, talking to a child.

Mr. Benjamin had wandered among the pews. The Reverend and I followed him, the Reverend talking to me more than Mr. Benjamin, which surprised me some. Even when we three joined up, Reverend Jones kept turned to me like Mr. Benjamin was the photographer they tell you not to look at directly. Flash hurt your eyes, they tell you, if you look straight at the camera.

"It's the best colored school in town, better than most of the white ones even. Teaching first six classes so far, almost thirty students. Hope to go up to eight in a couple of years."

Reverend Jones smiled at Lizzie. She didn't smile back.

"I hope it's not the best colored school in town, Reverend Jones. I do my best—we all do—but this is just a space in a church. It's solidly built. Better than Mr. Webster's school in Briar Hill, but he was the better teacher. Which made it the better school."

I felt myself flush at her praise, but she already turned away again. She pointed to a word and the child that wrote it started erasing so hard, I thought he'd rub a hole in the paper. She picked her head up. "Unfortunately the teacher they have now is not very good. So perhaps our school *is* better now."

Lizzie finally did smile at me, but just a moment. She turned stern to the Reverend Jones.

"But there are many good teachers in Lexington, Reverend Jones. Their school buildings might be half fallen down like Briar Hill, but they're good schools. Can't confuse the building with the school. It'd be like judging a congregation by how fancy their church windows were."

Reverend Jones thought he was just doing a bit of good-humored bragging, praising his teacher and his school. He should of known better. Lizzie was tough.

"Oh, no, no, no. I know lots of good colored teachers around. Didn't mean to say that."

Mr. Benjamin finally caught his eye. He held it.

"Lots of bad colored teachers, too, William. Which is why I'm glad you opened your school—though it's less than a half mile from the public school."

"A very crowded school, Robert. They have more than two hundred students and space for fifty."

"Renamed for your hero, Mr. Russell, isn't it?"

He stopped suddenly, aware he'd been caught.

"We do what we can, Robert. Mr. Russell's done a lot of good—I know you don't think so." He looked over to me and then looked away, probably remembering my part in all this. Poor man didn't know where to look. "We do what we can."

Mr. Benjamin looked grim.

"The problem is, William, you think people want good schools. The people in charge. They don't want good schools—not even good white schools. They'll educate their own children, but the rest can go begging. Colored and white. The elite only cares for the elite. And Billy Klair and Mr. Green Pinckney Russell, they only care about money. And power."

"You simplify, Robert. You might not like Mr. Cassidy, but he's working to better the schools. Even the colored schools. And what about Mrs. Breckinridge? Don't Maria and her friends work with her? They certainly are the ones in charge, as you put it."

Mr. Benjamin looked scornful. "Mr. Cassidy has built a few schools, knocked down a few others before they fell down. But he's part of the machine that is keeping us all down. And Mrs. Breckinridge? Real power has never been female. They are not the ones in charge."

I thought Mr. Benjamin doesn't really know Mamma. Or Miz Chiles. Or even Maria. But I didn't say anything. He would of said that wasn't the kind of power he meant. I understood that. But sometimes I thought the only power that mattered is the kind Mamma got.

I heard Lizzie sigh. The Reverend Jones turned away to bend down to a child working some addition problem. He made the child move over in the pew, squeezing out the child on the end. The Russell school wasn't the only one needing space. I heard his voice tremble a bit.

"You carry the one when you get a number this big," he said, too loud for Lizzie, who I could tell wanted to hush him, but she let it go. The Reverend was finally solving a number problem he could manage. All the other children were working hard. Lizzie had a moment.

"How come you didn't tell me you was in town?"

"I reckon if you was interested in that, you would of answered my last letter."

Her letter was a month old, laying on my dresser at home.

"I've been busy, but I was gonna write soon."

"Then I would of told you I moved to Lexington."

She swung away to another child then. I could see the top of her head as she bent low, that long black braid of hers only pinned in. I knew it wanted to break free, swing low. I yearned to reach out and unclip the pins myself.

But I didn't need Mamma to tell me that would of been a mistake.

"Could you use me a morning or two, Reverend Jones? I don't have much time to spare but I maybe can find some time when Mr. Benjamin don't need me. Can't be reading law books all my spare time."

The Reverend Jones looked surprised for a second, relieved probably that I wasn't calling his school a waste of time. Or accusing him of selling votes. Then I saw his eyes flicker over to Lizzie, adding it up. But he's a preacher. They might eat well, but they also know when to keep their mouths shut.

Mr. Benjamin was almost out the door. "I saw Maria out canvassing women to register for voting," the Reverend said, almost racing to keep up with us. "Between the two of you, colored be a force nobody will be able to ignore."

Maria. The second time her name was spoke in five minutes. I might spend days with Mr. Benjamin without him mentioning her once. She wasn't strong enough to be walking the streets. But Mr. Benjamin wouldn't like me saying that. Mr. Benjamin turned to the Reverend Jones one last time. "Maria does her best. We all do our best, William, except maybe the Reverend Hathaway and Noah's friend, Jake. Even you, I see, are putting in the effort. But we get tired. And you are wrong, William. There is no end to the ways whites can ignore coloreds in this town."

He looked tired for a moment. Mr. Benjamin almost never looks tired. Gets mad at me. At Maria. Not mad, maybe, but impatient when we wear out. But he looked almost worn out now when he turned at the door and gave a wave to the children.

"No end, William. No end."

CHAPTER 29

Noah Webster, January, 1900, Lexington, Kentucky

> Today tells the tale. Shall we have men whose party is mainly com-
> posed of Negroes to fill our offices, or shall we have men who are
> representatives of white men to fill them?

Mr. Benjamin held up the copy of *The Mt. Sterling Advocate.* "Here you have it. The voice of the new millennium in Kentucky. Sounds a bit like the old millennium, doesn't it? *The Leader* and *The Morning Herald* are too polite to run something like that, but they think it just the same. Now with William Justus Goebel as their champion, more and more people get to say it out loud."

I was puzzled. "But he lost the election."

"Does it look like he lost the election? He received fewer votes than Taylor did, but they'll fix that soon enough. He'll be sitting in the governor's mansion come the end of January. And we'll have a governor determined to strip us of the few rights we've managed to cling to. It'll be Wilmington, North Carolina all over again."

Wilmington was a sore point with all of us—a city ruled by Red Shirts as mean as the Klan ever was. Ran the coalition black and white city government out of town at the butts of their rifles. Nobody did a thing.

"Won't happen here, Mr. Benjamin. For one thing *The Herald* and *The Leader* both hate Goebel."

"They do. Desha Breckinridge thinks he'll bring on another civil war. But that's because Goebel is for regulating the railroads. And he's not one of them."

Not one of *them.* All those Breckinridges and their cousins mostly ran the town, still. The part they didn't run, Billy Klair did. Goebel was a wild card. If Goebel wasn't one of them, we sure weren't. Colored was as far away from being *them* as you could get. We off in the corner. *The Standard* make enough noise, they look over once in a while. Make enough noise, they send policemen with night sticks to quiet us down. That civil war Desha talking about is everyday life for coloreds in this town.

Mr. Benjamin part of the civil war. Said he could just about tolerate white Democrats who've been open about wanting to steal the vote away from coloreds. "But I cannot stand Negro Democrats who have degraded themselves so as to rob the black man of the only right that makes him feel he's a man."

"We calling every colored Democrat a traitor? On the front page of *The Standard?*"

Mr. Benjamin just looked at me steely-eyed. Like I can't read. When they ain't shooting at us, we shooting at each other. Same old millennium.

Not that Mr. Benjamin happy with the Republican, Taylor.

"A terrible choice," Mr. Benjamin called it. He chose "the Westerner." Didn't like him, either, but the Goebelites too scary. "White sheet scary."

"We for the railroads?"

"It's a terrible choice," he said again.

Terrible choices are what colored folk get. Only the whites don't seem too happy, either.

Nobody was talking about the school board election. Last I heard they hadn't even counted the women's vote—they got separate booths.

"What's to talk about?" said Mr. Benjamin. "The Democrats swept every post and why not? The Republicans put all their energy into Taylor and the non-partisan ticket didn't even get on the ballot. Maria and her club ladies went around with lists voters were supposed to write in. Above the official stamp. Or below it! Maria herself seemed to change stories. If we want to be taken seriously, we must be serious. "

Wrote that in *The Standard*—about being taken seriously—right near to where he called colored Democrats traitors. Saw Maria reading it when she'd come by the office with both children. Mr. Benjamin and me been working long hours.

"Didn't want them to forget what their daddy looked like," she said to me. He was playing hard with both of them, like if he played real hard they wouldn't notice he wasn't home much. Saw her sigh when she looked at the editorial. I'd set the type myself, knew every word by heart. Wished I didn't.

"He don't mean it to sound that harsh," I said.

"Robert always means what he says," Maria answered, as if I been attacking him somehow. Then she smiled at me. "But you're right. Sometimes he sounds more harsh than he intends."

"At least the bond bill passed," I said to him later. "Fifty thousand dollars, money for one colored and one white school."

"Of course, the bond bill passed. That money's already been spent. And you think they're going to split that money in half? Colored school lucky to get ten thousand of it. More like five."

So that wasn't much comfort. Still, the Republicans found out they needed the colored vote and that was something. *The Leader* ran articles just about every day talking of one Republican Negro gathering after another. Even *The Morning Herald*—where a colored man usually had to be on one end of a shooting to get any notice—ran columns about the Goebelites trying everything they knew to scare off the Negro vote. Both *The Herald* and *The Leader* ran a box on their front pages almost daily, telling Negroes how there was a Federal law against trying to keep coloreds from voting.

Usually it just *The Standard* talking about Negro rights. Mr. Benjamin allowed it was something. Federal judge in Louisville even indicted a half dozen Lexington Democrats.

Still, on election day, the Goebelites did everything they could to scare coloreds off. Didn't open the booths till the afternoon in some colored wards. Challenged folks who were born and raised five steps away and hadn't moved ten steps their whole lives. Even Judge Bullock fit to be tied with some of the challenges. If challenges didn't work, they step right into the voting booth and try to scare folks off.

And if none of that did the trick, they just out and stole the votes.

"Stole the actual ballot box in Athens. Went to look for the box and the election clerk said he had taken the box home to count the votes but somebody stole it on the way!"

It was *The Leader's* headline. *The Morning Herald's*, too.

Mr. Benjamin stared at me hard, holding both papers, like I had some answers, or maybe I knew where the ballot box was. I almost started laughing. Mr. Benjamin wouldn't of liked that. *Stole the ballot box?* I kept my head down while I got control. Of course it was Goebelites who took the box, that whole part of the county turning Republican. Or at least they don't like Goebel. A lot of white votes in that ballot box.

See? We was getting equal rights, finally. Kentucky fashion. Steal the votes of white and colored alike.

Other news wasn't so funny. Had a riot in the 20th—over by Fifth and Race. Neighborhood changing. About fifty coloreds showed up to vote. Whites didn't like it. More than fifty shots fired but nobody shot so mostly blowing off steam, I gather. Maybe in the new millennium we shoot up in the air. That'd be something. Arrested a dozen, all colored. I guess coloreds must of been the only ones shooting. That's the Kentucky I know. The civil war we live.

Nothing to do with Goebel and Taylor.

Haven't counted those ballots yet, either. But at least the ballot box ain't missing.

Only recognized one name from the ruckus in the 20th—Zeke Taylor, the same Zeke who almost hoisted Mr. Benjamin on his shoulders over in Yellmantown. After he almost slugged him. Got pulled in for hitting a cop with a stick. I pointed his name out to Mr. Benjamin, reminded him he was the fellow who he made that rousing speech about standing up for colored voting rights. Mr. Benjamin nodded.

"Lot of good that did."

He's been in a bad mood since the election. The whole state's in a bad mood. Frankfort's an armed camp, Mr. Benjamin says. Newspapers saying they expect thousands to march on the town—Goebelites and anti-Goebelites if the legislature does what it says it's gonna do—throw out Louisville's vote altogether. Those Democrats in Frankfort ain't amateurs like the fellows who stole the ballot box from Athens. They steal votes by the thousands.

Mostly a white man's fight, but shooting starts, it won't be just white men getting shot.

Won't be shooting in the air either.

Middle of all this an ex-congressman bumps into somebody he feuding with from the army. Nothing to do with anything about the election but they start blasting away at each other like they on San Juan Hill instead of eating lunch in the Capital Hotel lobby. Congressman shoots six, kills three. Got shot himself. Paper says half the legislature diving under tables, reaching for their own guns, probably thinking here it is, the war finally on us.

Looking over their shoulders.

"Now they know how colored men feel. Half this state is carrying," Mr. Benjamin says. "The wrong half."

"I guess they'll hang the congressman," I said. The men he shot were high up in the state—two Commonwealth attorneys, an assistant postmaster .

Mr. Benjamin shook his head at me. "When's the last time a white man who knew anybody got hung? Look at Goebel. Shot a judge down in the middle of the afternoon. Didn't even call it a duel. Would have kept him out of office. Self-defense. Doesn't matter if he was the one starting the shooting—others shot back. That's called self-defense in Kentucky."

He corrected himself. "For a white man. For a colored man, it's an invitation to a lynching."

I was headed over to the Quinn Chapel school. Mr. Benjamin wasn't sure he approved of my volunteering, but things had finally slowed down after the election.

Least we're not walking the streets since the election, as much good as that did. Registration day, October 3rd, we were up at dawn. Mr. Benjamin said Maria and her club women were up, too, trying to get people to their precincts places. Only one day to register. I thought I'd go down in September when I turned twenty-one, but I have to wait until October next year.

"That's crazy," I said. "People move all the time in this town. And then there's new voters like me. Got one day to register?"

"Boy, where do you think you're living? This is Kentucky. One whole day to register is a lot better than it was ten years ago. If the Democrats hadn't signed you up already, you had to scramble to do it in a couple hours. And the Democrats didn't register colored men."

"They still don't. Or they try not to." We'd had challengers questioning men who spent their whole lives in Lexington. It'd been real mean in the 32nd, Irishtown. We got six men registered but didn't think we'd get out of there alive. The cop on duty, Doyle, wasn't happy to see me.

"I thought you left town."

"Bad penny showing back up," I tried to joke.

"Bad copper penny. You here to register?"

"Not old enough."

He looked disappointed almost, like he waiting for the fight. But he smiled. "Not white enough, either."

Mr. Benjamin made a formal complaint over that remark, but of course, it didn't do nothing. Said it was intimidation against Federal law. But the election board folks you make your complaints to the same folks you complaining about.

Don't have to worry till October about registering. Enough worries for the day, Mamma says. Or the Bible says. Hard for me to keep them straight sometimes, what the Bible says and what Mamma says.

Mr. Benjamin doesn't much approve of the volunteer schools. That's one of the reasons the Reverend Jones so leery of him. "We starve public schools—white and colored though the colored's down to skin and bones—and we make do with these church schools. People settle back, think things just fine."

"Nobody's settling back," I said. He looked surprised. Only thing I ever used to say to Mr. Benjamin was amen. "But the children can't wait until we get the public schools up. They got to be educated now."

Maybe I was feeling a bit touchy because I just got word that Willy might be able to come to the Quinn Chapel school. He and the new teacher at Briar Hill didn't get along much, my letter praising Willy not helping much. Only thing it did was let him know Willy'd been a favorite of mine, which meant he weren't no favorite of his.

"The road to Hell paved with good intentions," is all Mr. Benjamin said when I told him.

"Maybe I should go talk to that teacher," I said, feeling rather sore.

"That's a good idea," Mr. Benjamin said. "Bring a gun. Settle things the Kentucky way."

Mamma tried to soothe my feelings some by saying Willy could come stay with us, though I don't know where we gonna squeeze him in.

"Sleep in the front room." That's the room Mamma do her sewing in, have lady friends visit when she got two minutes' leisure which she almost never do, but she wave that off. "He'll be up and out before I need that room. He a farm boy, used to early hours."

He ain't the only one.

I went out to Briar Hill to pick up Willy. Buster, my old boss from horse mucking, let me have a horse and rig for the day. I was worried he might get into trouble but he just waved that thought off.

"That filly needs walking and the owners too lazy to give her any. A nice country walk just the thing for her."

The rig looked brand new—fancy roof and shiny black wheels. I wondered if the owner would think a country walk just the thing for it, too. But I didn't say anything more. Buster reminds me coloreds ain't always fighting each other. Sometimes we aid and comfort each other. Only way we gonna survive.

I felt right in style. That filly stepping up made me feel like I was in a parade. Or a funeral. I only passed a couple of farm wagons—it pretty quiet in January—moving hay to one field or another. One wagon had a load of pigs. Didn't understand that. Slaughter time almost two months overdue. The pigs stared out through their slats like they as surprised to see me as the farmers who wondered at the high-stepping display I put on. The farmers nodded to me—can't hardly not nod when you meet on a country road—but their eyes stayed suspicious. I felt better knowing I'd brought the gun.

I decided not to swing 'round the school, as much as I wanted to see the other children, Luella especially. The best way to avoid the Kentucky solution is not to go out of your way to find it. Shouldn't of brought the gun, maybe, but I'd be coming back in the dark. Fayette County ain't Alabama, but it's close enough. Willy tells me later Luella doing just fine—my letter didn't seem to hurt her.

"New teacher's pet," Willy said.

I don't think so. Luella nobody's pet. She more than a pet.

When I get to the Chiles' place, the new teacher's there, a Mr. Joseph Bryant. About a year older than me but carry himself like he already settled. Even Mamma won't call me settled. He'd heard Willy was leaving and come to talk the Chiles out of it. Mamma said a Kentuckian—it don't matter white or colored—rather get a whipping than made to feel he was being rude. Or forward. Shoot the fellow but don't be impolite. Mr. Benjamin don't understand that, coming from up north or the islands. Nothing hurts feelings worse than saying something straight out.

The five of us meeting in that yard was like we was caught in some kind of Kentucky nightmare. Even Willy, and he a child. Children usually free from all that politeness, but Willy old for his age. We all looked like a whipping be a blessing, even Miz Chiles. The teacher nodded when he was introduced to me.

"Call me Noah," I told him when he said Mr. Webster to me. He didn't invite me to call him Joe. Or Joseph. Don't think I could of managed Joe. He Mr. Bryant, and when he say "Noah", it's like I some truant student he need to talk serious to.

Conversation went downhill from there. More a speech than a conversation.

"It's unfortunate—though I do not blame Noah, he was put into the classroom with no training and received no guidance—but still it is unfortunate that when Noah taught, or rather when Noah was in charge of the classroom this summer, the children were subject to the most frivolous of curriculums. Poetry, and as I understand it, not even the classics such as Longfellow or Whittier. Poems from Noah's present employer, a somewhat scandalous figure in his own right, were the subject of at least half the subjects presented. I do not say taught. Poetry, even good poetry, would be a waste of precious classroom time when the children need drilling in all the basics of language arts and mathematics. Our children need to be taught what is useful in their lives, what will enable them to make a living in a hard culture. As colored children they will face many obstacles in life. Poetry will not help them succeed."

He looked over to me and nodded sadly, like a preacher mourning a sinner's descent into damnation. One thing I grateful about, though. That speech freed me from the shackles of politeness. I felt them drop off me like I was a native-born New Yorker.

"That's just not so, Joe." His eyes bulged at the Joe. I let him have it again. "Poetry is gonna set you free, Joe."

"I prefer that you call me Mr. Bryant."

"And I'd prefer that you didn't try to 'drill' the life out of our children, that you try and teach them something about who they are rather than turn them into some kind of hewers of wood and drawers of water for some factory. Or maybe just to keep them in the tobacco fields. Your hewers got to know how to read enough to do they's work but not enough to get any ideas above they station. Poetry just too dangerous, ain't it, Joe?"

The politeness shackles were dropping off Mr. Bryant, too. No sweet mournful preacher anymore. More like a hell and damnation one. He turned to Miz Chiles. She and Mr. Chiles looked a bit sick: two teachers fighting in their front yard.

"Listen to his language. 'Ain't' and 'they's work.' He can't even speak the language and he's a teacher? Your boy, Willy, as badly taught as he's been, would make a better teacher. Least he wouldn't do as much harm. Wouldn't teach bad poetry like it's holy scripture."

Mamma says the closer you get to the truth about a person, the madder they get. Maybe that's why I swung at Mr. Bryant. Joe. When your fist hits a fellow's jaws, you ought to be on a first name basis. He was getting too close to what I thought, that I'd done more harm than good. That I didn't teach them what they needed.

Didn't even knock him down and I a big fellow. He swung back and loosened a few teeth. At least they felt shaken. But then he'd been on a first name basis longer. We came in close after our two punches and fell to the ground, rolling around like those pigs I saw off to market. Willy was jumping around us, so close he almost make it a threesome. His eyes and mouth open so wide, his face hardly got room for his nose. Two men teachers fighting in his folks' front yard. Don't get more entertaining than that in this world.

Only Mr. and Miz Chiles didn't seem to think it that much fun. Miz Chiles leaped into our heap with Mr. Chiles right behind her. They pulled us off each other rough, like we two scraggly dogs. Which we felt like. Least I did. Joe did, too, I think. Anyway, he didn't look like the settled Mr. Bryant he started the day off as.

"Don't know if poetry good or bad, though I always liked it myself," Miz Chiles hardly looked winded, though we young men both were breathing like boxers after going fifteen rounds. "But two teachers fighting on the ground like two eight-year-old scamps, I know ain't good. Mr. Bryant, Mr. Webster, stop this now. Remember who you are."

I looked over at Mr. Bryant. He was remembering. I don't think he was ever gonna forget. He brushed himself off and climbed into his rig. Wasn't nearly as fancy as mine.

"I believe I was only defending myself, Miz Chiles, but I apologize for this display." His dignity was coming back on him, settling like road dust after a whirlwind passes. "I meant only the best for your son and for all the children." He bowed like he hadn't just two minutes earlier been trying to gouge my eyes out. "I wish you good day."

Willy was the only happy face among the four of us left. He waved gaily at Mr. Bryant like they'd been the best of friends, though we all knew better. Mr. Bryant had said his adieus and did not return the wave. Miz Chiles just shook her head at me. I couldn't help feeling relieved that she and Mamma didn't really know each other, though with Willy staying with us, I know they'd be meeting. She was sending food and a thank you note along with it.

But the note was writ already. I didn't think she'd be adding to it.

"You a good teacher, Mr. Webster. And a good man. I just sometime forget how young you be."

If my teeth didn't loosen with Mr. Bryant's punch, they felt a little shaken then.

I wanted to go back that night but Miz Chiles thought it too late. "Day light stretching every day but dark still comes early. Don't want Willy out on these roads when it's murky."

Didn't want him out on the road with a crazy man is what she meant.

"Storm coming, too," she added, sniffing the air like the country woman she was. Storm and darkness, good reasons to stay the night. And maybe I'd be calmed down by the morning.

"Not too much," Mr. Chiles added. "Just a brushing. Maybe an inch." They looked to the darkening sky as sure of their forecast as Christians waiting the Second Coming.

Waiting for that, too.

Miz Chiles fed us such a breakfast I felt like going back to my loft and sleeping the morning away. Even Willy looked like he'd had enough and that didn't happen often. Mamma said later that feeding Willy was like trying to fill a sack with a hole in it. Miz Chiles must of known that because she loaded us up with three sacks of corn meal and enough green beans to almost sink the axle into the snow. "You gonna need it and more," is all she said when I protested.

I think it might have been an inch and a half of snow so their weather predicting was off a half inch by my reckoning. Of course there was a good stiff breeze working.

"This be your chance. Take it," is all Miz Chiles said to Willy, standing there straight with that X scar on her face like a crossroad on a map. The scars had faded some but you could still read them. His mamma let him hug her but pulled him off when he lingered. His daddy just shook his hand. Men folk didn't hug.

Miz Chiles didn't let us start until the sun up so it almost eight before we got started. The snow wasn't much but it made things slippery and slow going. I figure Buster wouldn't much appreciate it if I brought his fancy rig back with a wheel busted or with his frisky filly limping. I told Willy to sit in back, on top of the corn meal sacks. Warmer there, out of the wind. But he wanted to sit up next to me and I let him. He squeezed in close so the wind bit less.

I saw Mr. Bryant's rig making its way up the other road, the main one coming down from Cadentown. I heard he was boarding up that way. The little weather we'd got not enough to cancel school. Cancel school with every snow brush, might as well not open it in January. We'd already spotted three, four children trotting across a field—Willy and my old shortcut. The way one girl was bouncing, I knew it had to be Luella though it was too far to tell for sure.

I hoped Mr. Bryant and me just pass each other with a nod—or without one if that what he wanted. But his rig had stopped.

I thought, *What now? Didn't get a chance to finish your lecture?* But I remember what Miz Chiles said. Time I grew up. I put on my best Kentucky smile.

"Howdy, Mr. Bryant. Weather nippy."

He looked about as put out as when we were wrestling on the ground. Surely he didn't want to pick up where we left off? Especially not with snow. Then I saw his trouble: his back wheel had slid off the road and lodged behind a rock. He was wedged in. Wasn't half surprising, the snow was frozen to a slickness that felt more ice pond than road. I got down and half-skated myself over to view the damage.

"Willy will hold your horse, and you and I get behind the wheel and lift it over the boulder. If we can get a grip, shouldn't be too bad."

Mr. Bryant hadn't even said howdy yet. Even Northerners polite enough to say howdy to the man who's helping you out of a ditch. I saw him working himself, breathing deep. Then his mouth got real grim like he suffering an attack of the appendix. He turned to me. "I thank you for your help."

I almost laughed but I keep it in. Getting so grown up, Mamma hardly recognize me. I thought Willy looked disappointed, like he'd been hoping for a rematch. "Hold the horse steady until we say go. Pull too soon, she'll rip the wheel right off."

Didn't go as easy as I'd predicted. Almost nothing ever does. For one thing, neither Mr. Bryant nor I could get a grip. The bank sloped down about three feet where he'd gone off and we kept sliding down ourselves. Only thing that kept Mr. Bryant's rig from going all the way down was the boulder. We'd both landed on our faces more than once—Miz Chiles see us now she'd think we'd been wrestling again. I looked over at Mr. Bryant's school suit. He dressed like a school teacher should, which I never had. Second set of clothes ruined in two days.

Imagine he held that against me, too.

"I'm gonna have to back my rig up. I got some rope to tie them together. You keep my horse steady. She's frisky so you got to watch her, Willy can't handle her. I've got to crawl on my belly since we can't stand up. I'll just dig out that boulder. Thank the Lord Buster—he's the fellow that lent me this rig—put just about everything in the back that anybody need. Soon as I dig that boulder out and tumble it down, your rig's gonna want to follow so you got to pull hard, Joe."

I waited for him to raise his eyebrows at the Joe, but I give the man credit. He didn't flinch. Needed to put in that Joe. Can't grow up all at once, Mamma.

I'd just started digging at the boulder when I spotted some riders almost galloping about a half mile off. About three wagons clipping along behind them, too, going way too fast for the way this road was slicked up. I doubt they saw us. Wasn't anything around them but open fields and we were backed up to a grove of trees—blended right into them. Our two buggies took up almost the whole highway so there was a good danger they might plow right into us. I threw my shovel down and scrambled up to the road. There was a big bend in the road about halfway between us. If Willy ran across the field, he could get to them as they rounded it—they'd have to slow down at the curve or go flying into the meadow.

"Willy, Willy, run to that bend there. Warn them to slow down. Quick, quick."

Mr. Bryant—Joe—or I would of been flat on our faces if we tried to cross that snow-covered grass, but Willy flew like he had skates on, like he'd been raised a Dutch boy instead of Fayette Country colored. He made it in plenty of time. I saw them pull up and listen to him. They looked over at us. I waved.

They didn't wave back. Should of said something to me. Mamma right about Kentucky polite and country people got it worse than any. But at the time I thinking a group of men would solve our problem a lot quicker than me trying to dig up a boulder in frozen Kentucky ground.

I heard them shouting even when they was a half mile off. The shouting got louder as they got closer. When they disappeared for a few minutes as they rounded the bend, I finally made out what they were saying. I looked over at Mr. Bryant.

"Goebel? They shouting Goebel? Something happen to Goebel?"

"Maybe the legislature finally do the right thing and elect him governor."

My heart sank. I sure hoped not. I didn't say anything more to Mr. Bryant. I should of known: a colored Democrat.

We waited for the riders and the wagons to appear. I don't know what made me reach for the gun right before they showed. Mr. Bryant's eyes got wider as I tucked it under my coat but he didn't say anything. Willy didn't see. He was still halfway coming back from the curve. Taking his time. I wanted to wave to him to stay where he was but he wasn't looking at me.

The riders trotted up first. They made way for the wagons which pulled up the last moment, almost touching my rig. They were a crowd. I counted around twenty white men— not a number two colored men and a boy want to meet on a country road. Meet anywhere. Something happen to white men when they get into groups. I see'd two or three fellows I recognized from the country store in the summer. Used to nod howdy to each other.

They weren't nodding howdy now. They all looked mad.

"What we got here?" A tall skinny fellow stood up in the front wagon. Willy must of told them what happened but they still looked surprised. I heard a last shout of Goebel before it got silent. The fellow spit out tobacco juice onto the snow. It lay like a yellow finger on the white surface. "Why you niggers blocking the road?"

The man sitting next to him—short fellow who'd been shouting Goebel—spoke up.

"Maybe they stopped to celebrate Goebel's shooting. Happy about that, ain't you? All you niggers hate Goebel."

These boys sure done a good job overcoming that Kentucky politeness. I felt Mr. Bryant stiffen next to me. He didn't hear that kind of talk too often. We might both be colored, but sometimes I wondered if fellows like Joe and I lived in the same world. I saw Willy almost to us. *Lord, keep him off*, I prayed. *Hear me, Jesus.*

"Something happen to Goebel?" I said to the man. He spit again. Must of stuffed his mouth full. Evil stuff, tobacco, Mamma calls it. Stain everything around it.

"That's Governor Goebel to you, boy. Soon as the legislature get off its ass and do what they should of done a month ago." He looked at us up and down. "That's a fancy rig you driving, boy. Fancy filly, too." He looked over at Mr. Bryant's rig. Didn't impress him much. Turned back to me.

"You steal it, boy? We catch ourselves a couple of horse thieves?"

"That's the colored school teacher. Both of them." One of my nodding acquaintances from the school finally spoke up.

The skinny fellow shook his head. "Two nigger school teachers. What you doing here? Holding a convention? I heard about them colored conventions—you all get together and pretend you as good as white men."

"Better," said the short fellow next to him.

"That's right, better." He turned to spit again but he'd run out of juice. Hadn't stuffed it full enough. Nothing came out but air. He scraped his throat till he got the spit he needed. He lay another yellow line on the snow. He kept looking at the rig. Its black wheels shone bright against the snow.

"They must pay nigger school teachers real good to buy a rig like that." All twenty men were looking at it, none of them could of afforded it. Top of the line. I wished Buster given me something raggedy. Though I gloried in it.

"Not mine. Borrowed it." Just then Willy reached us. He climbed into the back of the wagon. "Taking the boy to work at John Fielding's place. He expecting us soon. In a hurry."

Willy looked at me confused but I willed him silent. Colored boys learn to read signs like that early on. He kept quiet. I could see the skinny fellow wasn't buying it, but the short fellow next to him changed the subject.

"What you think about that, boy? Goebel getting shot. I bet you happy."

Mr. Bryant been silent the whole time, like he knew it wasn't time for one of his or Mr. Russell's speeches about Negro uplift. But he spoke up now.

"That is terrible, news, sir. Terrible news. I voted for Mr. Goebel. I hope and pray that the shooting is not fatal. I know he will make a splendid governor. A splendid governor."

Only thing grate a poor white man's nerves worse than a Negro speaking like he some actor talking Shakespeare is a Negro talking about who he voted for. Even if he voted the right way. Only right way for a Negro to vote is no way.

You gonna get us all lynched, I'm thinking.

All twenty white men stared at Mr. Bryant for a good ten seconds. Maybe more. Then the skinny fellow turned back to me.

"Who'd you vote for?"

"Not twenty one yet. I'm too young to vote."

"You're too black to vote," said the short fellow.

Second time I been told that. Must be a saying among the white folk.

"Who'd you vote for if you could?" The skinny fellow wasn't letting it go.

"The best man. I'm an independent."

Well, I knew it was the wrong answer soon as I said it. Independent. An independent colored man choosing the best man. About half of them twenty white men flinched like I was Deputy Sheriff Siebrecht hitting them with a whip.

"Let's get going—we need to be in Frankfort," one fellow in a back wagon yelled. "Get them nigger wagons out of the way."

And before I knowed it, those twenty fellows done solved our problem just like I knew they could. Rolled both wagons over onto their sides, shiny black wheels busted, corn meal spread like a winter feast for the black birds.

"Don't know if that fellow's gonna let you borrow any more fancy rigs when he gets this one back," the skinny fellow yelled at me as they careened on down the road, going way too fast for the conditions. Break your neck going like that.

The good Lord willing.

I felt a rage in me I wasn't about to grow myself out of. Same rage I felt when Miz Chiles got whipped. When Tommy got shot. When they ran poor Eddie off his horse and crushed him. My filly started to pull back, raising her front legs like she was gonna rear up. My arms were shaking. I was spooking her. Willy was looking at me, like he was more afraid of me than the white men. I took a breath. I steadied my arms into steel rods. The filly still trembled but she was calming. I smiled at Willy.

"It's gonna be alright. Don't worry."

We sent him off to get help. Mr. Bryant helped collect the corn meal—wasn't much the worse for wear. Had to scare off a couple birds. One man's famine another man's feast. Or a bird's. Mr. Bryant didn't say much. Both of us felt too bruised for words. I looked at him in his ruined school suit standing next to his ruined rig, both of us soothing our fillies as best we could.

He still a Negro in the South for all his Shakespeare tones, I thought. I looked over the fields, Willy just a black dot against the white meadow. His daddy and the other men come soon. Don't know if Mr. Bryant make it to school after all. He kept whispering to his filly. Wonder if he talked Shakespeare to her. Or if he just speak that colored talk—not proper English at all. I shook the thought away. Old Joe and I ain't never gonna be friends. But I reckon we live in the same world after all.

One thing: the skinny fellow wrong about Buster being upset. He upset but not at me.

"Oh," he say after I told him my story, "white men. Worse than tornadoes, white men. Tornadoes just come spring time. You never know when white men gonna show up."

CHAPTER 30

Maria Lulu Benjamin, March 15, 1900, Lexington, Kentucky

"You cannot expect spring to arrive simply because the calendar leaf turns from February," Robert tells me sternly as if I am an unreasonable child. I stared out the window at the frozen wasteland of our yard. The doctor—and Robert—had forbidden me to go outside. I felt like a prisoner. "Kentucky," he continues, "Lexington at least, is not Alabama."

Not St. Kitts, either, I almost tell him. I know that. But February, even January, was so mild. And then this ambush—that's what it felt like. This frozen mush. This ice coating the windows and the trees.

"We will take a trip to see your father when spring truly arrives—we will take the children. It will do you good."

I smiled at the thought. I didn't tell Robert that when spring comes finally to Lexington, it will already be summer in Alabama—already hot with a heat Kentuckians cannot conceive of. His thought is sweet, though I know he will not, cannot, find the time for such a trip. I smiled at the thought of the trip doing me good.

If I cannot leave the house to see the world, I will invite the world in. I have asked Miss Lizzie Price to tea, the teacher at the school that the African Methodist Episcopal School operates. Robert half disapproves. "Private schools will not reach our children," he says. But Emma Bisou has asked me to determine whether our club should help this school. And I would like to talk to Miss Price. After last year's disastrous school board election, we need help from ladies out in the county. And Noah speaks so highly of her.

She was so much younger than I expected—perhaps twenty. Noah's age. The March wind whipped in through the open door like an uninvited guest seizing its chance. Sheila struggled to push it shut again. Miss Price turned to help her.

"Oh, where's our spring? Jesus, this *is* March, isn't it? You think it's still February?"

I was startled. Someone else might think Miss Price a blasphemer but I recognized her immediately: a Jesus talker. I hadn't heard one since Alabama. Never one so young and pretty.

"Please, Miss Price, come by the fire. Sheila, please hurry Miss Price some tea."

"Oh, yes, tea, Sheila. Something warm inside us. Let me help you." Miss Price is ready to roll up her sleeves.

"No, no," Sheila says and laughs. I feel a little jealous. Of whom? I shake it off.

"Sheila won't even let *me* in the kitchen, Miss Price. I'm afraid you're going to have to sit and wait like the rest of us." And play the lady, not easy for a colored girl from the country. I should know. I smiled at her and steered her into the parlor. We chatted of acquaintances—the Reverend Jones and his wife. Miss Emma Bisou. Noah. I watched her closely. She was not so young as she first appeared. She knew that she was being watched.

"It must have been dreadful—that whole affair at Cadentown. Were you arrested?"

"I have the bald spot at the back of my scalp to show, where the sheriff dragged me by braid. Just a little bald spot, thank you, Jesus. My sister, Suzie, is the only one who's seen it. But I didn't get a whip across my face. Didn't get a scar like a cross that everybody sees. Then those men came in and took our school anyway. But we'll get it back. Jesus, you better be there! We'll get it back."

She shuddered at the memory—a different shudder than the one she had brought in with the cold. No playfulness now in the shake of her limbs. Her face grew stern, her jaw clenching. A young warrior. An Amazon. Her black hair shone as if she'd woven sparkles into it, her thick braid rounded into a bun now, so thick and abundant I couldn't imagine the bald spot.

Her hair was all too much for the small hat she wore, a cloche that looked new for all the wear the March weather had inflicted. Her attempt at being a lady, I guessed. It reminded me of my silly shoes. Her hair had begun to spill out from the hat. It would all collapse before too long.

"Oh, goodness. I knew this hat was the most ridiculous thing—Suzie made me buy it." She pulled it off and her hair fell around her stern young face just as Sheila returned with the tea. Sheila rushed to help her but the hair had a mind of its own—it would not be contained.

"Oh, leave it, Sheila. It's Jesus' spite on me for spending all that money on this silly thing. Vanity. Serves me right."

She flung the hat in front of her and I could not help it, Sheila, either. We both laughed hard though we feared to hurt her feelings, but after a second, Miss Price—Lizzie—joined in.

"Oh, Miss Price, Jesus is not that hard on us. And the hat is precious, truly. If I had your hair, I certainly would have been tempted."

She made no response. It was time to move on from the hat.

"We need your help, Miss Price."

She looked surprised.

"My help? I thought I was here to solicit your help—your club's help—for our school. I've brought a list of things we need. Pencils. And paper. I don't understand how we go through as much paper as we do." She looked flustered, more than with the hat. She dove into the bag she carried with her, a carrier bag big enough to stuff a whole class's papers into.

"That's wonderful. Please leave your list with me if you can. I am sure that among all our ladies, we will be able to fill all those needs. It's other help we require."

She stopped fussing and waited for me to explain.

"We need your help to take back your schools, the ones in Cadentown and Briar Hill, I mean. All of our schools. You have thirty students and hardly room for more in your church. But it is the public schools that must rescue our children."

She looked confused. "Are you saying I should leave our school and teach in the public school?"

"I hope you will someday. But you help many now. You set a high standard for the public schools. Mr. Benjamin and I hope to send our boy, Charlie, to your school when he's older."

I wasn't being clear but I liked the way she waited—calm, expectant. She *calmed* me. I understood now, understood why Noah's eyes no longer had the hunger in them when we met, a hunger that crawled at me. He was a son now, a brother. As it should be. I was glad.

"We want your help out in the county, and the ladies who led the gathering at Cadentown. We must vote in a Republican school board. Take back all the schools that those men took from you. From us."

The blast of cold air almost blew over our tea cups—it stirred the fire to new heights. Robert and Noah sounded as if they had crashed into the front hall, as if they had sailed their boats with a thump onto the sands. The wind had gotten stronger; it blew through the house until the door was finally shut. Robert's lilt traveled with the wind into the parlor.

"The only time I miss the islands—wretched places. But such soft breezes. Not this miserable blowing."

"What about hurricanes, sir?" Noah was laughing just as Miss Price had. Such fun. Only I feared the icy wind cutting into my lungs.

"Yes, Robert," I called from the parlor, "what about those hurricanes?"

Robert smiled in recognition when he spotted Miss Price. Noah's eyes glowed like he'd been given an unexpected gift.

"A hurricane is God's broom. Sweeps everything clean and we start anew. This icy blast is just miserable winter clinging on. Like the school board I imagine you and Miss Price are discussing. Billy Klair and company. Time for them, and winter, to be gone."

If Miss Price was surprised that Robert and I discussed strategy, she did not let on. I liked that, too, about her.

Our parlor, so to speak, was a small room right off the entry way. Robert is not a big man, but Noah is. Four felt like a crowd; it disrupted what little formality I had managed. I let it go. The men squeezed in, their knees almost touching ours, and Sheila—somehow—managed tea and scones for us all, the small table angled between us like a small life raft. My illness had isolated her, too. She was happy that the world had taken refuge in our parlor. So to speak.

Noah, too. So happy. He picked up the cloche from his seat and puzzled at it a second. Miss Price snatched it from his hands like he was a pesky younger brother touching her things. But he kept smiling, kept looking between the two of us. To my shame, I felt a twinge of jealousy. I shook it off.

We sat there, the four of us, and plotted the campaign to take our schools back—Briar Hill and Cadentown and Russell School right here in town. Plotted ways to save our children. Plotted in a space as tight as an embrace. Noah looked at us in turn and each look was a caress. I knew he loved Robert. I knew he was fond of me. Miss Price pushed her rebellious hair from her eyes and let it be. When Noah bent his head, she lifted hers. I caught her eye. I smiled.

What could I do?

Time for the old school board to go, we all agreed, and spoke of the lady who had been whipped, Mrs. Chiles, and others who would struggle with them. I grew silent and listened. Robert and Noah could explain it all so much better than I could. Colored women united, Robert said, and Miss Price glowed in agreement. White women, too, I wanted to add, remembering the dream we had shared in Ashland with Madeline McDowell Breckinridge and Sophonisba. When was that? October a year ago. Women, colored and white together, for our children. *We must stand together.*

"White women, too," I finally whispered for the wind that had brought them strength had taken mine. But Noah heard me—he always heard me.

"Yes, Maria's right. We need white allies. We need each other. We can take the school board but we need white allies."

Together. Black and white together. Sometimes that dream seems further and further away. I was stronger then.

Sheila kept bringing in more tea, whispering that she'd put a something extra in the gentleman's tea because, "Really, gentlemen can only take so much tea. And it's so cold out. Would the young miss like something, too, to warm her?"

No, Lizzie smiled, she needed to go back to teach and wouldn't that be something if the Reverend Jones or, worse, Mrs. Jones smelled liquor on her breath?

"Jesus and your tea have warmed my heart."

Robert startled when she said that. He frowned as if Miss Price had made some social gaffe, mentioning Jesus out loud. Too country church for Robert. Noah didn't flinch at all. I imagined he was used to it. I saw the tiny bald spot on Lizzie's head as we finally managed her hair back to the top of her head, a light brown dot in the middle of a black island. I wanted to touch it, to gently caress it. A small battle scar.

I did not carry Miss Price's Jesus with me. I never spoke His name out loud except on formal occasions, but I murmured to Him, now, under my breath.

Protect her, Jesus, and Noah, too. Cover their bald spots with Your warm breath, even in March's icy winds.

"What did you say, Maria?" Robert asked.

"Oh," I said, "I think spring's finally on it way. I feel a little warmth trying to sneak out from all the cold."

CHAPTER 31

Judge Frank Bullock, July 15, 1900, Lexington, Kentucky

My office is the wonder of the new courthouse and the courthouse the wonder of the town. Its four large corner windows face two directions overlooking what used to be the slave market but is now the courthouse square. It's quite a pleasant little park, though a bit empty most days. My windows go from floor to ceiling. Designed, the architect told me, to capture every passing breeze, cooling rich and poor alike.

Or to suffocate us all together—democracy's revenge. No breeze has been felt in Lexington since the middle of June. And, of course, no one is in the square. What sensible person would be? I tell Grace I can remember the slave market, right below these windows. Perhaps that's why it seems so odd to see it vacant. Every inch was taken up then by slave and seller. Grace wonders how I can recall those days—I could not have been more than four or five. But I remember. One hot day in particular. Hot, but everyone dressed. Even little boys were made to dress for town in those days. Little boys of good families, at least. Not little ruffians, of course. And not slaves. I remember being very surprised at how few clothes they wore—some naked—even the women.

Father had taken me to the slave market, of course. He took me several times. Wanted me to see it before it all disappeared, for everyone knew that slavery was ending. Even the idiot buyers snatching up their "bargains" must have known that they were buying a rapidly diminishing commodity, though their greed kept a strangle hold around their common sense. Common sense so often yields to greed.

What a messy, stifling business that was, what a trial for buyer and seller alike. I remember envying the slaves in their undress, my clothes a misery on me. Though even the babe I was could see that their misery was worse. I looked up at father.

"Why don't they have clothes?" I asked him.

"Clothes are extra," Major Bullock told me, splendid in his own uniform. Ladies and small boys agreed: Morgan's Raiders were the most dashing of all our soldiers. "Besides, you need to see the merchandise. Lots of traders in this town try to pass off a sick nigger for a healthy buck. Look before you buy. You remember that, son."

And so I looked. Father wasn't buying. He was not a fool. But he looked, too. A young girl was trying to cover her breasts. Mother would have died if she had known where Father was taking me. But they weren't breasts on a woman, Father would have told her.

Just part of the merchandise.

Oh, the humidity is unbearable—each breath feels as if one were sucking air through a wet towel. And all these massive windows simply glare massive sunshine. The whole place is a mausoleum designed to entomb us alive, as if we were some Pharaoh's slaves sent before our time to wait on him in the afterlife.

"Please, dear," Grace urged me. "Come with me to the mountains. It must be cooler there."

But I am stuck here in this damn town in these robes that would defeat any cooling breeze that dared show itself. The more clothes, the more dignity. That is why the slave had none. My dignity is such I am about to suffer a heat stroke.

An election is coming—when do we not have an election coming? And my dual role as judge and Democratic official demands my presence. Or so says Billy, and, as even Grace acknowledges, Billy Klair's opinion carries more and more sway these days. Certainly more than the wishes of a spouse or the lure of the cooling mountains. He was in my office now. Even Billy cannot look cool in this weather. He was smiling, though I was not fooled. He was not happy.

"Well, Judge," he said, standing by an open window to no purpose, looking down at the square, "soon the niggers will be selling us down there like we used to sell them. I'm still young enough to get a fair price, but I don't know that you'll bring much."

"I wasn't aware, Billy," each word an effort, "that slavery for either race was still an option. But do judges sell for less than state legislators these days?"

He laughed. "Depends on the judge. And on the legislator."

"Well, then, Billy, I'm sure you'd sell for more."

He didn't answer. People didn't stand up when he entered the room or call him "your honor." And his clothes were casual, almost slapdash. He would have been considered a ruffian in my youth. Those who don't know him might still consider him one.

But we both knew who was worth more.

"I'm serious, Judge. It might not come to being sold in Cheapside, but things are turning 'round—and not to our benefit, either. You see this paper?"

He showed me the copy of *The Morning Democrat*. Since *The Morning Herald* had become less partisan, the slack had to be taken up by someone. He read it aloud like he was reading a Longfellow poem:

> Shall we have men whose party is mainly composed of Negroes
> to fill our offices, or shall we have men who are representatives of
> white men to fill them?

I looked at him. "Billy, I have been reading that same line my whole life and as you kindly pointed out just a moment ago, I'm no spring chicken. Every election since the Fifteenth Amendment was passed, white hysteria shows its pasty face."

Billy actually looked offended. "You ain't a nigger-lover, are you, Judge?"

"No, Billy. But I *ain't* a nigger-hater, either."

Billy was smiling again. "Oh, me neither, Judge. Me neither. I pal around with bucks all the time—they know how to have more fun than a church full of Irish men. But you know there's places they don't belong. You know it yourself. And Judge, I wouldn't call whites pasty-faced around too many other fellows. They might get the wrong idea. I know we're always worrying about something, but I'm telling you it's serious, now. Serious. Know how many colored women registered to vote? About twice as many as white women. We're gonna lose the school board."

"You'll figure something out, Billy."

Billy not smiling was a startling sight—something missing—as if he'd shed his derby or the cigar butt perennially stuck in his mouth.

"I am figuring things out—I can always shave a close thing. But two to one—that's something you can't really shave. Need a meat cleaver then, and that gets messy."

He sat in one of the four upholstered chairs scattered around my office. I watched carefully where he put his stogie. Grace would have a fit if he burned a hole in the chair. But he took care. Billy only looked casual. He always took great care.

"But that ain't what I'm worried about this election. Even if we lose the school board in the city, we'll keep the county. And I got plans for the women. Not this year, though. Frankfort's still wrapped up in knots over the Goebel mess. Least we ended with a Democrat, though Beckman ain't much. No, that's not what I'm worried about. It's colored men, not colored women—or any women—that's keeping me up nights. And you know who's the cause of me tossing and turning till Katie's just about ready to toss my tail right out of bed so she can get a little sleep herself? Your old friend, Robert O'Hara Benjamin."

I winced. I couldn't help it. I felt a deep abiding distaste for Benjamin. And he seemed everywhere. In my courtroom, at the race track. In the newspapers. His own and others.

"He's not running for Congress again?"

"No." Billy's smile came back. "I wish he was. Waste all that energy he got so much of. He's doing worse, really getting colored men ready to register. Got people helping him, ready to register bucks in almost every precinct in town. Even precincts that ain't seen a colored face ever."

"Irishtown, you mean?"

"Yep. Irishtown but the 20th, too, and the 19th. Coloreds taking over. We're gonna have to scramble to keep the city. Some precincts we can still shave—delay the voting. Lose a few votes. Challenge some others. Other places we gonna have to do some meat cleaving."

I was very uncomfortable with this kind of talk. Billy knew that.

"These are my chambers, Billy." I pulled my robes around me as I were chilled. "My chambers do not have the full official distinction of the courtroom, but they are not the party's backroom, let alone a saloon. You must not bring up subjects like this here again."

Billy was almost always respectful. Always called me Judge. But his eyes grew hard at my admonition. He stuck his stogie back into his mouth and relit it. He took a breath.

"Let's get something straight, Frank. This 'subject' is power and how to keep it. It ain't *my* business; it's *our* business. And I'll bring up the subject here or any goddamned place I choose."

He let that sink in for a few moments, puffing on his stogie as if that were the only task at hand. Then he smiled at me.

"The problem, Judge, ain't this election. That's what wrong with most politicians. They're always thinking about the election right around the corner. Most times, ain't much you can do about that. It's the next election you got to be thinking about. Benjamin ain't just getting colored men registered, he's getting them to think they can win. He's getting them excited. And he's right. Coloreds almost half this town. Put them together with the pasty-faced good government crowd and they got the town. Might get us a colored mayor. A colored county judge."

A colored county judge. I looked down at the square. I tried to imagine what Major Bullock would think of that idea. I pulled the robes away from my throat. Billy had gotten my attention. I felt a bit of what I had labeled white hysteria.

"It won't come to that, Billy."

"Why not? He's a smart man, Benjamin. Your kind, Judge. Never thought a German-Mick like me would ever make it, never be worth even thinking about. When word got around that I was running against Colonel Roger Williams of the Iroquois Hunt Club, he just laughed. Everybody laughed. I ain't bitter. I'm glad they laughed. But the Polacks I told about it didn't laugh. Neither did the Micks."

We both turned as a flash of lighting struck across a blue sky. Not a cloud in the sky. Heat lighting. It hadn't rained in weeks.

"I don't like the coloreds. We got to live with them, but I don't like them. I imagine the same way your kind don't really like us. But I ain't making the same mistake you and the Colonel made. I ain't laughing. The coloreds ain't any dumber than the Micks I go to church with or the Germans I drink with. Ain't much dumber than you, Your Honor. And with a man like Benjamin leading them, no reason they can't take over this town. Or enough of it to make the rest of us real uncomfortable. All I had was some sorry Micks and Germans and a few Polacks. And he's an educated man, Benjamin, something I ain't never laid claim to."

A thunder clap snapped through the air. So strange in a clear sky. We needed rain badly, not just to break the heat. Our bluegrass was already turning brown.

"What do you intend to do, Billy? As long as we're talking plainly, I will tell you: I will not countenance killing."

"Killing? Whoa, Judge. Nobody's talking killing. We're not Republicans, conspiring to gun down the governor. We're just fellows meaning to help Benjamin remember who he is and where he is. We ain't Alabama, but we're still South. We got to bring him down—and that might mean a little roughing up. But nothing more than that. The coloreds getting too comfortable in this town, going places they never went to before. They're crossing boundaries like they ain't there clear as day. Look how they carried on about the street car bill. Now they're squawking about colored teachers getting less pay than white ones." Billy shook his head. He was shocked, looking, for all the world, a bit like Grace did the two times he's graced our parlor. "Can't have that, Your Honor. And when they come crying to the court—when Benjamin comes crying to court or heckling you in his paper, or the other papers—you got to do your job, Judge. Our job."

I felt a breeze finally, a gust blowing into the office so strong and sudden, it blew Billy's stogie out. He murmured a small cuss as he relit it. But the wind just made the heat worse. A hot wind. A bitter wind. A wind with no hint of rain, no balm of Gilead.

Our job. Keeping power. Keeping ourselves wrapped in our robes even if the robes made it hard to breathe. Only a slave got to strip himself naked, only a slave was permitted to let her breasts hang freely in the afternoon heat.

"I'll do what I can, Billy." I looked down on the square and could see Father there in his splendid uniform. His body man, Toby, always kept him primed, prepared to lead a cavalry charge. Or a cotillion. A man should be ready to do both. He'd look at me, always a bit skeptical I'd be up to either task. "I'll do what I can."

CHAPTER 32

Noah Webster, September 21, 1900, Lexington, Kentucky

Lizzie turns twenty-one tomorrow, old enough to register in October. "A younger woman," I tell her. I turned twenty-one earlier this month.

She gave me a look she gives me a lot, like I'm not being serious enough even when I need to be. Or like she's thinking about what I've said even when it ain't nothing. Mamma says she's ballast.

"That make me flotsam?" I say.

"No," Mamma says. "Not flotsam. Just someone who needs a little ballast."

Miss Price looks hard at me before she flicks me a tiny smile.

"I don't feel young. I haven't felt young for a long time."

I want to tease her out of the mood. Sometimes I think she wants me to. Other times, Mamma says just to listen. "Keep your mouth closed and your ears open," is the way she put it.

I'm trying.

"You know where you register?"

"Miss Fannie Anderson at 53 Georgetown Street."

"A white lady?"

"I imagine so. Printed in *The Leader*. *The Leader* doesn't usually label colored ladies 'Miss'."

The children were running around the small grassed area behind the church. Well, it started out grassy—their boots and shoes more or less reduced everything down to dirt. The two flower beds, too, that some church ladies had planted along the edge of the carriage path, yielded now mostly to the power of trampling feet. I apologized to one of the ladies one day as she tried to rescue some rose mallow, their faded pink petals drooping onto the ground.

"Oh," the lady shushed me. "Children got to run somewhere, cooped up in those little rooms all day. Besides, we never get enough sun. Look how spindly they all look, stretching their necks out till they almost all stem. Children almost a mercy. Put the sorry things out of their misery."

Just then Willy dashed right over the flower border, the border I been yelling at them all morning to watch out for. Not only him, but two boys and a girl chasing two inches behind him. What was left of those rose mallow was gone. Smashed. Thin necks broken. The lady and I just stared down at them like mourners over an open grave.

"Well," the lady said, laying down her little shovel. "Rest in peace."

I worried about Willy when he first came. Town children just love to taunt a country boy and Willy was country. Everything surprised him, everything was new. But Willy was more than country and the children saw that. He laughed at their teasing. He'd never been teased for being country before—never been around anyone who wasn't country. Well, except for me, of course.

Before long everybody forgot about where he came from. He was Willy. I began the stories again about all the colored heroes and soon Willy got them playing them, running around the playground freeing slaves. I don't think anybody mentioned slaves to town children before this. Oh, they heard about them. Grandfolks born slaves. But it was shameful, not something anybody talked about.

Town boys wouldn't play a woman, though, not even a daredevil one like Harriet Tubman. That confused Willy some at first, but he just shrugged.

"Guess that's what they do in town," is all he said. He didn't really mind. He got to play Sojourner as often as he wanted. I thought for sure he'd come to grief over that but he didn't.

Almost came to grief myself with the Reverend Jones about colored heroes.

"I do not think Professor Russell would approve of taking valuable school time for history that is not in the curriculum."

"Professor Russell's not even the head of the Russell School since the new school board kicked him out. We're a private school anyway; he never was head of us." I was walking on thin ice. Lizzie gave me an eye. The Reverend Jones was one of just about three respectable colored men in town who admired Green Pinckney Russell. I don't know why especially since he—or his toadies—had slandered every colored woman voter in the county. Called them illiterate. Immoral. Worse than immoral. Said a whole slew of them was prostitutes.

But Mamma's always warning me not to jump into fights I got no business fighting, at least not fighting them until I had to. Lizzie giving me the eye, like Mamma sent her special. Ballast.

"Of course, Professor Russell's a fine educator." Lizzie opened her eyes wide. I was going too far. I turned away from her so I couldn't see her face. "But, Reverend, do you see anybody who looks like us in the curriculum? I'm just asking because I know we were there— we didn't spring out of nowhere—but far as I can find, we weren't there. The way the history books tell it, the Civil War didn't even have much to do with slavery or us. Now I know you were born a slave, Reverend. I know it because I know you forty-four years old. You almost ten years old before you free—1866." I could feel Lizzie's eyes on me but I kept my back turned from her. "I want to say to the children, 'you know when the Reverend Jones was your age, he still a slave. My mamma, too, and my daddy. Slaves longer here in Kentucky than just about any place in the whole United States because Kentucky didn't have to free them until the Thirteenth Amendment was passed. Kentucky didn't want to free them and didn't free them until it had to.'

"Don't you think the children need to know that, Reverend, as much as they need to know about George Washington and the cherry tree? Though that cherry tree's real important—takes up three pages in the curriculum—maybe Frederick Douglass is somebody they need to know about, too."

The Reverend Jones gave me a slant eye with that stuff about the cherry tree. Sure wasn't gonna turn around to see what Lizzie was doing. Already seeing Mamma in my mind's eye. But I give the Reverend credit. He took a breath before he answered.

"As long as you leave sufficient time for their other subjects: mathematics, reading, gospel studies. I see no harm and, perhaps, it might even do some good."

Might even do some good. I smiled and nodded and said nothing. Nothing. Didn't have to turn to feel Lizzie's shoulders relax behind me.

I only could come into the school two mornings a week anyway. Mr. Benjamin grabbed all my time. He was making a push, preaching in the saloons and arguing in the pulpits. They listened to him everywhere, but they liked him better in the saloons. "You need to come register to vote." And he'd wave his finger at the drinkers. "You might as well sell your children as sell your vote. For that's what you're doing. Selling your children's future."

He thundered from the pulpit. "You think you're good people because you go to church? You think you're respectable because white folks say you are? You're not respectable till you make them respect you. Vote. All of you. Men and women."

"Make sure your vote counts," he told saloon and church. "Make sure you count. It's a new century. We're done with the nineteenth century. We're tired of slavery and separate coaches. You want to change things? You want to keep them from getting worse? We're half the vote in Fayette County. More than half when some good white folks join us. They're few in number but they're enough if you vote.

"Vote. Vote. Vote."

Oh, he got everybody excited. Preachers who I know hated him more ways than a Methodist hates sin couldn't keep from amening him. He was our Moses, our own Harriet, leading the way over all those little Ohios keeping us from freedom. He was our jockey, our Eddie riding Bluegrass Funeral the home stretch to freedom. Only this time, Bluegrass wasn't just galloping, he was a jumping horse, too, leaping over all those fences Fayette County keeps putting up.

It wasn't just me Mr. Benjamin had working like he was determined to wipe out sleep time. He had Lizzie walking the neighborhoods. Maria, too—past her strength, I tell Mr. Benjamin, but he just waved that away.

"She's almost twenty years younger than I am," as if that meant anything. But you don't argue with Mr. Benjamin.

People were getting excited. Of course, freedom didn't come easy. Harriet Tubman could of told us that. Plug-uglies all over this town. Mamma said don't call them that. "Just poor Irish boys," she says, "just like you a poor colored boy."

"I don't go looking to beat up poor Irish boys," I tell her, but she wave me off.

Billy Klair's people getting nervous. The cops real nervous, like they seeing colored patrolmen in their future. Somebody always looking for a fight. Got in more than one myself. Mamma takes each bruise personally, fussing at me for not getting away. She make me raise my shirt and spot a big ugly map of a bruise where I got whacked with a baseball bat. I heard her gasp.

"Stay away from them plug-uglies," she say.

"Two of them standing right in front of me and swinging at my face, Mamma."

"What you doing in that neighborhood? Coloreds don't live on that block."

"Coloreds live two blocks over and they vote there."

She shake her head but Mamma excited, too. She heard Mr. Benjamin speaking, preaching at the Reverend Pickering's own church. She just wary, too. Mamma always got something she worrying about.

"Somebody gonna shoot at that man. Hope the bullet misses him. Hope it don't find you."

"Nobody's gonna shoot Mr. Benjamin, Mamma." I stopped worrying about that long ago. "They don't kill coloreds like Mr. Benjamin. Just poor saps like Tommy. Or Eddie. They know we all tear down the town if they shoot Mr. Benjamin."

Mamma just look at me like I ten years old. But she don't say anything. Mamma knows how to keep her mouth shut, too. Especially when she's wrong and she knows it.

It a new century like Mr. Benjamin say. I watch Willy lead the children to freedom, full of hope, the city children shouting out the names of colored heroes, names they never heard before. They ain't weighed down by the past. Willy's leading them to the future.

I can't help it. Mr. Benjamin make me feel just like that, full of hope. I see Lizzie swing that braid of hers, talking to women old enough to be her granny. Telling them about the vote and how we're gonna change the schools, change the city. Change the world. I see Maria barely able to get the strength to stand but finding it to walk up and down the streets, talking to mothers just like her. The women look at Lizzie and Maria like they creatures from another land, but I see their faces light up. They can't help it. Grannies who've watched their babies cry for food, who never had anything they could call their own—not even their own selves—hear of this thing they owned called a vote now. A vote that let them choose who run the schools, schools they never saw or even thought of when they were young.

They couldn't help it. Their hard old faces pulled in when Lizzie or Maria started talking to them, but they just couldn't help it. Hope started to relax the deep lines around their mouths, hope worked like fingers soothing their brows. Hope made them think things might change. Could change. Would change.

Even Mamma. "Well, don't go on those blocks by yourself. Take a friend. Take two friends. I don't believe in fighting. But when somebody swings two fists at you, you swing three back."

"That don't sound Christian, Mamma."

For a moment, she looked like she might swing a fist at me. "It's not Christian, but even Jesus whipped the money changers out of the temple. I'm not saying the voting booth's a temple. It's not the way to salvation. But in Lexington, Kentucky, it's the way we're gonna save ourselves."

Chapter 33

Noah Webster, October 2, 1900, Lexington, Kentucky

Mamma woke me up, shaking the bed. Shaking herself.

"That boy Tom Blevins is dead." I looked dazed, not awake yet. "The jockey. You know him."

I remembered. A pal of Eddie's. One of his casket bearers.

"A horse accident?"

"No." Mamma looked down. "Shot at Showalter's saloon." The Showalters was one of Lexington's German gangs posing like a family. They owned a couple shoddy holes coloreds drank at. Cheapest whiskey in town. Roughest, too. Mamma didn't know saloons but she heard of Showalter's. The Reverend Pickering mentioned it just about every other Sunday. "Not even his fight. Just trying to keep another man from being shot—then got shot himself. His poor mamma."

"Who shot him?"

"One of the Showalters. Mose or John. Shot him for trying to keep one of them from shooting another man."

"A colored man?"

Mamma took her hands away from her face and looked at me.

"Of course a colored man. You don't get shot trying to save a white man. His poor mamma."

Get shot in Kentucky for just about anything. But I kept my mouth closed. Mamma was right. The odds go up when you're colored.

I told Mamma to wake me early—registration day. Didn't ask her to bang me awake with a hammer. I was gonna be walking all day with Mr. Benjamin. Felt worn out already. I looked out the window. Still dark, a trickle of light on the curtains from the candle Mamma left. I tried to picture Tom Blevins—a little fellow. All those jockeys little fellows. Had to lift his corner of Eddy's casket higher to keep it level with the rest of us. Showalter's saloon over by Goodloe and Warrock, a neighborhood folks stayed clear of. Especially after dark.

It was still after dark. Before the light at least. I carried the candle over to the basin so I could see my hands as I dipped them into the water. I cupped them full and splashed my face. I felt myself wake as the water rested on my eyes. Tom Blevins' face rose up in me. *What were you thinking, Tom? Interfering with a bullet meant for another colored man?*

Mamma was whipping up eggs and fatback and biscuits with porridge on the side—a Sunday breakfast and it just Tuesday. She was moving so fast you wouldn't know she was still shaking unless you knew that she didn't usually beat the porridge like it was a rug caked with six months' worth of dust. I sat down quiet.

"I thank Jesus every day you don't work at George Thomas no more. Them saloons are death-traps. I don't want you ever in one of them again. Ever. You got to promise me."

I kept quiet. Saloon about the only place a colored man got to sit easy in this town. Most times, leastways. If you stayed out of a dive like Showalter's. And when bullets weren't flying. But I wasn't gonna argue the point with Mamma. She turned away from the porridge. Just in time. It'd been beat to a froth, peaks whipped up like hands raised in surrender.

"You won't promise your mamma to stay out of saloons? Won't let her have a little peace?"

Mamma never did fight fair.

"He didn't get shot because he was in a saloon, Mamma. He got shot trying to save a colored man. I shouldn't try to save a colored man, Mamma?"

She looked hard at me, her spoon held over the pan of porridge, ready to attack again. "Noah Webster, you do what a man need to do to stay a man. Don't need to do none of that in a saloon."

She plopped my Sunday breakfast down then. "I'm going to Tom Blevins' house now. Try to do what I can for his mamma. Ain't nothing to do but sit there, but I'll do that. You think about what I said. Don't want no promise you can't keep—or won't keep. But I want that promise. You think about it."

She was gone then. I saw Miz Inez—the lady next door—leaving, too, joining up with Mamma. Miz Inez's boy, George, was sitting three bar stools away when the bullets started flying. That's about how fast news travels in this town. I imagine his mamma got him promising never to go there again, or any saloon. Probably didn't take too much urging. Bullets passing overhead a good argument.

"Thank Jesus none of them hit George," Mamma said. *Jesus want Tom Blevins shot instead?* I almost asked, but knew better.

Both women off to go sit with Tom Blevins' mamma. Not time enough to bring cooking. That'd come later. Just sitting and crooning. Just sitting and crooning.

Colored ladies real good at that. Got lots of practice.

Mr. Benjamin was waiting for me, tapping his foot as if I was late. The sun was just up, but filtered still. Trees still full of leaves, but starting to drop.

"You've heard the news about Tom Blevins?" He didn't even wait for my nod. "I passed a half dozen groups of men—colored and white. They're fixing to go after each other. We got to get over there quick."

I was confused. "We gonna try to stop the fight?"

Mr. Benjamin looked at me like a disappointed teacher.

"We're going to register those men. It'd take us all day to gather a third of those men. Showalter's saloon right in the center of the 19th Precinct. This is very good luck."

Not for Tom Blevins, I thought. But I didn't have time to think of him. Mr. Benjamin was halfway down the street. I scrambled to keep up with him. The precinct headquarters were over on Megowan and Coral. That whole area opened up to coloreds a few years ago. The powers-that-be pass the word and coloreds can move onto a block. Sometimes the powers close off a block and coloreds got to move. I asked Mr. Benjamin once about who decided all that. And why. He quizzed me like a schoolboy.

"Who's interested in housing?"

"Real estate people."

"That's right. And politicians who are beholden to them. And why?"

Didn't take much thought. "Money."

Mr. Benjamin just nodded. "Race just a way to get to the money for most of them."

Megowan was mostly colored now, though a lot of Irish still lived in the small homes pushed up against each other, as crowded as a streetcar at closing time. The Separate Streetcar Law was supposed to keep everybody separate but it didn't really. How you gonna keep separate when you practically sitting on each other's lap?

Nobody was separate on Megowan Street, either. Not yet anyway. Take a few years for the Irish and the Germans to move out. Kind of like Showalter's Saloon. Started out mostly German. But then the drinkers turned black and the whiskey turned sour.

Only the money stayed white. The money almost always stays white.

The Irish and Germans hated the coloreds moving in and hated the downtown crowd that let them move in. Would of moved out yesterday except most of them didn't have the ready money. And some of them had bought those sorry houses and were stuck. Coloreds moving in hurt their value considerably. Except to the coloreds.

Billy Klair said he'd turn that all around, send the coloreds back to where they used to live. Except the word is he owns about half the houses on Megowan, or his friends do. Somehow they make the money when everybody else is losing it.

We turned down Constitution Street. It's spitting distance away from all those shotguns over on Race Street but it's a different world. I've been up in the balcony at the Opera House. When they opened the curtains the crowd just gasped, even the white folks down below. They built a whole make-believe street. You knew it was cardboard and paint but you believed it anyway.

Constitution was like that—those homes so big and solid. But like they weren't real. So quiet. Streets I've lived on—streets most people live on in this town, white and colored—just spilling over with people. Homes too tiny to keep inside: too hot in the summer, too full of coal dust in the winter. Somebody always yelling at somebody. Neighbors ain't really neighbors. They know your business better than you know your own. I know more about the women George Inez seeing than he do, or as much. The whole neighborhood do—his mamma always yelling it out.

Mamma don't do that, but they know about me anyway. That's just the way it is.

But Constitution Street private. The windows shut. The doors closed. Spooks me a bit, to tell the truth. Like you walking through a graveyard.

Mr. Benjamin woke me up. "You are registering today also?"

"Yes sir. But in the 32nd."

"We'll go there in the afternoon."

We turned onto Race Street and ran into our first plug-uglies. About eight of them. I recognized a couple of cops but not in uniform. They carried their police bully clubs. A couple others had baseball bats—the poor man's billy club. I pointed to them.

"We need to get out of here, Mr. Benjamin."

"Why would we do that? We are citizens walking peacefully on a public sidewalk."

They spotted us then. Not just spotted us, they recognized us. "That's Benjamin! The nigger newspaper man." It was one of the cops dressed like a bullwhacker. He turned to the others. "He's always stirring up the niggers, trying to take over the town."

They started running towards us. Mr. Benjamin raised his head calmly, like I've seen him do before speaking to a difficult crowd. Like these plug-uglies were gonna stop and listen to him, calmly consider his points. I grabbed his arm.

"Mr. Benjamin, we got to run now. Run!"

They were half a block off and he still wasn't budging. Like he Martin Luther. *Here I stand.*

I couldn't run without him running so there I stood, too. *Sorry, Mamma,* I thought, *I'd run if I could.* I'd run if I could and still be a man.

They weren't a hundred yards away—so close I could almost smell them—that sick smell of sweat cooled and warmed up again. Or maybe that was me. It weren't Mr. Benjamin. He looked as cool as if he was sitting in a shaded park in May. "Men!" he shouted out, like *that* was gonna stop them. They did pull up a moment, like a herd of wild mustangs startled by a gun shot. But just a moment. They kept on stampeding right at us. *Oh, Jesus,* I prayed.

Mamma must have been praying, too. Jesus don't usually pay much heed to me. About twenty colored men came off Megowan Street. They were behind us. The plug-uglies saw them first and stopped dead. I think Mr. Benjamin thought his "Men!" had done the trick till something told us to turn our heads. They carried bully clubs, too. Homemade billy clubs that looked like they could do the job just fine, and iron pipes that could smash heads even better.

They waved at us to move aside so they could charge direct at the plug-uglies. I tugged at Mr. Benjamin's arm.

He wasn't moving. "Men!" he shouted at the colored fellows and they did pull up. Both the plug-uglies and the colored men weren't twenty yards apart. All Mr. Benjamin had to do was pivot between the two of them—like a preacher set down among the sinners—more of that good luck he'd been talking about. I figured any second both mobs'd rush at each other swinging their clubs and not too particular about whose heads got smashed, but Mr. Benjamin looked like he weren't worried about that possibility.

Mr. Benjamin likes to quote Shakespeare about a coward dying a thousand deaths while the valiant only die the once. I must of shed a dozen or so lives as Mr. Benjamin commenced to speak.

"Put down those clubs, men. This is registration day. We don't fight in the streets in America. We vote in the election booth. That's how we settle our disputes. Put those clubs down, men. Put them down."

Nobody put them down. But they stopped charging. I think they might have been more confused than convinced. This is America? We don't fight in the streets? Seems to me that's all we did. Mr. Benjamin turned to the white men.

"I know that some of you don't like that idea of settling disputes in the ballot box— or rather, you don't like the idea of colored men getting to settle those disputes. I know some of you would rather the colored didn't have the vote at all. I know the sentiment. You should, too. Your English landlords preferred your parents didn't have the vote so most of them never got the franchise. You moved here—or your parents did. And you have the vote. But like your English landlords, you'd prefer we did not. Your English landlords were wrong. You have the right to vote. But you are wrong, too. We also have that right."

Mr. Benjamin always thought his logic win over anybody, even plug-uglies. But their faces got even harder, their breathing so heavy it was like they had run a three-mile steeple chase rather than less than a block. Comparing them to us poor coloreds was one thing; comparing them to English landlords was almost enough for them to disregard the odds against them.

But the odds were there. *Thank You, Jesus*. Mr. Benjamin turned to the colored men next.

"Look at you! A good solid crowd of colored men. You got the clubs ready and you got the numbers. You can beat these white men. Why not? Enough of their white mobs have beaten plenty of coloreds. We would have been beaten if you hadn't shown up. Enough of you to break every white man there—send him crying back to his white saloons. Send them crying back to Ireland maybe—or Germany. Leave the land to us who've been here a whole lot longer.

"Only you know it doesn't work like that. Beat this white mob; a bigger white mob will come looking for you. The police on their side. The police already here," and he pointed his finger at the two I'd spotted. He recognized them before I did. "I told you about settling disputes at the ballot box. It's the only way. How many of you men are registered to vote?"

He looked over them like the stern preacher that he was. Three of maybe twenty raised their hands. "Come with me now. We'll register right now." He swirled back to the white men. "You," he pointed to one of the cops—the biggest man there. Flannigan, I remembered. Cousin to the Doyles. He carried a club but he didn't look like he needed it: his fists were clubs. "Tell your men to break up and go home or I'll turn this crowd on you and they won't stop until you'll be begging to be back starving under your English rulers. And tell them not to just turn the corner and mob again if they don't want to end up in that death hole folks call a hospital."

The man got a face like a smashed-in-pumpkin—like he'd been in more bar fights than my old friend Jake. But you don't survive that many fights without picking and choosing when you can. He looked like he wanted to tear Mr. Benjamin apart, but he didn't. He said something we couldn't hear to the other white men and they started walking off in different directions. Two even walked around the edges of the colored crowd who stared at them like wolves eying the sheep sheltered by the guard dogs. Mr. Benjamin the guard dog here. Mamma was wrong. Mr. Benjamin could survive anything.

About fifteen of the men followed us to the precinct headquarters. The four white official challengers in the 19th Precinct didn't know what to do when we barged in. The men hid their clubs inside their coats. Needed to prove they lived in the precinct boundaries or be validated by someone who did. Validated each other mostly, which wouldn't of passed muster but the clubs sticking out of their pockets might of carried the point. Most had lived in the neighborhood since it opened up to coloreds. And then some: one old man almost twenty years.

When the challengers started asking whether they could read, Mr. Benjamin stepped right in.

"That's not the law. A man doesn't have to read to vote in Kentucky. And a man doesn't have to tell you who he works for or who his father works for. Why would you need to know that? So you might inform his employer? It's a form of intimidation and it's against the law."

I could tell the white challengers wanted to tear Mr. Benjamin apart just like Flannigan did. But the odds were still with us. The better part of judgment is discretion. They were the discreetest white men I ever saw.

Mr. Benjamin followed the law himself. Three other colored men showed up while we were there, confused as to where they needed to register. They keep changing the precinct boundaries so that's not hard to do. Turns out all three needed to register in my neighborhood, the 32nd Precinct. Mr. Benjamin told them to come with us.

"Have to register young Noah. Free, black, and twenty one. Get you registered at the same time."

It'd taken most of the afternoon to get the fourteen men registered. One fellow was visiting his folks but lived in Louisville. "Not the law," Mr. Benjamin told him. "Have to wait until next year."

Past four o'clock when the five of us left started heading to the 32nd, the Bloody B—called that for all its broken heads. The Bloody Battlefield. The heart of Irishtown.

"Maybe we should ask some of the men to come with us?" I said. I meant some of the big men Mr. Benjamin had talked out of smashing that white mob. I was the only young man left in our group of five. Two looked in their sixties. One man about Mr. Benjamin's age was so thin he just about disappeared sideways. Didn't look like he'd be too handy in a ruckus. But Mr. Benjamin didn't see the need.

"We're not an invading army. We're registering voters, not taking over a saloon."

I'd feel safer taking over a saloon.

I spotted Mike Moynahan a block off, loafing at the corner of Water and Spring. He was the fellow who'd thrown the rock through our window down at *The Standard*. Only I didn't see him throw the rock, Patrolman Doyle told me—just seen him running away, in the dark from the back. "Wouldn't be able to point him out in the courtroom," Doyle told me.

Except I couldn't forget that face just seeing it that once. Wasn't that different than other Irish boozers. Same red lines running out from the eyes, like pink creek lines on a face-map left out in the weather. Same nose ballooned up from the booze or a fist. Colored drunks got the same face, only you can't spot the vein lines so easy, and their noses just squash in.

But nobody got eyes like Moynahan—colored or white—hard blue with a ring of yellow. Mean eyes. Malice eyes. Hate eyes.

After I wrote that article about the window-breaking and him being a friend of Patrolman Doyle's, I heard Moynahan was looking for me. Somebody passed the word to Mr. Benjamin. Why I hid out there for a few weeks. Shamed me. Shamed me worse that I was afraid. But I was.

"Nothing to shame you, Noah," Maria said to me. "I've seen that hate in white men down in Alabama. That's why I'm here. That hate will destroy anything in its way. You need to run from hate like that, Noah."

Her words shamed me more. "Colored men have been running from men like Moynahan too long. We need to stand up and face them. We can hate just as hard."

She looked at me a moment. She said the words again. "You need to run from hate like that, Noah."

I waited for Moynahan to recognize me and I tensed, but he glanced at me and away almost as quick. He didn't know me from any other young colored man. He got his gaze fixed on Mr. Benjamin. He knew him. Mr. Benjamin kept his head high. He was walking so briskly, it was like he was some colonel marching in some military parade. Only he didn't turn to wave at anyone, certainly not to Moynahan. Just another disheveled private, drunk and disorderly.

Moynahan did look drunk—not much past four but time enough if your breakfast was an egg in a tumbler of whiskey and your lunch a beer and a chaser. But he wasn't falling-down drunk. He was a drunk looking for the insult so he'd get a reason for the fight that was building up in him.

A black man marching past him like a colonel all the insult that Moynahan needed. He scrambled into the precinct right before we did. Bloody B. The 32nd.

Somebody must of sent word we were coming. Two cops was standing guard, almost blocking the entrance. I squeezed by one who turned his head away from staring at Mr. Benjamin for a second. His breath smelled like Moynahan's must of, like he'd been drinking his meals.

"Young Noah," Patrolman Luke Doyle said to me. "I heard you was back in town. Still keeping bad company, I see."

Three vote challengers occupied one wall and two precinct officials at the table. Moynahan and two other plug-uglies stood holding up the walls. Kept their eyes fixed on Mr. Benjamin. I counted ten to our five. The skinny fellow turned around and walked out as soon as he saw the numbers.

"Wait," Mr. Benjamin said to him, but he was gone before we could even tug at his sleeve. Turned sideways and disappeared.

"Smart fellow," said Patrolman Doyle.

Down to four—two old men, Mr. Benjamin, and me.

One of the challengers waved one of the old men over to him. The challenger looked familiar, though I don't think I knew him.

"I'm John Doyle, an official sanctioned by the City of Lexington to examine and challenge all men who wish to register to vote in our state. I have some questions to ask you."

I turned to look at Patrolman Doyle, who grinned at me. Doyles everywhere we looked.

Mr. Benjamin walked over to the table and stood by the old man waiting to be questioned. John Doyle looked annoyed.

"I'm just questioning him, boy. I'll talk to you if I need to."

"I'm here to advise him how to answer and to reject questions that are not legal questions."

190

It was like Mr. Benjamin had slapped every white face in the room. The men by Mike Moynahan held him by both arms. John Doyle was silent for a second. He kept his head turned to Mr. Benjamin as he questioned the old man in front of him.

"Your name? Legal question?" he said to Mr. Benjamin who didn't reply. Mr. Benjamin stayed silent the first few questions as the old man told his age and his address and how long he'd been living in the place he rented.

"Your occupation?"

Mr. Benjamin snapped to.

"Not a question allowed by law."

"I am asking the man what he does for a living. He could be a burglar. He could be a felon. We don't want them voting in this precinct."

"You have his name listed as a felon? You do not. You may not ask him about his employment or who employs him. It is not a legal question."

Mike Moynahan had pulled free from his handlers.

"Who do you think you are? A raggedy old nigger comes in here and interferes with the man doing his job—keeping some other sorry nigger from coming here and stealing the election. Dead men voting."

Mr. Benjamin turned briefly when Moynahan started talking but turned back to the challenger.

"This man will answer any legal question. I will vouch for his living at his address for the last two years."

Mike Moynahan didn't like being ignored.

"One nigger vouching for another. Like one whore claiming another's the Virgin Mary."

There were murmurs at that. "Watch your language, Mike," Patrolman Doyle said. The Irish don't like the Virgin Mary mentioned if she's not in some prayer.

John Doyle continued. "I'm going to read a passage from a Kentucky statute. Tell me what you think it means."

Mr. Benjamin leaped forward to the table and started to shout. "No, no, no. This is not a law school. The man is here to register, not to take a test. This is not only illegal, it is harassment. You cannot ask these kind of questions—neither the law nor the city nor the Commonwealth of Kentucky give you the right to ask these kind of questions. You are interfering with his civil rights. Register the man and let him go on his way."

John Doyle flushed red, but before he or anyone could open his mouth, Mike Moynahan pulled a gun from his waistband and was beating Mr. Benjamin over the shoulders, aiming at his head.

"Here's your fucking civil rights, nigger," Moynahan shouted. With each blow of his pistol. Mr. Benjamin was covering his head with his arms as he sank to the floor. Moynahan kept beating.

I started to run to Mr. Benjamin but the two thugs grabbed me. Big men, bigger than Moynahan. One hit me on the side of the head. I sank slowly to the floor. I lay there dazed and watched, like a waking dream, Mr. Benjamin being hit again and again. Finally John Doyle tried to pull Moynahan away, but he couldn't budge him. Mr. Benjamin lay on the floor with his hands covering his head. He didn't groan. Or I couldn't hear him.

Finally, Patrolman Luke Doyle pulled Moynahan off, whispering to him, but breathing heavy.

The two old colored men we came in with went the way of the skinny fellow, out the door. I pulled myself up from the floor. I swayed for a few moments but I held steady. I went over to Mr. Benjamin and pulled him up from the floor. His face was bruised but he wasn't bleeding.

"Where did Mr. Thompson go?" he said, talking of the colored man he'd been trying to register.

"He's left, Mr. Benjamin. Got scared, I guess."

Mr. Benjamin pulled his shoulders up. "Can't be scared. Can't stay scared. Not much of a life if you're going to be scared. Not if you're a Negro in the South."

But I was scared. He was speaking choppy, like he didn't know where he was. The white men in the room tensed when he got up, but they looked confused at his speech. Mike Moynahan still held his gun like he wanted to start hitting Mr. Benjamin again if he got the chance. Mr. Benjamin looked at me like he didn't know me.

"We gotta go, Mr. Benjamin."

"Go? Go where?"

Mike Moynahan let out a snort. "You been drinking, nigger? Maybe they should close the saloons on registration day, too. But you probably got a private stash."

Mr. Benjamin didn't even glance at Moynahan as he turned to John Doyle again. "Legal questions only," he said to Doyle but had to grab the table to keep from falling.

"Let's go, Mr. Benjamin," I said again, and grabbed his arm. "Home, Mr. Benjamin," I said, loud as if he had gotten hard of hearing all of a sudden. "Home."

Patrolman Doyle grabbed Mike Moynahan who struggled with the two plug-uglies. "You're under arrest, Mike," I think I heard him say. I was surprised. But Moynahan wasn't.

CHAPTER 34

Noah Webster, October 2, 1900, Downtown Lexington

We had gotten quite a few blocks from the precinct, trailing up Spring Street in silence. Just Mr. Benjamin heavy breathing and me half-carrying him up the streets, wishing I could get a wagon to give us a ride. But there weren't any colored drivers around and a white one would never pick us up. We needed to stop after a few blocks. We had made it to Limestone across from the old St. Peter's, the church Catholics use just for special occasions. This was a special occasion.

"Let's catch our breath in there," I said. If Moynahan or Doyle was chasing us, he wouldn't look for us in a Catholic church. Probably never heard of a colored Catholic.

Mr. Benjamin turned to me like he was seeing me for the first time.

"We didn't get you registered, did we? We need to go back." He took a breath. "I need to go home and rest. But this evening, young Noah. We're coming back this evening. You can't wait a whole year to register. You wouldn't be able to vote. And we need your vote."

I didn't think it was a good idea. "That fellow Moynahan might still be there. He might use that gun like a gun, not a hammer."

"Arrested. Won't be there."

I didn't think he'd heard that—didn't think he half-noticed Moynahan for all his beating on him. Arrested didn't mean jailed. I didn't press it. Maria would help me persuade him to stay put. I just needed to get him home.

But we needed to rest first. I liked St. Peter's. The Catholics were planning on a big cathedral—so many of them in town now what with all the Irish and the Germans. Old St. Pete's too small, more cabin than church. You could see the chinking. I'd ducked in it before, just to sit and rest and look at the Catholic statues of their saints. Nobody there in the middle of the week. Don't think the Irish would much like it if they knew I came there. Mamma, either. She wouldn't like it if I sat by myself in a white church and she sure would hate it if she knew it was a Catholic one.

Mr. Benjamin was getting his second wind. "I don't know that I've ever been in a Catholic church before. Not even in New York and they're on almost every other corner there. Not even in St. Kitts, though the Anglican churches probably closest thing to this." He looked around like he was a tourist. "Look at those saints. Why do people need saints, do you think?"

He looked at me like I was supposed to answer that. I thought for a moment. Mr. Benjamin didn't like easy answers with no thought to them. He was like Mamma in that.

"I think we need people to look up to. I think we need examples. So we can try to live our lives like them."

He thought himself a bit at my answer. "You? You got any saints?"

That was easy. "Frederick Douglass. Sojourner Truth. Harriet Tubman." Mr. Benjamin nodded at each of my choices. "You."

"Me?" I surprised him. "Oh, you got that wrong, Noah. You got that wrong." We were sitting next to a statue of a grizzled man whose beard looked shaggy even in plaster. Mr. Benjamin pointed to him. "St. Peter, I imagine. Name of the church. Peter. Rock. To build this church out of this rock." He looked around at the modest cabin of a church. "More like a few pebbles here. Ran away twice from *his* saint, Jesus. Fell asleep in the garden. Maybe I'm a saint like Peter."

"Came back in the end, didn't he?"

Mr. Benjamin gave a shrug. "In the end. The end. Is that what it's all about? The end?"

I didn't know how to answer that so I stayed silent. Mamma'd be proud.

"We all come to that. The end. And maybe you're right, Noah. Maybe the end tells us who we are. Tells others who we be."

His voice had taken on the singsong of St. Kitts—something that usually only happened when he got mad. He didn't sound mad. If it wasn't Mr. Benjamin, I'd say he sounded almost sweet.

"But Noah, I don't want you to be taking me for a saint. Not the plaster kind. And not the kind like Frederick Douglass. There's a saint, boy. Kept at it all his life, through all the dark times. Dark times when he was a slave and dark times when he was free. Those last years of his life when all that freedom he fought for was slipping away, the amendments being ignored like they meant nothing. But he kept on. Told us to keep on."

He grew silent, so silent that in the dim light of the church, I thought maybe he slipped into a doze. I worried about Moynahan's pistol blows to his head. But he roused himself.

"And Sojourner. An ignorant woman. An unlettered woman who let the truth of genius seep into her like sun and water seeps into a tree. But she did what no tree could: spoke to us with words like the sounds of angels. Full of wisdom and love. Ain't she a woman?"

He took a breath. I held mine. "Harriet. She's still alive. She'll get there. She's already Moses, leading her people to the Promised Land. But you got to be dead to be a saint, don't you, son?"

He laughed, holding up his hand to me, telling me to slow down. Like I was hurrying him on to sainthood before his time.

"And what have I done to be a saint, son? Wrote a few books, gave some speeches. Preached at folks from my newspaper. Got some colored folks registered to vote. Things I've done private, Noah, I wouldn't want anyone to know. Devil's advocate might flush them out someday. Iconoclasts sure to smash any plaster mold if my sainthood got that far."

I lifted my shoulders. I wasn't even much of a Baptist. What did I know about the rules for saints? Just knew Mr. Benjamin was the finest man I knew. Just knew I loved him. Would of told him that but he wouldn't of liked it. This time I knew what to say. But I kept my mouth shut.

"Another thing, son. You can't be imitating somebody else's life, saint or not. Won't work. Harriet had to get her folks across Maryland's Eastern Shore. Freedom. Frederick had to get across the Ohio. Freedom. But folks across the Ohio—even folks way up in New York state—they're not free, Noah. Not free here in the Commonwealth of Kentucky. No Underground Railroad to get them free. Frederick knew that and told us so until the day he died. Got to figure out a new way to freedom, Noah. Not their way. Not my way. Your way. I've been figuring out new ways to freedom all my life. If you want to imitate that son, I'm all for you calling me saint."

We rested then, silent. If somebody had peeked in, they would of thought we was praying, to one of the plaster saints, maybe. Or to the Virgin Mary Catholics always going on about. Some countries, Catholics paint her brown. A brown Mary would be easier to pray to.

Maybe we was praying to the October light filtering through the high nave window of the cabin church. It laced down on us like Maria Lulu's silver shawl, Mr. Benjamin's wedding present to her. The light patterned all about Mr. Benjamin's face as if Maria had wrapped her shawl special around his head. If it wasn't a halo, it was the closest I ever came to seeing one.

I looked over at Mr. Benjamin and it was like someone painted his face with sparkles that crisscrossed up and down his cheeks like prison bars that would crumble with the first shade.

But you need more than shadow to break prison bars. I don't know what you need. Mr. Benjamin say it my job to find out. Maybe it's a fist, maybe it's a vote. Maybe it's something else. But it's something solid. Just know you need a whole lot more than shadow to ease the bars to freedom.

CHAPTER 35

Maria Lulu Benjamin, October 2, 1900, Lexington, Kentucky

I was angry when I saw Robert. "How did you let this happen?" I yelled at Noah. It is his job to keep Robert away from harm. He flinched as if I had slapped him—which I wanted to. Robert was bruised all about the face. I did not know if the hurt went deeper than bruising. I wanted to send for Dr. Horner but Robert would not let me. I turned to Noah who urged the doctor, too. Of course, Robert does not listen to him, either.

I wanted him to go straight to bed. I would bring up some light broth. Sheila was gone for the day. But again he would have none of it.

"Woman, it's still light out. Where are the children? Let me see the children."

They came running in, both of them, excited that he wanted them. It is not his fault. He has so little time. I was almost as happy as they were that he was making time for them on such a day. But I was afraid that they would take the last of his energy, Charlie, especially. I hovered around the edges of the play, fearful that they might hurt him in some way. Neither child could imagine that they—or anyone—could hurt their large, strong daddy. He yelled and they yelled back. He rolled on the floor with them. I thought Lillian might have a fit, she was so excited. Robert did not roll on the floor with the children. It was all very strange.

Finally, I saw Robert sag a bit. "Enough! Daddy must rest." No one—not even the children—had energy to protest. "Noah, take the children to their room."

Robert bent down to kiss them both, even Charlie whom he has taken to shaking hands with. As Noah scooped Lillian up, her head plopped on his shoulder. She was out already.

We were alone.

"You must rest, Robert."

He took my hands. "I will. I will. But we must talk a little."

I was as surprised as the children. Robert talked. But inviting me to talk? I reached out to touch one of the bruises. He frowned but let me do it.

"Maria. You are not strong. I need for you to rest, deeply so that may recover the strength you had when we first met. You are so much younger than I am, Maria. You should live many years beyond me."

Upstairs, Charlie let out a squeal. Over-excited. I hoped that Noah wasn't getting him even more so. I turned to Robert. "I have been poorly for almost a year. I sometimes thought you did not notice."

"I sometimes did not."

We heard Charlie's noises subside, like a storm whose winds gradually slowed down. We listened as only parents can listen to the sounds of their children growing fainter and fainter. Robert turned to me. He touched my hand and lifted it, almost as if he were going to kiss it. Of course he did not. Just the thought of him doing that tickled me so I almost laughed. Though looking at his bruised face made me want to cry more than laugh. Our talk had ended, I gathered.

"I sometimes did not." The words hung there, warmer than a kiss.

"I will lie down if you will promise to wake me in an hour."

"An hour? What are you doing in an hour? Surely work can wait."

"I need to take young Noah back to the polling booths. They are open until nine p.m."

I have heard that a punch in the stomach will take one's breath away—that for many seconds air will not enter the lungs—like life itself is suspended. The horror. Robert returning to that place? How could he think it? But I could not utter a sound. He saw my face.

"I cannot let the day go by, Maria. Noah has to be registered. If he is not, if he must wait another year, it would be another defeat. Noah is the race, Maria. He has the right to register. We have the right."

I found my breath and with it came my words. I poured them out at him like sharp pebbles spitting from my mouth. "I do not care about registration. I do not care about the vote. I care about you, Robert. I care about our children. If you care, if you have finally noticed us, Robert, you would not go. But you do not care, Robert. You care only for your place. You care only for your reputation."

He drew himself up. I could have attacked nothing more sacred. His reputation.

"Please, Robert."

The "please" pricked his skin, but he did not bleed. Or I did not see it. One more bruise, one more smudge on his heart. His face tightened. He got up slowly.

"I do not believe that you do not care about the vote, Maria. You have worked as hard as I have. You registered yourself, today, at Miss Willard's. You are upset. The little scuffle I suffered has disturbed you more than it should have. I know that battles will have to be fought, but this was nothing. You have nothing to worry about."

He took his hand away. I felt the warmth of his touch fade slowly.

"I will lie down. It is doubtful that I will sleep in any case."

The hour passed. I sat there as my children slept and my husband lay on his bed, resting. Eyes open, staring at the ceiling. Thinking. Of what? The right to vote? Colored freedom? Us? He sometimes did not notice. But then he noticed. Was that enough?

Noah crept into the living room, not knowing where to light, looking as if I might still slap him. As if he could protect Robert from bruises. Or me. As if anyone could. I nodded my head towards a chair and he sat in it, waiting. He already knew Robert's plans. He had already argued against them, I was certain.

But Robert only listened to the voice inside his heart.

And that voice was not mine.

CHAPTER 36

Noah Webster, October 2, 1900, 7 p.m. 32ⁿᵈ Precinct, Lexington, Kentucky

I tried to get Mr. Benjamin to carry a gun—I knew he had one—but he wouldn't.

"When I say we need to fight battles for the right to vote, I did not mean literally. I will not carry a gun and I will not let you carry one. This is not George Thomas' saloon. We are going to return to the 32ⁿᵈ and register you to vote. That does not require weapons."

I wanted to tell him that Mike Moynahan beat him about the head and shoulders with what looked like a weapon to me in the middle of the 32ⁿᵈ Precinct and that the policemen standing about didn't seem too upset about the brandishing of the weapon. Of course, Mike Moynahan was a thug Irishman, a plug-ugly, not some out-of-control colored lawyer.

"Mike Moynahan…" I started but he waved the name away. "Mike Moynahan's been arrested and, while I am not hopeful that much will come of it, I am certain that he will at least be detained for the evening. No more delays, Noah. We need to get you registered."

For one moment, I thought of refusing, telling Mr. Benjamin that I wouldn't register. Wouldn't vote. No need to go back to the Bloody B. Not for me. I was done with it. The hell with it. Registration. The vote. Freedom. The hell with it all. It wasn't worth it.

But, of course I couldn't do that. Couldn't of done that if Mr. Benjamin put a gun right to the side of my head. Couldn't of done that if Maria Lulu had begged me to. Which she had, kind of. Only not with words.

The length of Water Street has about fifteen saloons, all squeezed up against the railroad tracks, all looking for the thirsty man. Trains run by and you got to shout to be heard. You get the shouting habit, it don't much matter if trains are passing or not. All that shouting makes you thirstier. Colored saloons and Irish. Not too many serve both. Some do—especially when the supply of drinkers starts running low—then the color of your money is all that matters. Of course, most Irish saloons wouldn't serve a beer to a colored man if their license depended on it.

License depended on lots of things. I heard the Mayor has suspended Showalter's. Showalter's like George Thomas—white-owned, colored-drinkers. Always rough places. They all rough places.

Saloon keepers in slow times out on the street, hustling people in. Saloons only closed on election day, but somehow word passed 'round that they closed on registration day, too. Weren't true but the rumor hurt business some. Spotted Ed Chennault out there—he's a colored saloon owner and a politician.

Of course he's a politician. All the saloon owners are. If they want to keep in business. Got enough votes in your pocket, you okay with the law, or you okay after a few dollars. Leastways if you refrain from shooting at your customers, or keep your customers from shooting at each other. Then you get closed down and got to go to all the trouble of opening somewhere else with a different name. Timmy's Place. Same owners, same drinkers, even. What's in a name?

Ed Chennault stopped waving when he recognized us. Ed Chennault thought the world of Mr. Benjamin and not just because he got a dozen colored voters in his pocket because of him. Mr. Benjamin didn't put them there, just got them registered. What they did with their vote was their business.

"Mr. Benjamin, don't come back here, sir. Trouble. They let Moynahan out of jail. Don't know that they even put him in it. He's back, Mr. Benjamin."

Just then Mrs. Lavery popped her head out of her place. She's the only woman saloon keeper on Water Street, though there's another woman down on Spring. Her saloon's practically the Democratic headquarters. Men in there drink too hard to care if you're colored or white. Long as you're not Republican. Hard drinkers. Mrs. Lavery's husband showed the way. Keeled over in the middle of the day. Drinkers stumbled over him all afternoon. Didn't know he was dead, she said later. Wouldn't of let him lie there if she'd known that. Not decent.

She took one look at us and ducked back through the doors.

Mike Moynahan came out next. He'd been drinking the last time we seen him. Didn't look like he'd stopped since, except for being arrested and such.

"You back here, boy? You didn't learn your lesson last time?"

Mr. Benjamin looked at him. "You're already under Federal indictment in Louisville, Mr. Moynahan, for interfering with a man's right to vote in last November's election. You beat him over the head, too. A colored gentleman. But he went on to vote. And I am going on to vote. Your friends here might let you out of the city jail, but the Federal government will protect our rights. I advise you to step aside before the Federal government puts your ass behind bars where it belongs."

I've seen Mr. Benjamin in many tight spots. I've seen him face down bigger, meaner men than Mike Moynahan. He was just a city thug, part of that mob Billy Klair keeps on the city payroll. A foreman at the quarry on the city farm, working prisoners to death. White prisoners, colored ones. Doesn't much matter the color of the back that gets broken. Smiling Billy Klair don't care. Billy tells Mike Moynahan to take care of things out in the 32nd.

Get things done. Don't let him know too much about how they get done.

When Moynahan pulled the gun out of his pocket, I was ready. No way that man was going to beat Mr. Benjamin again, no way he was gonna bruise that face that already had too many bruises. I couldn't stand it. I couldn't face Maria Lulu one more time. I started to run forward, ready to jump on Moynahan, to grab that pistol from his hand.

Then Moynahan shot him. I saw Mr. Benjamin's right arm flap out like a wild duck's wing that's been snapped in two. I saw dark blue spread like ripples on his jacket. We were ten feet from Moynahan who had opened the chambers to his pistol and was fumbling with it.

"Run!" I yelled at Mr. Benjamin who looked at me just a second before he turned and ran up Water Street. It was dark—must have been close to 7:30—Mike Moynahan ran by me three seconds later, panting with the drink he had in him. He didn't see me, though I felt the wind of his running, smelled the stink of his breath. "Run," I yelled again as Moynahan fired another shot. But it missed. Mr. Benjamin was still running, his right arm swinging.

A policeman came out of the 32nd—not Doyle, the other one, Hawkins—running towards Moynahan. "Stop! Don't do that!" he shouted at Moynahan, who kept running after Mr. Benjamin. I could just see Mr. Benjamin's back, though he was a half a block away by now. Moynahan fired two more shots.

I saw Mr. Benjamin crumple to the sidewalk.

Hawkins stopped running. Luke Doyle opened the precinct door and walked slowly to Moynahan.

"I surrender," Moynahan said to Doyle, who nodded to Hawkins. Hawkins led him away. I saw Doyle walk towards Mr. Benjamin laying still upon Water Street. Like an eagle who's been shot. Doyle hovered over him, turning him, Doyle's hands moving.

I couldn't see. It was dark as midnight though it wasn't eight o'clock at night yet. No stars, no moon. Dark as if the sun had left us for good.

But early. Maria Lulu wouldn't expect us home for another hour. Mamma'd be over still at Tom Blevins' house, sitting with his mamma. Gone home and cooked something and come back. Mamma'd expect me to stop by, too. Show my respect though I didn't much know Tom Blevins.

I'll stop by then—to give Tom Blevins' mamma comforting. To whisper to Mamma that she was needed somewhere else; someone else needed some comforting.

"What now?" I can see her asking, half-mad and half-worried. "What you gone and done now? Or your Mr. Benjamin? I swear one of you is gonna get shot one of these days. You mark my words. One of these days."

CHAPTER 37

Judge Frank Bullock, October 4, 1900, Lexington, Kentucky

Billy was waiting for me when I arrived, not smiling. In fact, he looked as upset as I've ever seen him. He was not as upset as I was. Patrick was chatting with him.

"Tell Mr. Klair I am not in to him, Patrick. Escort him from the premises." Patrick looked as if I had just instructed him to slap his mother. Or his brother. Of course, Billy had gotten him his job.

"Judge, I know you're upset. Let's talk about it."

I wanted to shout that the last time we talked about it, a man ended up dead. Murdered. But Patrick looked like he was going to have a stroke. I nodded at the office door and Billy entered.

"Last time you were here you were talking about people doing their job. I did not realize that doing one's job involved actual murder."

Billy Klair actually winced.

"Not murder, Judge. Self-defense. That's what I'm here to talk to you about."

"I'm a judge, Billy, and justice is going to happen. Don't talk to me again about my job. My job is justice and your man will find that out soon enough. You should not be here at all. We have nothing to talk about. It is not proper."

Even I knew I sounded pompous sometimes, but I did not care. I remembered very clearly our last talk about taking care of Robert Benjamin. He had been taken care of. My skin crawled. I heard the conversation as others might hear it: as a planned assassination.

Billy waited while my breathing calmed. Billy's chief strength as a politician wasn't his glad-handing, his ready smile. It was his ability to wait. He waited while I bustled at my desk; he waited as the picture of what was coming formed a picture in my mind. A dread filled me.

"Judge, I never wanted this to happen. He was supposed to have been rustled up a little—scared off. But Benjamin didn't scare and Moynahan…" Billy paused and shook his head, "Moynahan isn't one for half-measures. Maybe not the best man for the job. That's on me, Judge. On me. But we're in it now, Judge. And I need you to know what's at stake."

"What's at stake is that your man, not the best man but your man, killed Benjamin when he was running the other direction. Shot him in the arm and when that didn't work, shot him in the back. Killed him. How you think you can construe self-defense out of that when your own witnesses have Benjamin running as fast as he can away from Moynahan is a construction that just won't stand."

Billy waited again. A good ten seconds. "It's gonna have to stand, Judge."

I listened then as I knew I should not—listened to Billy spell out his "evidence" that I should have heard firsthand in court. The threats Benjamin had made towards Moynahan earlier in the day.

"Who heard these threats?" I asked.

"Mrs. Lavery. And several of her customers. After Moynahan beat Benjamin in the afternoon, he stopped by the saloon. Benjamin told Mrs. Lavery he was gonna kill Moynahan."

"I did not realize Mrs. Lavery's saloon served coloreds. Or that she was a confidante of Benjamin's."

"Sure, she serves coloreds. Especially on a slow day like registration day. And it's not like he told her special. He was shouting it out. That's why the others heard him."

We just looked at each other. What was there to say? I cut to the core.

"No one saw Benjamin with a gun. No one, other than Moynahan, saw or heard him shoot."

"That's unfortunate. But he had a gun. Cops found it on him. And a bullet had been fired."

"Yes. I've heard. Luke Doyle found a gun on Benjamin's body. A lucky find. And a chamber was empty. But that chamber is rusty. That would suggest that the gun had not been fired for a few days at least. Maybe longer."

Billy Klair was shaking his head. "No. I got an expert gunsmith ready to testify that that gun's been fired recently—that night."

"I'm to believe Luke Doyle then, that he found a gun on Benjamin. I'm to believe Mike Moynahan that Benjamin fired that gun though no one else saw it. I'm to believe your gunsmith that a rusty chamber is not evidence that a gun has not been fired. And I'm to believe Mrs. Lavery, the grieving widow, and her faithful customers that Robert Benjamin made dire threats towards Mike Moynahan."

I felt calm now. I looked out my office windows. The view of the square always calmed me. "Why, Billy, am I to believe all this?"

Billy glanced at the closed door. He did not whisper, but I had to strain my head forward to hear him.

"Because if you don't, if you find Mike Moynahan guilty or even if you hold him over for trial, he's gonna tell a tale that will send us all rolling, that will have the Federal government indicting us all for vote interference and maybe the governor holding us on trial for murder. Even you, Judge. The least we can expect is to be turned out office—all of us. The worst is that we end up in jail. Because Mike Moynahan is going to say I sent him to scare off Benjamin and a lot of the other colored voters. A court in Louisville's already trying several Democrats from Lexington on just those charges. Mike Moynahan's one of them. John Doyle, the other challenger, is another. They've been loyal and shut-mouth so far. But if things go wrong, I can see myself headed down the same path.

"But on my way down, I'm gonna have to recall our last conversation, Judge, where I let you know I was interested in discouraging the colored electorate and you didn't object. Not out loud. I'm no lawyer but I know something called proximate cause. It's the thing the law says set everything in motion. Some do-gooders, some Federal judge maybe might think our conversation was the proximate cause. I don't think that's reasonable, but the law got its own way of thinking."

He took a breath. "Here's another proximate cause: you saying or practically saying by not believing him, that Patrolman Doyle—the brother of that shut-mouth John Doyle— kind of produced that gun he found on Benjamin's body. That's a serious charge, Judge. How do you think that might go over in the municipal police department? They've been loyal to us—the Democratic Party—not just the police department, but the whole crowd that surrounds them. If you don't believe the very convincing story I laid out to you... well, Judge," Billy shrugged, the long shrug of the man who is just telling us what the world is, not what we might want it to be, "well, Judge, all hell will break loose."

I sat in my splendid office a good hour. Patrick knocked twice, telling me I had a full court waiting. Packed. Everyone from the mayor to the alderman's assistant, waiting for the Judge to convene the court. Waiting for justice. They could wait.

I sat there wondering what Father would make of this situation, how surprised he'd be to see his shrimp son the center of all this hell breaking loose. The Major and his fellow Morgan's Raiders loosed old-fashioned blood and guts hell on so many peaceful hamlets. Slashing with his swift sword, as righteous as a battle hymn and with as little doubt. Certain.

Beneath his fury, calm. An island of resolve. No matter the innocents he killed. Father stayed pure.

I had resolved to leave that world. His world. I was resolved to uphold the impartiality of the law, its fairness. Brutal arrogance would be subsumed in the certainty of justice. The weak and the strong together. Judged. Together. Balance. Fairness.

Noah Webster has written me, the young aide to Benjamin. I had already read his letter several times. He begged to be heard. The Commonwealth's attorney did not choose to call him to testify, though I could summon him myself. He contradicted everything in Billy's play, shredded the story from beginning to end. All hell would break loose.

I smiled, imagining the look on all their faces if I called Noah: the aldermen, the mayor. Billy. Call Noah, I'd say to Patrick. Tell him to bring his ark. We'll cross the River Jordan on it. Flee to the Promised Land. We'll escape this Hell. This Hell of our own choosing. This Hell we've made.

Where ere you went, Father, you made a Hell.

I, too. Where ere I go.

Myself am Hell.

I walked into the courtroom. "All rise for the Honorable Frank Bullock," I heard Patrick intone.

"All rise for the Honorable Frank Bullock."

Not even Father had ever had a courtroom rise in his honor.

CHAPTER 38

Maria Lulu Benjamin, October 8, 1900, Lexington, Kentucky

I was surprised when Sheila told me who was calling. I could not afford Sheila. I told her that. Robert had always handled the money. I never worried about it. There was enough. "Enough was a feast," Mamma would say, whipping out meals from the air it seems to me now. What could a colored lawyer in Alabama have made? Enough. Like Robert, Mamma carried us day to day. Until she was gone. And then there was nothing. Or not enough.

Sheila—maid, cook, nanny, nurse—says she will stay. Announce my callers. Prepare my feasts.

"Will you follow me to Alabama?"

"Alabama? You can't be going back to Alabama, child. That's the wrong direction. Everybody headed North."

"I gather that's a no."

"Miss Sophonisba Breckinridge," Sheila announced.

She came into the parlor, wide-eyed and scared. As if she had never made a mourning call before. I am sure she never made a mourning call on a colored lady. I saw her eyes take in the furnishings, surreptitiously, for Sophonisba was the soul of politeness. But still, it was a foreign country, a colored lady's parlor. When would she next have an opportunity to observe?

"Mrs. Benjamin—Maria. I am so sorry."

"Miss Breckinridge. Thank you. You are the first white lady to have called on me. Bless you."

She almost stumbled under the words "first white lady," and it was unkind of me to say them. But I did not feel kind. Robert had been killed because he was colored—killed by a white man who was let free by a white man. Let free because he was a white man. No white person had come near me since his death and his killer's acquittal. Did they fear my rage?

They were right to fear it.

Sheila came in with a plate of cakes. I was inundated in cakes. Let them eat cake. She poured our teas. I was such a lady. It did not matter that when the cakes were gone, I would have a hard time finding the bread. Sophonisba's hands trembled as she encircled the cup with both of them. The warmth of the tea must have felt good. The weather had turned, a cold October rain tearing the leaves from the trees.

"The weather has turned," I said and Sophonisba faced me gratefully. We discussed the oddities of October for a few minutes. But I was not done.

"Mrs. Breckinridge was unable to come?"

October's treacheries were forgotten as more pertinent betrayals were examined. This time Sophonisba did not try to escape.

"No. I asked her but she could not bring herself to come."

"Because I am colored?"

She considered before she answered. She nodded. "Because you are colored. But she sends her warmest sympathies. She does."

"Oh, Miss Breckinridge, not her warmest sympathies, I think. Those she must reserve for white widows whose husbands have been gunned down in the street."

My words hung there. I had to admire Sophonisba. She did not run. She let my anger settle on her like October's rains. She looked down for a few moments and then met my eyes. That could not have been easy, meeting my eyes.

"I am sorry. Very, very sorry."

Her "sorry" enraged me. I could barely choke down hot words of anger. How dare this white old maid, this dried-up spinster express her sorrow for my loss? My husband? My children's father? Did she think I would suck on her genteel condescension like a hungry babe sucks on her mother's teats? Suck on her dried teats? Was she apologizing for the murderer Mike Moynahan? Or Judge Bullock's ruling? Her cousin. They were all cousins. Breckinridges and McDowells, Clays and Bullocks. Running the town. Pretending this town was better than Mississippi or Alabama. They didn't hang their niggers from the lamp posts. They shot them in the street.

Or perhaps she was apologizing for the whole damned white race? My rage choked me. I have trouble breathing on the best of days. I started to gasp.

"Are you alright?" Sophonisba was by my side, her handkerchief on my face. "Girl! Girl!" she called out to Sheila, who came running in. She bent my head down and whacked my back with a blow that forced the air into my lungs. I breathed slowly. Sophonisba's face still hovered two inches from mine. She looked sorry. Very sorry.

"I know you are sorry, Sophonisba. I thank you for your sympathy."

I expected her to run then, to make her excuses and go, but she sat there, still. We listened to the October rain but felt no need to comment on it further.

"Was Madeline pleased with the registration totals? Women turned out in much larger numbers than last year, Noah tells me."

Sophonisba looked the question at the mention of Noah's name.

"Robert's young aide," I explained. "He brings me all the political news. Colored women, especially, registered in record numbers. Was Madeline pleased?"

She stayed silent a second. "Madeline is happy when any woman assumes her rights. That is what we are fighting for. I hope when you are stronger you will continue the fight with us."

"No. I am done with that. Done with Lexington, too, I fear."

She turned to me again, her large eyes glistening a light sheen.

"Where will you go?"

"Alabama. My father's home.."

"Your friends here cannot help?"

"They help. But they are too young or too old or too poor to help as much as I need. As much as my children need. I never thought to return to Alabama. Sheila, my girl, thinks it's the wrong direction for a colored person. But what direction is the right direction for a colored family in 1900? Lexington certainly has not proven a good haven."

She winched a little at the words "good haven" and finally began the movements of leaving. "I am so sorry that your circumstances will separate us."

My circumstances. Such a big word for nothing. No, not nothing.

Not enough.

"My circumstances, Miss Breckinridge? You have always been kind. You are kind now. But our circumstances are a wedge between us, Sophonisba. Tell Mrs. Breckinridge, Madeline, that I remember her words at Ashland. Just two years or so, though it seems a lifetime. 'We must stand together.' Do you recall? When my silly shoes fell apart in the snow? Tell Madeline that I remember her words and that I am sorry she was unable to come, that *circumstances* have kept us apart. 'We will stand together.' Do you think, dear Sophonisba, that we ever will?"

Chapter 39

Jake the bartender, November 10, 1900, Timmy's Place, Lexington, Kentucky

First time I saw Noah in here I thought he'd just come to say hello. "Hey!" I yelled at him. I don't bartend much anymore. George Thomas got me running between his three bars supervising and I got my own little place over near Spring Street. Bad times and good times in Lexington, but it's always drinking times. Noah already drinking by the time I spot him—look like he'd been drinking a while. *That ain't like him*, I thought. At least it didn't used to be like him. He barely look up at my hey.

"Hey, yourself," he managed, and lowered his mouth back to his drink. I know that look. It a look that say "I'm here to drink, not talk. Keep your heys to yourself." A man needs a drinking night like that every once in awhile. A good bartender leaves him be.

I was gonna have to move on anyway—go check on one of George Thomas' bars up North Upper. George Thomas suspected the bartender stealing from him. I know the bartender stealing from him—just about all the bartenders stealing from him. From me, too, in my little drop-in even, and it's my wife's baby brother bartending. It just go with the territory. But George Thomas' man on Upper getting greedy. You supposed to let your fingers do the skimming, not shove your whole arm in up to your elbow. George Thomas always appreciate my light touch, so to speak. And he know I know how to spot a skimmer.

"Takes one to spot one," he says.

"Got that right, boss."

Of course, Noah never did no skimming. It irritate me some. I tell him as best I could when I count his till. "Good God, almighty. George Thomas gonna think he won the numbers. Till never this high before."

"Yeah, it was a good night," Noah would answer. "But not much more than usual."

"I just hope George Thomas don't expect this as usual."

But he still didn't get it. Or he didn't want to get it. Couldn't hardly come out and say "You ain't stealing enough, boy." I have to skim his till just to keep George Thomas' expectations reasonable. Didn't like to do that. Made me feel like I was stealing from Noah. I try to slip him a ten note sometime, saying something like how George Thomas appreciate his work so. But he wouldn't take it. Just look at me steady.

"George Thomas handing out bonuses?"

And Jesus moved into the new courthouse, gonna hand down justice to all God's children.

It irritate me so I finally had to come out and say something.

"You don't think George Thomas make enough money? You worried that George Thomas' family gonna suffer if he don't get every nickel a poor colored man pays for a beer that don't cost George Thomas a penny? You must got a soft heart. Or maybe a soft head. Why you care so about George Thomas getting his due?"

Noah looked surprised, like he didn't know what I was talking about for a second. But he a smart boy for all his not taking my clues. That don't mean he didn't understand them.

"George Thomas? I don't think anything about George Thomas. George Thomas sell whiskey that will slick your way into Hell almost as fast as a bullet to the heart. Or the brain. First it make you a fool and then it kill you. George Thomas' due? I wish I could give George Thomas his due. It ain't got nothing to do with George Thomas. It's about me."

I just wait. He hadn't been working with me more than a couple months back then, but already I knew he usually got something to say worth waiting for.

"I'm not judging any man. Well, maybe I judging George Thomas. But nobody else. This is a hard town, especially for coloreds. You do what you got to do to survive. My mamma already hate it that I work here but I tell her it more money than anyplace in town and I got to earn some money. But that don't mean I got to steal it. George Thomas ain't gonna make me a thief."

He hang his head then and look like he wanted to drop through the floor. He even reach out and touch my arm, and then pull back, like I some woman whose rear end he just pat and he waiting for the slap. I know he thinking that I thinking he just call me a thief.

Well. He did call me a thief, but then I gone and asked him to explain himself. And hell, I was a thief. George Thomas a thief, too, and I stealing from a thief. My wife's baby brother is stealing from a thief. We all thieves.

Except for Noah.

I know I said a good bartender leaves a serious drinker be if he ain't making no commotion, but this was Noah. I slid over near him before I had to leave.

"Noah, if you gonna drink like that, come on over to my place. Jake's. You know what they serve here. Hell, you used to serve it yourself. Slide yourself over there. Tell Casey, that's Suzy's baby brother, I said to take care of you. You tell him that."

But he wouldn't budge. Thanked me kindly. Said he was used to George Thomas' stock and doing fine.

That weren't good. Nobody used to George Thomas' stock, not men who been drinking it twenty years. Of course after twenty years, ain't many around to offer an opinion.

Noah was at another of George Thomas' establishments not two nights later, like he was making a tour of all the low-life spots in Lexington. This time I didn't even suggest my place. Figured the way he was going he'd make it there soon or later. But I went up to him. Sorry drunk or not, he was still Noah.

At least I hoped he was still Noah.

"I remember you telling me once that George Thomas make you a thief. Maybe not. But he sure doing a good job making you a drunk."

First, he look at me like he don't hear me, or the way you look when you think you hear a sound way off and ain't sure what it is. He straighten himself out a little.

"George Thomas got a lot on his plate. Making me a drunk ain't one of them. That's on me."

I decided to break my own bartending rule which is never tell a man he drinking too much. Spitting in the wind. Cut him off or let him be. But this was Noah. I pulled up next to him. When a fellow sat on Noah's other side, I gave him a look that said he was two seconds from a truncheon on his head. Man looked confused but skedaddled himself off that stool real quick.

"What's going on, Noah? You drinking like somebody tell you it's a race and you six drunks behind. You in trouble, boy?"

He paused before he took another sip of his drink, which is about as polite as a serious drinker gets. But his answer was rough.

"Of course, I'm in trouble. Mr. Benjamin shot down just a block away. I know: old news. Colored men shot down all the time. Remember Jimmy? Of course you do. Caught in that crossfire with the Mayor. What was his name? George Broadus. Poor old George Broadus. Did everything the man wanted and still got shot. Kind of like you, Jake. You do what the man wants, take a little for your troubles and keep all your other troubles—all those colored man troubles—far off. Even got your own place. Ain't that something? Jake's. He takes. But not too much. He the man. Well. He somebody's man. But I ain't nobody's man, Jake. Used to be Mr. Benjamin's man. But he got shot. Trying to be his own man. Can't do that in this town. Not if you're colored. Sure, I'm in trouble, Jake. The question is why ain't you in trouble?"

I don't know another man I would of let talk to me like that—not George Thomas for all Noah think I in his pocket. Another man even look those thoughts and his head split three ways to nothing. Other men in the bar hear half what Noah said and start for the exit doors like it gonna be a shootout in some wild West saloon. I look at him and I ain't lying. I'm thinking of slapping him up the head. I'm thinking of kicking his rear end into the street and keep kicking till I kick him into his mamma's front parlor. Then she can take his sorry self to bed and keep him there until he know that you don't talk to a man like that—any man. And sure not Jake.

But I don't. I take a breath and the rest of the bar just scatter. Even the bartender hiding over at the far end of the saloon, about as far as you can go and still be inside. I take a breath and put my hand over Noah's drink. He don't fight me. Thank the Lord he don't fight me.

"Enough. That's a feast. Your mamma tell you that? No? I thought all mammas said that. When you half-starved with the half-food they spent their whole life hustling for you, they tell you it was enough. And enough was a feast. Make you half-believe it, too. Because they were your mammas and what you gonna believe? Your own eyes or your mamma? What you gonna listen to? Your stomach rumbling or your mamma telling you that you had enough?"

I pulled Noah's drink over in front of me but I didn't drink from it. Even Noah, peace-loving Noah, might of had to fight me if I done that, take another man's drink. He pulled his head up and looked at me. I liked that. Noah weren't a fighter, but he weren't no coward, neither.

"You ask me why I ain't in trouble. A colored man in Lexington, Kentucky and not in trouble. Man, Noah. I got brothers I got less use for than you, and you say that to me." I took another breath. "Of course I in trouble, Noah. I handling it. I ain't saying I handling it the right way, but it's my way. I ain't strong like you. I don't mean the kind of strength that'll break a man in two. I got that. I mean the strength that keep you straight when straight so narrow you don't got room to put two feet side by side. You got that strength. I ain't smart like you. Oh, I smart enough. I know what's what. I got a head for figures that match you any day, Noah. But you got a different smart. You got an old man's smart like you lived a life already and a young man's smart, too, knowing what that old man forgot. You got a woman's smart. I don't mean that wrong, just that you feel people and most men don't."

A few of the men in the bar started to inch in closer. I guess they figured the chances of a shooting had lessened considerably. But I felt them listening to me, too. Can't remember the last time anybody listened to me other than a loud drunk to get himself out before I got him out. Felt good. But I kept my eyes on Noah.

"You got a smart that's gonna figure out a way to get out of trouble. And the way ain't in that bottle. Just more trouble. Then you gonna figure out how the rest of us—all us coloreds—can get out of trouble, too. Or at least a way to live with trouble. Live with trouble and still be men and women. Grown up colored men and women in Lexington, Kentucky. Won't that be something?"

I felt real tired—giving speeches wore you out. Most times all a bartender had to do was nod and murmur. "You got that right." "Ain't that so." "Lord almighty, what they gonna do next?" Don't even have to listen, just roll on out those handy sentences. Once in awhile the man looks confused and you realize you done rolled out the wrong words so you quick throw in a few others till he calm down. But this speeching—having to think hard of what you said—made me feel like I was trying to dig through rock. Still, I wasn't done. I reached deep.

"I met Mr. Benjamin several times. He was a fine gentleman. Educated. I bet you he read more books than any three white men in town. And he could write. Oh Lord, he could write. And talk. And preach. He was a man we all looked up to. Even when he sometimes bothered folks, they looked up to him. Now why in all that's holy would a man like that choose somebody like you to not just be his all-around man, but his friend, too? Because you was cheap labor? Hell, we all cheap labor. And Noah, you don't speak much better than me. I know you got two years more schooling, but that ain't much. You ain't no scholar. I know you can write, but you ain't write enough to make much difference. So it a mystery, Noah, and one I ain't the only one asking. Why Mr. Benjamin chose somebody like you?"

I let the question hang, like I seen preachers do. The whole congregation pushes forward, necks strained as they wait for the answer. *My* congregation—the six fellows who had made their way back to the bar—got their necks out, too. We all got our necks out.

"Because he knew you got what it takes, Noah. He knew he might not make it to the Promised Land, but you might. Or you might help us make it. My way ain't the right way. I know that. But that way," I pointed to the bottle—like I was that preacher again, pointing to demon rum, instead of a bartender and a saloon owner myself whose whole living depended on men reaching for the bottle—"ain't the way, either. At least, it ain't the way for you."

I swear I heard one of the fellows murmur an amen. I don't think he meant it funny, either. At least nobody clinked glasses.

"That don't mean you should stop drinking. A man sees trouble like you, maybe he got to drink. So go on drinking if you want to. Drink till your head ache so much from the booze that you can't hardly tell if your heart is hurting, too. Drink till everything hurt and then nothing hurt. Then drink some more.

"Then stop. Pick yourself up and lead your life. Help us lead ours. Show us how just like Mr. Benjamin tried to show us how. Just like Mr. Benjamin knew you would."

Then I did hear an amen! I looked hard at the fellow to see if he was joking. But he weren't. I must of been the only one who thought that speech funny, coming from me. Till I looked back into Noah's eyes. I looked hard and I saw he thought it funny, too.

Only he weren't laughing.

CHAPTER 40

Noah Webster, February 20, 1901, Lexington, Kentucky

Lizzie say she don't want me to come 'round anymore.

"Men in my family don't drink."

"Never?"

"Not around their families."

I came by after school. I waited a bit. Wanted to make sure the children were all gone. Especially Willy. He'd moved in with the Reverend Jones' family since Mr. Benjamin's shooting. Mamma was sorry, but she couldn't feed him and me, too. That's what she said. But mainly she didn't want Willy to see me like I was most of the time. He'd already seen me drunk two or three times. His daddy didn't drink. Imagine that? If I didn't know better, I'd say half the colored race was teetotaling. At least Willy got a uncle who drank. He told me that the last night he spent with us, looking at me wondering.

"But Mamma don't let him come 'round when he's drinking. Closed the door on his face. And it was raining."

My mamma nod her head, like she thinking of doing the same thing.

The children be asking me all sorts of inconvenient questions as to why I stopped coming around. But Lizzie was almost as inconvenient.

"Well, I'm not a man in your family."

She looked at me, that hard look she got. Maybe a little sad, too.

"That's right. You're not."

I gave it one last try. "Thought Jesus wanted us to get together."

Her mouth got even tighter on her face. Didn't think that was possible. Lizzie was worse than Mamma about disrespecting Jesus. She disrespected Him plenty I thought, calling Him a bad cook with His head off in the clouds when the stew's burning, saying He was like a student reading poetry when He should of been adding sums.

"Jesus just like your daddy," I couldn't help pointing out. She didn't deny it.

"Just like Daddy," she said.

When I called her on all that, she said she wasn't being disrespectful. "Jesus is family. He gets on my nerves, just like family. I imagine I irritate Him some, too."

But when I mentioned Jesus, she heard a mocking. She didn't go for mocking. I expected hot words from her mouth. I wanted hot words from her mouth. But when she spoke she was more sad than mad.

"Guess I misheard Him. I thought He meant for us to be together, but Jesus doesn't always say things clear. I get on Him about that, but that's how He is."

All I got left is Mamma and she about to throw me out. I see her come right to the edge and then draw back. I try not to sleep home nights when I real bad, just to give her a break from me. One time I tell her she spoiled.

"A whole bunch of colored women been dealing with drunken husbands all their life. Daddy maybe take two drinks his whole life. You spoiled, Mamma."

She knocked me on my tailbone for that one. I was teetering anyway, but she finished the job with a blow to the head. Ears ringing for near two days.

Don't drink in any George Thomas place, either, or at Jake's. Not up to sermons from Preacher Jake. Wears thirty-dollar suits, selling rotgut, and preaching about the evils of drinking. Plenty of other places. More than one hundred and fifty saloons in the mile circle around the courthouse. Some don't serve coloreds. But plenty do. Figure it'll take me years to work through the ones that do.

Of course sometimes you got to work through the jails, too. That slow you down some.

"When you gonna stop?" Mamma ask, the last time she come get me. She says it the last time, but I know better. "I know you hurting but this ain't the way."

"I'm not hurting, Mamma. Feel good. Not this morning so much. But last night I felt real good."

She look at me. Paid the man the fine. Out of my school-teacher savings, she tell me. Running low. Seem like a long time ago. She ready to cut me loose. Wish she would. Then I'd be free.

Free as a colored man gets in Lexington, Kentucky.

Still got my job at *The Standard*, but it's wobbly. Didn't publish the week after Mr. Benjamin's shooting. Then we put something together. Then skipped another week. Get paid one week and not the next. Skip two weeks and then a little something. I thought Mr. Johnson from Louisville who sold the paper to Mr. Benjamin back in the early nineties would come back. But he's too busy with his papers in Louisville. Rumors kept circling that Maria was selling the paper and she kept denying that. Truth is, she told me, she didn't own enough of it to sell. Just debts. And the debt men kept sending editors who didn't know a news story from a rumor, a fact from a wish. "If wishes were fishes," Mamma'd say, "we'd fry catfish tonight." Editors kept frying catfish when they didn't even have bait. Maria wanted them to hire me as the editor, but I was too young, they said. Too green.

Too close to Mr. Benjamin is what they meant. Mr. Benjamin scared away the merchants with all his radical talk. They wanted someone who got along with white people. Got along with white merchants at least. Kept me around for the mechanics. Not one of them knew how to typeset. They'd handle the words.

But one thing white merchants hate more than a radical paper is a paper nobody reads. I saw people still picking up the paper, looking for something. Looking for words that meant something. Looking for Mr. Benjamin.

The last pay I got was about half what I was owed. I felt lucky to get it.

"The name's worth something," I said to Maria.

"The name's worth everything," she said. "And nothing."

We were sitting in her front parlor the week before Christmas. She was leaving for Alabama two days past the holiday, "If the weather lets me. But then I'm headed south. It should get better by the mile."

"I guess it depends on what you mean by better. You headed south, remember."

I was trying everything I knew to get her to stay. I couldn't say everything—not two months after Mr. Benjamin's death. But I hinted it. I looked it. Maria wasn't blind. She knew.

She knew other things, too. About Lizzie. I didn't know what she knew about Lizzie. I didn't know what I knew about Lizzie. She hadn't told me to stop coming by yet, but I figured a couple more drunks should do it.

"How is your lady friend?" Maria asked.

"Not my lady friend, Maria. I don't have a lady friend. Hasn't been possible until now."

She blushed and looked down. She shook her head.

The children let out some shout in the kitchen where Sheila had hustled them. "Mamma needs to visit with Mr. Noah," is all she said. She let them grab the two small presents I held out and stick them under the tiny tree. Already about two dozen wrapped gifts circled it like a wall—the colored community wasn't about to let these new half-orphans want anything this Christmas. At least not presents.

Maria lifted her head. "Please, Noah. Don't."

I felt slapped though she said it in the gentlest of tones. I couldn't say, "*Why not? Why not tie yourself to a man on half-pay from a half-job who's been drinking a whole bunch lately? Who lives with his mamma who feeds him even when he spends the little money he got on booze. Take a chance, Maria. Why not?* I couldn't say any of that, couldn't make the promises I needed to make.

But if Maria would of taken that chance—a bad chance, a bet that Mike, my old bookie, would of never taken—if Maria would of taken that bet, I would of made it work. It would of pulled me out of that bottle faster than Mamma's pleas or Jake's sermons. Those children shouting in the kitchen would of dried me out quicker than a southeaster blowing August.

But I guess Maria wasn't a gambler. Or maybe she was and already lost all she could afford. And more. All she had left was two children, and a train ticket to Alabama. Maybe she wasn't gonna risk that on another child.

Or maybe she just didn't love me like I loved her.

I sat there quiet for awhile. We both did.

"Maria, you won't survive Alabama. Bad as Lexington is, it ain't Alabama."

She tightened her mouth. "A whole lot of colored people are surviving Alabama. Last I heard they're more than half the state. And you forget, I grew up in Alabama. I know the state. I will do fine. My father …"

She stopped. *What was the point?* her stopping said.

You don't go back to Alabama after living ten years in a freer place, I wanted to say but I didn't. *What was the point?*

Sheila let the children surround me as I said goodbye. I think she might of thought me the last hope. I kissed them both, even Charlie who I think thought he was a bit old to be kissed by a man. But even though they were too young to really understand what goodbye meant, the rest of us did. "Let Noah kiss you," Maria admonished Charlie as he tried to squirm away. Sheila grabbed me in a hug, though she wasn't going anywhere.

Maria just held out her hand. "Goodbye, Noah," she said, as if I made some afternoon call. But she didn't say, "Please come again." Just "Goodbye, Noah" and the smallest squeeze to her fingers, the squeeze you only give to your best friends when they're going away.

For good.

CHAPTER 41

Mamma, Fanny Webster, February 20, 1901, Lexington, Kentucky

I don't think I lay hands on Noah since he twelve, and then just a swat or two he hardly feel through his britches. And I never seen Joshua touch the boy except to sweep his hand up the boy's neck, more soft pat than cuff. Every minister we ever went to warned us about sparing the rod, spoiling the son, whatever that meant. My mamma, too. But Noah such a sweet boy, nobody—not even my papa who thought a mule's education started with a blow to the head—could think he needed hitting. Don't mean he didn't do wrong—he was a boy who thought rules made for other folks—but hitting him just didn't seem the way to make him mind.

"A lot of them rules need breaking," Joshua said to me. That was after Noah decided to borrow a couple of books from John Fielding's private library. I ain't seen John Fielding use that library for anything but show, but it was his to show, not Noah's to use.

Joshua said that there were a lot worse bosses than John Fielding and I'm sure he right—Noah's George Thomas come to mind. But John Fielding was bad enough. He got real touchy about things he owned. Had to keep reminding him he didn't own us. Not anymore. But he owned them books. We sneaked them back in the dead of night, breaking in to put back, like some kind of backward burglars. I said to Joshua he was gonna have to whup the boy.

"They catch him stealing books, no telling what they do. You got to whup him."

"Whup him for wanting to read? Ain't like he got any books in that school he go to."

"Whup him for being a colored boy who end up hanging from a tree if he don't watch out. Or if we don't watch out for him."

Joshua's mouth grew grim, but he took the boy out back and did something to him. Didn't see any bruises, didn't hear any crying, but he did something. They both came back as gloomy as broken-down horses.

"Ask John Fielding to borrow the books," I said to them. "Can only say no."

Didn't say no. Just made Noah work. Noah muck out stalls for an hour, he get a book for a day. Our own lending library. Noah said it made him a fast reader.

"Did you whup him?" I asked Joshua.

"Woman, that my business. Between me and my son."

That meant no. Neither Joshua or me seemed able to do what needed to be done. It weren't about sparing some rod. It was about needing to keep a colored boy safe in a white world. It was about teaching him what fences he could jump and which ones he'd be sure to break a leg trying. Or a neck. It was about teaching him that he needed to break some rules if he wanted to do anything in this world, but that's there some rules just weren't worth stretching.

How you teach that? Like telling him to hurry up and slow down at the same time.

So, when I smacked Noah up the side of the head and sent him tottering to the floor, he real surprised. Oh, I was mad. Telling me I spoiled because his daddy weren't a drunkard. All colored men natural-born drunkards? I almost wish his daddy *was* a drunkard. Wouldn't been so hard him leaving me to raise a no-good son on my own, without enough money to raise a puppy, let alone a boy.

Only he ain't a no-good son. Just pushing me. Trying to get me to push him out to the street. Mr. Benjamin gone. His wife, Maria, too. I been watching Noah moonstruck for years. But she a grown woman. She know better. Don't look like she long for this world anyway. Poor woman. Don't know what's going on with that girl, Lizzie, but she don't look the type to take too much nonsense. Good for her.

That leave me, his mamma. Get me to push him out and he can fall as far as he want, fall harder than when I knocked him down. Maybe that what he need, me pushing him out. Maybe that what it come to.

But not yet. His daddy gone. He would of knocked him down, too, him disrespecting him. Or me. But pushing him out? No, his daddy too soft-hearted to do that. It might not be the right thing to do, but I can't help it. Joshua couldn't either.

I remember the Reverend Pickering come 'round to stick his finger in both our faces. "You hate that boy? The Bible says if you hate the boy, you spare the rod. If you love the boy, you use the rod."

We didn't argue with the Reverend Pickering, though Joshua never did much care for the man. Would of been like arguing with the Good Book itself. But I thought even then that the world must sure love colored folks because it don't spare no rod for them. Must hold colored boys special tight in its embrace. Crush them to death. And I thought to myself, even then, *Ain't the world rod enough? We got to be rod, too?*

For the world's been one big rod on Noah. And maybe he needs someplace soft to land, needs someplace safe to hide. And maybe I doing this all wrong. The Reverend Pickering still telling me I too easy, that I'm opening the gate wide to Noah's destruction, that I'm clearing the broad path to Hell.

But Noah seem like he finding his own way to Hell. Or the world finding it for him. I watch him drinking and fighting and pushing everybody further and further off. He trying to push me off, too. But I'm his mamma. I don't push easy. If he going to Hell, he gonna have to drag me with him. Won't be long now.

We halfway there.

CHAPTER 42

Maria Lulu, January 5, 1901, Birmingham, Alabama

I wrote Emma Bisou as soon as I had arrived, thanking her for raising the money for my trip. A public subscription. Robert would have been humiliated, but there was no choice. Emma had not wanted me to leave, or so she said. So everyone said, but what was the alternative? Even the most cheerful of friends could see that I was fading away. And like everyone in Lexington, Emma had built up Alabama in her mind as a place so evil to coloreds that the very air would burn them to breathe it.

The air I breathe always burns, I could have told her. And one can learn how to breathe anywhere.

"You won't stand it in Alabama," she warned me.

"It's only for a little while," I told her, which I shouldn't have. Even Emma Bisou looked stricken when I said that. "It will take only a little while for me to accustom myself," I amended, but the damage had been done.

The policeman who greeted me as I debarked in Birmingham was there to prove my fearful friends right.

"What you doing out in the middle of the day, girl? Ain't you belong in some kitchen somewhere? You taking the day off? Playing fancy lady?" He was looking at my dress with deep suspicion and dislike. "Why you dressing like some white lady?" Just then the porter handed down the children. "These your children? You dressing them like some fancy white children. Where you come from?"

The children were looking up at him wide-eyed and fearful. Lillian was two heartbeats from a loud wail. Even Charlie's eyes filled with tears. They had never heard their mother addressed so.

"We are from here. We are visiting my father."

"You from here? Then you should know better than to dress like that. You ain't no white lady. Ain't no lady. Next time I arrest you. We don't like our niggers putting on airs. If you can't remember that, better put your tail back on that train and take your fancy-ape children with you."

I wished I *could* put myself back on the train. We were to wait for my father on the platform, but he would come dressed in his suit for the occasion. That would make the policeman angrier.

"Yes, officer," I said, and bowed my head. I hurried from the platform, leaving the luggage. Real suitcases. Not cotton or potato sacks. What would the policeman think? What had I done? Bringing my children back to this.

Well, it's just for a little while, I comforted myself.

Just for a little while.

CHAPTER 43

Noah Webster, March 9, 1901, Davis Bottoms, Lexington, Kentucky

The dog licking my face awake looked half-disappointed, got that sad look dogs get when you scold them. I was lying in a gully where folks tossed their garbage and by all rights he should have found something to eat, but other critters must of beat him to it. Not as much as a dry bone to gnaw on. On the other hand, he'd found me and I was one of them human beings—or at least I looked some similar to one under all the dirt—and sometimes human beings fed you. The Lord knows why.

"Sorry, mutt. Nothing here for you." He kept licking me anyway. Just loved human beings, I reckon. Or maybe I got some bacon grease stuck in my stubble. I gave him a scratch behind his ears for his troubles. Least I could do.

A normal March would of washed me away where I was laying, but it'd been dry. Dry as the roof of my mouth. Davis Bottoms. The bottom of the well. Spring floods usually swept away a couple of the houses. Then folks built again, sometimes using the same boards.

The Lord knows why.

I know why, too. Poor people why. White and colored. Build on land nobody else much wants. Good fertile land maybe because of all that flooding. New March green just peeking out at the end of branches, buds thickening. A garden scratched out by somebody on the slope. Lettuce mostly, looked like, maybe some carrots and some turnips. Don't have a garden where we live now. City crowded. Colored crowded. Mamma loves turnip greens. Could move over here. Like the country in the city. Real nice. Except for the flooding.

I pulled myself up, found myself being stared at by an old woman leaning over a porch railing that looked about as steady as I did. Must of been the gardener. I had to squint my eyes to make out if she was colored or white. Colored, I thought. Hard to tell after a certain age. I waved, but she didn't wave back. Just shook her head. She threw some scraps over the porch and my mutt abandoned me in a heartbeat. *Ain't that just like a friend,* I thought. The old woman kept a suspicious eye on me, like I was gonna fight the mutt for the leavings. I waved again and this time she picked up her hand and shook it some.

Ain't come to that, old woman. Not yet.

The last time I'd been in Davis Bottoms was when I walked it with Mr. Benjamin, when he was running for Congress. That didn't last long. Nothing seemed to last long. Hope the old woman didn't recognize me from then. Probably not. Mamma'd have a hard time recognizing me under all the dirt. I stretched, aching like an old man. Tried to remember how I got here.

Daddy called it a Methodist hangover, when folks couldn't remember—or said they couldn't—what they did the night before when they were carousing. I wished for one of them now as memory just passed over me—clear as a Baptist sin—me crawling through Yellmantown and then over to Irishtown, first the colored bars and then the bars that didn't much care what color you were. Like that old woman. After awhile, couldn't much tell what color a drunk was.

I was looking for plug-uglies on their own, or with maybe just one fellow in tow. I could take on two of them if they weren't expecting it. I'd jump in swinging, with my fists if it was just the one, with a homemade truncheon if it was two. Once I took on three. They didn't know what was happening to them, one crazy colored fellow jumping on three plug-uglies.

Only got a couple of licks in before the third fellow ran yelling up the street. The other two just lay on the sidewalk, covering their heads. I beat them like a rug that'd been rolled in the mud.

The plug-uglies didn't all lie there. Some fought back hard. I didn't ache just from lying on the ground.

Jake couldn't believe it when I told him what I was doing.

"You done lost your mind. And about to get your brains blown out. Just like the Mayor. How you know these fellows plug-uglies? They wear some sign or something?"

"They white."

"They white? Listen to you, man. You gonna fight every white man in town?"

"Not every white man. Just every white man I can find alone by himself or almost alone. Figure I can break a lot of heads before they stop me."

Jake looked like he couldn't take it in for a second. Like he didn't know what to say.

"Noah," and he tapped a finger to my skull like you tap a pumpkin to see if it's ripe, "this the head that's gonna be broken." Then he put his fingers 'round my throat. "And your neck snapped. Is that what you want?"

He wasn't gonna understand, Jake. I didn't want my head broken, but I didn't much care. And nobody was gonna snap my neck, or shoot me in the back, either, running away. What I wanted? I wanted Mr. Benjamin to have brought a gun with him, really, not get one planted on his dead body. I wanted Maria living in Lexington, not dying slow in an Alabama hell.

"What I want is to make them pay. As many as I can. That's what I want."

"Make them pay? How much you think they owe? How much Mr. Benjamin worth?"

The sun was barely up. Not enough leaves on the trees to block it. The tree shadows looked like boney fingers stretching out on the ground. My own shadow grew as the sun hit me, crawled up my body. Felt good. Felt the chill melting. I brushed the dirt off much as I could. Wondered if the old woman knew of a pump I could use to wash off some. I smelled terrible. Mamma would be off cleaning houses by now, but I didn't want to trudge home looking like I'd slept in some dump. Which I had. Didn't want to shame Mamma in front of the neighbors. More than I done already.

Now I remember why I ached. The last plug-ugly I jumped—a skinny, red-headed fellow. Thought he'd be an easy target but it was like he was half-waiting for me. Maybe he was. Word probably out about the crazy colored man beating on young white men. I only jumped young ones. Didn't take no money though sometimes they offered it to get me to stop. Just wanted them to hurt. When they yelling, whimpering, it calm me. Just a little. Like I don't feel it all. Just a moment. Then it start again.

Best when they fight back, though, like that little fellow did. Best when I feel their fists hitting me as I hit them. The world all disappear then. That little fellow got in two, three licks before he went down. I only kicked him once when he fell. Good fighter like that, least I could do.

I went closer to the porch but stopped about six feet off. Didn't want to scare her. "Missus!" I yelled out. "Missus, you know where I can use a pump? Wash up some?"

She came back outside. This close I could see clear. She weren't colored—wrinkled and real dark, but not colored. Italian maybe, though I could see some red hair still sparkling in the dawn. Mostly gray, though. She pointed to a pump half hidden by a lilac bush—no purple showing yet but full of buds. Hope it didn't frost out before it bloomed.

"Use that one. Good water. Good drinking, too. You want soap?"

I nodded. She brought out a bar of lye soap, the kind that peels the skin off along with the dirt. A tin cup for drinking, too. "Got to push the pump hard. Don't want to come up chilly mornings, but it's good water."

217

I felt my arm half drop off from pumping, but finally I heard the gurgling. And it was good water, smelling of Bluegrass limestone. I poured it over my head and scrubbed all my sins away. Scrubbed the dirt, at least. The sins stayed hid, beneath the skin. Then I drank, tin cup after tin cup, till I felt the water sloshing around in my stomach. I brought the cup and soap back to the porch. I was gonna leave them there and go but the old woman was waiting for me. She handed me a towel about as rough feeling as the soap. She had a plate waiting for me with a hunk of cheese along with some bread and a wizened old apple. She nodded approvingly at my appearance.

"Now you're looking like a person, not some mud-creature. Get your woman, if you got one, to scrub those britches, though I don't know anybody can save them the state they're in. Here's some victuals. Sorry about that apple. Don't have more than a dozen left and they're looking kind of sad. Taste good, though."

I didn't know what to make of it. I mumbled out some thanks but she waved it off.

"Oh, I could see you were a good boy, even under all that dirt. Out gallivanting. You boys. Why you do that? Can't be that much fun. And you worry everybody, especially your mammas. I got my own boy out there—didn't come home last night. Didn't see him, did you? Skinny little fellow, but tough. I don't worry about him. Well, not too much. Red-headed boy? Like me, except I'm mostly gray, now. Oh, well, he'll show up. Couldn't kill him with a stick. Want more? No, that's okay. Maybe your mamma's feeding my boy. Go on home, now. Don't drink so. You young now, but that's a way of getting old real quick."

One kind old white woman don't make up for a world of evil, I said to myself as I walked off—slunk off, really, quick as I could, fearful I'd run into her son before I could get away. So maybe her son weren't a plug-ugly, he was white. No telling what he'd do to a lone colored man, especially if he'd a bunch of his pals around him. But it didn't do me any good. Couldn't summon up a Methodist hangover to save my life. Or my soul. "Maybe your mamma's feeding my boy." If he was hungry, Mamma'd be feeding him, plug-ugly or not. Turnip greens if she had them. I shuddered, remembering that last kick I gave him. Felt kind of plug-ugly myself.

I wanted to go home and sleep. Wanted to go home and think. Mamma and Jake and the Reverend W. C. Jones, all been hammering at me. But that old white woman with her moldy apple and her hunk of cheese, that old woman waiting up for her no-account son—listening for him in the half-sleep of the early morn and getting up to help wash the no-account son in front of her, to feed him and chide him and love him. That old white woman was shaming me, peeling at the callus on my heart like her lye soap peeled my skin.

"Oh, Jesus," I murmured, "just leave me alone. I ain't done hating yet. I ain't done hating yet."

It was like the Lord answered my prayer. Patrolman Luke Doyle stepped in front of me like Pharaoh's army, blocking me from the Promised Land of sleep and forgiveness. I don't know if he planned Mr. Benjamin's death or just helped it happen. I know that I hated him, hated him more than Mike Moynahan. Moynahan was a rabid dog. You shot a rabid dog, but you didn't hate it. I hated Luke Doyle.

The Lord's love just sank like water down a sinkhole at the bottom of Davis Bottoms. Doyle was the real thing. That old woman's red-headed son just a substitute.

"Noah! My old friend, Noah. What you been doing since the high and mighty world of colored journalism done let you down? Christ, look at you, boy. You're a mess. And soaking wet, too. Fall off your ark, Noah?" And he laughed, like he the first man who thought of that joke. "Or maybe you've been swimming? Only pond nearby is the one over by Bolivar, where they do the baptisms. Getting yourself baptized again? Never figured out why you Baptists feel the need to dip yourself in over your head every couple of years. Catholics just sprinkle a couple drops on a baby's forehead and leave it at that. Well, whatever it takes. Maybe you all need more baptizing. Things I've heard about you, you sure do—soak yourself in the River Jordan. 'Cross over Jordan.'"

He sang those last words: "Cross over Jordan." He was happy, showing off. Look how smart he was, even knew the old time music. He'd hear it on a Sunday or a Wednesday, pouring out of the windows of the colored churches on his beat. He was smiling wide like we really was old friends. Old enemies. Hard to tell the difference sometime. I should of smiled, too, given him some of his own back. Asked him about his pal, Mike Moynahan. He wouldn't of liked it, but he would of let it go. But I couldn't do it. Just couldn't do it.

"Ain't been baptized in awhile," I said. "Probably could use another dip. But I hear the pond over at Bolivar ain't just for baptizing. People throw things in there they don't want anymore—or don't want to be caught with. You find all sorts of things if you dredge that pond. Old wagon wheels. Broken farm plows. Even guns. People throw in pistols they don't want people knowing they owned. That where you find your old guns, Patrolman Doyle? Imagine you find a use for them—even rusty old guns."

Funny how quick he stopped smiling. Like I slapped the smile right off his face. Like we crossed over Jordan the wrong way and we were headed back to Egypt.

"What you saying, you black bastard? You saying I planted that gun on your nigger boss, may he roast in Hell? Say it out loud if you got the balls. Say it clear. I'll cut them black balls off and stuff them in your lying mouth. I'll haul you off to jail so quick you'd think you landed in the middle of a May twister."

Sometimes you get to step back before you do something. Sometimes you look at yourself before you move, and you think, *Am I really gonna do this? Is this a good idea?* And then you jump in anyway, feel the cold water touch your toes and know it gonna wash over your whole body. You gonna be baptized. You gonna be born again. I watched Luke Doyle's mouth shrink that smile, watched his face blotch red and green and purple and all those colors white people get when they about to fit out and it felt good. The sun was up full now. Saw my full shadow behind me and there was two of us and I was swinging away with everything I had. It felt real good. Better than pounding on ten plug-uglies, a whole lot better than kicking a skinny, red-headed boy whose mamma was waiting up for him. Felt so good I didn't want it to stop. Felt so good I needed one more fist to his face. Only I kept my hands strict to my side.

"Just saying what you and I both know happened, Doyle: that you put that gun on Mr. Benjamin's body after your pal, Mike Moynahan, shot him in the back. That you stood there in court and lied under oath, so help you God. Maybe that Catholic sprinkle didn't do its job. But I don't think a Baptist dunking would do much good, either. You're a lying, murderous prick. Ain't enough water in Kentucky to wash your black soul clean. Your white soul."

His eyes got so wide, I thought he might stroke out. He tottered like he was about to fall over. "You, you…" he mumbled and finally grabbed my shoulders.

"What?" I said. "Am I under arrest, Officer Doyle? What's the charge? Telling the truth? You got that right. That will get you arrested in Kentucky."

He couldn't speak, but managed to blow his whistle—three times—loud. Two other police came running from different streets. They looked around us, searching for the mayhem three whistles meant. Looked perplexed when Doyle, finding breath, managed to choke out "Arrest him. Arrest the black bastard."

"What's he done?" one police asked. He was young, so young the uniform looked strange on him. "Stab somebody? He got a knife on him?" He looked at me scared, like I was a bomb ready to go off.

"Drunk, disorderly," was all Doyle could get out. The young police and the older one with him grabbed me and held me tight though I just stood there. "Assault, too," Doyle added. "He assaulted me." Both cops looked at me standing peacefully there.

"He assaulted you?" the young cop asked, looking to his older partner for assurance. The older cop turned on the young police. "If Doyle said he assaulted him, he assaulted him. Cuff him hard or I'll be assaulting you."

They didn't wait for the police wagon—we were only four blocks from the city jail. They walked me there, the older police pushing me along, the younger one's hand tense on my shoulder. People made way for us, the white folks shrinking back like I was some pollution they soiled themselves with just by seeing—trying not to look at me, their day half-spoiled by me passing them by. A few colored folk like that, too. But they looked angry, too, and shamed. I'd brought shame on the race. Didn't know how I did it, but the police dragging me through the streets proved I did. They turned their backs. "Ain't one of us," their back-turning said to the whites, "don't have nothing to do with us."

But other coloreds didn't turn. Kept their eyes on me all the way. "Hang in there, brother," one whispered to me as I passed, and the older police swirled round and barked at him: "Don't talk to the prisoner!"

But he couldn't keep their eyes off me, and it was their eyes passed over me as cool as that old woman's pump water, as soothing as an Easter blessing, Mamma'd say. Somebody be sure to recognize me—Lexington a small town like that. Somebody be sure to run to Mamma, tell her about her boy in trouble again. Pushed through the streets like Barabbas. Looking a sorry mess. Don't know what he did, but he in trouble.

Mamma said last time was the last time, but she'd be there—at the jailhouse or the courthouse. She'd be there, and her eyes be the biggest ponds of all. Her eyes take me in and tell me not to worry about all the trouble I bringing on—not to worry now. Just lie on your back and float, and when you think to sink, just take a breath and rise up.

"I'm sorry, Mamma," I'd start to say but she wouldn't let me.

"I'm sorry, too, son, but don't worry about that now. Plenty of time to worry about things. Sufficient unto the day are the troubles thereof. The day's all full up with trouble. Don't go worrying about tomorrow."

CHAPTER 44

Judge Frank Bullock, March 11, 1901, Lexington, Kentucky

The same names on the court docket, week in, week out. The same drunks. The same sad women.

"We could save money, Patrick. Just change the top date on the docket."

He laughs heartily as if I hadn't already told him the same joke the week before. We are all of us like actors in some tired melodrama.

And I am the villain. The script is the same. Thirty days or thirty dollars. Most of the drunks have long since run through their poor families' money. If they are fit, I halve their sentence and send them to the city quarry, though most can barely walk, let alone swing a pick. Mike Moynahan's the foreman. No public drunkenness deserves his supervision for long.

The women have their pimps at hand—the younger ones, at least. They look more inconvenienced than arrested, though this being Monday, they spent Sundays in jail. Their day of rest. Thirty days' lost income is much more than a fine.

I wonder if the older ladies might almost welcome the respite in the city jails.

"Esther, are you returned again? Aren't you getting a bit old for this?"

"Oh, Judge, it ain't much work lying on your back."

Patrick thought that even funnier than my tired joke about the docket, but I cut his laugh short with a look. It may all be melodrama, but the public dignity of my court needed to be retained.

I scanned the names. Not all the names were the same. One name in particular stuck out: Noah Webster. I had not seen him since Moynahan's trial, his face staring at me from the back of the room. Judging the judge. And his letter. I looked over the crowd of prisoners. I motioned Patrick over, pointing to his name on the list.

"Where is this man?"

"Trial, Judge."

Almost no one chose a trial. I could go through a docket of fifty drunks and ladies in a morning. I looked at his charges: drunk, disorderly, assault upon a police officer—a felony. The police officer's name was another name leaping up to slap me awake: Luke Doyle. I looked at Patrick.

"Says he wants a trial, Judge. Gonna be his own lawyer."

He looked like he was about to laugh again at the idea, but one glance at my face changed his mind. An assault on a police officer could bring five years. His own lawyer. I had known that he read in Benjamin's office, but he could not have read much. Too young. His only other experience that I knew of was his standing up for those women in Cadentown, that so-called protest that ended in a near riot. This did not look promising.

As it was, lawyers were scarce in Morning Court. Rich drunks did not appear in court. In fact, they were rarely arrested. And shootings were deferred till the afternoon, and even then did not always involve lawyers. Unless the shooters were rich. So little to argue about in most cases. I insisted that a lawyer be involved if there was killing. Moynahan had had two for a mere hearing and several more waiting on the sidelines. Watching for a word from Billy.

Thomas Headley, the Commonwealth's attorney, was waiting for me in my outer office when I returned from lunch, holding the week's trial schedule. Another cousin, or our grandmothers had been. Cousins, removed or not, somehow always present in Lexington.

Billy certainly must feel we are everywhere. The schedule was unusually crowded: two fatal shootings and six less lethal ones. The names were the familiar ones, though an assault charge raised both our eyebrows: a lady of our acquaintance had stabbed another lady with her sewing scissors.

"I think I am related to both these ladies. You must be, too, Thomas. Can't you make this go away?"

He looked harassed. "I've been trying. The wounds barely broke the skin, but tempers are running high."

"Make it go away, Thomas," I said again, and he nodded.

"I've been trying to make this go away, too," he said, pointing to Noah's name on the list. He looked more annoyed than bothered now. "I offered him a year—the minimum for assault on a police officer and he won't budge."

"Did you talk to the officer? Perhaps reduce the charge to disorderly?"

"Tried. Real excitable fellow. Wanted to raise the charge to aggravated."

Aggravated. A maximum of twenty years for aggravated assault on a police officer. I'd say Luke Doyle *was* excitable. But I was annoyed. A trial would take too much valuable time. Lawyers in my court knew to be both succinct and prompt.

"All rise," Patrick intoned, and Noah was before me again—his case squeezed in between two shootings—one fatal. He was in manacles, both hands and feet, though both the first accused shooter and the second, stood there freely, unshackled.

The first shooter was Jack Brennan, a pickled forty-year-old who looked sixty. Sober in my court but floating in so much past alcohol he was like a bog that had had weeks of rain. The first sunny day was not enough to dry him. He pleaded self-defense. He worried, he told me, that sometime in the future, the man he shot would shoot him.

"Did he threaten that?"

"He did with his eyes, Judge. You could see it in his eyes."

"What caliber bullet do his eyes shoot?"

His lawyer objected, said his client had witnesses who'd witnessed the same lethal eyes. "Mr. Brennan was right to be frightened for his life."

His victim—a man whose name I also recognized as a regular from Morning Court, was still in the infirmary though not in serious condition. Alcohol facilitated shootings, but it marred aim.

I could not recall his eyes.

"One year in the state penitentiary, two years probation. Next."

Noah stood there, his eyes free if not his hands. I called Patrick over.

"Remove the manacles. If Mr. Webster is going to be his own lawyer, he might need the use of his limbs."

"Judge, the policeman who arrested him said he's a dangerous man. Needs to be held tight."

I looked at Patrick. He did not usually question my orders. He quickly removed the handcuffs, only glancing up at me before he removed the fetters from the feet. I waited as Noah rubbed blood back into his limbs.

"I am sorry to see you here in this condition, Mr. Webster. I thought you would prove a better credit to your race."

He smiled at me like he was happy to see me. Then he started speaking like the lawyer he claimed to be and not the defendant he was.

"No credit, Judge. Just debt. All debt. The race's credit been shot down in the street, trying to kill the fellow shooting at him running away from a bullet. Never know what's gonna kill you in this world. Surprised you just convicted that fellow who told you about those eyes.

222

Everybody knows eyes are deadly, kill you sooner than a back will, running away. But I guess each case is different, Judge."

Patrick turned to me, wondering if I would order the shackles returned. Noah's speech had silenced the murmurings that continued throughout the day for all my gaveling ordering quiet. I saw that Luke Doyle had entered the court, along with several fellow policemen and his brother, John. I remembered them all from Moynahan's hearing. It was as if we were revisiting that day, absent the main defendant. Noah looked at me almost as if I were the defendant.

"Each case is different, Mr. Webster. I understand you are acting as your own lawyer. As you have declined a jury trial though you are entitled to one, I wonder at your opening statement. Proceed."

Patrolman Doyle smiled widely at my words and one of his friends laughed loudly, though the other men turned on him quickly and he quieted. They knew I would not tolerate such demonstrations. The choked-off laugh hung like a sour note in the courtroom. Noah nodded.

"Alienating the judge. You're right, Your Honor, probably not a good opening move. Mr. Benjamin would of been disappointed in me. I plead 'not guilty', Your Honor and I call myself as a first witness."

This time the laugh was general. I gaveled quiet.

The Commonwealth presented its case first, but I glanced at Thomas, who shrugged his shoulders—meaning I should let Noah testify. It might expedite matters. Noah's lawyer should have known better, but Mr. Benjamin's training had been cut short. I gave him leeway.

Noah told his story quietly and quickly, how he had met Patrolman Doyle who queried him on his wet hair which he had acquired from a pump in Davis Bottom—he could summon the lady whose pump it was if that was necessary. How Patrolman Doyle wondered if he'd been swimming in the pond on Bolivar, how that had prompted Noah to recall the many objects thrown into that pond—old guns among them. How Noah had wondered aloud if the pond was a source for Patrolman Doyle's own old gun collection. How Noah suggested that Doyle might need a constant supply of them as they seemed to turn up in all sorts of places.

How Patrolman Doyle had taken offense and ordered his arrest.

I looked at my cousin, Thomas, who seemed more than usually removed, as spellbound as the rest of us by Noah's quiet recitation. He had not objected throughout Noah's testimony, though Doyle and his friends could hardly contain themselves. They were jumping about in their corner, making as much noise as they dared. Thomas finally pulled himself up.

"It wasn't eight o'clock yet and you live a good ways from there. What were you doing up and in that neighborhood? Why were you using a pump in Davis Bottom?"

Noah glanced at a middle-aged colored woman before he answered. He spoke softly so that we strained to hear, though the colored woman's deep sighing made it clear that she had heard. "I woke up from a drunk the night before in some lady's yard, asked her if I could use her pump to wash up. She fed me some breakfast. On my way home when I met Doyle."

Thomas smiled, sure he had Noah now. "So, you admit you were drunk and disorderly."

"Nope. Not drunk. A lot less drunk than that fellow you just sentenced to a year. And not disorderly. Just not the neatest fellow on the street. And wet. On the outside. Insides all dried out."

"Some drunk states go on for days. Patrolman Doyle says you assaulted him when he tried to arrest you for being drunk and disorderly. Do you even remember what you did that morning?"

"Oh, yes, sir. I got a good memory. Remember you not questioning Patrolman Doyle too much about that gun he said he found on Mr. Benjamin, though it was half-rusted like it'd been lying in water a good while."

Thomas turned to me, too shocked to object. I slammed the gavel down. Everybody, even Doyle and company, jumped from their seats.

"Keep your answers confined to this case, Mr. Webster, or I will confine you for contempt. Do you understand me?"

"Yes, Your Honor. It just all seems to blend together. This case. That case. But I'll try, Your Honor. Only I wasn't allowed to speak that case so it kind of spills out this case. What I got to say. But I'll try, Your Honor."

He turned back to Thomas.

"Wasn't drunk. All sobered up—maybe I should bring in the lady, she'll tell you. Though it seems poor treatment for her kindness. Wasn't disorderly. Never touched Luke Doyle. He's lying."

Thomas shrugged in bewilderment as he dismissed Noah as a witness and called Patrolman Doyle to the stand.

A policeman's word was taken as bond in Lexington. They lied, of course. They lied all the time. Everyone knew that. Sometimes Thomas would walk them back from an all too obvious lie that would embarrass the city, embarrass the court. But if they insisted, their sworn oath carried the law, and all bowed before it. Only occasionally would I quarrel with their testimony and insist that they rethink their stories. They would retreat from the stand then and come back with something approaching credibility. I did not like it, but the integrity, the stability of the court, the structure of our very society, demanded that we accept the policeman's sworn words. Patrolman Doyle's face and manner reflected that stability. He knew we were required to believe his policeman's word as he told his story of Noah objecting to his arrest, assaulting him with his fists and kicking him. Noah knew it, too.

Thomas had only one follow-up question.

"When the other patrolmen came in response to your whistles, they said Webster was just standing there, quiet. They said he also didn't resist when they arrested him. Can you explain that?"

"I think he was shocked at what he done—knew he was in deep trouble. Didn't want to make it worse."

Noah looked quietly at Doyle before he began his cross-examination—both sets of eyes as lethal as the ones the shooter had described.

"Do you remember what we talked about that morning, Doyle?"

"Patrolman Doyle!" Thomas objected.

I raised my eyebrow. "Use the correct titles, *Mr.* Webster."

Noah smiled at Doyle whose face got darker than Noah's. "*Patrolman* Doyle? Do you remember?"

"You was talking a bunch of nonsense. Drunk. Lashing out."

"You don't remember asking me if I'd been swimming in Bolivar Pond?"

"Maybe. You was wet. Looked a mess. More than usual."

"You don't remember me asking you if that's where you found the gun you planted on Mr. Benjamin's body?"

Thomas was out of his seat, objecting that Noah was doing it again, mixing the cases. Doyle had stood up quickly and sat back down as quick, his whole body looking like he was about to lunge at Noah. His friends in the corner ignored my gaveling as they shouted at Noah. "Lying black bastard. Kill the nigger!"

I pounded all to silence at last. I was breathing as heavily as anyone. Only Noah stood there calmly. Only the black lady in the crowd sat still, her one movement the sighs that moved her bosom.

"I warned you, Mr. Webster, not to mix the cases."

"They are mixed up, Your Honor, like peas and carrots in a stew. Can't separate them after awhile. All one mess as my Mamma says. Me asking Doyle—Patrolman Doyle—that question about the gun-planting is why he got so upset. Why he got me arrested. Hurt his feelings with my question. Never touched him with my fists. Never kicked him. Just pricked him with a question. Like I done now. See how upset he is? How upset his friends are? They'd arrest me all over if they could. Charge me with murder this time, I reckon."

He turned back to Doyle. "You said that I must of been shocked, that's why I just stood quietly when the other police came up to arrest me. The young police asked you twice what I done. Didn't make sense to him, me standing there quiet and you saying I was assaulting you. Or been assaulting you. Ever arrest anybody else for assault who acted like you said I did?"

Doyle didn't answer right away, as if he hadn't understood the question. Or even heard it. Which was probable. Doyle kept staring at Noah, his hands almost trembling as he kept them to his sides. I prompted him.

"Answer the question, Patrolman."

He glared at me. I was part of the enemy now. I had let this happen.

"No. I don't remember. No."

Noah stopped smiling. "No, you don't remember. Because you usually make up better stories than this one. You're a smart man. Everybody knows that. The brains of the outfit. But you came up with this one too quick. Had more time when you planted the gun on Mr. Benjamin. Could plan it out more."

Doyle was on top of Noah in an instant, pounding him with his fists. But Noah kept his feet. Like a pugilist who knows how to let the punch meet him but not knock him over, he took the blows and didn't fall. He didn't hit back—he covered his face with his arms as Patrick finally peeled Doyle from him, then turned to block Doyle's friends from joining the fray.

I did not gavel. It seemed beyond my gaveling. Order in the courtroom was beyond anyone's grasp.

But quiet returned. It felt more like the quiet of the grave than the stillness of justice. Patrolman Doyle was back on the stand and Doyle's friends back in their corner. The lawyer for the second shooter—whose trial did not look as if it were going to happen anytime soon—approached the bench quietly and Patrick rescheduled him for the next day. Promptness be damned. We breathed. March light poured through the large courthouse windows. Almost spring outside, the light said. Whatever happened inside the court, it was almost spring outside.

Sufficient unto the day are the troubles thereof.

"Are you done questioning Patrolman Doyle, Mr. Webster?"

"Oh, all done, Your Honor. All done. Except one thing I want to point out, Your Honor."

I turned to him. The whole court turned to him.

"That's what assault looks like, Your Honor, in case you're wondering. That's what assault look likes."

I sentenced Luke Doyle to thirty days at the city quarry for contempt of court. I imagined his associate, Mike Moynahan, would take care that he wouldn't swing too many picks. Still the indignity would sting. I could hardly put him in a city jail. I didn't imagine Noah was the first prisoner Doyle had assaulted. A policeman as an inmate in our jails might not live out his sentence. And assault, for all Luke Doyle might think, is not a capital offense. I dismissed the charges against Noah.

Billy was in my office within the hour.

"You can't do that, Judge. You're taking the word of a colored rabble-rouser over a policeman of good standing."

"Not in such good standing, Billy. He assaulted a lawyer in my court."

"Lawyer?" Billy almost gaped. "That…" He couldn't finish. "Don't do this, Judge. You're making an enemy of every cop in town."

"Am I making you my enemy, Billy?"

There it was: Billy looked me square for a moment. He didn't come as far as he had without knowing when there wasn't any give left. His shoulders sagged a bit, but he was smiling.

"No, Judge. Hope it never comes to that. Just gonna make things harder, Judge."

"Then here's some more news that might make things even harder, from your view point, at least. I decided to hire Noah Webster as a clerk and have him read law in my offices. I understand that I may have to pay him out of my own funds if the city—if you, Billy—object to a colored clerk on the city payrolls. He showed true aptitude for the law in my court this morning… before things got out of hand. Of course, it may all be a moot question; he may not agree to clerk for me."

Billy just sat there, silent, perhaps stunned. "Why, Judge? Why would you do that?"

"I owe him, Billy. So do you. Besides, a good half of the people who stand in front of my bench are colored. They need a good lawyer of their own. We took away a good lawyer. Only right that we replace him. As much as we can."

Billy wasn't stunned anymore. He leaped up from his chair. "We don't owe him a god-damned thing, Judge. You want to waste your money, that's your call. You're right about that. Not one city penny is going to that nigger on my watch. And keep him out of the courtroom. Keep him out of sight. I couldn't beg, buy, or steal enough votes to get you elected if word got out. Or me, either. We're known to be political partners. I'd go down with you. The whole organization might go down with you. Nigger lovers. Kiss of death in this town. In this state. Far as I know, in this country."

He took a sip from his flask. He almost never did that in front of me—the dignity of my chambers, but dignity be damned.

"You hear me, Judge? You want to do this goddamn thing, you got to keep it secret. Irish voters put up with anything, the Krauts, too. But they got one thing in common, one thing they share with your people, Judge, though your people don't like to say it out loud. They hate the nigger. They hate him so much they'll live on two meals as long as the nigger only got one; they'll work a seventy hour week for coolie wages, long as the nigger got to put in eighty for even less. You think you don't think that way, but you do. You hated Benjamin as much as Moynahan did, or Doyle. More. Benjamin thought he was your equal. Hell, he thought he was better than you. And maybe he was. Look how far he got. Black, poor, foreign. I understand him better than you do. We the same except for his color. My people know that. We only one step up from the nigger. Just one step, but we're gonna keep that step."

He took another long draught. At least he did not offer me any.

"You got some guilty conscience over that man, Benjamin, as if he hadn't got just what he had coming to him. You don't want to think you knew what was coming—what had to come—but you did. You're a judge. You know how one thing follows after another. Your daddy knew what was what—didn't worry over much when he and Morgan raided a town and folks got hurt: children, women, colored, white. Folks got killed. Folks he killed. Knew what he wanted, knew what he had to do to get it. But your blood's got thin.

"That's why you got me. I've put up with your moaning for years and I'll put up with it for years more, 'cause we're a good team, Judge, your people who are used to running things and my people who make things work. But it'll all come crashing, Judge, if you let this out. Worse than if you had a shady lady on the side. People might understand that. They won't this."

He left then, too upset to work his way back to his smile and his easy manner. Smiling Billy left my chambers scowling. I had tried his patience, as Grace might put it. Might be for naught. Noah might not want to be my shady lady on the side. Billy was right. About the politics. About all of it. I had my father's ruthlessness in my blood. I simply lacked his honesty.

Benjamin was dead, shot in self-defense by Mike Moynahan. I had ruled it so. It must be so.

But I could do something for Noah if he let me. Because I did not hate the Negro. Billy's people might. My own, for all their politeness, might also. But I did not.

I did not.

CHAPTER 45

Lizzie Price, June 5, 1901, Lexington, Kentucky

Suzie says I'm spoiled—even her man, Bill, has been known to drink a little.

"He does his work. He's a good husband and father, but I smell it on his breath. What am I supposed to do? Kick him out of the house? Just 'cause Daddy never drank, you think all colored men should be some kind of half-preacher, half-teacher. Even Jesus drank. Why'd He make all that wine for the wedding if He didn't?"

"Because He got manners, which is more than some people have. And because His mamma asked him to. If Noah wants to drink a little wine at a wedding, that'd be fine with me. But I don't think Jesus bounced from saloon to saloon in Jerusalem, fighting every drunk who'd raise his fists to Him, and some who just looked Him cross-eyed. At least I haven't found that part in the Bible yet. But Noah can drink all the wine he wants at weddings. Just won't be our wedding he's drinking it at."

Suzie looked at me like she didn't think there was ever going to a wedding to drink at—not mine, at least. She probably right. I scare most men. Which is alright. Most men I want to scare. I thought Noah was the one who I didn't scare, who didn't scare me. A colored man as sweet as Daddy. But one with sense, one who wouldn't put his wife into an early grave worrying about how to put food on the table while her man is reading Shakespeare to his daughters.

I used to fuss at Mamma in my head, wondering why she didn't just put down what she was doing and come listen to Daddy.

"Was Shakespeare a colored man?" I asked Daddy once when I was real little.

He thought a few moments before he answered. Even Mamma stopped stirring the corn meal for a second to listen.

"Of course, he was a colored man. That's how come he speaks to us so."

I glowed with pride. I *knew* he had to be a colored man. Only a colored man could talk in sentences that wrapped you in quilts warmer than Mamma's. Then I noticed Mamma hadn't started stirring again. She kept looking at Daddy. He scratched his throat a little and turned back to me.

"Of course, he was a white man, too."

Mamma turned her eye on me, then, so I kept quiet. I didn't misbelieve Daddy. I never did that. I just didn't always understand him.

I understood him now. Daddy's Shakespeare was my Noah—everything to everybody. Only he wasn't.

I talked to Jesus about it. I shouted at Him so loud I walked around hoarse for days. I said, "Jesus, you got him into this mess. You let that man kill Mr. Benjamin. You get him out of this! Jesus! Do you hear me?" But Jesus in one of those deaf times when you can yell all you want and He don't hear. Or He's not listening.

"He's listening, daughter," the Reverend Jones tells me. "He's just waiting for the right time to answer."

No, Jesus is being mean, I thought but don't say out loud because the Reverend Jones wouldn't understand. Everything that passes through my mind don't come out my mouth, whatever Suzie thinks. He'd think I was blaspheming. And maybe I am.

Oh, I know Jesus can't be mean. But it feels mean. It feels like He doesn't care that Noah's heart is broken, or that Mr. Benjamin's wife and babies' hearts are broken. That He turning away just when I'm hurting more, more than I ever thought I could, hurting as much as Daddy hurt when he saw Mamma sinking and me yelling at him. Blaming him. And what for? For not changing the world for all his Shakespeare? A world where his woman worked herself to death and his daughters put in twelve hours on a good day. Yelling at him for raising them in a white Kentucky that saw them as cute little pickaninnies when it was feeling sweet, as uppity colored girls when it was feeling mean. And most days white Kentucky was feeling mean.

Daddy did the best he could. Mamma knew that. Mamma never blamed him. She looked at me soft in the end, too weak to speak, but I knew what she was saying. *Don't blame your daddy.*

But I did. I do. I want my white Shakespeare and my colored one, too. I want my Jesus right here and up in heaven where He belongs.

It's like Suzie says. I'm hard. I'm hard on Daddy. I'm hard on Jesus.

I'm hard on Noah.

I wasn't going to go to the trial, wasn't going to see him locked up for being a drunk. But Suzie told me different, said the policeman Doyle—the one who planted the gun on Mr. Benjamin—had framed him.

"Framed him? Nobody has to frame Noah with being drunk. Half the town's seen him drunk."

"He wasn't drunk that day or resisting arrest. You can't arrest a man because he's been drunk—be about six men left free if that's the case—white or colored. My Bill sure wouldn't be one of them. The man has to be drunk right in front of you. And disorderly. That's the law."

"The law? Maybe for white men."

Soon as I said that, I knew she had me. I had to go with her. I said I'd sit with her in the back. Noah's mamma was going, but I couldn't be with her. That'd look like I was her boy's lady friend, standing by him.

I wasn't his lady friend. I wasn't standing by him. Jesus might not be mean, but I was.

But maybe after I could pat Noah's mamma some, let her know I was grieving with her as they dragged him off to jail. I know Jesus will be there patting her, too. But sometimes you need a human hand trying to be Jesus just for a bit. Mean as we are, got to try to be Jesus sometimes.

Only they didn't drag Noah—dragged Doyle instead. Or at least pulled him off and sent him to the city quarry. Then the judge, instead of sentencing Noah, dismissed the charges, just warned him to stay sober. Said he wasn't allowed in any saloon in the city of Lexington for thirty days.

Thirty days? Noah could have got five years for assault on a policeman. Make that five years he can't go into a saloon, I thought. Make it forever.

But I was shell picking, Mamma would have said, fussing about somebody leaving a fleck of pecan shell behind and forgetting to enjoy the sweetness of the pie.

"Taste the pie, honey. Just spit out the shell."

We were all tasting the pie. Noah was telling them all: that policeman, that lawyer, even the judge. Standing up to them all. For us. We forgot all about his drinking then. Like the past six months hadn't happened. We could have carried him off on our shoulders if the judge's gaveling didn't quiet us down finally. We were quiet. Even me. I didn't yell out. I said my "Thank You, Jesus," real soft. I told Him it didn't matter about the shells, didn't matter if we broke our teeth. All that mattered was the sweetness. "Thank You, Jesus."

I didn't go over to Noah after, but Suzie did—and she pointed me out. He smiled so big at me I couldn't resist. I had to give him a little smile. I'm hard, but not that hard. But then his mamma turned and saw me, and you might as well try to resist a second slice of that pecan pie as not to laugh out loud with joy when she looked on you with all that feeling.

That feeling said *Give my boy another chance.* That feeling said *I know it ain't all settled, I know you gonna have problems, but look what he did here. Ain't he worth a few problems?*

I nodded to Noah's mamma and she nodded back. Noah was listening to something the judge was saying, something about his future, I didn't hear. His mamma and I were figuring out his future, too. His mamma, me, and Jesus. Jesus bending my head. *Nod,* He said, *and spit out that shell. Nod and you might get more than thirty days. Might get more than five years.* "You can't tell the future," my mamma said. "Can hardly figure out the day." *But bend that head,* Jesus told me. *Nod. And maybe you'll get forever.*

Soon as school let out, I was back at Daddy's store, like I never left it. But it was about to leave me. Us. A country store clings to survival like a chicken skirts disaster. The smartest chicken's going to meet his end before too long, and Daddy wasn't the smartest chicken. "Neither a lender nor a borrower be." Polonius might have been an old fool, but Daddy should have paid heed to his words. Mamma was the one who kept the store going. Somehow, she could smile sweet and still make people pay their accounts. Daddy grumbles but doesn't follow through. I told him he'd be better off farming our few acres while I was there. Some customers didn't like it much when they saw me behind the counter. I didn't have Mamma's sweet ways, but they paid up if they could.

Only most of them couldn't. We were going downhill fast, but at least we had company.

The whole idea of a country store run by coloreds was like that chicken deciding that it was cooking the dinner, not being cooked. Most country stores just part of the old way, piling up debts the landlords sign up for. The landowners didn't like it when their tenants shopped with us, wouldn't always let us collect the debt from the crops. Of course, we didn't have room for doodad, we only stocked candy at Christmas except for suckers. Kept our prices so low, we might even get a white farmer in, though he'd snuck in after dark like he was doing something shameful.

It was hard going even when Mamma was steering the boat. The only colored-owned store in the county, though I know of two in the city. Mamma always said I didn't give Daddy enough credit. Maybe he's not such a dumb chicken after all.

I was surprised to see Miz Chiles. She didn't do much store shopping, except for coffee and flour. Anything she could make herself, she did. Everybody did. It was mid-morning—everybody in the fields. I was about to close shop and join Daddy myself.

"Miz Chiles. Is something wrong?"

The X scar on Miz Chiles' face hadn't faded much over the year, but it no longer looked raw—more like a decoration—or like some face scar I heard some African heathens carved into themselves. Only this decoration was a cross, which was strange since Miz Chiles wasn't much of a Christian. She was too polite to say much when I talked to Jesus, but I could see she wasn't much for Jesus. I tried talking to her once about it.

"You believe what you need to, child. Jesus reminds me of a man who makes all sorts of promises but don't show up when he's needed. Like a white man."

Like a white man. I never thought of Jesus as a white man. He's more like Shakespeare. *Jesus, help her.* But I said it to myself, not out loud.

"I've come for your help. Your sister's, too, if she can spare the time. Twins don't give you much time, so I'll understand if she can't. We got another chance to take back the school board, take back our schools. And you can do it right here, right in your daddy's store. Talk to the women. Tell them we can do it this time."

I remembered Miz Benjamin and her tea, where she asked me the same thing. That seemed a long time ago. Poor Mrs. Benjamin. Last anyone heard she was fading quick.

"Jesus, help her." That one I did say aloud. Miz Chiles didn't ask me who I was talking about. I didn't tell her.

She had come with an idea for a giant sign telling the women—and the men, too—where they needed to vote. And who to vote for. She would visit the women who never made it to the store—make sure that all the parents would have somebody call. Me, if I could make the room for it, or Suzie.

"We can do this. Jesus helping us."

She didn't dispute me. "That's right, child. Jesus. Or we helping ourselves. We can do this."

After Miz Chiles' visit, seemed like almost every day somebody else made the rounds. The store became a kind of check-in for the school board election. Even Miss Emma Bisou and the Lexington Improvement Club made its way out to the wilds of eastern Fayette County. She made me close shop more than once or go get Suzie to bring her twins and settle behind the counter. Rainy days, Daddy came in from the fields and we'd head out to talk to folks.

Daddy liked us being the election center—he'd talk to the men. But he didn't hold out much hope. It made me mad.

"Daddy, why are you helping if you don't think it will change much?" It aggravated me. Reminded me of how we got him to go to church—he went when you pushed and shoved, but he wasn't a Jesus man, either, just like Miz Chiles. No faith. Or not enough.

He took awhile before he answered. "Flat times. Keep on doing even when you don't believe. Flat times."

When Daddy wasn't reading Shakespeare, he could be a silent man. I waited. But he wouldn't say anything more than that. "Flat times."

But he talked to the men and they listened. Or seemed to. Some of them had the same look in their eyes as Daddy. Flat times.

Miss Emma Bisou showed up twice driving her own one-horse rig, both days with enough rain to keep people indoors—the fields too wet to work—but dry enough so the roads didn't turn creek beds which they did on a regular basis. County took care of the main roads, but the small roads were private adventures. It was like Emma Bisou had her own personal Farmer's Almanac. She said it was her big toe aching with rain coming and a lifetime figuring out Kentucky weather.

The second time Miss Bisou arrived, there was another coach driving behind her, a fancy closed barouche with two matched gray mares. We didn't often see such fine vehicles in the country. I hoped it was planning to stay to the main roads, its finish wouldn't survive our small paths.

"My goodness," Daddy said. "Who can that be?"

I knew. Anyone in Lexington would know, especially anyone connected with the schools. Mrs. Madeline McDowell Breckinridge had visited our church-school, had parked her satin barouche out front with its black coachman, not noticing the awed glances our children shot her, and had limped her way through our two rooms, listening intently to the Reverend Jones' explanations. She asked sharp, sometimes uncomfortable questions of me and the other teachers.

"You have not completed your formal training, Miss Price? Do you feel yourself qualified to teach on so many levels? The colored public schools have wonderful teachers."

The Reverend Jones had busied himself elsewhere quickly and left me to fend for myself. Mrs. Breckinridge had not asked the question meanly—her large blue eyes looked at me curiously—her inquiries things she would wonder about herself if she were teaching. But they weren't new questions for me. I asked myself, often, and Jesus, too, if I was ruining the children instead of teaching them.

"I'm not qualified. I need more training. But the children seem to be doing better. They get more attention here than in the public schools. And I'm getting better, too. Jesus helping."

She looked a little surprised—I don't know why mentioning Jesus always surprises some people. Or perhaps she was surprised that I said I wasn't qualified.

Well, I wasn't. I needed to know more. That was a fact.

She came back twice more to visit the school, which surprised *me*. She rarely visited the colored public schools though, she was a regular at the white ones. She always stopped by to ask me what I was doing. I was reading Wordsworth's "Daffodils" her last visit: "A poet could not but be gay/ In such a jocund company!"

Her eyes grew even wider, but she said nothing.

Mrs. Breckinridge parted the curtain of the barouche's window. She did not seem surprised to see me.

"Miss Price! Miss Bisou says you are doing such good work."

She wouldn't step down—late, she murmured, meeting some ladies near Athens. "We will replace the school board. With your help and the help of all the colored ladies in the county."

Daddy stood by our store door, curious to see the grand white lady his daughter had brought calling. No, not calling. Perhaps pausing would be a better word. I couldn't help feeling flattered. But I needed to ask the hard question I'd been wondering about.

"*The Morning Democrat* says those colored ladies—the ones whose help you need—are not ladies at all. 'Disreputable' is the kindest word they use. They think we have too much power."

Daddy stopped gawking at the white lady and turned to look at his daughter. Mrs. Breckinridge frowned. She understood what I was asking. Would our white friends abandon us after the election? But Madeline McDowell Breckinridge did not only ask difficult questions, she answered them, too.

"*The Democrat* thinks all women have too much power. We do not have enough—white or colored. But this election will help with that." She smiled. "And your 'jocund company' will make it happen."

She waved at Miss Emma Bisou who had not descended, either. Mrs. Breckinridge's barouche quickly rejoined Richmond Pike. Emma's buggy turned itself, ready to branch up a country lane to find our people. "Hurry, Lizzie," Emma shouted. She must be late, too, though it was hard to tell with Emma. She was always in a hurry. I hopped in and hung on.

Folks always out on their porches or in their yards waiting for us, surprised at anybody visiting in the busy time. Recognized me but turned wondering eyes on Emma, the men and women both. When she spoke to them she must have seemed like a fire and brimstone preacher. Baptists don't allow women to speak in church, at least not from the pulpit. But Miss Emma Bisou was preaching Frederick Douglass, not Jesus, so I guess it was okay. It helped, too, that they already knew what the election was about: Green Pinckney Russell, the Lexington Supervisor of Colored Schools, back in power after being kicked out, reaching his Democratic machine hand out to the county. It helped that they were already mad about it. Emma didn't need to do much preaching. Neither did I.

"Keep that man's hands off our schools!" Miz Jackson, a big woman with six children, shouted. "Man goes around preaching about 'idle colored children.' I don't know no idle colored children. Ain't idle around me. Wants to turn our schools into workshops for his white bosses. Fire the good teachers we got and bring in his sorry bunch."

I thought we should bring Miz Jackson with us on our rounds, but she could barely spare the five minutes we were there. Six children and the busy time. She invited us down from our rig to refresh ourselves, though I know for a fact from her account list in the store that she barely kept those children fed. We thanked her and kept in the rig like politicians making the rounds. Which is what we were, I guess.

Miss Emma Bisou worked her poor old mare up and down the lanes, the rain getting thicker and the mud, too. Her big toe hadn't predicted a downpour. She didn't seem to mind the pace at all, but I was wearing out. So was the mare. She finally pulled the rig over beneath some trees during the worst of it and we rested. She looked over at me, a bit pitying.

"Well, you're stronger than poor Maria, at least. Of course, when Maria and I canvassed, we did it on foot in Lexington, not sitting down like we're doing now."

Sitting down isn't what I would have called it. Holding on would have been more accurate.

"Have you heard from Mrs. Benjamin? How is she?"

"Dying. Might be dead already. Haven't gotten a posting in a week or two. Sounded almost despairing the last couple letters. Hope she lives through the election. Hope we get good news to tell her. She worked hard on this. Robert, too. Would hope it weren't for nothing."

The rain started pouring even heavier—we wouldn't be making any more side trips this day. I began to worry even about Richmond Pike, and we were still on Boggs Fork, a tiny sliver of a road that led to Boones Creek.

"Flat times."

She looked at me, waiting.

"It's what my daddy calls the times when you don't have much hope. At least I think that's what he means. How you just have to hang on—just keep on doing. I think Mrs. Benjamin must be in one of those times. Jesus help her."

Miss Emma Bisou shook her head.

"Jesus better hurry up. Her husband got shot, her children are ailing, she has no money, and she's dying. I reckon that's flat times for anybody. What's Jesus supposed to do for her? Lift her spirits?"

Another person mad at Jesus. I knew all about being mad at Jesus, but this seemed different.

"Jesus didn't shoot Mr. Benjamin. And He doesn't have anything to do with money."

"The rest of us do. And I know He didn't shoot Mr. Benjamin. But He didn't keep it from happening, either. I'm tired of colored folks putting all their trust in Jesus and letting the white man shoot us down in the streets."

I felt like jumping out of the rig and making my own way home. But considering the state of the road, I might have to swim my way there. And Daddy would be waiting for me, Daddy who felt the same way Miss Bisou did. The same way Miz Chiles did. And Noah. Only Noah's mamma knew the same Jesus I did—a Jesus who maybe didn't keep bad things from happening, but helped make sense out of them. Pulled us through the flat times. I turned my face and looked at the rain.

I felt a hand on my arm.

"Well, child, I shouldn't have spoken like that. You're out here doing your best, not just leaving it all to Jesus, and any help He gives you is help I get, too. I'm glad you're a Christian. Forgive an ornery lady with too many opinions and too few places to give them."

She tapped the mare then, who—tired as she was—knew better than to try and dispute that opinion.

Boggs Fork looked a bit like Boones Creek had decided to join it—we guessed wrong when we stopped. Should have gone on. The rain wasn't letting up. I was just thanking Jesus we were the only ones foolish enough to be out driving in it when we spotted a carriage inching its way towards us. Jesus likes to toy with me like that. It was bigger than our rig with two horses. It took up a good two-thirds of the road. Neither of us could see much more than the outlines of each other, ghostly outlines at that. We stopped and let the mares nuzzle each other.

We could see that the driver was a colored man, and that there was a woman huddled beside him, wrapped in a coat like it was January and not a wet September. I knew how she felt, though. That rain cold cut right through you.

"Move out of the way!" the man was yelling.

Move out of the way? Boggs Fork was so slick and narrow, out of the way was in the drainage ditch beside the road, except the drainage ditch wasn't draining anything, more like it was draining what it had onto us. And nobody, not even Miss Bisou who handled that mare like she made her living trotting ponies on the side, was backing up. Might as well get out and push the rig over the side ourselves.

"Who is this fool?" Miss Bisou said, almost loud enough for him to hear us. "Sir!" she said, louder, "we cannot move 'out of the way' and neither can you. We will have to wait until the rain lets up. Then perhaps we can find our way around each other."

"I'm in a hurry, woman! Move out of the way! If you can't handle a one-horse jitney on your own, you shouldn't be on the road."

I put my hand on Miss Bisou's arm. She is a woman of great self-control, but this man might try a saint. I felt her relax a bit at my touch. "I know this man," she said to me.

"Professor Russell. Is that you?"

Green Pinckney Russell, out canvassing himself, perhaps. There was a moment of silence. I saw the woman lean over to whisper something. I imagine it is one thing to yell insultingly at strangers and quite another to berate someone you knew. He stood up before he spoke next, as if we were seated in a dry parlor somewhere and not perched precariously on one of Fayette County's least favored roadways. The mares moved nervously when he stood. Miss Bisou tightened her grip on the reins.

"Miss Bisou? I beg your pardon. I had heard that you were traveling the county. I did not think to meet you."

"No, I imagine not. But since we are out speaking to many of the same people, it is no great surprise. Is that Mrs. Russell with you?"

They had been shouting over the noise of the downpour. But the rain had begun to lessen. The words "Is that Mrs. Russell with you?" hung in the air as clear as a bell. A silence followed.

"No. This is Miss Henderson, a teacher. She has been meeting parents with me."

"A teacher? How do you do, Miss Henderson? How brave of you to travel alone on these roads with Mr. Russell."

Miss Henderson did not attempt to speak. She only nodded. *Brave and wicked,* I thought.

"Meeting parents?" The rain had slowed to a drizzle, no need to shout anymore though Miss Bisou's next question sounded like a shout though spoken softly.

"Have you met Mrs. Jackson? She's over near Todd's Road."

"Yes. We have met." He sat down with those words. "Some parents have the erroneous idea that we are here to ruin their children's schools instead of trying to make those schools useful and practical for colored children. These children need to find their way in this world."

"These children? I thought you were speaking of our children. And what world are you talking about? The white world?"

"Yes, our children. In a white world. You see a different world? The only way they're going to make a living is manual labor. We need to stop teaching so much book learning and train the children—our children—how to work in the only work that they'll be able to do. Your Mrs. Jackson wants the classics taught though she's too ignorant to even call them that. You think any of her six children are going to make a living with the classics? They'll make their living sewing and cooking, which our schools need to teach. Booker Washington knows what our children need. Tuskegee's graduates are known throughout the land. I have the good fortune to be able to hire a Tuskegee cooking graduate at a mere pittance to teach our children. We must ameliorate our children's industrial condition."

I had felt Miss Bisou tense up further during Mr. Russell's speech. Because it was a speech. He almost stood up again during it but thought better of it. Except for his reference to Mrs. Jackson, I am certain that I had read the same sentiments in his letters to the newspapers. The need to "ameliorate our children's industrial condition" stood out in particular. I didn't know what it meant when I first read it; I didn't know what it meant now.

Unfortunately for Mr. Russell, he usually spoke to the like-minded, especially the "white world" he extolled, who loved his message. His and Booker T's. But here he was stuck with us on Boggs Fork, his heavier carriage more entrenched in the road's mud than our one-horsed jig. Stuck with having to listen to Emma Bisou's answer.

"It's funny, Professor Russell, that you mention Mrs. Jackson's lack of classical education. You're right. My young friend beside me has a daddy who loves to read Shakespeare. I don't see Mrs. Jackson doing that with her children. I'd be very surprised if Mrs. Jackson knew any Shakespeare.

"But you know what Mrs. Jackson knows a lot about? Sewing. Cooking. Running a farm. Figuring out how to feed six children and a man on money that would starve those fine mares you're driving. Mrs. Jackson teaches all those things to her children—she could teach you if you were willing. What does she need the school for? Maybe for that Shakespeare she's lacking.

"You say we need to train our children how to work? Really? That's all our children know. They leave the breast and jump into the fields. You better come back from that white world you're living in, Professor. You better open your eyes. You're training our children to be maids and gardeners. They're already maids and gardeners. You're training them to be cooks or cook teachers for a 'mere pittance' as you put it." Emma paused. I saw her breathing deeply. She hadn't been shouting but she shouted now, shouted so loud Professor Russell flinched like she had struck him. Which she had.

"They don't need your damn schools for that."

I had never heard a woman curse and no man had ever cursed directly at me or even near me, except for deputy Sheriff Siebrecht when he arrested us. But I did not even ask Jesus to forgive Emma. Jesus had run the money changers out of the Temple. He might have cursed then. Cursed with Miss Bisou to get the slave masters out of our schools, the slave trainers. That's what "ameliorate our children's industrial condition" meant. I understood it now.

I gripped Emma Bisou's arm and squeezed it in solidarity. We would stand together. We would get them out of our "damn schools." Our schools wouldn't be damned anymore. Shakespeare? Why not? Why should Suzie and me be the only ones blessed?

"Thank You, Jesus!" Miss Bisou laughed softly, but she wasn't mocking.

After enough water had run off Boggs Fork, Emma and I both descended so we could lead our mare gently and safely around a very rigid Professor Russell, shocked at Miss Bisou's language. Miss Henderson pulled her head out from under her coat. I think she gave us a small smile. Perhaps I had been harsh. Perhaps she wasn't so very wicked after all.

But she was keeping bad company. Not "the jocund company" Madeline McDowell Breckinridge had teased me about, the band of women, colored and white, who were standing together to bring change. Though sometimes things Emma Bisou said made me think she doubted Mrs. Breckinridge, doubted that any white woman—especially one of Mrs. Breckinridge's high standing—would stick by us and our cause. I did not doubt.

"Wait till they group us all together. Wait until they don't just call colored women disreputable. They will stand by us. I am certain."

Miss Emma Bisou did not answer, but I felt her doubt.

Faith, I wanted to say to Emma. Have faith.

I prayed for Miss Henderson now. But I kept my prayer to myself. Our mare was gentle, but I didn't want to risk spooking her. I smiled back at Miss Henderson, what Suzie calls my prayer smile. Suzie's always wanting me to use the smile instead of shouting out His name. But it doesn't do the job, I tell her. Not most times. People need to hear the name of Jesus spoken. It shores up faith; it finds faith in the flat times. But the silent smile did the job that night. I could tell by the way Miss Henderson relaxed. It did the job that night.

Praise Jesus.

CHAPTER 46

Noah Webster, November 7, 1901, Election Day, Lexington, Kentucky

4:30 a.m.

Judge Bullock told me to keep out of sight as much as possible. I would of liked to keep out of his sight and he out of mine forever. But Lizzie says it's too good a chance to pass up. Even Mamma agrees, and she doesn't much like the idea of me lawyering.

"He's the man who let Mike Moynahan free. You think I should be doing his research for him?"

Mamma kept her head over the stove—wouldn't catch my eye for a bit—mulling over her answer.

"He done something bad, real bad. Now he's trying something good. You bent on lawyering. You think the people you gonna speak for all be good? Some of them are gonna be so bad you run from them if you meet them outside the courthouse. Judge Bullock could of locked you up. He didn't."

He didn't. That was good enough for Mamma. For Lizzie, too, though of course she had to throw in some Jesus. Sometimes I wonder if Lizzie thinks we need lawyers, long as we got Jesus.

I'd go in early to the courthouse if I had to go, five in the morning and be gone by eight. I'd take what I needed and do the work at home. About the only ones who'd see me were the night watchmen, the cleaners. Coloreds, mostly, so it didn't matter. Occasionally a white clerk would call out, "Hey, boy," but Judge Bullock gave me a letter to show them. They'd scowl when they read it, but nobody was challenging Judge Bullock.

Election day I was in the courthouse before polls opened at six, or were supposed to—and I needed to start making the rounds. The Judge wanted some paperwork done. I figured to be safe: four in the morning was too late for the saloons and too early for anything else.

But Billy Klair must of had the same schedule in mind, election day, almost bumped into each other, both of us scrambling and dropping papers. Always glad to see Smiling Billy, only he didn't look much happy to see me. Wasn't five years older than me and ran the town. Be my hero if he didn't hate coloreds. And if I didn't suspicion he was behind Mr. Benjamin's killing. Other than that, a real good fellow.

"Goddamnit. I told the Judge to keep you out of sight."

That surprised me—impressed me—Billy Klair knowing about me. But it riled me some.

"This building's as dark and empty as the Lexington Cemetery. As out of sight as I can get."

"Out of sight means nobody seeing you. You practically ran me down. Coloreds don't belong here. Coloreds ain't in Lexington Cemetery, either."

"We're there, just not buried. Digging, though, which is what I'm doing here, digging through files. As far as that goes, ain't no Catholics in Lexington Cemetery, either. Probably a few diggers, though, just like the coloreds."

A good way to irritate the whites in this town is to remind them how close they are to the coloreds. I saw the color rising on Billy's neck, but he didn't say anything right off. It was a sore point, not letting Catholics near Henry Clay's resting spot. Catholics had to rest themselves across the street. Coloreds had to bury themselves almost clear out of town, but most folks I knew figured that was okay. Couldn't figure laying down too close to white people. Wouldn't find it restful.

All of a sudden, Billy wasn't in a hurry. He looked at me.

"I hear you're helping the colored women with this school board election. You know the Judge is on the other side and here you are working against him. What's he say about that?"

What he said was to keep all my politicking as quiet as a Masonic swearing in, but I guess I hadn't if Billy knew about it. Of course, Billy knew everything politic in this county. In this state.

"He don't mind. As long as I do my work. Way I hear it, we got a good chance to kick your crew out, especially in the county. You picked the wrong colored hack to tie yourself to. Mr. Green Pinckney Russell is doing about three-fourths of our work for us getting out the vote. The women are so eager to kick him out—to keep him out—that they'd turn repeater if they weren't such honest voters."

That was one of Jake's jobs: rounding up repeaters for Billy in Yellmantown. They'd go from polling station to polling station, eating up legitimate votes like locusts on a corn field. Some repeaters might vote three, four times if they were fast enough.

Smiling Billy wasn't smiling.

"Everybody's got to make a living somehow. Repeaters got limited skills—got to use them when the need arises. But you seem like a real talented young fellow. You might be right about me picking the wrong colored in Green Pinckney Russell. He's giving us a lot of trouble. He knows what to do and he does it. But he upsets people. Causes all sorts of problems."

The way he kept looking at me made me nervous.

"You look like a fellow who'd know when to keep a low profile, when you ain't running into people. Or being arrested. And your people trust you. Maybe Judge Bullock got the right idea about you."

Here it was: the big time. Billy Klair offering me a job. Of sorts. At least feeling me out. How willing was I to sell out my people—sell out the women? If the price was cheap enough, I could be the next Green Pinckney Russell. Who knows? They might even need a black city judge at some point.

But I'm a constant disappointment. Mamma would of told Billy that if he'd asked. "The Judge is already ruing the day he hired me. If I could, I'd get enough colored votes to turn him out—though that don't seem like it's gonna happen anytime soon. I just got to aim at Green Pinckney Russell for the time being. Down the road a bit, you, maybe. I got a lady friend who'd put in a 'Jesus, make it happen!' right about now. Oh, what the hell. It can't hurt. 'Jesus, make it happen!'"

I laughed then, thinking what Lizzie would think of my using Jesus like this. Billy's eyes got narrow. He still wasn't smiling. Have to take away his nickname if he was gonna be so grim.

"Boy, you gonna need a whole lot more than Jesus on your side if you're coming after me. Your old boss never learned that. At least your new boss got more sense. He knows how to listen."

The courtroom hall where we were standing was wide enough for ten people to pass each other, but somehow Billy didn't find enough space, knocked my shoulder as he passed, and the papers went all over the place again. *Well, Mamma,* I thought, *there's another golden opportunity gone by the wayside.* Only I don't think Mamma would of been too disappointed. Lizzie, either.

For that matter, I didn't think Lizzie's Jesus would of minded, either.

"Billy!" He was at the end of the hallway by now, but he turned. Billy never could resist his name called out. "I see Mike got arrested again." Moynahan had gotten into another drunken brawl. This time he was beat up by at least five policemen and thrown into the wagon. "What's the matter, Billy, he stop listening? Or maybe it's just better that he's out of the way for awhile?"

"Mike Moynahan's a brute. Everybody knows that. But even a brute has the right to defend himself. Mr. Benjamin was a good lawyer. For a colored. He would of told you that himself."

He was smiling again. I wanted to smash that smile into his face so he'd be like a jack-o'-lantern the day after Halloween. But that'd be what he wanted. I'd be sharing a cell with Mike Moynahan in an hour.

"Mr. Benjamin *was* a good lawyer, and he would of said that. Every man has a right to defend himself. Every woman, too, as far as that goes. Colored or white. Think I'll see you out in the hustling today? Gonna be a busy day. Hope it stays peaceful. You think it will stay peaceful, Billy? Better chance this election with Moynahan behind bars."

"And Benjamin gone."

The words hit me. I didn't even try to hide that. Benjamin gone. *Mr. Benjamin, you son of a bitch.* I glared at Billy Klair and he glared back.

"Yes, he's gone, Billy Klair. Maybe thanks to you. Sure thanks to Moynahan. But he's not forgotten, Billy. You'll find out that even way out in Cadentown. He's not forgotten."

6:30 a.m.

Soon as I scooped those papers up, I headed over to Deweese and Main—the 19th Precinct. Two hundred voters were left waiting there last year's election. *The Leader* ran a picture of them. Almost all of them colored. Already about twenty men in line this year, a fellow named Charlie Taylor in front. He was banging on the door so hard, it looked like he might splinter it in no time.

"Charlie, you break that door, they'll take half the day replacing it. And they'll haul you off before you or anybody else gets to vote."

He turned around with his fists in the air, but put them down when he saw me. He used to be a regular at George Thomas before he found Jesus, as Lizzie might put it. I'd say it had more to do with his wife. She's the one who pulled him out of the saloon. Didn't see Jesus anywhere about.

"That you, Noah? I ain't gonna be stranded like last year. It's after time already. They open up or we open for them. Broken door be the least of their worries. Broken heads come next."

Wasn't light yet. Wouldn't be for another hour. A quiet time usually. We could see a light inside the precinct. Charlie and another fellow recommenced the banging. The light edged its way to the door, the face of a skinny old white fellow finally appearing above the lantern, not looking too happy.

"Stop that banging. Ain't nobody here but me yet. You got to wait."

"You got to open the damn precinct doors at 6 a.m.! That's the law!" Charlie shouted, and the thirty men behind him—the crowd growing by the minute—shouted with him. They were all of them colored except for two men way in the back. The white fellow inside looked scared, but opened up the door before the next banging.

"Can't do anything without the election officials but maybe the damn door won't get broken."

"The election officials." Just the thought of them made me want to break the door down myself. All Democrats. All Billy Klair's personal choices. The Republicans brought it to court, but it did no good—not with Democratic judges making the ruling. Their Judge Parker said the way the law was set up the Democrats could replace all the Republicans and the Independents, and they did. No remedy in the law.

"The election commissions are a law unto themselves," Parker wrote.

"That can't be right," I said to Judge Bullock. "Even you, Judge, wouldn't rule like that."

Lizzie can't believe I talk to Judge Bullock like that. Mamma, either. But I still don't know if I want to stay in his office. Toss me out, that'd be one less decision. He looked over at me. I don't know if he wanted to toss me out, but I know he'd like to slap me around some. He'd have to get in line for that.

"I don't know how I'd rule until I read the law carefully. The law doesn't right every wrong."

"A law unto itself?"

Judge Bullock shrugged. "A law unto itself until the next election cycle."

If there was another election cycle. Wouldn't be in Alabama. Last letter Maria wrote—a month now—she was talking about how the state was voting on a referendum to take away the black vote altogether. But Maria was hopeful. So many coloreds were mobilizing to vote one last time—her daddy, her uncles. And with the "good will of many whites," she wrote, "perhaps it will be enough."

Living in Alabama and still believing in the good will of whites. Puts Lizzie's faith to shame.

The two white men at the end of the line disappeared. Don't know if they had good will or not. Maybe they just figured they were in the wrong place.

It was close to nine before Billy's election officials showed up. By then the crowd had grown to over a hundred. They brought three police with them.

"Don't block the street," one of the police started shouting.

"We wouldn't be blocking the damn street if you had got here on time," Charlie said. "You trying to pull the same stunt you did last year. We ain't gonna let you!"

Two of the police started going for Charlie before he even stopped speaking, grabbing at him to pull him out of line. But he wasn't budging and the two men behind him took hold of his arms and held him in place. Then the third police came in with his billy club and started swinging. A fourth fellow grabbed the club halfway down and sent it flying out into the street we weren't supposed to be blocking. The policeman looked startled.

This wasn't the way colored men were supposed to act.

The two white fellows had come back, bringing a dozen other white men with them. They didn't wait to find out what was going on, just charged at Charlie and the three men near him. I saw another gang of white men running on Constitution and two of the police were blowing so hard on their whistles I thought everybody's ears were gonna burst. I could see two police wagons crashing up Deweese Street. I thought back to my asking Billy if he thought this was gonna be a peaceful day. Charlie landed a blow on a police's jaw and he went down.

Reckon not.

The police would end up arresting half the men in line. I needed to get out before I was one of them, but I turned back at a loud crash. The door. Being open hadn't saved it. The skinny white fellow was shaking his head like a mourner at a drunk's funeral. He'd predicted it. That's what happens when you give the coloreds the vote.

Well, when you give it to them and you try to take it back.

Poor skinny fellow's troubles weren't done: somebody's fist went out and he went down. Couldn't see the color of the fist that hit him, just know the blood that flowed from his nose was red.

CHAPTER 47

Jake the bartender, November 7, 1901, Yellmantown, 22nd Precinct, Lexington, Kentucky

6 a.m.

Twenty-three repeaters. I expected thirty, so we were waiting. We all gathered at Timmy's Place; the men lined up for their pay before we hit the first precinct.

"Five dollars? You told us ten."

That was from a big man named Sam, always on the edge of finding out what I was made of. If we got through the day without me smashing his head open we'd be lucky. He'd be lucky.

"Five dollars a vote. We hit another precinct, you get another five. We make it to a third—which ain't likely if we don't get moving—it'll be five more."

He nodded. "How about a free beer then? Seeing as we're meeting in a saloon."

"Can't. Against the law to open a saloon on election day."

"Right. Don't want to be breaking no laws."

Be more than luck, more like a miracle if I didn't break his head in by the end of the day.

We were headed to Vertner and Third Street—the 22nd Precinct. I had wanted to hit it six a.m. on the dot, election officials swooping us right into the booth, crowding in with us to make sure we marked the right ballots. Then we'd head over to the 32nd before the fellows with the names we used were half out of bed. But we were seven shy of thirty. George Thomas would be real unhappy with me. Billy Klair unhappy with him. So we waited.

When four more fellows showed up, I figured close enough. I paid them and we headed out.

But it was close to seven when we got there, and dang if there wasn't a crowd of men already waiting—about half of them colored. They looked at us like we were Morgan's Raiders come to take their last chickens. I banged on the door and at first the fellows inside waved me away until I yelled out that George Thomas done sent me. Then they opened just wide enough to pull me inside before they slammed it shut. The fellows in line were yelling to let them in, too. But they weren't yelling as loud as the fat election official who had yanked my arm in so hard the pain shot right into my jaw like he'd jabbed me with a right hook.

"Goddamnit, boy, where the hell've you been? The goddamned polls open at six. Now we got a goddamned line, and half of them are probably the men you're supposed to be. Goddamnit, why can't a nigger ever show up when he's supposed to?"

I'd been asking myself the same question, but it riled me to hear the fat bastard say it. When a man's selling his soul—or his vote—he expects a little respect.

"I don't know, captain. Sure don't. I'll just tell the boys to head on home, keep the five dollars for their trouble."

I smiled at him while he stood there, trying to figure out if I was an idiot or just mouthing him. But the crowd outside was getting rowdy and he couldn't wait to figure it out. Some of them were yelling at my men, asking where they lived and how come they were over here in the 22nd? Some recognized a few, knew they didn't live in the precinct. I had to scrape the bourbon barrel far afield to get my twenty-seven. A couple of my boys came from Frankfort, so it was no wonder they were late.

"You got a back way in, captain?"

"No, there ain't no back way in. Your men will just have to wedge in. We'll keep the doors open and squeeze out any coloreds you don't give the nod to."

"Wedge themselves in? That sounds like fighting, captain. My men weren't paid to fight, just to vote. Vote as often as you pay them, but no fighting."

"Then they should of got here on time, goddamnit."

I just waited. I knew he'd see the logic of the situation before too long. He glared at me. I reckon he concluded that I wasn't an idiot.

"How much?"

"Five dollars should cover the wedging. Twenty for me for getting them to do it."

I thought he might stroke out, but he dredged up the extra money. One hundred seventy dollars and about twenty goddamnits. I didn't tell him I was three men short. Figured I'd clear that up with him later. We pushed right on through that line though the men standing there got mighty upset with us, pushing back, and throwing punches. Even some of the white men, though most of them figured out what we were doing after a bit and weren't too unhappy. My bunch was real happy. Ten dollars and a day of voting stretching ahead of them like a long drunk on a summer's eve.

"How much they paying you?" Sam wanted to know.

"Nothing, brother, nothing. I'm doing this out of civic duty, out of my respect for the Fifteenth Amendment."

"For what?" he asked, and I just shook my head at the level of voter ignorance these days. Maybe I wouldn't be smashing his head in before the day passed. The few brains he got needed protecting.

"The Fifteenth Amendment, Sam. It's what's gonna free the colored man. That and a whole bunch of this." And I waved the cash in front of him. He grinned. He was a good ol' boy and knew what he needed to know to get by. We were all good ol' boys. White and colored together. Just a bunch of good ol' boys.

CHAPTER 48

Lizzie Price, November 7, 1901, Election Day, Cadentown, Fayette County, Kentucky

3:00 p.m.

The ladies would have walked themselves to the polling booths, but we were trying to give some rides—for the old folks, at least, and for the younger ones encumbered with child. Daddy gave us the farm wagon for the day. He'd built a make-do bench on both sides so eight ladies at a time could ride. Most waved us off when we offered rides.

I never would have believed how many colored women come out. We outnumbered the white ladies near two to one. Emma Bisou was proud. She was out in her rig, going from precinct to precinct, checking on problems.

"Told us they didn't know where the women could vote in Pricetown. Had to show them the official site and make sure they opened it up. When we got there, fifteen women waiting in line. *They* knew where the polling booth was. Then over in Athens, nobody showed up. Roused the so-called election officials out of bed. Didn't open till eleven. But our women are voting."

"But I don't see as many white ladies voting."

Emma Bisou pulled herself up. "We have done our job. Madeline McDowell Breckinridge needs to convince more of her race that 'intelligent' women do vote." That was the argument made by some in the legislature, that intelligent women did not want the vote. I never could understand what they were saying. If you had brains, wouldn't you want to use them?"

"Bad women," I blushed as I said it, but Emma's eyes opened so wide I couldn't resist. "Disreputable women are doing all the voting, I hear."

"And I imagine only good men vote!" She knew when she was being teased. She was in too good a mood to let it bother her. She paused as I helped a lady into the wagon—looked almost to her due date. She needed pushing and pulling to get up to the bench. It made us all feel hopeful, though, seeing her on the way to vote.

"Hope it's a girl child you're carrying," Emma shouted over. "You can tell her that she was in the election booth before she was born. And when she's grown, maybe women be voting for more than a school board."

The woman smiled at Emma and she smiled back. We were all smiling.

"Of course," Emma continued talking to me, "what's really disreputable to a lot of those white ladies is being put together with the colored."

"How are we put together? We're just voting. They're just voting."

"Put together in the public mind. Which is what *The Morning Democrat* wants to do. Make voting something only ignorant, dumb, disreputable colored women do. And judging from how few white ladies are turning out, they might have succeeded."

She looked somber a bit, but shook her head and smiled again.

"But somehow that don't seem to matter today. Don't even matter if they steal the election from us, which they probably will. I see that child in that woman's womb and I just got hope."

I needed to get going, but Miss Bisou still held back. Her smile had turned somber again and I knew I had to wait.

"You know Maria passed. Got a letter from her daddy the other day. Didn't want to tell your Noah until after the election. You don't need to be jealous about Maria. The way Noah loved her not that much different than the way I loved her. She never could recover from Robert's killing. Never could. Went back to Alabama to die. Only thing Alabama good for. They voting today to take away the vote from coloreds for good. I'm sure of it. Don't need to wait on the election returns. *The Morning Democrat* called us coloreds 'crude and ignorant.' That's what I think when I think of Alabamians. White Alabamians. I guess that just proves I'm as mean as they are, but I can't help it. Maria thought the good white Alabamians would turn the tide. Had more faith than I do, Lord rest her soul. Where all those good white Alabamians been hiding out the last thirty years? Behind those white masks?"

She looked at me fiercely as if I should answer, but I knew better. Miss Bisou wasn't done.

"The question for us is if there's any good white Kentuckians out there? Madeline McDowell Breckinridge says there are. We'll see. Coloreds only about a fourth the numbers of Alabama and Mississippi, but *The Morning Democrat* still talks about 'black hordes' overrunning the elections. Someday, they fret, Negroes might even want some of the offices they vote for—might be on the school board. Might even want to be sheriff. Wouldn't that be something?"

Miss Emma Bisou finally lifted her whip over her mare's haunches, preparing to go. "But won't be elected anything if we don't get moving," looking at me sternly as if I'd been the one holding us all back. The mare started her trot. "And who knows," she shouted as she receded from us, "maybe enough good white Alabamians will turn out to save the colored vote. And maybe the country won't have a giant bilious attack when the President invites a black man to dinner. Maybe," and we could hardly hear her for she was a good hundred yards away, "someday the President will be a black man and invite the white man to dinner!"

We all laughed at that last line, but Jesus willing, why not? I let Miss Emma Bisou get out of sight before I let out a "Jesus hold her" for Mrs. Benjamin, Maria. Emma was wrong to worry about me feeling jealous for Noah. Noah loving Mrs. Benjamin was one of the reasons I loved him. A loving heart never gets overfull, never runs out of room for more love. Emma keeps calling Him my Jesus. He's not mine. There's enough of Him for everyone. And enough love in Noah for Maria and me, too.

When we got to Athens, the election officials had decided to take a lunch break, but we lined up into the street and so they hastened back. Well, they didn't hasten, but they came back. A couple of white men made some comments and I was glad Daddy hadn't come. We just shut our ears. I believed that there are good white Kentuckians—I have met my share. They just didn't loaf around election booths. I thought of the voting going on in Alabama. I'm afraid I don't have much hope, though I wished for Maria's sake that I could think differently. But Kentucky isn't like Alabama. Kentucky wouldn't take the vote away, not from colored, not from white. Kentucky, for all the nasty men hanging around voting booths, is better than that.

It especially won't take the vote we have from women, though we have all heard the rumors. The good white people and the good colored people of Kentucky will keep that from happening.

Noah was waiting for us when we finally made it back to Lexington. It was so dark, the twilight fading and it barely six. I wanted to tell him about all the colored women who had come out to vote—old, young, pregnant—with all the hope of our new century. But he was full of news himself, and, though Suzy does not think so, I do know when to listen. I will tell him about the women tomorrow. I will tell him about Maria tomorrow. Tomorrow the votes will have been counted. Maria's news will temper our victory. And if we are defeated, we will remember what is really important.

He tells me of Billy Klair's offer, or half-offer. And I laugh. How could Billy Klair think that Mr. Benjamin's right-hand man would become his stooge?

How could he think that a man who loved Maria Lulu Benjamin would do anything to soil her husband's name?

CHAPTER 49

Noah Webster, December 10, 1901, Lexington, Kentucky

Billy Klair got a bill in the legislature taking away the women's vote. Lizzie can't believe it.

"They can't do that. Once you got a right, they can't take it away."

I just look at her.

"Where you been all your life, Lizzie? You so full of Jesus you don't see what's going on around you? They been taking back our rights for thirty years. You like Maria thinking the good white people of Alabama gonna come through and not vote to take away the colored vote. They came through alright. I read a piece in *The Leader* about how the Republicans should do better now in Alabama, now that they don't have the Negro vote weighing them down. But Maria died believing. I reckon you think that's a good thing."

"You don't?"

What I thought about Maria and her dying wasn't something I could put in words. Not words I could think of. But words scraped their way out of my throat anyway.

"I think she's just one more colored fool, going to her grave, hugging her Jesus."

I thought maybe Lizzie would do a Mamma and knock me on my tail for those words, "hugging her Jesus." But she didn't. She got real quiet, looked more sad than mad which hurt me more.

"You think I'm a fool?"

"Sometimes. I see too many coloreds just clinging to their Jesus, thinking if they pray hard enough, Jesus will turn the white man's heart around. But if his heart's turning, it's spun 'round right back to where it started. And so are we. We're right back where we began. Back to slavery time. Your Jesus ain't done a lick of good."

She nodded like I was making sense.

"I'm not a fool, Noah. And I'm not clinging to Jesus. He's clinging to me."

I knew better than to argue with Lizzie about Jesus. But I was sick. Election day come and gone, and the Democrats stole and bought and challenged just about every colored vote in the county. *The Leader*s shouted about it: "A Day of Infamy" it headlined and even *The Morning Herald* got embarrassed, and it's a Democratic paper.

> The ordinary Negro found it was almost impossible to vote at all.
> Scores of Negroes did not get to vote at all. The delays were such
> as to win the admiration of the corrupt and the contempt of the
> honorable.

I guess that even "ordinary" coloreds got to admire their pluck. Sure knew how to steal votes.

Judge Bullock lectured the Democrats about wasting the court's time with all their challenges, like he ain't a Democrat himself. Maybe he meant it. The men still lost a day's wages and most times still couldn't vote. Didn't vote. The Democrats would of stole them votes somehow.

Now they're talking of taking away the women's vote, because even with all their thievery, colored women voting out in the county scared them, made them steal extra and pay repeaters extra all to keep their hands 'round the throat of the schools. 'Round all our throats.

And folks keep hoping things will change. Mr. Benjamin kept hoping till they shot him in the back for trying to get colored men the vote, one of those rights Lizzie thinks they can't take away from us. Maria kept hoping, living in Alabama.

Even Jesus about lost hope spending forty days in the desert. It's been forty years since the Civil War and hope's sinking like water in hot sand. People hoping beginning to look like fools.

And I'm the biggest fool of all.

I waited to tell Judge Bullock my news.

"I'm going to Frankfort to talk to the legislators. Going with a group of women. Gonna change their minds about this women's vote. You got any names that might speak to us?"

Judge Bullock was looking at me like I'd lost the little mind he thought I had.

"Speak to the legislators? You and some colored women? They won't let you in the building."

"They'll let us in the building. Every voter's got a right to talk their legislator. That's the law, Judge. And the women are voters, still, till they pass that bill."

I liked telling the judge the law. I was right about the law, but he was right about getting in the building. But Lizzie and women from her club were going and I wasn't gonna let her go alone.

"Maybe you could get me in to see Billy Klair. I know you're close."

He narrowed his eyes at me. "He's told me you've already met. I heard it didn't go that well. Another meeting might not help."

"Never can tell. You can always hope."

He gave me a letter that I could wave at Representative Allen, the other sponsor of the bill.

"Might keep you from getting you arrested. Won't do any other good. Billy's not above arresting the women with you, too."

"For what?"

"Immoral soliciting. Surely, you've read the accounts. Republican bosses charged with driving colored women straight from their brothels to the polling booths."

The only brothels I knew were run by Democrats, or protected by them. But I heard the stories, read them in *The Morning Democrat*. I thought of all those rides Lizzie gave to folks. No telling how many brothels she stopped at.

"I don't put anything past Mr. Billy Klair. But even Billy might not arrest ladies, even colored ladies, if they're with other ladies. I know his partner in the Senate, Colonel Allen, sure wouldn't let ladies be molested like that."

"Ladies?"

I wanted to strike my fist into his face for that. That'd be the end of my clerkship once and for all. But I held back. He never in his life thought there could be something called a colored lady. Better to face a Luke Doyle—or even a Mike Moynahan—men who hated coloreds but right in your face. Judge Bullock would have had his feelings hurt if I put him with them. He figured he was way above them, and I guess he was. But he could say that still, "Ladies?"

"They all ladies, colored and white," I said. "But you're right. Colonel Allen might only be concerned about the white ladies. That's why I mean to get some of those, too."

I wanted another meeting first, one that could get me in a whole lot more trouble than meeting Billy Klair. Billy Klair'd just throw me out of the building probably. The person I wanted to speak to was somebody a young colored man took his life in his hands just looking at, let alone talking to. A white lady. Not just any white lady: a white lady who was part of the group that ran the town even when other people got the credit for it. So much pull, she might even turn Billy Klair's heart. Or his vote.

I didn't much care about his heart. I wanted to talk to Madeline McDowell Breckinridge herself.

She turned up at *The Morning Herald* two, three times a week. It was common knowledge that she wrote some of the editorials, especially the ones about education or women voting. Didn't sign her name most times. Didn't need to. Sometimes she traveled in with her husband, Desha. Sometimes, she came by herself. I'd have to plant myself in front of the *Herald* building and hope not to attract too much attention. Lizzie would have to plant herself with me. She knew Madeline McDowell Breckinridge. And she was a woman. I was less likely to get lynched if Lizzie talked to her first.

We waited three days before she showed up. Twice police started to shoo us away, but I pulled out Judge Bullock's letter and told them I was to wait for someone on the judge's instructions. That confused them some, but they left us alone. Or circled back and looked at us warily. We were dressed too good. Didn't look like servants, so what were we?

I thought Lizzie'd fuss about the whole idea of waiting, but she didn't. Calm as if we was picnicking on a pretty June day, not shivering in a December so gloomy half the time we could hardly see the steps in front of us. Sometimes I heard her praying, but she didn't shout. Like she talking to herself, even when she was arguing. With Jesus, I guess, but I couldn't hear.

Couldn't hear Him answering, either, but Lizzie says I got to listen a special way. I just nod. Tell her I'll just let her translate for me.

But she stood tall beside me and waited, holding vigil. Picture of a lady, only lady I needed. She told me she'd met Madeline McDowell Breckinridge more than once.

"She came out to Daddy's store last summer, with Emma. Daddy couldn't believe it. She didn't get down from her carriage, but we talked. She went off electioneering to the white ladies—Emma and I went off to the colored. But we were working together."

"You think you're still working together?"

"I don't know. I pray we are."

Lizzie spotted her first, stepping down from her fine carriage, walking that strange limp she walk with her false foot.

"Mrs. Breckinridge!"

I remembered seeing her far away in the race track stands, but I never seen Madeline McDowell Breckinridge up close. Just seen pictures of her in the newspapers, her husband's *Herald* mostly, but *The Leader*, too. Now she turned, startled to be addressed in public—and by a colored woman. She wasn't a pretty woman, but her face held the eye for some reason. I see why Lizzie wanted to believe her. I see why Maria did.

"Miss Price?" Her eyes, so large upon her face, grew even wider when I approached. A colored man did not approach a white lady, unless he shuffled. But I walked up with Lizzie like I had a right to be there. Lizzie wondered if confronting her was the right thing to do.

"Lots of promises made," I said to Lizzie. "To you. To Emma Bisou. To Maria. They needed you. Now you need them."

"We need each other."

"That's all I'm gonna say."

Mrs. Breckinridge hadn't said anything more than "Miss Price." Lizzie turned to me.

"This is my friend, Noah Webster. He worked with Mr. Benjamin on *The Lexington Standard*. Now he reads law in Judge Bullock's chambers. He was a friend of Mrs. Benjamin, too."

Maria's name broke the ice.

"I was so sorry to hear about Mrs. Benjamin. So young. Was it consumption?"

Mrs. Breckinridge hadn't looked at me, as if she decided that if she kept her face turned towards Lizzie, I'd disappear. But I jumped in.

"Consumption. And a husband being shot down in the streets. Combination, I imagine."

I doubt if Mrs. Breckinridge ever spoke to a colored man in her life, one that didn't have "Uncle" in front of him, at least. Short sentences, "Uncle, bring the carriage around," or "Uncle, do sweep the path." Old men, those uncles.

But I was young, full of life. It was dangerous. A colored man couldn't talk to a white woman like she was just another human being. Couldn't talk like *he* was a human being around her. No such thing as a colored man next to a white woman.

The two police down below on the plaza were getting tense. Only Lizzie's being there kept them from charging.

Madeline McDowell Breckinridge turned to me then and the look on her face said that she didn't know this world I had entered her into. She stayed silent for a few long moments. I started feeling tense myself. If she screamed, I figured there'd be a noose around my neck in minutes. If she screamed, I'd have to run. But I wouldn't get far.

But she didn't scream. Maybe because she'd done things other women hadn't. Maybe she was a new kind of white lady. Maybe she just curious. One more new place she was going.

"That was terrible. A terrible crime." She paused again. "But why have you approached me?"

I liked that. Direct. Maybe this white woman would help. Maybe we would stand together.

"Because of another crime that's about to happen: Billy Klair's bill to take back the women's vote. We want to join forces—we want to stand together."

Maria had told me those words, described that morning at Ashland. I could tell from Mrs. Breckinridge's face she remembered them. She looked at me now with a strange bitterness.

"You are a man, Mr. Webster. Your color does not matter. If you stepped off the boat yesterday, you would be among our rulers. As long as you were male."

I nodded. "But I didn't step off the boat yesterday. My people been here as long as yours. Maybe longer. And Lizzie would lose her vote. The vote she and Maria fought hard for—fought hard with you."

I showed her a copy of *The Leader* I brought with me, unfolding it to a whole page column protesting Billy Klair's bill taking back the women's franchise. Signed by the committee of one hundred, the "intelligent and home-loving women of Lexington." She and Laura Clay's names were way down, but that didn't matter. Everybody knew who the leaders were.

"How come there isn't one colored woman in the whole list of one hundred? And how come in this whole column you don't protest the name Billy gave those women, Maria and Lizzie?" I waved the paper in front of her like a flag. "You heard those names: ignorant, illiterate. And worse. Can't say them in front of you—in front of Lizzie. But you've heard them."

It was like the paper I'd been waving was red and the police below were bulls just waiting to charge. Madeline McDowell Breckinridge looked like she might charge, too. Away from me. I lowered my voice.

"No 'intelligent' colored ladies, Mrs. Breckinridge? They all illiterate? They all prostitutes?"

The two policemen were climbing the steps now—two at a time—for Madeline McDowell Breckinridge had one hand on her breast and was swaying. I doubt if she was ever the steadiest of women, but she looked in danger of toppling over now. If I caught her in my arms, I doubt if I'd get a chance to explain myself. If I let her drop, I might as well drop down myself.

But she steadied herself and waved the police away. She had to wave twice before they retreated. If she hadn't been Madeline McDowell Breckinridge, I doubt they would of. Lizzie held back a little, herself, but I heard her mumbling. "Jesus, catch her." Now Mrs. Breckinridge came two steps closer to me so that her soft voice was out of range of the police.

"I am not prejudiced, Mr. Webster. I am not responsible for every slander voiced against the colored. I've worked with many colored ladies. With colored gentlemen, too, indirectly at least. Professor Russell and I have exchanged several letters. But this was not the right venue to include colored ladies. This was not the time. Of course, there are intelligent, virtuous colored ladies. Maria Benjamin was among the best. Miss Price is another. But it would have hurt our cause to have included colored ladies in our protest. People would have used it against us. Against our cause."

I understood. Get to be known as a nigger lover in this town, you were dead, in politics, in everything. Imagine ladies didn't take tea with ladies who'd been known to stick up for coloreds.

Only I didn't buy it. Lexington run by the Breckinridges, the Clays, the McDowells. Even Billy Klair knew that, why he got Colonel Allen to run that bill with him. People would grumble, wouldn't like it. But they'd have to live with it. Because they couldn't live without the Breckinridges.

"Guess I don't know what your cause is, Mrs. Breckinridge. Way I see it, you're afraid white women might lose the vote if colored ladies used it. Or used it too much. Or maybe you think like Mrs. Stanton—or your cousin Laura Clay—that only 'intelligent' people should have the vote in the first place. 'Intelligent.' Sure don't mean colored."

She had grown rigid, her large eyes shrinking into her face.

"You say it's the time not being right," I continued. "It ain't the time. I say you just running away. You don't run as fast as some others. You limp so we think we might catch up, but you put the distance in just the same. You'd rather lose that vote than stand with us." I'd been trying to keep calm, but I felt my voice getting louder. "You shooting us in the back just like Mr. Benjamin got shot trying to keep the vote. You stepping over colored bodies for all your promises. We ain't standing together because you're white and this is a white town, for all Maria hoping different, for all Mr. Benjamin giving his life to change it."

I stepped closer so that I stood right next to her. I could feel her breath upon my face. Closer than she'd even been to a black man—a full-grown black man. She breathed hard. I lowered my voice. I whispered.

"Mr. Benjamin's Lexington let him lie in the street. Mr. Benjamin's Lexington said his killing was self-defense. And it was. Mike Moynahan defending white Lexington and Mr. Benjamin trying to change it. Mr. Benjamin's Lexington stepped over him like he weren't there, not worth caring about. Just one more dead colored in a town full of them. That's why you didn't have colored ladies sign that petition. Mr. Benjamin's Lexington said it wasn't time. Ain't be time. You that Lexington, Mrs. Breckinridge. Might as well have shot Mr. Benjamin yourself."

I'd gone too far. I meant to keep myself calm but I wasn't calm. The way she turned away from me at the last was too clear for anybody to mistake. She was affronted. She was insulted. I offended her. Wasn't a week since they hung a young black man down the pike in Nicholasville because a teacher said he'd assaulted her. Just three hours from the time she said that to when they hung him. After she allowed she wasn't sure he was the right man.

But I was the man. No doubt here. I'd assaulted Madeline McDowell Breckinridge. A young, black man had made her turn and scramble away, had made her run so hard you couldn't even see her limp. The police were too distant to hear what I had said but they charged up those steps as if I'd been yelling profanities. Nothing could of stopped them then—no mere wave from Mrs. Breckinridge. Might as well try to stop the Elkhorn from flooding in April as keep those two police from tackling me. Might as well try to turn back that Alabaman vote squashing the colored franchise as try and taint the committee of one hundred with colored blood. Might as well try to change Mr. Benjamin's Lexington into another town, a town where colored mattered as much as white, a town Mr. Benjamin thought he was on his way to making before they shot him down.

Madeline McDowell Breckinridge didn't wave at the policemen to stop this time. Didn't even turn when Lizzie called out to her that the police were arresting me, if that's what they were doing. I gone too far. I was on my own. We were both on our own. All Lexington's coloreds were on their own.

The good white ladies of Kentucky were gonna lose their vote, but it was a small price to pay for keeping pure. Whiteness didn't come cheap. You got to fight for it. Sometimes you got to bleed for it. It was me bleeding now as the two police hammered on me. Didn't know what I'd done, didn't know what I'd said, but I'd made a white woman run.

Lizzie was screaming, yelling for Jesus, but He wasn't listening. Or maybe *she* wasn't hearing right this time. The police would of arrested her, too, but they were too busy with me. Covered my head as best I could and settled in for the night's beating. It didn't matter.

I was a colored man in Lexington, Kentucky.

"Jesus, save him!" Lizzie kept shouting. But He wasn't listening or maybe just not hearing. Just one more hard-of-hearing white man. Needed a big horn in his ear but it wouldn't help.

What? What's that you wanted? Freedom? Freedom? Why?

Because it's ours. Ours! Because Mr. Benjamin's Lexington isn't a white town. It's our town, too. Because Madeline McDowell Breckinridge might not think times are right, but they are.

My feet dangling behind me pounded freedom each step the police dragged me down. *Freedom, freedom*, like a drummer's beat. Didn't matter if Jesus heard or not. Couldn't wait anymore for Jesus to clean out His hearing horn. He wasn't gonna save us. That drum beat hammering loud was clear enough for me, clear enough for anybody listening.

In Lexington, Kentucky, we were gonna have to save ourselves.

CODA:
WAITING ON JESUS

Judge Frank Bullock, February 11, 1920, the Courthouse, Lexington, Kentucky

"How many people you think down there, Judge?"

The boy—he couldn't have been much more than eighteen, not a veteran for sure—looked frightened. They had sent three boys to my office: the vantage view over the square was the best of the courthouse. They had stationed the veterans in the square itself, facing the mob.

Veterans? Of what? Who had ever seen a mob like this?

"Oh, six, seven thousand. Maybe more." The chant was so loud, it was as if they were in the room.

'Give us the nigger! Give us the nigger!"

"They seem rather agitated, don't they?"

I had never seen the square so crowded. I had seen it celebrate the 4th, bedecked in blue and red. And when the Daughters of the Confederacy erected John Breckinridge's statue, ten years ago now, the square had returned to antebellum times for the day—the ladies so festive—some of them even wearing hoops. A beautiful June day. Grace and I had flung open my office windows and thrown a large reception. Later-day Breckinridges and Clays—all our cousins—had strolled up from the square and into my chambers.

I remember the square further back, too—the sad savagery of the slave markets, the call of the barkers, the casual greed and lust of the buyers. The shame, the sadness, the despair of the slaves.

But this mass of white men shaking their fists and chanting hate was something I had thought foreign to Lexington. Every inch of the square was filled. Two boys perched on each of John Breckinridge's shoulders looking as small as pigeons from my window. They could not have been more than ten, but they waved their thin arms like the rest of the mob, their mouths moving in the same chant:

"Give us the nigger! Give us the nigger!"

"Do you think we'll hold them?"

All three boy-soldiers turned to me for assurance. They might be boys, but they were soldiers. It was not my job to give false words of comfort.

"If you don't, I imagine Will Lockett won't be the only one killed today."

Will Lockett, the poor deluded center of all this drama. *He* is a veteran. Just back from the big war. Back in time to be hanged. A colored veteran. That's what we do to colored veterans in Kentucky: hang them. A good dozen last year alone. We do not like the way they look in uniform. We shiver at the thought that the government has actually trained them to shoot.

Usually we hang them out in the counties, drag them from some rural jail built for drunks. The mob has come from those counties, in for Court Day. And a treat. A Lexington hanging.

Of course, many of those hanged had never made it to the jails, had never even been charged with a crime.

Will Lockett *has* been charged with a crime—the murder of a little girl. A little white girl. The black brute murdering an innocent white child. He has confessed. What else could he do but confess? We are more civilized in Lexington. We need our confessions.

The boy-soldiers are not from Lexington. Camp Zachary Taylor, near Louisville. I wonder if they find us more civilized. I told the mayor and the police chief to change the venue. Even passed word to Judge Kerr, though we are not currently speaking. "It would be prudent," I said.

But they are all idiots. The mayor even let out a statement that the trial "would demonstrate Lexington's devotion to the process of law."

"Give us the nigger! Give us the nigger!"

Mobs are so impatient. Thirty days the law says we have to wait before we hang him. The minimum to preserve our dignity. And our civilization.

The three boy-soldiers jump when the phone rings, as if the mob had breached the barricades. Country boys themselves, they look at the phone fearfully. It is probably Grace. Concerned.

But it is Noah. Worried about me, which is kind of him. Worried about Will Lockett, which is foolish. He has heard, somehow, that the trial is over. He thinks a thirty-minute trial unduly short. He suggests that Colonel Allen, Lockett's court appointed lawyer, had been unduly laggard. Thirty minutes *and* a lawyer. How often do county-coloreds get such amenities?

"It's not a fair trial," Noah shouts at me. He has to shout to be heard. He must hear the mob's chant. "It's not a real trial. It's just a legal lynching!"

"Not yet," I murmur. "It may turn into a real lynching yet."

But he cannot hear me. The mob is too loud. An old dispute between us anyway. The truth. Noah has been a lawyer almost twenty years and he still thinks the law is about the truth. The law is about order. If the truth creates disorder, the truth must yield. These poor green troops were not sent by the governor to save Will Lockett or to give him a fair trial.

A fair trial for a black man accused of killing a white child? It would enrage the city. No troops could save us. Noah might as well ask his Lizzie and her Jesus to save us. To give us fairness.

I sometimes think Lizzie has done more good as a teacher and principal these past twenty years than Noah, striving to save his poor clients. Fighting. What has it got him? Noah actually wanted to come down here today, actually wanted to represent Lockett.

Judge Kerr is an idiot, but he is not insane. Noah would have been lynched on his way to the courthouse. I sent Kerr another note. Told him to order Noah away from the courthouse under threat of contempt. Kerr issued the order. He is not insane.

The colored janitors have more brains than Noah. Not one has showed up for two days. The whole courthouse smells of stale spittoons. I did not know if Noah would obey the order. But perhaps Lizzie prevailed.

We do not talk often, Noah and I. His clients pass through my courtroom like pigeons through the square, one like another. Grace passes the whispers to me. She says people think I favor Noah. I do not. I simply listen to his arguments. Perhaps that is favoritism.

We are not friends. He's been to my chambers perhaps a dozen times in the twenty years since he stopped reading for me. I thought we'd be closer, though how that could happen has always eluded me. I cannot invite him to our receptions. Grace would not allow it.

But times have changed. He no longer has to sneak into my office. He walks there, upright, in full view of everyone, though some are still angered by his appearance. A well-dressed colored man. But there are others, perhaps two dozen colored lawyers in town.

Times *have* changed. Though the chant that comes through my chamber windows says not enough.

Noah came two days ago, angry that I had opposed his representing Lockett. I mentioned the progress to him.

"Yet you think I might be lynched if I represent this poor, deluded Lockett? Don't seem like progress to me, Judge. More lynching in Kentucky than I ever recall. Feels like Alabama. That progress, Judge?"

"Yes. The lynchings are a sign of the progress. Whites scared things are changing. They *are* changing."

He looked at me. I could tell he was caught between rage and laughter, as if he were a young man again and I had said something that I knew made him want to reach wide and knock me flat. I always wondered if he would do it. I always wondered how I would respond.

But he just shook his head.

"So, lynching is a sign of progress? Well, Kentucky is a leader of the nation, then."

Of course my argument was ludicrous, but there was some truth to it.

"No. We are behind. Thank God for Mississippi. I am only saying that this spurt of violence is a last-ditch resistance. Terrible, but it is a sign of change. And that is good."

Noah was calm now, looking at me like I've looked at lawyers trying to save desperately guilty clients with equally desperate arguments.

"Sounds like you're talking about the end times, Judge. Even Lizzie shies clear of those folks. And I don't buy your premise. My mamma and daddy grew up in a time of change. Progress. Than the Klan came down. Then Jim Crow. And change didn't happen. Change went away. Seems like they're trying to make change go away again, Judge. I worked for a man who worked hard for change. The only permanent change happened to him. Shot down in *self-defense*. That's Kentucky's way of changing. At least for the coloreds."

There it was again. Benjamin. Why we could never be friends. *In self-defense.* Noah did not have to physically assault me. We looked at each other.

"We do many things we regret, Noah. We hope we do not define our lives by them. We hope our friends do not, either."

"Friends?" Noah paused. "I think you're into Jesus talk now, Judge. Lizzie's territory. But I know what you mean by regret. I regret a lot of things. I regret never being able to get Mamma to retire from cleaning folks' homes. I regret half-believing her when she told me she liked it, that it kept her busy. Kept her busy till she died. On her knees cleaning. Praying. So I know all about regret. But tell me, Judge, you regret being a judge these past twenty years?"

I pulled myself up. It was my life. "I do not."

He kept nodding. "That's what Dante say about the fruit. Remember? If you hold onto the fruit, you can't regret the act. Kind of like saying you were real sorry you robbed that bank, but the money was fine where it ended up."

"They're charging!"

The three boy-soldiers stuck their rifles through my office windows. They were all equal rank, though one boy had been designated leader. Like telling a child he was in charge while the grownups were gone. The grownups were gone. I looked below.

"Stand back, Judge!" the boy in charge told me. Six thousand people were pushing at the thin column of soldiers, the men in front being pushed by the men in the middle who were being pushed by the outer rows. Court Day. Most of them here for Court Day, a peaceful bartering of their farm wares with each other and with city folk who paid in cash for what they could not grow. It was not a peaceful barter now, and they would pay in more than cash. I looked for the two small boys on the statue, worried they'd be trampled but they were gone, swept off Breckinridge's shoulders into the arms of the mob.

"Stay calm, men," I said to the boys, but my judge authority meant nothing to them. They had their eyes zeroed in on a colonel standing at the edge of the troops. His right arm was raised.

He lowered it. The blast that followed was louder than I had ever heard, but I had missed our wars. Too young when Father and the rest of Morgan's Raiders ravaged the countryside, the same kind of countryside these poor Court Day folk came from. Father had gone out from the city to pillage their stores. They had come in from the countryside to savage our pride.

253

The troops below kept firing though the mob was trying as hard as it could to turn itself around—to turn from the charge to a frenzied retreat—the front pressing the middle, the middle pressing the rear. The rear scattering to the winds. The chant had been replaced with screams. We could no longer make out individual words. Only one long sound of horror and fear. Only one long curse. Some turned their faces upward towards my office and shook their fists. They kept their mouths open in a howl.

The three boys were firing still. "Enough, men. Enough. They're done," and they turned toward me, looking at me for a second as if I were one of the mob snuck past the lines. The enemy. I wondered if they might use their guns on me.

Gradually color came back into their faces. They pulled in their rifles. Their shoulders sagged, a gloom like a fog settled into their eyes. They no longer looked like boys. *This is how we become men,* I thought. *We kill other men.*

I looked at Noah when he made the Dante allusion. I felt a certain pride in my tutoring. He was one of the best-read men I knew in Lexington. Lizzie, with her Shakespeare, was certainly the best-read woman. Of course his logic followed: my ruling on Benjamin's murder had let me stay a judge. Any other finding and Billy Klair—the whole Democratic machine—would have turned on me. Probably impeached me. Certainly not put me up for re-election. The notorious 1901 election. But I won fairly in that election. My totals were honest, for I was known as an honest judge.

I am an honest judge. As honest as any judge in the Commonwealth of Kentucky.

And so it follows. I cannot regret betraying Benjamin. I might as well regret the fine view from my office chambers on an April morning when Kentucky dogwoods bloom their week of glory.

But it was February and the view from my chambers was not one I wanted to see. Not one anyone wanted to see.

And I did regret. I do regret.

Noah as a man, should know that a boy's moral judgments are too sharp. A man is a mix, a terrible blend of old and new, sordid and fine. Not unlike our Commonwealth. Not all North or South. Not all one thing. Noah is a Kentuckian, too. He should understand. He should forgive.

"Of course, I do not regret being a judge. It is what I have done. It is who I am."

We stared at each other. I felt it would be a long time, if ever, before he returned to my chambers. Grace wanted another reception in the spring. Perhaps I could prevail on her to invite Noah and Lizzie. Grace would resist. Not think it proper. Not think the time was right. And Noah and Lizzie would not come.

Noah had to get home early that day, just two days ago, though it seems longer. We'd heard reports of colored men being attacked by groups of marauding white men. A white child murdered by a black man. The town was inflamed.

Noah was not safe. I thought of asking a policeman to escort him home. Noah laughed at me.

"Police gonna escort every colored home? Not enough police. And who's gonna protect us from the police?"

Coloreds have pulled into their homes like Jews hiding in Russia's shtetls. Lexington's shtetls.

Noah is right. It does not feel like progress.

"Noah," I said just as he was leaving. I had spoken it louder than I meant to. Like a shout. Like a cry for help. He startled. I held out my hand. "We *are* friends, Noah," remembering how he had questioned the word.

254

He looked at my hand and it hung there like a plea stuck in an appellate court. The light from the windows had already begun to dim, though the days were longer, February promising April. I felt its weight as I stretched my arm out, the early twilight blurring the colors of a white hand reaching for a black one. The ache in my arm traveled to my shoulder, but still I held it out, the pain reaching into the tendrils of my neck, but still I summoned the strength. I kept my arm out even as the terrible hurt clouded my eyes.

Noah took my hand just as my arm began to bend slowly downward, rescued it from its descent. I waited for his words.

"No, Judge, we're not friends. Not yet. But Lizzie tells me one day maybe. Lizzie tells me we're all gonna be one people, one family. Someday. Even in the Commonwealth of Kentucky. That's what Lizzie tells me, Judge. 'Hurry up, Jesus!' she shouts. Right out loud. You've heard her. Mamma would slap me when I tried to shush her. 'She's calling on Jesus. Let her speak.'"

He gave my hand a squeeze before he let it go.

"We're all calling on Jesus, Judge. But He better hurry up. You ain't the only one getting old. So we ain't friends, Judge. Not yet. But someday maybe. Jesus willing."

*   *   *

Jesus willing. The mob below was no longer one din of screams. It had settled into a moan, a dirge of cries and weeping. Figures dressed in white were moving among the fallen, taking the wounded to the waiting gurneys. Covering the dead.

No. We could not wait for Jesus. I'll tell Grace that my friend Noah and his lady, Lizzie, must be invited to our next reception. Grace is a mainstay of First Presbyterian on Mill Street. I'll make Noah and Lizzie see that they must accept the invitation. For all of us. We cannot have more bodies in the courtyard square. We cannot be this place we've been. Hurry up, Jesus!

Come to our reception, I'll say to Noah and Lizzie.
Jesus wants you there.

And so do I.

AUTHOR'S NOTES

Partial list of characters. Characters existing in history are marked with an asterisk (*).

Beatty, Miz: Older lady who joins demonstration at Cadentown
*Benjamin, Robert O'Hara: Journalist, lawyer, politician, writer, poet, preacher, civil rights advocate
*Benjamin, Maria Lulu: Wife of R.O. Benjamin.
Bisou, Emma: Black club lady and activist.
*Breckinridge, Desha: Editor of the *Lexington Morning Herald.*
*Breckinridge, Madeline McDowell: Prominent Bluegrass aristocrat and suffragette.
*Breckinridge, Sophonisba: Pioneer social worker.
*Broadus, George: "Mayor" of Yellmantown.
Bryant, Joseph: Teacher who replaces Noah in Briar Hill.
*Bullock, Frank: Judge in Fayette County.
*Bullock, Grace: Wife of Frank.
*Bullock, Major: Father of Frank Bullock. one of Morgan's Raiders.
Buford, Eddie: Sixteen-year-old black jockey, rider of Bluegrass Funeral.
Chiles, Mrs.: Mother of Willy and activist in Cadentown.
Chiles, Willy: Twelve-year-old student at Briar Hill. "Ain't I a woman?"
*Doyle, John: Election Challenger, brother of Luke.
*Doyle, Luke: Patrolman. Found gun on Benjamin.
*Graves, Professor: Teacher sent by Democratic machine to teach in Cadentown.
*Klair, Billy: State legislator and political boss of Fayette County for decades.
Jones, W.C. Reverend: Pastor of AME and head of Quinn Chapel School.
*Littlefield, William: Black Mississippian who shot the sheriff *and* the deputies sent to dispossess him from his family farm. Fate unknown.
*Lockett, Will: Black WWI veteran, convicted of murder. Hanged.
*Moynahan, Mike: Acquitted killer of Robert O'Hara Benjamin.
Price, Lizzie: Teacher, activist, friend of Noah, twin sister of Suzie.
*Russell, Green Pinckney: Supervisor of Negro Schools in Lexington, 1890s.
Sheila: Maid to the Benjamins.
Webster, Fanny, Mamma: Mother of Noah, husband of Joshua (deceased.)
Webster, Noah: Benjamin's assistant, bartender, bookie, teacher, and lawyer.
Winslow, Jake: Jake the bartender.

 The Standard column cited in the novel's opening concerning William Littlefield and the shooting in Mississippi comes directly from the paper as reprinted in *The Morning Herald* in 1898. All other *Standard* columns are fictionalized.
 The poem used by Noah in his county school is by Benjamin. It was published in a collection of his called *Poetic Gems* in 1883.

*   *   *

 It is challenging to write a novel based on so much historical fact. *A Wounded Snake* blends accurate historical data—the killing of Robert O'Hara Benjamin—with imagined responses: the rest in the church on the way home. It does the same with the school "riots" in

Cadentown, which did take place. The women were arrested on Judge Frank Bullock's orders under the infamous KKK law. However, all of the circumstances around that disturbance have been imagined. Judge Frank Bullock was a real figure who both presided over Mike Moynahan's pre-trial and released him, and did rule in favor of hundreds of challenged black voters. Bullets did come from his windows in 1920 at the Will Lockett race riot. He was even accused of shooting them himself, though the explanation of soldiers posted in his office was finally accepted.

Much of the novel's perspective is shared by completely fictional characters such as Noah Webster, Lizzie Price, Jake the bartender, Mamma, and also real-life figures, such as Maria Lulu Benjamin, whom we know nothing about except that she was married to Benjamin, had two children, and went home to Alabama to die. Even the historic characters such as Billy Klair, Judge Bullock, and even Robert O'Hara Benjamin, are in many ways my novelistic creations. These characters talk of real things, notably the treatment of black jockeys and their removal from the sport they once completely dominated. They get into real fights such as the one over the approaches to black education, as espoused by Booker T. Washington and W. E. Dubois.

The long struggle in Kentucky over women's suffrage took on a local character as the limited franchise for school board elections and its repeal (initiated by real-life Billy Klair) has both fictional and historical accuracy. Madeline McDowell Breckinridge's role in that struggle and her perceived racism are still a topic of great debate. The novel's characters express their own judgment.

I have tried to be faithful to my reading of history even as I let my novelist's imagination create and extend drama. The snake of racism took different form in Kentucky, a border state, than it did further south or further north. Sometimes that racism took on a virulent and violent form, as some characters' use of the "n-word" demonstrates. Often, though, that racism was more subtle and "polite," but nevertheless accomplished the work of exclusion and debasement.

The wish to make real and current that historic struggle to cross the borders set by race, gender, class, is the main objective of my fictionalized story. I hope I have told it well.

About the Author

Joseph G. Anthony moved from Manhattan's Upper West Side to Hazard, Kentucky in 1980. Anthony, an English professor for 35 years, regularly contributes essays and poems to anthologies, including a poem and story in *Kentucky's Twelve Days of Christmas.*

His most recent novel, *Wanted: Good Family* (Bottom Dog Press), was described by the *Lexington Herald-Leader* as "masterfully written and well grounded in Kentucky history and mannerisms [exploring] race, class, relationship and the potential for change."

His previous books include two short story collections, *Camden Blues* and *Bluegrass Funeral*, plus two novels—*Peril, Kentucky*, and *Pickering's Mountain*. *Appalachian Heritage* said of *Pickering* that, "Anthony balances multiple voices with restraint…[he makes] us feel for their individual pain and sorrow, their prejudice and greed and lack of guile and fully-realized humanity."

Anthony lives in Lexington, Kentucky with his wife of forty years, Elise Mandel. They have three grown children.

Books by Bottom Dog Press
Appalachian Writing Series

A Wounded Snake: A Novel, by Joseph G. Anthony, 262 pgs, $18
Brown Bottle: A Novel, by Sheldon Lee Compton, 162 pgs, $18
A Small Room with Trouble on My Mind, by Michael Henson, 164 pgs, $18
Drone String: Poems, by Sherry Cook Stanforth, 92 pgs, $16
Voices from the Appalachian Coalfields, by Mike and Ruth Yarrow,
Photos by Douglas Yarrow, 152 pgs, $17
Wanted: Good Family, by Joseph G. Anthony, 212 pgs, $18
Sky Under the Roof: Poems, by Hilda Downer, 126 pgs, $16
Green-Silver and Silent: Poems, by Marc Harshman, 90 pgs, $16
The Homegoing: A Novel, by Michael Olin-Hitt, 180 pgs, $18
She Who Is Like a Mare: Poems of Mary Breckinridge and the Frontier Nursing Service,
by Karen Kotrba, 96 pgs, $16
Smoke: Poems, by Jeanne Bryner, 96 pgs, $16
Broken Collar: A Novel, by Ron Mitchell, 234 pgs, $18
The Pattern Maker's Daughter: Poems, by Sandee Gertz Umbach, 90 pgs, $16
The Free Farm: A Novel, by Larry Smith, 306 pgs, $18
Sinners of Sanction County: Stories, by Charles Dodd White, 160 pgs, $17
Learning How: Stories, Yarns & Tales, by Richard Hague, $18
The Long River Home: A Novel, by Larry Smith, 230 pgs, cloth $22; paper $16
Eclipse: Stories, by Jeanne Bryner, 150 pgs, $16

Appalachian Writing Series Anthologies

Unbroken Circle: Stories of Cultural Diversity in the South,
Eds. Julia Watts and Larry Smith, 194 pgs, $17
Appalachia Now: Short Stories of Contemporary Appalachia,
Eds. Charles Dodd White and Larry Smith, 178 pgs, $17
Degrees of Elevation: Short Stories of Contemporary Appalachia,
Eds. Charles Dodd White and Page Seay, 186 pgs, $16

BOOKS BY BOTTOM DOG PRESS
HARMONY SERIES

Taking a Walk in My Animal Hat, by Charlene Fix, 90 pgs, $16
Earnest Occupations, by Richard Hague, 200 pgs, $18
Pieces: A Composite Novel, by Mary Ann McGuigan, 250 pgs, $18
Crows in the Jukebox: Poems, by Mike James, 106 pgs, $16
Portrait of the Artist as a Bingo Worker: A Memoir, by Lori Jakiela, 216 pgs, $18
The Thick of Thin: A Memoir, by Larry Smith, 238 pgs, $18
Cold Air Return: A Novel, by Patrick Lawrence O'Keeffe, 390 pgs, $20
Flesh and Stones: A Memoir, by Jan Shoemaker, 176 pgs, $18
Waiting to Begin: A Memoir, by Patricia O'Donnell, 166 pgs, $18
And Waking: Poems, by Kevin Casey, 80 pgs, $16
Both Shoes Off: Poems, by Jeanne Bryner, 112 pgs, $16
Abandoned Homeland: Poems, by Jeff Gundy, 96 pgs, $16
Stolen Child: A Novel, by Suzanne Kelly, 338 pgs, $18
The Canary: A Novel, by Michael Loyd Gray, 196 pgs, $18
On the Flyleaf: Poems, by Herbert Woodward Martin, 106 pgs, $16
The Harmonist at Nightfall: Poems of Indiana, by Shari Wagner, 114 pgs, $16
Painting Bridges: A Novel, by Patricia Averbach, 234 pgs, $18
Ariadne & Other Poems, by Ingrid Swanberg, 120 pgs, $16
The Search for the Reason Why: New and Selected Poems, by Tom Kryss,
192 pgs, $16
Kenneth Patchen: Rebel Poet in America, by Larry Smith,
Revised 2nd Edition, 326 pgs, Cloth $28
Selected Correspondence of Kenneth Patchen,
Edited with introduction by Allen Frost, Paper $18/ Cloth $28
Awash with Roses: Collected Love Poems of Kenneth Patchen,
Eds. Laura Smith and Larry Smith with introduction by Larry Smith, 200 pgs, $16
Breathing the West: Great Basin Poems, by Liane Ellison Norman, 96 pgs, $16
Maggot: A Novel, by Robert Flanagan, 262 pgs, $18
American Poet: A Novel, by Jeff Vande Zande, 200 pgs, $18
The Way-Back Room: Memoir of a Detroit Childhood, by Mary Minock, 216 pgs, $18

BOTTOM DOG PRESS, INC.

P.O. BOX 425 / HURON, OHIO 44839
HTTP://SMITHDOCS.NET